The Red Scholar's Wake

ALIETTE DE BODARD

First published in Great Britain in 2022 by Gollancz
an imprint of The Orion Publishing Group Ltd
Carmelite House, 50 Victoria Embankment
London EC4Y 0DZ

An Hachette UK company

This edition first published in 2023

5 7 9 10 8 6 4

A CIP catalogue record for this book
is available from the British Library.

ISBN (MMP) 978 1 399 60136 8
ISBN (eBook) 978 1 399 60137 5
ISBN (audio) 978 1 399 60146 7

Typeset by Deltatype Ltd, Birkenhead, Merseyside

Printed in Great Britain by Clays Ltd, Elcograf S.p.A.

www.gollancz.co.uk

To my friends, for their support

1

Bargains

'The Red Scholar is dead.'

The words, at first barely a whisper, passed through the fleet, gaining strength as they went — from the largest mindships to the smaller three-plates craft, from the open-the-voids to the planet-hoppers.

'The Red Scholar is dead.'

There were defiant firecrackers; noisy, screaming processions of mourners; drunken meals which degenerated into fights; all the while, Xích Si, leaning against a wall in the darkness of the hold where the pirates had imprisoned her, prayed to her long-dead ancestors to be forgotten.

She was one of their only captives: taken from a small and insignificant scavenger the pirates had attacked almost as an afterthought, charring her battered-down ship and breaking her bots with frightening ease, then marching her into this small and suffocating space. Of course they would not expect ransom from such a poor-looking ship. They would press her into service as a bondsperson on their own ships, using her until she broke, if she was lucky. If she was not ...

There were other, darker uses for bondspeople, especially

once wine had flowed freely, and if the pirates were in the mood for pain or pleasure, or both.

Please please please.

At least she was alive — unlike Diệu Ngà and her former crew-mates from *The Leaping Carp*, the ship that had been boarded and pillaged so long ago. At least she had a chance of being used, rather than being tortured or killed. She remembered fleeing in the escape pod with the sound of battle still raging around her, back to the safety of Triệu Hoà Port; remembered the vids of Diệu Ngà's body when the militia had found the wreck of *The Leaping Carp*, the eyes shrivelled in their orbits, the broken texture of the lips, the teeth rattling loose and refracting starlight like jewels — and the wrists and ankles chafed where she'd struggled against the magnetic holds. They'd pinned Ngà to the ship without an unreality suit, and jettisoned it into deep spaces, and Xích Si hadn't been there for any of it, hadn't been able to defend her the way Ngà had defended Xích Si's presence on the venture to the ship-owners and merchant families.

At least Xích Si was still alive — but Ngà had been alive, too, before they started on her.

The door opened, the stench of cheap wine and the din of firecrackers blowing in.

No, not so soon. Please.

Xích Si tried to fold herself as small as possible against the bulwark, hands scrabbling for purchase against smooth, oily metal.

'So you're the one.' The voice was low, and cultured. For a moment its owner was only a dark silhouette in the doorway, and then the lights came on in the hold, and some kind of ambient filter descended, silencing the noises from outside.

The newcomer was a mindship — and not with a ship's usual avatar, but a human shape: a female official with long flowing robes and a topknot – except that where the hair flowed down and met the cloth, there were stars and nebulas, winking in and out of existence – and her eyes had no whites or irises: they were the colour of the void, dark with no glimmer of light.

'You're the ship,' Xích Si said.

The ship on which she was imprisoned, her prison cell only one room in a vast body, the avatar only a fraction of the ship's full attention – everything else focused on passengers, on moving between the stars, on bots repairing tears on the hull or maintaining recyclers, filtration systems and airlocks.

The ship. The pirate ship.

'My name is *The Rice Fish, Resting.*' *Rice Fish* used 'child' to refer to Xích Si, 'elder aunt' to herself. A gulf, but not such a wide one, between them.

Xích Si knew the name. This was not just any ship. *Rice Fish* was the Red Scholar's wife. Her widow, now. The Red Consort, they'd called her in Triệu Hoà Port. The Red Scholar and the Red Consort. Legendary pirates. A ship and a human, the founders of the Red Banner pirate alliance that plagued the Twin Streams, the two asteroid groups stretching in the shadow of the Fire Palace, the red-hot mass that was a long-dead civilisation's destroyed homeland.

What could someone like *Rice Fish* want with someone like Xích Si?

Behind *Rice Fish* was a woman of indeterminate age, her hair shorn close to the scalp – she'd have looked like a reprobate monk if not for the harshness of her expression, the gun and knives in her belt, and the lavish haphazardness of her clothing: a magistrate's winged hat; an elaborate cloth in five layers, two physical ones, and three in overlays, showing clouds and rain, and half-bitten peaches, and other faintly suggestive images. She stood as if at rest, one hand nonchalantly resting on a knife's hilt, her role as a bodyguard clear.

3

The ship's hands moved, smoothly and far too fast, throwing something towards Xích Si—not just hands. Bots. She must have had her own bots behind the overlay: for even an avatar with the full overlays of perception adjustments couldn't physically move anything. Something metallic clattered on the floor.

'Pick them up.'

Restraints? But then Xích Si looked up and saw that they were her dead bots.

What kind of ordeal was this meant to be?

'I don't understand, Lady.' She used a pronoun reserved for high officials, abasing herself as abjectly as she could.

Rice Fish's face shifted, briefly. Anger? Annoyance? Any moment now, she was going to stride into the cell, or order Xích Si dragged out of it.

'I'm sorry, I didn't intend any impertinence!'

Xích Si crawled across the floor, picking up her bots. The weight should have been familiar in her hands, but they just felt . . . light. Hollow. They'd been charred, and then gutted; in proof, their broken innards spilled in sharp fragments on Xích Si's palms. She turned them, seeking something, anything that had survived – the myriad legs she'd so painstakingly assembled were snapped off, the sensors crowning the bodies removed, the round, small bodies themselves scored over and over.

Broken and charred, like everything taken by pirates. Like *everyone* taken. She closed her eyes, trying to hold back the tears.

'You killed them,' she said. Her mouth tasted of salt.

'So they *are* yours. You built them.'

'Yes.'

Xích Si opened her eyes. She was kneeling in the middle of the floor, and there was no cover or shelter for her any more.

'Good.' *Rice Fish* moved – one moment she was in the

doorway, and the next she was kneeling in front of Xích Si.
'Look at me,' she said.

A gentle pressure under Xích Si's chin: *Rice Fish* wasn't in
the physical layer, of course, but the sensation was passed on
through the overlays, becoming a perception on Xích Si's skin,
a feeling of oily warmth spreading from *Rice Fish*'s fingers, just
as *Rice Fish* would feel the cold, shivering touch of Xích Si's
own skin. How Xích Si wanted to pull away, but she couldn't
afford to.

Rice Fish's face was a matriarch's: weathered and lined, with
dark brown skin that shone as if lit from within. It looked
human, almost — the eyes were black from end to end, and
her lips, slightly parted, revealed teeth that weren't white or
yellowed, but the fractured, sheeny colour of metal in deep
spaces. She breathed, or appeared to, but what Xích Si heard
wasn't air inhaled and exhaled, but the distant sound of
motors, and a faint, haunting melody on an instrument that
wasn't flute or zither.

'Look at me.'

She couldn't look away. She might as well have been trapped
in a black hole's gravity well, slowly and inexorably drawing
close, her own lips parting, air mingling with *Rice Fish*'s ether-
eal breath — close enough to make contact, close enough to feel
the warmth . . .

The ship withdrew her hand. It felt as if she'd cut a pup-
pet's strings: Xích Si sagged, struggling to gather her confused
thoughts again.

'You'll do,' *Rice Fish* said. She was still kneeling, but she
did it like an empress.

'Do what?' Xích Si said. 'Please, don't . . .'

'I'm not here to torture you.' *Rice Fish*'s voice was faintly
amused, though beneath it lay that same anger. 'I need your
services.'

5

'As a bondsperson?' Fear made her reckless.

This time it was unmistakably amusement. 'No. As my wife.'

The words made no sense, no matter how many times Xích Si turned them in her head.

'I don't understand,' she said.

The Red Scholar had been *Rice Fish*'s wife, and she was dead now. Why would *Rice Fish* want another wife?

'Consider it ... a business proposal. There's no love involved. This is a matter of contracts.' There was a flicker of something Xích Si couldn't read, changing the colour of her eyes to indigo blue for a moment. 'Of ... protection.'

'Protection.' Xích Si's voice was flat.

'I said I wouldn't torture you or harm you. It'll hold true within the Red Banner – which is my fleet, now the Red Scholar is dead –' again, that flicker of colour. Grief? No, that didn't seem right. '– but not everyone here will be so considerate. There are four other banners in the pirate alliance.'

'I don't want to get married!' She ... Oh, ancestors, she wanted to go home. She wanted to hold her daughter Khanh in her arms, hug the small wriggling body of her six-year-old, hear her peals of laughter – what she wouldn't have given for even one of Khanh's tantrums. 'I have a family.'

Rice Fish didn't move. 'You did.' And, not unkindly, 'You know the process.'

Unless she could prove that she'd taken no part in piracy, either as a pirate or as a bondsperson – which meant being ransomed, and no one in a tribunal or the militia would believe that a small-time scavenger would be held for ransom – she'd be deemed a pirate, and the penalty for piracy was death. It might be a swift or slow one, depending on the magistrate's mood. There was no going home. Not now, not ever. Khanh ... Khanh was lost to her, and that was like a blade of ice in her belly.

'You didn't have to take me! You didn't have to break everything ... You didn't have to ...'

She was crying now, struggling to form words. How dare they? How could they snatch everything that caught their fancy, with the same greed as corrupt officials, as venal merchants – how could they tear apart even her small, unambitious, utterly unremarkable life, for no other reason than because they could?

'Why did you ...? Why?'

'I didn't take you.' *Rice Fish*'s voice was distant. 'The banner is in disarray after my wife's death, and they take comfort in pillaging. It's familiar.'

Familiar. She remembered Ngà's brutal death.

'And that's what you'd protect me from? I don't even know why ...'

A raised eyebrow. The ship hadn't moved, and didn't show any sign of discomfort. Her hair spread in a pool of blackness on the floor, and stars slowly wheeled and changed within it. The bodyguard was still in the doorway, but she might have been light-years away.

'Your bots,' *Rice Fish* said. 'And your ship. You like technology. You're *good* with it.'

Xích Si tinkered, because there was only a knife's edge between survival and death, out there between the asteroids in the Twin Streams. She didn't have the supplies, or the time or the money to pay a bot-handler. So she tinkered.

'I'm no one.'

'I disagree. Everyone is someone.'

'I don't need your pity! I don't want ... I don't want to get married.'

'We seldom do what we want in life.'

'You haven't explained to me what you want me to do in it. Or why I care.'

'Careful now. You're growing bold, aren't you?'

'Or what? You'll silence me?'

A shrug. 'Prisoners are not a rarity.'

'I get the feeling you needed me specifically. And my bots. The ones you broke.'

Laughter. 'Some spunk at last? Better.' And, more seriously, 'I won't make the threat, but remember that anyone from another banner might. Make sure you know what they need from you. Specifically – bot-handling doesn't require you *whole*.'

Whole.

Xích Si's innards twisted. 'You—'

'I said I wasn't going to make the threat.' *Rice Fish* shifted, slightly. So did the pool of stars around her. 'Huân – my wife – shouldn't have died.'

Xích Si clamped her lips on the hurtful reply.

'The imperial censor's ships, the ones that ambushed Huân on her return from raiding season, shouldn't have known where we'd emerge from deep spaces.'

'So you have an informant on board. I don't see where I can help.'

A smile, showing radiance as dazzling as the Fire Palace. 'Oh, I don't just have an informant on board. There's someone within the alliance who is trying to tear it apart, and I know who. But I don't have proof.'

Movement behind *Rice Fish*. The woman with the suggestive robe had winced at those words, and was hastily trying to hide it by turning away from Xích Si.

Politics. Intrigue, and way above Xích Si's capabilities.

'I'm just a scavenger!' She belatedly realised she'd just admitted she was expendable. 'I didn't . . .'

Rice Fish raised an eyebrow. 'Scared?' she asked, her black-on-black eyes entirely too perceptive.

Never admit fear to a predator.

'Of course not.'

'Good.' *Rice Fish* watched her, for what felt like an infinite time. 'I want you to find my proof, which will require being ... creative. I can handle people, but no one is going to hand me a confession, or at least not one that's worth much of anything, politically speaking. I need your bots to watch and listen to people. To trawl the network for information. To follow and incapacitate them, if needed.'

Technical expertise. Xích Si forced herself to breathe. Of course. That made sense.

'As I said, it would be a partnership,' *Rice Fish* said. 'Our marriage will ensure you have status and protection, but there's nothing else involved.'

A twist of the lips, and suddenly Xích Si's confusion resolved into the truth that of course nothing else could be involved. This was a grieving, angry widow looking for revenge.

And a pirate, like the ones who'd killed Ngà. The words came welling out of her, and she knew exactly how wounding they would be.

'No forcing me to sleep with you? I suppose I should be thankful for that.'

Rice Fish's face didn't move. 'Rape isn't allowed in this banner. The penalty is death by spacing.'

'Now you're going to tell me it's different in other banners.'

Laughter. 'Hoping I'll get annoyed enough to kill you? That's a dangerous path. I might decide to do something smaller and more painful to you instead.'

'Why marriage? A partnership doesn't require marriage.'

'It shouldn't. But things ... are in flux at the moment.'

'In flux?'

'Dangerous. I did say the Red Scholar's death had thrown the banner into disarray. Some of ... the usual codes have been forgotten. Marriage is the oldest contract. The kind of

9

protection and status everyone will respect. The best I can offer you. So?'

Xích Si didn't want to choose. She didn't want to be responsible for setting aside her entire life. It would have been easier if she'd been forced. If, from the moment she was taken, everything had been out of her control. If she hadn't been in the middle of this ship — of the ship kneeling in front of her — being offered a *choice*.

The last time she'd made a choice of similar import, it had been Ngà and her offer to trade on *The Leaping Carp* instead of scavenging, to get larger profits, earn a new life. It had all turned to fractured, bloody pieces, and Ngà herself had never come back.

Reaching out for more always ended up in broken hands.

'What if I say no?'

A shrug. 'As I said, prisoners aren't a rarity.'

'But you won't protect me.'

Another smile. 'Why would you need the protection? An obscure bondsperson toiling in the belly of our ships ... you might never come to the attention of another banner.'

Xích Si shivered. No rape, she'd said. Only there were so many other ways to be hurt.

'I want to know what's happened to my daughter.'

'I told you. She's part of your old life. Your dead life.'

'I know I can't be in contact with her or she'll be sentenced to death as my accomplice. But I want to make sure she's provided for.'

Auntie Vy would take Khanh in, but she wasn't Vy's flesh and blood, and who knew if Vy — another scavenger, and about as poor as Xích Si — could feed her? Or would want to? It was easier, and so much more convenient, to sell children into indenture or concubinage, fates that sent chills down Xích Si's spine.

A shrug. 'It might be a while before we can locate her. It's not that easy to move within Triệu Hoà Port — too many sentries, too much empire surveillance on that habitat. But I could try. So?'

She was waiting. Stars wheeled and glittered, her hair merging with the cloth of her tunic. Her eyes were dark again, the anger she'd shown tamped down.

Choose.

She could say no, and become one of the countless bondspeople given menial jobs, their only way out becoming pirates themselves — which was the very escape route *Rice Fish* was offering her now. A partnership. She could say no and keep her pride, but she guessed she'd never had much pride to start with.

Or much choice.

'I'll do it,' she said. 'I'll marry you.'

2
Ceremonial

Rice Fish wanted a small and intimate wedding ceremony, though she knew it wouldn't make everyone happy: Tiên, in particular, advocated a grand occasion.

'You need to unite the fleet,' Tiên said. She was sitting in her own rooms, sipping tea. She had offered *Rice Fish* a cup — ships couldn't feed, but food and drink in the overlays were more than just taste; they carried memories and connotations. 'If you're really going for marriage . . .'

'Yes.' *Rice Fish*'s hand hovered over the tea. It smelled of rain, and of Huân laughing at the night sky on one of the large habitats — Bình Mạng, probably, the Đại Việt one, one of their allies. Not a safe place, but not an unfriendly one, either. At least, it hadn't been, but now the Đại Việt empress was dying, and who knew where the Việt stood any more? 'It's only fair.'

'She could be a bondsperson. Or freed.'

'You know that wouldn't give her the protection or status necessary to deal with the banner scholars.'

There was another reason she had offered marriage — one she wasn't speaking aloud: this was the offer Huân had made her, once upon a time. A partnership, proposed because she

12

didn't quite know what to do with the gaping hole in her life. Because she needed to be less lonely.

'Hmm.' Tiên didn't sound convinced. But she was wise enough not to press the subject. 'In any case, the Red Scholar's death has shaken the banner. They need something they can stand behind.'

'I don't think they need another festival. Huân's death banquet was more than enough.'

'You've always hated pomp.' Tiên's voice was fond.

She'd changed out of the clothes she'd worn in the hold: the inner layers remained, but the outer ones were now banyan trees and moons which managed to be just as irreverent and suggestive as the layers they had replaced.

'I understand it serves a purpose,' *Rice Fish* said.

Part of her awareness was following the navigation sensors. They weren't far from the Citadel – on Huân's death, it would have become a nest of scorpions and poisonous centipedes, all vying for a chance to become her consort, or to displace her as head of the Red Banner.

Tough luck. She was in control, and she would have a wife again by the time she got there.

'It does,' Tiên said. 'There might be few rules in the banner—'

'You know that's not true.'

'Mmm,' Tiên said. She knew how sensitive *Rice Fish* was about public displays, and deflected. 'Consider this a need for reassurance, then. The Green Banner will try to make out that you and Huân have been doing unaccountable work in the dark. A secret wedding and a hidden bride will just support this.'

Rice Fish thought of Xích Si – of how abjectly she'd crawled, of how ready she'd been to abase herself – of how angry *Rice Fish* had been, at the way fear broke people.

'I don't think it would be fair.'

Tiên frowned. 'To her?' She was silent for a while. 'She's a scared little thing, isn't she. I wonder how she got that way.'

'I don't know,' *Rice Fish* said. 'But I do know if I push her too hard, she'll break.'

'Perhaps. Or perhaps not.' Tiên drained her tea, staring into the cup as if she could divine the breath of the universe within it. 'You're the boss. Have it your way.'

It was only after she left Tiên's quarters – after she dematerialised her avatar altogether and was, for a moment, just the ship, just flying through the void and monitoring her passengers – the faint chatter of her bots in the background, the myriad feedback from her sensors, the comforting flow of information lulling her to something almost like sleep – that *Rice Fish* realised she'd lied to Tiên.

She wasn't just thinking to spare Xích Si. She couldn't bear to have another grand wedding, the way hers and Huân's had been a grand affair, their boisterous insult thrown in the face of the world.

She'd been young then: a small, scared creature Huân had found in the harbour of what would become the Red Banner's quarters in the Citadel, broken by her captors and towed back to the shipyards in a body she could no longer command, to be rebuilt, to be made obedient by viruses and shadow controllers. She'd been so young when Huân had thrown open the door of her broken airlock and set foot on her deck – and looked up and laughed.

'I see you,' she'd said. 'I see you, big sis.'

Always and forever, except that she'd not foreseen her own death.

Rice Fish hadn't thought she'd miss Huân so much.

*

14

When someone came again for Xích Si, it was the bodyguard – who introduced herself as Tiên, and looked at Xích Si with a particular expression Xích Si couldn't quite make sense of, a mixture of pity and disapproval. She held out something: a red and yellow áo dài.

'She's said she's not sure if you want a wedding dress,' Tiên said. 'Some people find having the ceremonial reassuring, and some people prefer to be reminded of the substance.'

They didn't sound like her words, but like *Rice Fish*'s. The substance. Obviously. A wedding dress for a wedding that was merely a business partnership.

'No,' Xích Si said, before she could think. She didn't need the trappings of a wedding. Not for this.

Tiên nodded, grimly. 'Thought so, too,' she said.

'Where is she?'

Everywhere, technically – they were standing on *Rice Fish*'s body, and every bot, every sensor was her eyes and ears.

'She's waiting for you,' Tiên said, which wasn't an answer, and she must have known it. Tiên gestured for Xích Si to follow her. 'Come, then.'

Outside, the corridor was empty, and oddly silent. Things had been oddly silent for a while – ever since *Rice Fish*'s visit and that fateful acceptance, but as Xích Si stumbled towards wherever Tiên was taking her, it was now obvious that the noises of firecrackers and mourning celebrations were gone. No, not gone; it wasn't likely the celebrations had halted. But the ship could, as she had in the cell, filter them out. The corridor she was in was deserted: a long straight thing with a half-moon section, its walls decorated with ... For a moment they'd been drawings of ship docks, but the moment Xích Si looked, these faded away, and became paintings of the aster-oids of the Twin Streams, the places she'd mined for scraps of metal and ores – and the silhouettes of small ships, such as the ones scavengers would cobble together.

For her. It was intended for her. To show her things could change – to reassure her? She wasn't sure. Some thought had obviously gone into this. She was seen – paid attention to, utterly naked and vulnerable in a way she hadn't been inside the cell.

By the time the door at the end of the corridor opened, Xích Si's breathing was coming in fast.

Inside the featureless room, small and cramped, were only two chairs, and an overlay of scrolling text.

And *Rice Fish*.

She was leaning against the wall – no, not so much leaning against it as coming out of it, her long hair flowing into it and the embroidered cloth of her robes becoming the overlay of the starscape on the wall behind her. And she was *there* – the weight of her presence filling the room with a particular focus, as if the air were made of cloth and someone had pulled it taut, and Xích Si could hardly draw enough air to fill her lungs.

'Child.' She gestured towards the chair.

Xích Si moved towards it in a daze, staring at the text.

As we enter this partnership, we promise that though we weren't born on the same day, on the same month or in the same year, we vow to stand where the other stands, to go where the other goes ... To safeguard each other to the best of our abilities ...

It was a contract. The marriage contract. A list of obligations, of commitments, phrased as a binding oath of sisterhood. A guarantee of her safety – which featured prominently – in exchange for her skills. She was used to selling her skills and parts of herself to survive, but this was on another level entirely.

This ... This was final in so many ways, though hadn't it been final from the moment she'd been dragged from the wreck of her ship?

'Here.' A touch on her wrist, which made her look up, startled – it was *Rice Fish*, standing over a tray which held dumplings and two teacups. The bots that had brought it were already scurrying away. 'Eat something. It's a long read, and you'll want to make sure you understand all of it.'

Ten thousand emotions warred within Xích Si, and the one that won out was not anger, but a deep-seated curiosity.

'You said you didn't need to keep me whole. There's no need to be so considerate.'

Surprise crossed *Rice Fish*'s face, and was swiftly extinguished.

'It's not part of the contract, no. But surely you'd prefer decency.' She smiled, and it was edged and bleakly amused, a minute star glinting for the briefest of moments in her eyes. 'Also, you'd hardly be any use to me if you're burned out from stress.'

'How do you know—?'

That same edged smile. 'I have eyes.'

And bots, and sensors.

'Of course. Keeping a watch on me.'

A silence. When *Rice Fish* spoke again, it wasn't to answer Xích Si's unspoken question.

'Drink,' she said, and it was almost gentle. She picked up one of the two teacups that were in overlay, and sipped at it.

Xích Si, feeling absurdly contrary, went for the dumplings instead, the translucent dough that melted in her mouth, the shrimp filling inside plump and chewy – rich people's food, not the powdered dust with vat-grown algae they had in the outer rings. She reached out for the tea, sipped it as she read through the contract.

For all its length and flowery language, it was, at heart, brutally simple. They swore to take care of each other, and to safeguard each other and each other's interests: for *Rice Fish*, the safety of the banner; for Xích Si, her own safety and her family's safety.

Khanh. A world she couldn't come back to.

Xích Si's eyesight was wavering and blurred. She took a deep breath, forcing herself to focus. To be in the present, where the task at hand mattered. Then – before she could think, before she could change her mind – she signed with her fingerprint and retinal scan, and watched as *Rice Fish* detached herself from the wall – the way that the starscape *flowed* to her hair, leaving the surface behind her blank – and came to sign.

'There,' she said.

It felt strangely anticlimactic.

'That's it?'

A silence. *Rice Fish* had dismissed the overlay, and she was already turning towards the door – Xích Si rose, ready to follow her, when a voice rang out in the small space.

'You should kiss.'

Rice Fish turned, whiplash-fast, staring at Tiên – who was the one who'd spoken.

'We are not,' she said, and her voice cut like a vacuum-blade, the atmosphere in the room going from tight to unbreathably tense. Xích Si fought an urge to throw herself to her knees. It wasn't her *Rice Fish* was angry at. It wasn't her. Not for now.

Tiên appeared utterly unfazed. She moved to stand closer to *Rice Fish*, the peaches on her dress shifting from whole to half-bitten as she did so.

'You know what this is.'

'A business proposition.' *Rice Fish*'s voice was tight and angry, the skin on her face translucent, showing the shape of the ship behind her. 'As you well know.'

'To protect her from the rest of the fleet. Which will only work if they don't think this is a ... pecuniary matter.' Tiên spread her hands. She seemed obscurely delighted by something – perhaps simply by watching *Rice Fish* get angry. 'You know this. I know this.'

'And you think this is going to solve anything?'

Tiên turned to look at Xích Si. There was no anger in her gaze, or pity, but simple thoughtful calculation.

'I think it'll help keep her safe,' she said. 'Signing a contract in a featureless room looks exactly like what it is – business. But a kiss ... then she becomes the successor of the Red Scholar. A love match. And you know the power of that story as well as I do.'

'No one is going to believe I fell in love with a captive within two days of my wife's death.'

'Then they'll believe you have a new toy. Someone to comfort you in your grief.'

Rice Fish's anger was making the room feel smaller and smaller.

'This isn't who I am.' She turned towards Xích Si, the anger leaving her face, leaving it once more that smooth, unreadable mask. 'And this is absolutely not what I offered you.'

'I know,' Xích Si said. Her voice felt tight, alien to her. 'But I'll do it.'

'You ...' *Rice Fish*'s anger slowly abated. She was facing Xích Si, staring at her. Her face softened. She finally said, 'I disagree with Tiên. It's not necessary. Your safety can be guaranteed in other ways. You don't have to do anything which makes you uncomfortable.'

The bots had come out of their alcoves, slowly crawling towards the table. Uncomfortable. And Xích Si suddenly realised, chilled, that she wasn't the one uncomfortable. *Rice Fish* was.

19

She said, simply, 'There's nothing real there. Nothing that matters. But I want to be safe. And we signed a contract where you pledged to safeguard me.' She stood straight — it cost her. 'You said you'd go where I went.' And left the rest unsaid.

Rice Fish's gaze was burning. At length she threw her head back, and laughed — a genuine, fond noise that suddenly made her seem younger and more carefee, and Xích Si found herself bending to catch just another peal of it, in spite of her better instincts.

'Trying to twist the law around me? You forget — it takes two for consent.' And, before Xích Si could say anything: 'But I'll do it, if you think it's necessary.'

One moment she was standing near the door; the next she blinked out of existence, and reappeared in front of Xích Si, one hand reaching for Xích Si's face, a gentle push upwards that Xích Si followed, tilting her face up to stare at her new wife. Their eyes met; in *Rice Fish*'s gaze there was nothing but mild curiosity. She held Xích Si's gaze a fraction longer than necessary, and then bent slowly, one hand still under Xích Si's chin, the other one at Xích Si's nape, an odd, electrifying kind of warmth — and the same kind of cold on Xích Si's lips as *Rice Fish*'s lips brushed them, a touch that shifted into a firmer pressure, becoming a weird, tight feeling in Xích Si's lower back and womb.

Then *Rice Fish* broke away, turning back towards Tiên with barely a pause.

'Satisfied?' she asked.

Xích Si was not satisfied. The diffuse feeling of desire she'd had was only slowly ebbing away, and she felt as though something precious had been wrenched away from her without warning. Which was absurd. They had a contract. A binding agreement. Nothing more.

'That will do,' Tiên said. 'It's very convincing.'

In overlay – where the contract had been – was now a picture of both of them kissing, gazing into each other's eyes as if they were lost soulmates and the thread of fate had wound itself tightly around them. Xích Si's stomach churned. Half of her wanted to walk away from the picture and never look at it again, and half of her – the half that still felt the warmth of *Rice Fish*'s lips on hers – was tempted.

Rice Fish's voice was cool and composed.

'Good. Then we're done here. Come.'

Absurd. Utterly absurd. Xích Si should follow *Rice Fish*'s example – much as it galled her to be following a pirate's lead – and put the whole matter out of her head.

Rice Fish tried not to think about the kiss.

It meant nothing. They had signed a contract. That Tiên was right – that the best way to guarantee Xích Si's safety was to follow appearances, to have at least a formality of a kiss, something to make it abundantly clear that Xích Si wasn't to be touched on account of being not just useful, but cared for – didn't change the nature of what had happened.

But, for a bare moment – when Xích Si had leaned into the kiss, when she'd breathed harder, not from fear or stress but from reflexive desire – when she'd softened and her entire being had seemed to change – *Rice Fish* had felt something. Like a drop of water on parched lips, a stirring of something she'd lost a long time ago.

Something utterly forbidden. It wasn't what she'd offered Xích Si; and even if it had been on offer, the differences in their statuses – and Xích Si being barely out of her prison cell, a cell *Rice Fish* had held the keys to – precluded anything.

No. She couldn't – wouldn't – go there.

Instead, *Rice Fish* walked slowly through her own corridors and cabins, with Xích Si behind her, a burning presence that she did her best to focus on. To soothe and comfort.

Part of *Rice Fish* wasn't there: part of her was flying through the Jade Stream towards the Citadel; part of her was monitoring bots; and part of her was sitting, stiff and upright and unsmiling, at her wife's mourning ceremony, listening to overblown songs about the Red Scholar's exploits that were so out of proportion Huân would have laughed in embarrassment. *Rice Fish* could maintain two avatars with a little effort, but interacting with people on a more than superficial level required more attention − and she'd rather keep all of those processing threads for Xích Si.

As Xích Si walked behind her avatar, *Rice Fish* changed for her, as she'd changed on her way from the cell to the marriage room: the paintings on the walls becoming the asteroids of the Jade Stream, the silence broken by faint folk songs of the An O Empire. She didn't know what would be a comfort to Xích Si, but she owed it to her to try. Her bots' legs clicked on the floor − she didn't need their sensors to see Xích Si's tense muscles and accelerated heartbeat. This wasn't just marriage, for her; it was a tearing away from her old life, an acknowledgement it would never return. *Rice Fish* had seen so many recruits and bondspeople go through it − the denial and the anger and the grief. She could remember, like a distant echo, what it had been like when Huân had picked her, when she'd signed her own contract: the feel of the table at which she'd sat; the smell of incense; the heat of Huân's bots next to hers. It had felt like being on the edge of a leap into deep spaces, a gesture that once started couldn't be walked back or erased.

'Here,' *Rice Fish* said, in front of a door with the double happiness symbol shimmering on its metal.

Xích Si pushed it.

It was the room where *Rice Fish* received her bannerpeople,

22

and dignitaries. The overlay was rich and formal, and half the furniture was physical — not *Rice Fish*'s preference, but some envoys liked to occupy the physical rather than the virtual layers. Half the room was occupied by a large bed, and on that bed she'd spread the bridal gifts: three red boxes with the golden traceries of two fish slowly turning into dragons. The boxes were open, showcasing what they contained: bridal jewellery, and new bots for Xích Si to bind to her.

'These are for you,' *Rice Fish* said.

Xích Si was breathing hard; *Rice Fish*'s sensors caught the frantic sound of her heartbeat, the fast blinking, the way her hands clenched and unclenched, the stress worse than the one she'd experienced when she'd signed the contract. She turned to face *Rice Fish's* avatar, but *Rice Fish* had already seen the pallor of her face.

'I didn't expect that reaction to gifts,' *Rice Fish* said lightly.

'The bed.' Xích Si's voice was shaking. 'There's only one.'

Oh. It had been obvious to her, and it would have been obvious to anyone within the Red Banner, or anyone used to dealing with the pirate alliance, but Xích Si was a poor scavenger, and mindships might as well have existed in another universe.

'I don't sleep,' *Rice Fish* said. 'And technically I'm no more present here than anywhere else. I'm not monitoring these rooms other than for critical life support breaches, and you can invoke privacy privileges if you want to be sure my bots or sensors aren't activated in here. I ask that you not do it too often — I need to maintain this room as much as the rest of my body.'

Xích Si opened her mouth, and closed it. The fear in her eyes was slowly receding.

'Present. Your body. You—'

'I told you. You're safe here.'

At the mourning banquet, Huân's son was now pouring wine in a virtual overlay — he had his own command and was on his own ship, and thank Heaven *Rice Fish* didn't have to deal with his anger and grief, just with his beamed-in holo. She pulled her awareness away from that avatar, let it be little more than bots running on low-level automatic routines.

Xích Si was breathing hard. She took one, two faltering steps towards the bed — reached for the bots, cradled them in her arms as they activated. There was a workbench nearby: just a materialisation of the access privileges that *Rice Fish* had given her. She rose, made her way there, the bots spreading across her shoulders — one stretching and melting to cover her palm, and form three rings on her fingers — and stared at the bench for what felt like an eternity.

'I'll leave you,' *Rice Fish* said. Of course she'd need time, and solitude. 'I've already asked someone to locate your daughter. But for now, you need sleep ...'

Xích Si raised a hand. The bots followed it, flowing up her arm. For a long, stretched, silent period — time that *Rice Fish* could count, blink by blink — Xích Si stood stock-still, her breath rising and falling. *Rice Fish* could see the minute shift in her chest muscles, the way she slowly, deliberately got her breathing under control, from the near panic to an even and slow rhythm, an act of sheer strength of will managed while standing absolutely unmoving, and with no other hint of the turmoil that must have been going on inside.

When Xích Si turned back to *Rice Fish*, her face was hard.

'Tell me,' she said. 'Tell me how your wife died.'

Rice Fish struggled not to take a step back ... but she wasn't about to give way on her own body.

'It's your wedding night,' she said, slowly, gently.

The corners of Xích Si's lips rose, but only a fraction. 'And it's not that kind of marriage, is it? Tell me.'

Rice Fish had misjudged her new wife; she'd thought Xích Si would be bewildered, or lost, or soft — but there was nothing of softness in the way she faced *Rice Fish* now, with the bots on her, body as taut as a leaping dancer's. She was ... incandescent and proud and utterly, dazzlingly beautiful. Something long forgotten twisted in *Rice Fish*'s innards — in her heartroom, where the organic core of her was plugged into her body, where she was most vulnerable, something expanded and missed a beat. She found herself faltering, as she had during the kiss.

Not that kind of marriage.

Never that kind of marriage.

She and Huân had had mutual respect, and some fondness, but that was all that could be expected. All that she deserved, now and forever.

'I'll tell you what happened,' *Rice Fish* said.

She moved closer to Xích Si, conjured a chair and sat near the workbench, well away from Xích Si's enticing tautness, far enough away that she didn't have to feel or touch her. But of course Xích Si's feet rested on the floor of one of her cabins, and she felt the minute pressure as she shifted position and walked to the bench. She didn't sit; she stood in front of it, biting her lips, and finally summoned a screen overlay keyed to both of them — the kind used for a vid or a picture, except that it was empty.

'Show me,' she said.

It was an invitation, but one as sharp and as cutting as a knife's blade: a call to battle.

Rice Fish conjured, one after the other, screen overlays: maps and ships and pictures of the banners and the empires — everything Xích Si would need to make sense of the world she now moved in.

25

'Here,' she said, laying it out like a peace offering. 'Here is what happened.'

Xích Si cocked her head, and stared, not at the screen, but straight at her. Her eyes were a brown so dark it was almost black, intent and piercing.

'Thank you,' she said, holding *Rice Fish*'s gaze.

I see you, big sis, Huân's voice whispered in her thoughts.

Do you? She shut it down, mercilessly – redirecting it to the avatar at Huân's funeral banquet, where it was drowned by rice wine and the weeping mourners. *You're dead, li'l sis. A corpse fractured by deep spaces. Let the living take care of themselves, and of what you left behind.*

In her thoughts, Huân laughed – because she knew, as did *Rice Fish*, that the dead couldn't be put to rest so easily.

3

Wedding Night

Xích Si inhaled, and stared at the screen.

Everything was dancing and wavering, her thoughts saturated with too much information, too many people, too many grievances and old records. What steadied her was the job: the analysis of the data so she could find the proof *Rice Fish* needed. It might not be something she'd ever thought she'd do for pirates, but it was a familiar job: a steadying task she could keep focused on.

Rice Fish was watching her, sprawled in the chair she'd pulled out. She was sharply defined from head to waist, and then the red and golden wedding robes slowly darkened and sharpened until they became the metal of the egg-shaped chair, and her long hair below the topknot was shadows on the metal. Her gaze was ... not predatory or heavy, but simply curious.

'You don't have to take it all in now,' she said, gently.

Affectionately, Xích Si would have said, except that she was a pirate, and she wouldn't have risen so far if she was weak. She was a pirate, and her kind had killed Ngà.

But when she'd told Xích Si she'd be safe, her voice had

been soft, and even: a quiet statement of the way things were, an utter certainty – a hard, comforting fact to which Xích Si could cling.

It'd have been easier if Xích Si could trust her.

'You'll want me to hold up on my end of the bargain,' Xích Si said, more sharply than she meant to.

A raised eyebrow. 'You're no use to me if you crash and burn.'

'And I'm of no use to myself if I go around like a backwater planet bumpkin.' Xích Si closed her eyes. Her bots nested on her shoulders and hands again; they felt worn and comforting. They shouldn't have – not when she'd seen the previous ones gutted and burned, had held their corpses – but these had the same feel and the same heft, recreated with painstaking attention to detail. An apology, of sorts; and of course she couldn't work without them. 'Tell me again.'

'Everything that led up to it?' *Rice Fish* considered. 'On the surface, it was an uneventful raiding season. The usual number of merchant ships that weren't careful enough, weren't protected enough.'

It almost sounded bloodless. It almost sounded ... fair. Which it couldn't be. It was pillaging and blood and pain, parasites taking what they wanted and destroying the rest. It couldn't be fair. It would never be.

'You said "on the surface"?'

'Yes.' *Rice Fish* sipped a cup of tea that had materialised out of nowhere. 'We have our own rules. The alliance has five banners, out of which the Red Banner is only one. And each smaller pirate craft owes loyalty only to their banner scholar. In turn, the council oversees the banner scholars.'

'And you're the Red Scholar.'

'Not officially. Not yet,' *Rice Fish* said. 'It's likely that I will be, but the council would need to confirm me as Huân's heir first.' She considered. 'I said "on the surface" because things were happening in the background. Little things at first. High tension within the Citadel. Arguments at flower-poetry contests. Too many brawls, too many incidents between banners in teahouses. More raids than usual that ended in slaughter. Larger targets.'

'Because you don't slaughter outright?'

Rice Fish paused, and Xích Si tensed, but she merely went on.

'Not as much as you seem to fear. We do this for money. But some ... Yes, they seemed to be doing it for cruelty's sake. And at first it was one banner, and then it was several. It was starting to look like someone in the banners was making a power play.'

Xích Si frowned. She called up the display again, looked at the ships that had killed the Red Scholar. Massive open-the-voids and the smaller three-plates. They moved far too smoothly, without any of the lags she was used to in the Twin Streams. They were too sleek, too smooth.

'Those ships aren't pirate ships. They're official. So why talk of banner politics?'

'No, those ships weren't from the banners. You're right. They're imperial. They belonged to Censor Trúc. I think someone in the banners – someone who wanted Huân dead – found a common cause with the imperial forces, who want all pirates dead as a matter of principle.'

'Imperial ships. The empire.'

'There are two empires, but yes. The one you come from.'

Her voice was even, dismissive.

How could she?

'It's my home,' Xích Si said.

A quirk of *Rice Fish's* lips.

'You think I should be making one here.'

29

'I think birds have wasted away in cages looking south,' *Rice Fish* said.

It was one scholarly metaphor too many.

'You're the one holding the keys of the cage!' The words were out of her mouth before she realised what she'd said, and to whom. 'I'm sorry, I shouldn't have ... Please don't—'

'Don't what?'

Rice Fish rose, and stretched. As she did, her hair lengthened and changed, became the Twin Streams, the river of stars across the sky. She wasn't an imperial mindship; she wasn't a wife or a friend. She was a pirate consort, one who pillaged and burned and killed. Why would she spare a mouthy scavenger who'd offered her nothing of value?

Xích Si threw herself to the floor – or tried to, because *Rice Fish* was suddenly there, and her bots were holding her immobile, pinned to the chair, Xích Si's own bots swept aside and clattering to the floor.

'*Don't,*' *Rice Fish* said, and this time the anger in her voice was unmistakable. 'Not ever again. Don't *ever* think of degrading yourself as a solution to anything again. Or apologising for your anger.'

A heartbeat; her eyes holding Xích Si's; her hands replacing the bots, a soft and warm touch that spread to Xích Si's body. It was relayed through the perception layers, a touch that wasn't physical and no longer prevented Xích Si from rising. She could have shaken *Rice Fish* off with a shrug. She tried to say something sarcastic or wounding, but the expression in *Rice Fish*'s eyes stopped her.

'Your old life ended when you were captured. I can't give it back to you. I can't turn back time. I'd say it's not my fault, but it was my banner, so it is my responsibility.' Her eyes filmed red, like the heart of a star, like bridal clothes. 'You don't want to hear it from me, but … you have to make the most of what you have.'

Something Xích Si had heard so many times, from so many condescending elders and officials. Except that *Rice Fish*'s voice wasn't contemptuous or dismissive, but worried.

She cares.

So few had. Parents, long dead, worn to nubs by the scavenging life. Ngà, once. Auntie Vy and her wife. Thấy An Sơn, a nun at the pagoda who'd given her scraps of metal for her bots, and taken Xích Si's own offerings with utter seriousness, no matter how small and inadequate they'd been. Her scavenger friends, Hoa and Vân and Ngọc Nữ, who'd always known when to bring braised dishes and spare rice.

Rice Fish had withdrawn her hands and taken a step back, but she was still staring at Xích Si with an intensity that could have seared metal, and around her the room was growing darker and warmer, with faint flashes like a storm on the sun's surface. Xích Si could still feel the imprints of the ship's hold on her, and part of her – the treacherous, oblivious, primal part – longed to be held; not pinned in the chair, but wrapped in someone's arms and held as though she mattered.

Don't ever think of degrading yourself as a solution to anything again.

Everyone is someone.

'We're business partners,' she said, finally, because words had fled and all she had left were scattered thoughts. 'I understand that.'

Rice Fish stared at her, for a little longer than necessary. Xích Si saw a flicker of hurt in the depths of her eyes.

Why?

'A business arrangement,' she said, finally. Her voice almost sounded smooth – but not quite enough.

'You said someone from the banners was making a power

play,' Xích Si said, returning to their safer and more innocuous conversation, though it was still filled with so many landmines. She had work to get to. 'And ... two empires?'

'We're attacking the An O Empire's merchants. The Đại Việt are on the other side of the Twin Streams. Their dynasty is younger, beleaguered and in desperate need of money, so they train us and let us loose in return for a percentage of the profit.'

Xích Si had seen many Việt merchants in Triệu Hoà Port. She was vaguely aware of them, and of the hostility the empire had for them – they'd been at war once, a long time ago.

'All right. When you said someone in the banners, it sounded like you had someone very specific in mind.'

'Mmm. The first banner that started behaving ... oddly was the Green Banner. Kim Thông, the Green Scholar, is a long-time enemy of Huân and I.' *Rice Fish* moved slightly, her hair and the chair shifting with her.

'What happened?'

'I don't really know,' *Rice Fish* said. 'But she's always wanted the power Huân and I were wielding, and she's always been resentful. She started becoming more and more aggressive in council sessions, and then outright trying to displace us. So it would make sense.'

'What about the other banners?'

'The Black and White Banners are neutral, but their scholars are weak,' *Rice Fish* said. 'The Purple Banner ...' A hitch, in her voice. 'The Purple Scholar is our son. Mine and Huân's. We don't get on, but I have no reason to doubt his loyalty.' The words were a little too quick: there was pain there, buried deep, and Xích Si didn't feel brave enough to probe. 'And the last member of the council is the Đại Việt envoy. She doesn't head any banners, but she represents the empire bankrolling us, so she's entitled to a seat.' There was amusement in her voice. 'The Green Banner is the one you should focus on, for the time being.'

'To find your proof.'

'Yes.' *Rice Fish*'s voice was hard. 'If Kim Thông is indeed in communication with Censor Trúc and the An O Empire, then I have a problem that goes beyond a political struggle. The whole alliance would be at stake, because Censor Trúc wants to destroy us. But the council would never dismiss the Green Scholar without evidence.'

Without the strongest kind of evidence.

Xích Si didn't need to be told how it worked, for the powerful. But this in turn told her that *Rice Fish*'s position might not be as secure as she projected it to be. That, for all her cool self-confidence, she might be ... No, she couldn't afford to see *Rice Fish* as bewildered and fearful. She was a pirate, and that was all Xích Si needed to remember.

The Green Scholar, Kim Thông. And Censor Trúc.

Xích Si stared at the screen again, at the map displayed on the overlay. The pirates had been headed back to their citadel – and its satellites, the myriad hideouts dotted in the asteroids of the Jade Stream. Raiding season had been almost over. They'd berth at their private ports and weather the calmer months while the merchants were busy marking festivals and planning for the future: negotiating rates; mapping out diving expeditions in the Fire Palace; and renting hold-space on ships headed to the centre of the empire. And Đại Việt, the empire's neighbour and the pirates' allies, would be busy with its own festivals and pageants. The Red Scholar, coming home with a ship full of stolen Ashling artefacts and debris, hadn't expected to find a fleet of imperial ships, still less Censor Trúc, the imperial officer who'd made it her business to destroy the pirates in the Jade Stream.

But Censor Trúc had clearly been expecting her.

'They knew where she'd be,' Xích Si said. She bit her lip, sweeping aside the map to call up the sequence of the battle. 'Exactly where she'd be. And which ship she was on. I don't mean they received a message prior to the battle – there's something more involved. They're tracking her too well. Here.' She pointed to the final moments of the Red Scholar's life, when the small three-plates ship she'd been on had attempted to escape the mass of open-the-void crafts surrounding the pirate fleet. Two ships had immediately turned to follow her. 'It was a three-plates. A ship that's small but not fast, and not heavily armoured. It's the worst possible option to flee a battle zone. They shouldn't have expected her to be on it – but there's no hesitation, and they address her by name before they open fire.'

She looked at *Rice Fish* as she was speaking. She wasn't sure what to expect; the Red Scholar had been her wife, and all that pent-up anger had to include some grief. But *Rice Fish*'s avatar stared straight ahead, and her expression only hardened.

'A spy in the Red Banner, then.'

'Mmmm.' Xích Si stared at the battle overlay. 'I think someone's tracking her messages. If it's a spy, it's not a human one. How much of her data log and bots did you recover?'

Rice Fish's lips thinned. 'Not much. She tumbled into the vacuum of space from a ship which was torn to pieces by energy weapons. Frozen pieces, and no one bothered to track down the bot-fragments. But there are backups.' Her voice was steady and cool, but keeping it that way clearly cost her; Xích Si had been in similar situations, staring down tribunal officials and not letting them see her upset or her anger. 'I'll see that you get them before we reach the Citadel.'

'The Citadel.' The pirates' hideout, in the empty zone around Triệu Hoà Port – too many asteroids in the Jade Stream, and not enough empire militia to scan them all. The fabled heart of piratehood. 'Of course. Raiding season is over.' Now Xích Si worked to keep her voice steady. All that stood between her and every pirate in the Citadel was a contract, and *Rice Fish*, and it seemed pitifully inadequate.

'It's not one place.' *Rice Fish*'s voice was kind, and disturbingly perceptive. 'It's a collection of habitats on different asteroids, with extended avatar privileges. You won't have to leave Red Banner space if you don't want to.'

She needed to ask – she needed to know, right now – what the terms of her captivity, her *marriage*, were.

'And if I do?'

A cocked head. 'I'm not your jailer. I'll make introductions for you, to the banner and outside it. And I'll assign ships to you.'

Xích Si stared, again, at the battle spread in front of her: at the ships crowding each other in what seemed almost a dance – except that everyone was in thrall to orbital mechanics – and it was more akin to the theatre, where everyone's skin colour and expression defined the roles that they couldn't escape.

'Ships. For my protection?'

'For whatever you deem them useful for,' *Rice Fish* said. 'You're my consort. That comes with power of your own.'

Xích Si said, 'What do you want?'

'I told you. A partnership. Proof of the Green Scholar's guilt.'

'I know this. And I know you'll go to the council with that evidence. That's not what I'm asking. What matters most to you? Avenging the Red Scholar, or safeguarding the alliance?'

Rice Fish blinked, and stared at her. Xích Si suddenly felt the ship's entire attention shift like a palpable thing, the room becoming smaller – no, it wasn't the room, it was merely that *Rice Fish* loomed larger within it. Her gaze held Xích Si, transfixing her like a harpoon – until Xích Si had to look away, flushed and flustered.

35

'Smart question,' *Rice Fish*'s voice was light and ironic. 'You mean — am I turned towards the past or the future? I was never one for vengeance.' A thoughtful silence. 'The alliance must stand. The Green Scholar has turned, which makes us vulnerable. We're only strong so long as we stand together.'

So they could attack more ships and hoard more ill-gotten wealth, and continue to prey on and torture the weak?

'You still think we're monsters.' *Rice Fish*'s voice was mild. 'I'm not reading your mind. I have more advanced perceptions than human beings, especially when you're on my body.'

Xích Si clenched her fists — she was tensed for an explosion from *Rice Fish*, but nothing happened. It was ... disturbing.

'This is a safe place,' *Rice Fish* said. 'A place where you don't have a choice between starving or selling yourself or your children into indenture. A place where there are no greater or lesser spouses, merely partners and lovers. Where everyone has rights.'

'Even the bondspeople?' She shouldn't have asked, but it came out like blood from a wound.

'In this banner, yes,' *Rice Fish* said. 'As I said — not everyone approved of my wife and our policies.'

That anger beneath her words wasn't aimed at Xích Si — again, a disturbing realisation. How could she be so calm, so ... civilised?

You still think we're monsters.

She did. She knew who she'd married, who her life belonged to. Who she was inextricably tied to — not by choice, but because she had no other alternatives. As *Rice Fish* had said, her old life was now dead to her.

It hurt. Xích Si made space for the pain — in the same way she had after Ngà's death, going back to scavenging, swallowing the bitter ashes of her dreams, knowing she'd never be wealthy, and she'd never be a partner on a merchant ship. As she'd always done, she'd accepted the inevitability that the world would always turn against her; that ambition was and always had been a poison. But it still hurt.

She channelled it the only way she knew how: into her work and obligations.

'Can you get me those logs? And those ships you mentioned, my honour guard.'

'Of course.'

Rice Fish was still watching her; the entire room was still saturated with her attention. Her eyes were black once more, and her clothes were shifting, the golden embroideries of the phoenixes spreading their wings, flying amid a sea of stars. She seemed surprised, and interested. She hadn't expected Xích Si to react like this.

Well, tough luck.

There was no way under Heaven that Xích Si would show her more weakness than she'd already displayed.

'What's your idea?' *Rice Fish* asked.

'I have lots of ideas,' Xích Si said. 'The problem is determining which ones are worth following up on.'

Rice Fish laughed. It was a crystalline and carefree sound — twisting in Xích Si's chest in some odd and unexpected way. She had no right to be so ... so genuinely pleased. So genuinely proud.

Partners. They were partners, and *Rice Fish* was Xích Si's protector, and that was all there was to it. That was all there would ever be.

4

Wanderings

Two days before they arrived at the Citadel, Xích Si called *Rice Fish*.

'Yes?' the ship asked.

She didn't materialise in the middle of Xích Si's cabin – instead, her voice echoed around the room, as if she were standing right beside Xích Si. The effect was uncanny.

'Is anyone out at this time of night?'

An uncertain pause.

'What do you mean?'

'I want to go out,' Xích Si said. 'On the ship. On ... you.' She'd stared at logs until her eyes ached – tried to find threads of logic within the Red Scholar's death that stubbornly refused to materialise. She was frazzled and exhausted, and feeling cooped up in a small, vaguely friendly space in the midst of an ocean of uncertain goodwill, if not outright hostility. 'Find out what you're like. What it's like.'

But the thought of walking into a den of pirates weighing her up just paralysed her.

A silence.

'I see,' *Rice Fish* said. She didn't quite sound like she did, but it didn't really matter. And then, slowly, 'At this time of night, most people on this floor are asleep. And I can provide you with filters.'

'Will they help?'

'They will make you less conspicuous. People never turn off the physical layer – and there are safeguards so no one can sneak up on anyone unseen – so they'll still see and hear you. Would you like to do this?'

They could still see her. Hear her. Xích Si fought the brief rising wave of panic. But she was here now, among pirates. She was married to a pirate. It was her future – and she couldn't spend all of it shut in a small room because of fear. She needed to do what made the most sense.

'Yes,' she said. 'Do you have a map?'

Brief, amused laughter filled the space around Xích Si.

'Of course.' A further silence, as if *Rice Fish* were chewing on something. Then: 'Remember, you are my wife. They will not touch a hair on your head, or there will be consequences.'

And before Xích Si could answer, the sense of *Rice Fish*'s presence vanished like a popped bubble, but her words remained.

There will be consequences.

She was safe. As safe as she could be, and she couldn't hide forever.

Xích Si took a deep breath, and headed out of the cabin.

It was silent and deserted outside: a corridor decorated with scrolling calligraphy. She could hear snatches of sound, very distantly – laughter and songs, and wailing from the last of the funeral banquets. There were no pirates that she could see, yet. And even if they were, she was *Rice Fish*'s wife. They wouldn't touch her.

The map – which she glanced at in overlay – placed her near the centre of the ship, close to the heartroom, the place where

39

Rice Fish's organic core was plugged in. A mindship's highest vulnerability. Heading that way felt ... too charged, too intimate. Too much outside of the bounds of their marriage.

The other way, then.

There were five floors on the ship, the map said. Four hundred people on board the ship. Xích Si, wandering the floors, found them all merged into a bewildering series of corridors, some sloping upwards, some downwards – some folding back on themselves until she was no longer sure which way was up or down. The walls were decorated with calligraphy, with alcoves containing jade ornaments, celadon cups, asteroid fragments, star maps – a dizzying mix of physical and overlay that changed as Xích Si walked, as it had changed on her wedding night, the ship adapting herself to be more comforting.

At the next octagonal intersection, there was a pirate.

Xích Si tensed, readying herself to flee; but the pirate stared back at her, briefly noting her and nodding at her. They were an elderly person with grey hair in a stern topknot – not a stray hair out of place. Their dark, wrinkled skin was tanned with starlight. They could have been an elder, except for the gun in their belt, and the suggestive way the large sleeves of their unadorned silk robe bulged: the promise of further weapons.

Xích Si stared at them, but the pirate had already looked away, their distant gaze absorbed in an overlay: they were reading or watching a vid, and Xích Si was just another person on board the ship.

No one will touch you.

Xích Si had expected hostility or a desire to hurt her, but not this matter-of-fact indifference. Her stomach still felt empty, her heart hammering too strongly against her chest.

Focus. Focus.

Nothing was going to happen to her. She knew nothing was going to happen to her, except that her stomach felt empty and her heart was hammering too strongly against her chest.

More intersections. Two women, smiling, staring into each other's eyes – they barely noticed Xích Si as she crept by, bending towards each other for a quick kiss, and then running forward, towards a cabin with an open door, giggling and already trying to take each other's clothes off. More people, yawning and on their way to their beds, barely paying any attention to Xích Si or to the frantic beating of her heart. How many people were on board the ship?

A handful of pirates stood by a glittering overlay fountain, laughing and nudging each other, lifting wine cups. They were a ship – their avatar a humanoid figure with a small model of the ship held in a second and third set of hands – and three younger women, two of whom were very obviously drunk, and the last one keeping a wary eye. Xích Si walked past them, heart in her throat – as she neared the fountain, she must have made a noise, because the watch-woman looked up, sharply, finally noticing Xích Si.

'You're new,' she said.

The ship with the six arms laughed, waving an overlay cup in Xích Si's direction.

'Come and join us!'

Join us.

The watch-woman was still staring at Xích Si, face hard – she could have been any of the people who'd grabbed Xích Si and dragged her off the ship – weather-beaten and lean, her gun on her knees and her eyes glinting in the darkness.

Join us.

Xích Si panicked.

'I'm ...' she said. 'Good. I'm good.'

But when the watch-woman spoke, her voice was soft, and kind.

'Oh, I see. Very new.' Her face remained hard, but there was concern in her eyes. She gestured towards the fountain, as one of the drunk woman produced a cup out of nowhere. 'Have a drink.'

Xích Si's heart rate spiked. She wasn't drinking with pirates. She ... She wasn't going to make small talk with people who killed for a living. She couldn't ...

She breathed out, tensing herself to run – and felt a touch on her shoulder. It was the mindship, staring at her, the dark, deepset eyes the only visible feature on their humanoid body.

'It's all right,' they said. 'You can say no if you don't want to come with us. We can do this later. Or not at all.'

The touch on her shoulder vanished. The ship took a step back and waited, head cocked.

Xích Si stared at them, suddenly unsure of what she could say. Or should say.

'I'd rather be alone,' she said, finally. They were still looking at her. 'But thank you for the invitation.'

A shrug, from the watch-woman. 'We've all been there.' She held out the full cup to Xích Si. 'Do you want this one anyway? To enjoy the night.'

Xích Si walked away slowly, holding the cup, with an odd, uncomfortable feeling in her chest. She went back to where she'd come from – to the more deserted areas of the ship, closer and closer to the heartroom. The corridors still had people in them, but it was clear there'd been some kind of change of shift: fewer faces around, and many doors closed with light filtering through them, and absolutely no sound coming from inside, thanks to the privacy filters.

She stopped, at last, in an empty area some way from her cabin – a corridor with scrolling texts, where she sat down.

'Ship?' she said. 'Elder aunt?'

'Child.' *Rice Fish*'s avatar coalesced in front of her: translucent at first and then gaining more and more solidity from the

42

floor up, the sweep of her hair made up of stars and scrolling texts. 'What do you want?' She cocked her head. 'You're less scared than you were earlier.'

'How ...?' But, of course, she could read Xích Si's body language. 'You were watching me.'

'I'm always watching you,' *Rice Fish* said. 'I did say there would be consequences if someone touched you. And the marriage contract guarantees your physical safety.'

Xích Si exhaled. It felt ... so clinical and distanced, and so intensely frustrating in a way that made her want to scream. It wasn't what she'd hoped for — but she couldn't name or pinpoint what she would actually hope for.

'You can change the decorations for a single person, can't you? You were doing it for the wedding.'

'What you see in overlay can vary, yes.'

A silence.

'Can you ...? Can you show me the stars outside?'

A smile, swift and quickly extinguished, that seemed to light the entire avatar from within.

'Of course.'

The overlay in front of Xích Si shifted, became a large window across the length of the wall. The text faded into darkness — and in that darkness, gradually, shone stars. Not just pinpoints of lights, but moving, pulsing swathes intertwined with a faint, distant sound. And the larger, darker mass of asteroids around them — the Jade Streams, the larger of the Twin Streams — not just masses of rocks, but hard, edged things that added their own harmonies to that intangible song. 'Is that how you see them?'

'Yes,' *Rice Fish* said.

'That's ... That's beautiful.' The words were out of Xích Si's mouth before she could think.

She felt the tenseness, then. *Rice Fish* had moved closer to

43

her, the weight of her presence palpable. Xích Si reached out, and touched the ship on the shoulder. Unexpected coolness spread to her fingers, as well as a distant pulse that felt deeper – and she suddenly realised it was the pulse beneath her feet.

'I'm sorry,' she said. 'I didn't intend to cause offence.'

Rice Fish was still looking at the hand on her shoulder. At length, she reached out with a hand that was trailing starlight, and held it for a fraction of a second longer than necessary.

'It's all right.' She turned her gaze again to the window. 'How did you find it?'

The ship. The pirates. Everything that had to mean so much to her.

Xích Si thought for a while.

'Not what I'd expected,' she said, finally.

She held out the wine cup, watched the fractured starlight reflect itself on the surface of the liquid. It felt cold, faintly reminiscent of *Rice Fish*'s sharply cold touch when Xích Si had touched her.

'Better, or worse?' *Rice Fish*'s voice was faintly sarcastic.

'Different.' Terrifying, and yet ... And yet it was a place where people lived. Where people laughed. Where ... Where people could offer her the kindness of a wine cup. 'Not unsafe,' she said, finally.

A silence she could have cut with a knife. Then *Rice Fish*'s hand, holding hers again, squeezing briefly.

'I'm glad to hear that.' A moment's hesitation. 'Li'l sis.'

Xích Si's heart leaped into her chest. She hadn't misheard. She was sure she hadn't. In one pronoun change, *Rice Fish* had made the gap between them so much smaller, from casual verging on formal to almost intimate.

'Big sis?' she said, feeling as though she'd swallowed live electricity.

'We *are* partners,' *Rice Fish* said, and there was an edge to it Xích Si couldn't quite interpret.

'Are you sad about your wife?' she asked, finally.

Rice Fish was silent, for a while, watching the starlight.

'A little,' she said. 'But it's more like ... some people leave large, gaping holes in the world when they leave.'

Ah. Grief.

Xích Si said, finally, 'It's hard to let go.'

A sigh. 'Yes. For you, too, isn't it? Not of the dead, but of the life you had before. The one that ended when you ran into us.'

Out of all the things she hadn't expected, compassion and pity was high on the list.

'I don't ...' she started, and felt *Rice Fish*'s hands holding hers. Pity. Compassion. 'Yes,' she said, finally, exhaling. 'It's hard.'

Rice Fish nodded, and said nothing more – and for a time that felt like ten thousand years, they remained side by side, looking at the stars.

5

Accountings

As they approached the Citadel, *Rice Fish*, inevitably, turned her thoughts to banner business.

This close to the Citadel, there shouldn't have been much prey, but the banner ran into a handful of foolhardy merchant ships without much of an escort; they had probably gambled on raiding season being over, and on the death of the Red Scholar throwing the banner into disarray. A disastrous gamble, as things went.

'Slim pickings,' Tiên grumbled.

She was calling *Rice Fish* from the wreck of one of the ships – she was physically there, which wasn't surprising, given that Tiên much preferred physical presence to anything involving overlays.

'You sound very annoyed,' *Rice Fish* said.

'You'd think people lacking the common sense to avoid banner space would have a little more in the way of valuables,' Tiên said.

She was standing in the midst of corpses, in a bulwark stained by burn-marks and blood, a testament to how much resistance the merchants had put up. Behind her, two bannerpeople were leading away two of the survivors, now prisoners – two middle-aged women with wrists and legs chained together. Their gazes moved towards Tiên's – and for a moment it seemed to *Rice Fish* that they were looking straight at her through the comms-link, terrified and trying to make themselves as small as possible.

And for a bare moment *Rice Fish*, staring at them, remembered what it had been like, all those years ago, before Huân found her, when she'd just been captured herself, broken and immobile and tied to a dock by multiple restraints: knowing that she was doomed, that they would do what they wanted to her; that they would rebuild her, install viruses that would make her utterly obedient – *pleased* to be serving them. For a bare moment she remembered the weight of that despair. What would have happened, if Huân hadn't found and freed her?

And then the moment passed, and she was herself again, Huân's widow, the Red Consort. The de facto head of the Red Banner, far, far removed from these traumatic beginnings – wondering how to stay in power, how to protect her own people rather than narrowly focusing on her own survival. Those two women would be indentured or ransomed; it was a harsh but fair system.

'Anyway,' Tiên said, 'we'll process the corpses to make some fertiliser.' She sighed, looking at the burned walls around her. 'And probably take the ship apart, too. There's no salvaging this.'

'I'm going to need an accounting,' *Rice Fish* said.

'Of this raid, or of the overall banner situation?' Tiên's voice was sharp. The half-bitten peaches on her robes flickered in and out of existence.

'Everything,' *Rice Fish* said. 'The council has accepted that I lead the Red Banner, but they haven't confirmed me as the Red Scholar yet. They still hope they can displace me.' It wasn't altogether surprising: weakness was a thing to be taken advantage of, at this level in the banners. 'The more I can demonstrate that the fleet is bringing in money and resources, the less successful an attempt is likely to be.'

It wasn't as much of a preoccupation as figuring out what the Green Banner was up to, but having to deal with Kim Thông from a fragile position wasn't ideal.

Tiên pursed her lips. 'You'll have it.'

Rice Fish found Xích Si in her room, in front of the console. She was poring over what looked like data from the recordings, but her vitals remained elevated, her heart rate still faster than the norm – and it jumped further when the other people with *Rice Fish* came into the room.

'We can do this another time,' *Rice Fish* said to Xích Si, over their private comms channel.

She'd given Xích Si ample warning and Xích Si had said yes, but *Rice Fish* measured how stressful it had to be.

Xích Si pursed her lips. She did that thing again – a long breath and a straightening of her spine, her bots riding in a slightly different way, shifting in one blink from frightened captive to empress in her own palace – that thing that left *Rice Fish* a little giddy and a little amazed, feeling too large and too tight for her body to contain her.

'No. Now. Ahead of the Citadel.'

'This is *Crow's Words on the Loom*. He's the head of your bannerpeople.'

Crow's Words was a smaller mindship, his avatar a hazy, iridescent human-shaped silhouette that pulsed, and in the space behind it was a vast hulled silhouette that was glimpsed only in pieces – reflections on metal, wings, exhaust holes blinking in starlight ... He cocked his head, staring at Xích Si, who levelly stared back at him. At length he bowed.

'Looking forward to working together.'

'And here are Tấm and Cám. They're among the best pirates we have.'

Rice Fish had the sisters' tally in Tiên's reports: on their small three-plates they had out-earned every other pirate in the banner, in terms of captives for ransom, for indenture, and general wealth plundered from merchants. Like *Crow's Words*, they were both named after the fairy tale.

The sisters bowed to Xích Si. Tấm was small, dark-skinned with shaved hair and jewelled bots; Cám was more extravagant, wearing her hair long and unbound, even in battle.

'A pleasure,' Tấm said.

Rice Fish was keeping a large fraction of her attention on Xích Si, and saw her heart rate going up. *Crow's Words* had to see it, too, though he would have far fewer access privileges given that Xích Si wasn't on his body. Should she shield Xích Si's vitals herself? But no, Xích Si wouldn't thank her for it. She said, finally, in private comms, 'You can hide your vitals from him. If you want.'

Xích Si's lips tightened, and she mouthed a 'no'.

'Looking forward to working with you, too,' Xích Si said, formally. 'What can you do?'

Crow's Words laughed. 'I have several other ships under my command. We can board smaller merchant ships with minimal damage. And take prisoners alive and with minimal hurt.' He must have seen the way Xích Si's bots froze. 'Ah. Not that. Sorry.'

Xích Si's face did not move. *Rice Fish* measured the effort it must have cost her — that supreme control that she exerted over her own body and reactions. She was going to be completely burned out by the time this short interview was over.

'Let's talk about something else,' Xích Si said.

Tấm said, 'We're here for everything you might want of us.

Including protection, if you're worried about the rest of the banners.'

Crow's Words leaned against one of the walls. He didn't sit down much or do human things, unlike *Rice Fish*, who'd had a lifetime of existing in mixed spaces and had adopted many of the mannerisms.

'I've got good knowledge of banner politics. If *Rice Fish* isn't available to help you – and she's going to be much busier than I am – I can help. She told me you were an expert in bots?'

Xích Si relaxed a fraction. 'Yes. I'm trying to figure out the final battle. The one where the Red Scholar died.'

Crow's Words' posture drooped. 'That should never have happened.'

Rice Fish said, '*Crow's Words* was in the final battle.'

'Oh. Are you all right?'

Crow's Words was visibly taken aback.

'Er . . yes. Battle is . . . er . . . fairly standard here.'

If he'd been human, he'd have blushed all the way to the roots of his hair; as it was, only the colour of his avatar changed, cycling through several shades of the rainbow.

'I see.' Xích Si's position was rigid again, her temperature elevated. She was afraid, or upset, or both. 'Can you share your logs with me?'

'Absolutely,' *Crow's Words* said.

After they left, *Rice Fish* was tempted to go as well; the bulk of her attention was going to be on navigating the asteroid fields around the Citadel, monitoring her passengers, and compiling the reports Tiên had sent her. She almost asked Xích Si if Xích Si wanted her to stay – and then she got a good look at Xích Si, whose heart rate was too fast, and who held herself upright only with a visible effort. No, she couldn't leave Xích Si like this.

'Li'l sis,' she said.

Xích Si was staring straight ahead, not seeing her. *Rice Fish* summoned bots for food. What would Xích Si want? Something to bring a shock of warmth into her system. Soup-filled buns? Clear flour dumplings? Fried rolls? In the end, she settled for cloud swallows: ground pork, shrimp and spring onions wrapped in dough so thin it turned translucent, floating in a chicken broth lightly seasoned with sesame oil. She paired it with a delicate jasmine tea, its leaves still redolent with the aroma of the flower petals.

'Li'l sis.'

Xích Si sighed. 'I can hear you,' she said. 'I'm just not sure I can move right now.'

'Do you want some food?' *Rice Fish* gently touched Xích Si, bracing herself for Xích Si to shake her off or for her heart rate to go up again – if she'd done either of those things, *Rice Fish* would have backed off. She didn't need to scare Xích Si half to death. Instead, Xích Si did something far scarier: she relaxed into *Rice Fish*'s grip, letting *Rice Fish* guide her to the table by the bed – and, when *Rice Fish* made to move away, Xích Si continued leaning into the touch, clearly unwilling to let go.

Rice Fish's own heartbeat skipped, and then went faster and faster. She sat by Xích Si's side, summoning a chair in overlay, one she could lounge into with her hair trailing on the floor.

Xích Si ate in silence; but it wasn't quite as uncomfortable as it had been. *Rice Fish* watched her: the way her hands rested on the chopsticks; the slight twist of her wrists; the lips parting to inhale the broth; the slight exhalation of breath, almost like a blessing or a kiss. She felt the slight weight of Xích Si's feet, resting on her floor and gently swinging back and forth, the slight give and warmth of her touch and presence.

No. No. She wasn't going there. She really wasn't going there. The terms had been clear – and she wasn't going to be that kind of captor. Xích Si – mistress of a mindship, two

51

pirates and a few other bannermen, all under the shadow of *Rice Fish*'s grace – could give her no meaningful consent.

'Thank you,' Xích Si said, finally.

She was smiling, and probably utterly unaware that she was doing so. *Rice Fish* had never quite seen her that way, not scared or angry but comfortable. *Happy.*

'You're welcome,' *Rice Fish* said, trying to banish the rising heat within her. 'Did you need anything else?'

'An answer.'

'Anything.' *Rice Fish* wasn't quite sure of what she was promising any more.

Xích Si said, 'How many ships have you taken?'

Rice Fish felt as if cold water had been thrown into her corridors. She forced her avatar to keep its composure.

'The banner as a whole, or I personally?'

Xích Si's hands clenched. 'Either. Both.'

'I don't know about the banner totals over my own lifetime as a pirate,' *Rice Fish* said, mildly. 'There are around five thousand people in the banner, and over this raiding season, we boarded one thousand, five hundred and thirty-eight merchant ships, and made around six hundred and fifteen prisoners.'

'And the others?'

'Didn't survive.'

Rice Fish focused on facts. On the contents of Tiên's report. It was easier than facing Xích Si's obvious upset – an upset she couldn't relieve.

Xích Si's face was hard.

'People you killed. People you pressed into service.'

Rice Fish said, 'The habitats have plenty of indentures.'

'Not . . .' Xích Si breathed, hard, her bots descending on her hands. 'We don't take people by force.'

'Don't you?' *Rice Fish* kept her voice low, level. She and Huân had seen it all. They'd resolved to build a society where

52

none of this could happen. 'If you cannot bribe an official, if you cannot afford to feed your family, then you'll either be seized by the tribunal, or forced to sell yourself—'

'It's not the same!'

'Really?'

She'd had the argument before, with so many new recruits. It was so familiar she could quote it, word for word. And yet … And yet, for some reason, Xích Si – upset, incandescent with hurt – felt as though she was pressing on the rawest of wounds. *Rice Fish* wanted, so desperately, Xích Si to see what she and Huân had built: the value of what they'd put together; the sanctuary of the Citadel. And instead, Xích Si saw only violence and greed – the worst sides of who they were.

'You just survive on killing others! And on the labour of those you don't kill.'

'We're not the habitats,' *Rice Fish* said. 'We might be harsh, but we're fair. An indenture is redeemed. Every raid you take part in earns you a little more towards your freedom. Every one of us started as a bondsperson.'

'Even you?' Xích Si's gaze was burning.

Rice Fish remembered the docks – the restraints holding her in place, the sense of bleak despair, of being at the utter mercy of those who would have no mercy.

'I built this,' she said. 'But once, I was a prisoner tied down to the docks of the Citadel. A long, long time ago. Does that answer your question?'

She was sharper, more unpleasant than she'd wanted to be. She was *hurt*, and she wasn't even sure why.

Xích Si set her chopsticks atop the bowl of soup, with an audible click that felt like a slamming of doors.

'Yes,' she said. 'It answers the question.'

Rice Fish wanted her to be relaxed again, to lean into her touch. To trust her and smile at her.

Oh. Of course. *Rice Fish* had wanted ... something from Xích Si. Understanding. Intimacy, even if it wasn't a physical one – that one was forever out of bounds.

A kiss, some part of her whispered, thinking of Xích Si's lips on hers – the way it had felt like a shock of electricity straight into her heartroom. And another, sharper part, watching the anger in Xích Si's face, knew that this would never happen, for so many reasons. 'I'll leave you, then.'

And she fled, pulling her attention back to her manoeuvres and her banner reports, and leaving Xích Si alone – trying to compose herself and utterly failing.

6

The Citadel

The logs arrived in Xích Si's inbox as the ship made its final approach to the Citadel.

With her extended access privileges and her new bots, Xích Si could program and send delvers — tiny packages that could make connections on their own, and follow through on those in a matter of centidays, a fraction of the time it would take Xích Si if she had to manually sift through the data. She set them to monitor the comms between the Red Banner's ships across the five battles prior to the one in which the Red Scholar had died, looking for any unusual patterns.

Then she turned her attention back to the rest: a message from *Rice Fish*, reports, and vids. As promised, *Rice Fish* had located Khanh.

Xích Si took a deep, shaking breath. The vids were all of Khanh with Aunt Vy, and Aunt Vy's wife Mei, all carefully shot from within crowds — Khanh laughing as she took a fried sesame ball apart, a sound that tore big chunks of Xích Si's heart. She wore an unobtrusive white mourning band in her hair, which she kept trying to tear off because it bothered her, and she seemed even more of a handful than usual.

A mourning band. Khanh thought Xích Si was dead. Of course. She'd been taken by pirates and not come back. It didn't really matter if she'd died or not, if there was a body or a grave or not. Xích Si couldn't return, and she'd carry the taint of piracy with her if she tried. Any contact — any attempt to let Khanh know she wasn't dead — opened her daughter up to being tried and summarily executed. Officials took 'gifts from the void' with glee — pirate bribes and merchant escort money — but scavengers like Xích Si wouldn't even be given a chance to defend themselves before being put to death.

Khanh was alive. She was being taken care of. She was loved. It was all that mattered. It was all that *should* have mattered, but it hurt. How was Xích Si supposed to let go of her daughter, the heart of her heart?

She saved the vids to her personal space, and pinned a picture of Khanh with the sesame ball smeared across her face on the console. She could ask *Rice Fish* for more pictures, later — if there was a later. She could watch Khanh grow up from afar, somehow.

It would do.

It had to.

The very last thing with the logs was *Rice Fish*'s accompanying note. It was short, and courteous, a carefully penned note that included a poem about starscapes and what looked to be *Rice Fish*'s personal seal: a red square filled with the broad strokes of the Việt alphabet, a language as alien to Xích Si as that of the long-gone Ashlings. The poem featured two distant scholars staring at the slightly different stars: a tactful invitation that *Rice Fish* could be present with her, if Xích Si willed it, and a callback to that evening when Xích Si had explored the ship and they'd ended by each other's side, holding hands.

Xích Si had been saving this note for last, because she didn't quite know what to do with it. Work sounded more fruitful.

Nevertheless . . .

She penned a quick, impersonal note thanking *Rice Fish* for the updates on her daughter, and carefully not addressing any of the points in *Rice Fish's* message. Then she opened up a secondary overlay, asked to see the view outside the ship — and braced herself.

At first, it was nothing but a field of debris. *Rice Fish* was gracefully navigating between them: scattered bits of rock and ice, some of them dwarfing the ship. They were far away on either side of the ship but habitat-sized, shadowed in the light of the sun — and in the fainter light from the Fire Palace on the other side. The planet was still burning from the conflagration that had fractured it aeons ago, the debris of which had formed the Twin Streams. *Rice Fish* manoeuvred slowly and carefully; as a mindship, she was theoretically able to enter deep spaces to swiftly move from one point to the next. It would have been the swiftest way to get to the Citadel, but this required her to have space, and there was no space within that debris. So, instead, she was approaching a slow, long-haul drive, in a straight line born out of her momentum. As she did so, the pieces of rocky debris got closer together and more numerous. It felt like being caught between the shrinking walls of a collapsing habitat. Xích Si took a deep, shaking breath. That was bad enough, but what lay at the other end . . .

Ahead was a jagged circle, with other debris in the centre. *Rice Fish* was making straight for it. The overlay of her sensors highlighted the sentry towers — they were barely visible until they moved, and the differential was caught by the ship's eyes.

That was it. The pirate citadel. The stronghold no imperial troops had ever taken. The base from which they did their blood-soaked work.

Xích Si's bots pinged her: her search on the Green Banner

had returned results, and quite complex ones. She dismissed the alert, entranced by the view.

Rice Fish passed beneath the circle. Beyond it, more rocks, pressing even more tightly together. The ship slowed down to a crawl. The orbits of the asteroids shone in overlay: a tight ballet of chaotic mechanics that never seemed to coalesce into anything making sense. And then, as they got closer and closer, dots and glints of metal: little pieces that didn't seem to quite belong, fuzzed-out images slowly resolving.

The habitats weren't in some central harbour, but scattered across those asteroids: small berths, and even smaller living spaces linked to them. There were ships everywhere, a haphazard scattering of metal planes on the ice and rocks. Some of the larger ones still had the oily sheen of deep spaces clinging to them – and the smaller ones were no larger than specks. Xích Si would never have noticed them without the overlay.

So many. There were so many, all of them labelled with their names and affiliation, a dazzling profusion of unknowns, and the ship she was on was too small and too flimsy, and it wouldn't save ...

A knock, on her door. Two visitors, and not ones she knew, either: not *Rice Fish*, and not Tiên or any of the bannerpeople *Rice Fish* had assigned to her, the pirates that Xích Si still couldn't bring herself to face. The query was tentative, clearly leaving her the option of acknowledging the visit later; it looked as though neither of them were in physical space.

Xích Si took a deep, shaking breath, and opened the door.

A young man with an elaborate topknot and purple robes, and two different seals on his shoulders, worn like shoulder pads. Both were in Việt and both equally unfamiliar – no, wait; her bots flagged the leftmost seal as *Rice Fish*'s. His robes in the overlay had tigers, slowly unfolding multiple tails like fans, their eyes burning as bright as the Fire Palace. When he bowed to her, it was slightly faster than physical human movement, an unsettling effect.

The other one was a mindship, their avatar a small and translucent version of their body: a large, almost spherical craft with just the hint of a prow, slightly blurred as if going too fast for a human eye. They were floating at eye level, large enough to fill the doorway. Their avatar even included bots: a small and translucent patch of them, legs silently moving in virtual space. It was odd; she'd become used to *Rice Fish*'s human avatar, she realised, and to not seeing the bots hidden beneath it.

'Yes?' she asked.

The man looked at her, cocking his head as if at a curiosity – but it was the ship who spoke.

'So you're the new consort. I'm *Stilling the Mulberry Sea*, the envoy from Đại Việt, and this is Hổ.'

She used the pronoun for an elder aunt to refer to herself, and of a younger uncle for Hổ.

Hổ: Tiger. No full name, title, or other introduction, but he had *Rice Fish*'s seal on his shoulders. She couldn't afford not to know who he was.

'Hổ. Who are you?' Xích Si asked.

A sharp-toothed smile from Hổ.

'I'm Huân's son.' And, because she must have looked blank, 'The Red Scholar's son. Can we come in, elder aunt?'

Hổ. Leader of the Purple Banner. The one *Rice Fish* had been feeling so conflicted about.

We don't get on, but I have no reason to doubt his loyalty.

And now he was in her rooms.

Not just a dangerous visitor. He was a black hole of epic proportions.

Could she refuse them? Probably not, but she could call *Rice Fish*. The ship had to know these two were there on her decks

– and she wasn't intervening, just as she'd said she wouldn't. Xích Si wasn't sure whether to be reassured by this.

She could call the ship. She could let *Rice Fish* handle them and take the pressure off herself.

But doing so would require calling *Rice Fish*. Would require *asking* a pirate to come to her rescue.

No.

'Come in,' she said, smiling brightly, knowing she couldn't keep her face blank. Instead, she focused inwards, hastily cobbling together a program to search for information about Hổ.

As Hổ sat down at the low table in Xích Si's quarters, the answers came back, overwhelming her with information she couldn't hope to sift through without aid. He was busy.

She got the bots to prepare and pour tea for them all: an acrid tasting wu long for Hổ, and the softer green tea which *Mulberry Sea*, the Đại Việt envoy, requested. She had a flat metal table in her rooms on which she conjured an overlay: a lacquered one of a dragon and phoenix. Safely classical and innocuous. Hổ sat down, and *Mulberry Sea* hovered lower. They enjoyed the tea in silence; Xích Si had no idea what memories it called up for *Mulberry Sea*.

In the other screen they were approaching a larger habitat: a crescent-shaped structure with a dazzling profusion of ships on either side, dotted across the ice of one of the larger asteroids.

'The Red Banner quarters,' *Rice Fish* said in Xích Si's ear, except that she wasn't really there; she felt distant and impersonal.

Which Xích Si wasn't going to feel sorry about.

'What can I do for you?' she asked.

She'd expected one or the other to equivocate, but when Hổ spoke up, he was quite candid.

'I wanted to meet you,' he said.

He sipped at his tea. His topknot was decorated with a metal flame ornament – and in overlay, that ornament was surrounded by the ghostly, unmoving images of ships.

Xích Si tried to weigh the cost of being candid with him, and gave up. If *Rice Fish* couldn't protect her here, in Red Banner territory, then where would she?

'You came to gape at the scavenger?'

Hồ flinched. *Mulberry Sea* didn't move. Her voice, when she spoke next, was gentle.

'You're aware of the politics involved?'

'Yes,' Xích Si said, not because it was true but because it would have been suicide to say no. And, because she felt cornered, 'Your mother died.'

'She did.' Hồ's voice was flat. With grief? 'Few pirates die in their beds. Not unless they're stabbed there.'

Mulberry Sea made a small coughing sound, and her attention shifted to Xích Si; it was nowhere as strong as when *Rice Fish* did it, but it was still perceptible.

'Younger aunt ... you understand that your ... elevation causes concerns.'

Xích Si didn't know how to answer, so she turned to her tea and sipped it – and felt a small, almost imperceptible ping at the edges of her consciousness: *Rice Fish*, asking if she could come in. If she needed her help.

'I thought you weren't listening.'

'I'm not,' *Rice Fish* said. 'But I did see them come in. I won't listen unless you ask me to.'

The invitation was obvious. Tempting.

'No, Xích Si said. And then, although she already had too much information to process, 'Tell me about your relationship to Hồ.'

A silence, matching the one in the room.

Good.

61

Then, unexpectedly, 'I'm sorry to put you in this situation.'

Xích Si was distracted, with *Mulberry Sea* and Hồ in the room. But this virtual conversation was the safer of the two, so she replied with the truth.

'I didn't ask for your help. If you solve every situation for me and make all the decisions and never leave room for me, how different is that from my being your captive?'

A panic spike – how dare she speak to *Rice Fish* that way – swiftly tamped down, as she remembered *Rice Fish*'s touch on her skin.

'Touché.' The pirate ship's voice was ironic. 'Hồ and I have been estranged for a while.'

'Why?'

Another silence, this time longer and more definite. *Rice Fish* didn't want to answer.

To *Mulberry Sea*, Xích Si said, 'What concerns?'

'Ma and *Rice Fish* have always held us back.' Hồ's voice was sullen; the edged charm of his smile had gone. *Rice Fish*, not 'Mother' or 'Mom'. They were estranged all right. 'Telling us to be careful. To be prudent.'

Mulberry Sea radiated scepticism, in that way that mind-ships did: something in the way the ship held herself, in the way she moved.

'There's nothing wrong with being prudent.'

'We're pirates! We've never got anywhere by being prudent.'

Xích Si decided, then and there, that she *disliked* Hồ intensely – and she didn't see why she should go out of her way to be kind to him.

Mulberry Sea said, 'It's not unheard of for pirates to make marriages with captives or bondspeople, but the custom died out some time ago. Everyone expected *Rice Fish* to pick someone from the fleet. Someone with ships under them already.'

And she was the scavenger – a powerless, scared one.

'Some time ago.'

Keep them talking. She didn't know what else to do, other than throw them out of her rooms. She was here for bots and to search out the information *Rice Fish* needed, not politics!

Information. Fine. If *Rice Fish* wasn't going to answer her, and if she wasn't going to request the ship's presence, then she could request something else of the ship.

'Can you sort through that for me?' Xích Si asked, pointing towards the mass of undigested data that had come up when she'd asked for information about Hồ.

'Of course.'

'Thank you.'

'Any time.'

She caught an emotion she couldn't quite pinpoint from the ship – something like fond amusement or laugher, but with an edge. Not anger. It was something that made her sit straighter, sending shivers down her spine – as if, reaching out, she could *touch* the ship. In fact, she could. She could lay her hand on the floor and feel the steadying coolness of it under her fingers, feel the faint, slow heartbeat in the heartroom – more shivers and a tightening in her chest ... How much more intense would it be to touch other, more intimate, places?

No, what was she thinking? The terms of the marriage had been very clear, and this had been ruled out. She couldn't possibly yearn for *that*.

Rice Fish made no comment – she must have seen Xích's Si's moment of arousal ... but no, she'd said she wasn't listening. It seemed absurd to trust her word, and yet Xích Si realised that she did that, already, as naturally as she breathed.

A barrage of images and sounds overwhelmed her – too fast, too confused, too jumbled – and then it slowed down, and she could breathe again.

'Sorry. I haven't got the hang of your reaction times yet.'

Hồ. Head of the Purple Banner, a post he'd only taken after his estrangement from his parents. A hothead, enamoured of adventure – he was so young, but his naivety and recklessness were hurting people. He wanted to be set loose. To pillage and kill as he wished.

He didn't look particularly close to *Mulberry Sea*; perhaps they'd only pooled forces for this visit.

Mulberry Sea had been talking for a while. Xích Si refocused her attention on the physical conversation with a start. She caught only the tail end: 'There is a lot of political jostling.'

'And you want to know where I stand?'

'That's only fair, isn't it?'

Xích Si said, 'Only if you tell me where you stand.'

A silence. *Mulberry Sea* had gone very still, the layer of motion blur completely gone, a pirate ship's stillness before it dived towards a merchant ship. Xích Si leaned back, trying to calm the frantic beating of her heart. They weren't there. Not physically, not with bots, and not with any kind of access privileges. They couldn't snatch her. She was safe, or as safe as she could be within a pirates' den.

Then the ship laughed. It was a low and good-natured sound, and without any hint of bitterness.

'I go where my master's interests take me.'

'Your master is dying.' Xích Si was bad at politics, but she had a good memory for details. 'What of the master-in-waiting?'

A layer of movement across the ship's avatar – very much like a dismissive shrug, except it involved the whole body.

'We'll still need the alliance. The money it brings us. The constant thorn in An O's side—' more laughter, without malice, a pure expression of amusement '– something to keep the censors and generals and troops busy during those long lull months.'

Which told Xích Si very little.

'You go where the interests of your master take you. I go with my wife,' she said, finally. The word tasted odd in her mouth — not bitter, as she'd thought it would, but uncertain — a mouthful of a plump lychee that could be sweet, or collapse into sour rottenness.

'Your wife.' Now Hồ was dismissive. No, more than that: angry.

'I have to go,' *Rice Fish* said.

Her attention, which had been diffuse and barely focused, completely vanished. It left a vacuum in the room, and left Xích Si surprised and wrong-footed, and feeling oddly abandoned.

'We have a contract, that's all,' Xích Si said, thinking Hồ was angry his mother had been so easily replaced. 'I'm not her lover.'

Hồ's lips thinned and his eyes blazed. He rose, setting the teacup roughly on the low table they'd been using.

'A contract. Not her lover. That's funny.' His tone suggested it was anything but. 'That's exactly what they were to each other, too.'

What? She'd assumed ... The way *Rice Fish* was grieving, the anger, the despondency, the determination to uncover how the Red Scholar had died ...

From the corner of her eye, she saw *Mulberry Sea* move towards Hồ, and some sort of silent communication between them. Hồ's body moved, gesticulating in an argument she couldn't hear, the ship remaining impassive and unmoved. Finally Hồ huffed, and turned to her.

'I apologise, elder aunt. I was out of line.'

'We'll take our leave now,' *Mulberry Sea* said, and then they were both gone, leaving Xích Si staring at two empty teacups: a virtual, perfect cup drained of tea, and a physical one put so roughly back on the table it had spilled droplets all over the lacquered overlay. She dismissed it with a gesture, and stared at the metal beneath, pristine and quivering with *Rice Fish*'s heartbeat – but not with the ship's attention, for she hadn't returned.

What's going on, big sis?

Rice Fish hadn't intended to leave.

Most of her attention, it was true, had already been elsewhere: focused on the delicate manoeuvre of docking, some of which couldn't be delegated to low-level threads. The switch from the lower-burn long-haul drive to the more manoeuvrable bright drive, the precise alignment with the habitat's dock – knowing that she'd have to get it right or risk having to pull out and move again, wasting precious fuel – had loomed large in her thoughts. Helping Xích Si with data analysis had been reflex, barely enough to keep her busy.

At least, that was how it should have been, but she'd chafed at it. For all her professions of not interfering, she'd *wanted* to help Xích Si – how could she pledge to protect her, and then stand aside in such a loaded situation? She'd forced herself to be silent; to only listen to the private comms channel she had open with Xích Si; not to monitor what was going on in her rooms – cutting off access to an entire part of her body.

And, for a while, it had worked. The missing room had been a gaping hole in her perceptions, an odd emptiness because her brain kept insisting there was something there – something she couldn't quite perceive – no, that wasn't it. She could perceive the room, but her perception of it – empty and with none of her bots – didn't match what she knew was happening inside. She'd eased slowly, gracefully, into the docking bay, finally killing off the drive and coasting on inertia – a familiar, mildly unpleasant feeling of being paralysed and restrained as the habitat's safety procedures locked on, followed by the connection to the docking bay, and the habitat's network opening up to her on a full bandwidth and high privilege accesses – and she could breathe again, and start up routines to collect messages and news from the heart of piratedom, from the tribute offices to the tribunals, from the Ministries of War, Works and Recruits to the quarters of the other banners.

It had worked. But then she was idle, with no way to move and nothing of interest yet in the network, because it was all being collected and processed – mere blinks of time to a human, but an eternity to a ship such as *Rice Fish*. And that missing room – that place where she couldn't tell who was moving, who was disembarking, whether physically or virtually, where all she knew was that no one was in danger of dying ... that missing room became a black hole that sucked in her thoughts. She couldn't know what was going on. She shouldn't know, because she'd asked and Xích Si had told her it was none of her business. But she wanted to.

Hổ being on board was like an itch she needed to scratch, and it was worse because he was with Xích Si. She'd dodged the subject when Xích Si had asked – had said she was sure of his loyalty – but that wasn't what mattered, was it? What mattered was how he felt about her – which she hadn't known since he'd walked away from her and Huân when he'd turned sixteen.

What words were being said? How was Xích Si feeling? What was Hổ feeling? Did he still hate her? Had Huân's death altered the chasm between them? She was going to drown if she didn't do something, and so she did the worse possible thing. She listened.

'I go with my wife,' Xích Si said in a level voice, and *Rice Fish* could feel the frantic heartbeat, the coiled panic within her – the way she expected anger in return.

'Your wife.' Hồ's voice, cold and dismissive, the surge of anger through his vitals: a rise of heartbeat, a rise of heat in his neck and face, fists that had started to clench – lips opening on something else, that he got under control only with a hyper-visible effort. He was in pain, and he hated her so, so much – and she shouldn't be here, she shouldn't have listened, what had she been thinking?

'I have to leave,' she blurted out – and fled, cutting herself off from that room again. She retreated closer to her heartroom, feeling her panic pulse through the walls of her body, spiking and turning into a clenched, ugly thing in her heartroom, an uncomfortable vacuum – like the bite of the safety systems locking her into place, but ten thousand times worse.

Calm down. She could do this. She could . . .

But all she could see was Hồ walking away from her – and an older, deeper hurt: Huân flinching as *Rice Fish* bent and kissed her – the way she'd pulled away and then stood, smiling sadly.

I love you, big sis. But not in that way. Never in that way.

Huân hadn't meant to hurt her. She'd wanted to let her down as kindly as she could. But she'd pulled away, and in the moment *Rice Fish* had felt her surprise, her confusion – and a brief spike of aversion.

'You think it's unnatural,' *Rice Fish* said, 'because I'm a ship?'

Such relationships had been heavily judged, in An O society. But surely not here, not in this new world they were making together, this safe place where they could be themselves.

Huân's face had gone still; there was just sadness left now.

'Because we're *business partners*. This is a marriage of con-venience, not a relationship.'

'I thought . . .' She'd been babbling like a baby, feeling as though someone had ripped her out of the heartroom and left her leaking blood and oil on the floor. 'I thought we had something.'

Or a chance at something. *Rice Fish* had wanted a relationship with Huân, something more than their business agreement as joint founders of the Citadel. She knew that some people found sex without romance fulfilling, and some people the opposite, but *Rice Fish* needed both. That kiss had been an expression of hope for something deeper – for the intimacy she craved, and hoped Huân could give her.

Huân's face had softened. 'We do. We always will. I ... care for you.' She'd picked her words with care, as if navigating an asteroid field on high-burn. 'A collaboration such as ours is about working together. It's about reason. Detachment. We can't—'

'Sleep together? Enter a romance?' Anger, making *Rice Fish* shake, had stilled the words on her comms system.

'Passions destroy,' Huân had said gently. 'They burn bright and spend themselves, and then we'd have to stare at each other from the ruins of a relationship. We can't afford that. There are *people* depending on us, big sis.'

Pirates and scavengers and bot-handlers, and menials and servants, all arbitrarily condemned by the magistrates – sentenced to decades of penal servitude for theft of the rice and fish sauce that would save them from starvation, or branded for defending themselves against corrupt civil servants. Huân herself had become a pirate after she'd tried to stop the militia from beating a confession out of a scavenger – and, in the resulting fight, had turned the captain's own energy weapon against her, burning the left side of her torso. Then she'd run, because the tribunal would at best have exiled her.

'I know,' *Rice Fish* said.

'Do you?' Huân had looked at her. Her expression was sad, her heartbeat slow and even, and *Rice Fish* had felt the flush of shame that she'd broached this subject at all. 'Would you sit by me now, big sis? Would you still be focused on this?'

She'd pointed to the couch where they'd been sitting – side by side, studying multiple overlays showing their plans for the expansion of the Red Banner habitat. Ships moved beneath it all: pirates returning with supplies and wealth, everything they needed to keep the Citadel going.

Rice Fish had wished she could disappear.

'You know I can't. Not now.'

'Yes. I do. You're ashamed, and that's just because we don't feel the same way. Now imagine how it would be if it went wrong. If we both agreed, and then one of us no longer felt that passion. Think how it'd be.'

They could weather this. Surely they could – but she felt so ashamed, and so small. Could she bear it, if she did get to have an intimate relationship with Huân, and Huân changed her mind? She'd feel so dejected, so angry she wouldn't be able to even materialise in the same space as Huân.

'You're right,' she'd said, finally.

There was a place for romantic love and for sex, and that place wasn't marriage.

Over time, they'd grown past it. *Rice Fish* wasn't loved – not in the way that she wanted to be. She'd taken lovers outside the marriage, but it was for sex and nothing more meaningful. Huân, for her part, had collected flings the way scholars collected books and vids – and one of these flings had led to the accidental pregnancy that made them Hồ's parents.

Over time, it had hurt less; or at least *Rice Fish* had convinced herself it did, layering over the old memory until it didn't sting any more.

And Hồ, too, had been fine with this, growing up – until he became a teenager and something broke. He'd finally snapped and walked out, yelling about loveless contracts and soulless

70

business, and how she and Huân were both shrivelling inside, heading for destruction ... and on, and on, every word a knife reopening *Rice Fish*'s old wounds.

Your wife.

Hồ still hated her, and nothing had changed: she was alone, and she didn't love, and no one loved her, and that was the way of things. That would always be the way of things, no matter that Huân was dead now, and that she'd entered a new contract.

I go with my wife.

No matter how fascinating, how entrancing, how attractive *Rice Fish* thought Xích Si was, she was off limits. She would always be.

7

Judgement

Someone was pinging her insistently on her comms. Tiên – her virtual self – was in the common part of the Citadel, where the council rooms and the tribunal were located, though her body remained where she'd disembarked, in Red Banner physical space.

'Elder aunt, elder aunt!'

The honorific, and the taut panic in Tiên's voice, snapped *Rice Fish* back to the present.

'What's going on?'

A silence, but one tinged with panic.

'It'd be best if you came.'

Rice Fish stretched, and moved to the Citadel.

Unlike in the empires, there was no overarching habitat-mind controlling access to the Citadel the way *Rice Fish* controlled access to parts of her body. The space was considered free to all, and everyone in the pirate banners, whether mindship or human, could project their avatars as they wished.

Rice Fish, like most pirates, had bots on board the Citadel, stored in a vast locker room tied to her ID. These activated as she manifested her long-haired avatar in front of Tiên, and started moving towards her — if she chose to focus she'd have access to their perceptions, but corridors and underground rooms were utterly boring.

Tiên was in the central plaza, in front of the tribunal. The public overlay was a downward slope of scree, as if the asteroid held a huge valley, except that stars shone in the hollows of the rock, minute pinpoints of light, and overhead was the shimmering image of the Fire Palace — the fractured burning planet filled with incomprehensible ruins. It shone over them all, and whenever its light touched, there was a faint shimmering of Ashling characters — a reminder that it was the trade in Ashling artefacts that ultimately sustained them all.

'In here,' Tiên said.

She was still carrying the remnants of a fried sesame ball, the smell wafting up to *Rice Fish* and reminding her of her first journey beyond the Twin Streams to the Twenty-Third Planet. She remembered the loud pop the balls made as they puffed, the smile on the street seller's face as her bots withdrew them from the oil.

Rice Fish hated projecting. It was one thing to be an avatar on her own ship, but in someone else's space she had no privileged access, no physical body, and she was acutely aware of how fragile bots were — she'd destroyed so many when taking other ships. Her bots had reached her, dancing around those physically present in the crowd, and were now sheltering beneath her.

The tribunal was downwards, in the central zone, which meant taking the corridors: physically they were corridors inside a dome-like habitat, but the overlay had been designed to make them look like canyons stretching downwards through the asteroid. They were packed with people — both physical and avatars — pressing themselves into the narrow space. Nothing unusual. Outside raiding seasons, bored pirates were always looking for excitement, and five elders arguing about the finer points of pirate law was a free spectacle. Extravagant clothing and body-mods abounded: tattoos that shifted on the skin; dragons rearing from the back of spines; wings and horns and metal protuberances; modified faces superimposed on the ghosts of the original ones . . .

Here and there, a bondsperson, with the marker of their indenture over their heads. Those whose ships' captains allowed it had extravagant displays; others were wearing drabber colours, with restricted access to the overlays. Some, the most recently pressed into indenture, walked in chains and with no access to bots.

Pirates were dragging prisoners held for ransom towards cabins and compartments, jeering and laughing. Not all of the prisoners would make it out unscathed – it had been a long raiding season ending in the death of the Red Scholar, and many pirates were going back to the familiar. There was pleasure in hurting others – in exerting the control and power they'd lacked in the matter world. It was only natural, and that way the Red Banner would vent their anger and frustration on someone else than their fellow bannerpeople: on the merchants who'd owned and mistreated them; on the officials and imperial soldiers who'd inflict the slow death on them given half a chance. The bannerpeople would come back with bloodied knives and guns smelling of residue, swapping anecdotes about who of the prisoners had screamed the loudest when cut, who had struggled the most as their fingers were broken. The entire Red Banner would relax, their anger vented at others, unlikely to brawl on board the ships and cause a disturbance.

'Talk to me,' *Rice Fish* said to Tiên.

She swerved, to avoid a pirate woman dragging a chain of indentured bondspeople behind her – they walked with heads bent, trying not to draw attention to themselves, and with a stiffness which suggested they'd gone through a lacerator. Small hands aboard a ship – who worked hard, with every mistake swiftly disciplined, and not earning enough from a raid to make any kind of significant dent into their indenture – they might never earn their freedom, and they knew it.

Tiên was busy elbowing the crowd aside – and, judging by the way people recoiled from Tiên as if burned, her elbows were sharp.

'No time,' she said, and, abruptly, dumped an entire case file into *Rice Fish*'s memory, the virtual equivalent of punching her in the face.

'I have to protest!'

'You'll thank me later,' Tiên said, sharply.

Within *Rice Fish*, several threads were already working, worrying away at the information to distil it into the essentials. She focused on following Tiên's wake.

The first party to this complaint is a scavenger by the name of Ái Nhân, as captured by the crew of the open-the-void ship *The Burning Pearl*, affiliated with the Purple Banner ...

The corridors ended abruptly; they'd reached the tribunal.

It was a vast space. In the virtual layers the dome above it was invisible, magnifying the space and altering everyone's perceptions to match it; it was an odd sensation – like hanging, weightless, in the deep spaces that mindships used for faster navigation.

The second and opposing party is Chi Lan, captain of *The Burning Pearl*, and, through her, Linh, captain of *The Peach-Sword Song*, who as Chi Lan's protector bears moral responsibility for Chi Lan's actions ...

Stars twinkled, brighter and closer than in the physical layer, and the ruin of the Fire Palace stretched above them, the burning and fractured planet forming a permanently broken sunrise. They'd made some changes since the last raiding season: the Ashling characters were sharper, and the seats had been replaced by lacquered pews.

Ái Nhân paid her protection dues to the alliance's officials, and as such claims to have been wrongfully captured for ransom ...

Rice Fish's processing threads finished taking apart the information as Tiên led the way to the dais where the five elders sat, watching the conflicting parties − no kneeling before the majesty of a tribunal here: both Ái Nhân and Chi Lan sat cross-legged, lower than the elders, a mark of respect for knowledge but not abject reverence.

It is this court's opinion that scavengers who venture into the path of raiding parties are and have always been fair prey, and that Ái Nhân's dues only afford her a reduced ransom ...

Anger, slow and cold and deliberate, was rising within *Rice Fish*, a constricting feeling from prow to stern, sending the bots on board her scattering in a frenzy.

How dare they?

How dare they take everything that the alliance had stood for and squander it all, and call it justice and fairness?

The elders rose. There were only two of them instead of five − not so unusual, but alarming, given the decision being made. It was also alarming to see the figure by the side of the dais − clearly not on it, sending a clear message that she wasn't an elder or involved in the course of justice ... Only both she and *Rice Fish* knew that for a lie.

76

'Elder aunt,' *Rice Fish* said, keeping her voice as neutral as possible. 'What a surprise to see you here.'

'Child.' Kim Thông, the Green Scholar, bowed to her with nothing of humility or respect. 'An unexpected pleasure.'

She wore robes the colour of nebulas, the colour of the sea: a shifting green-blue, with a hint of fire beneath. Her bots were impeccable, chosen for their sleekness. Having seen Xích Si's bots, *Rice Fish* knew these were for show rather than for practicality.

Rice Fish bowed to everyone in turn: the scavenger Ái Nhân, the pirate Chi Lan, and the two elders. They were all physically there — the tribunal excluded the use of avatars for any parties to a case and for the elders. Kim Thông was the only one present in virtual space; she was cautious and would be unlikely to put herself in danger with physical presence.

'We're almost done here,' Kim Thông said, sweetly.

'I know,' *Rice Fish* said, curtly. The two elders wouldn't meet her gaze, and it wasn't just a question of being respectful. They were *ashamed*. 'I read the case file, and the tribunal's deliberation.'

Behind her, she knew the variegated crowd would be listening, avid not only for spectacle, but for any hint of how Huân's death was going to play out in the council. She also knew, because of her good memory and capacity to parallel-track, that Hổ was in the audience, pretending disinterest — but that he was angry and disappointed; he'd expected her to stay away.

Which led, in turn, to a question she'd wanted to avoid: to what degree was he in cahoots with Kim Thông?

She wasn't ready for an honest answer.

Speaking of cahoots, the elders' behaviour made it clear that they had been suborned. She didn't know why, but it didn't matter.

'You know the law. You know that dues afford not only

safe passage, but an escort from pirate ships when deemed necessary.'

Perhaps not for a scavenger, but certainly for a merchant fleet that would be targeted by unaffiliated bandits if not defended.

A cough, from the elders.

'This is a special case . . .' one of them said – the eldest, Dinh. He'd done time on the ships and finally retired when wounded; the arm he'd lost had regrown in culture tanks, but he'd never fully recovered.

'*Special case?* You know the precedents as well as I do. The only question we should be asking ourselves is to determine whether Chi Lan and her protector will survive this,' *Rice Fish* said, sharply – and Chi Lan flinched.

Good.

The youngest elder – a smooth-faced girl who looked barely old enough to hold this post – looked up at *Rice Fish*. Minh Loan. *Rice Fish* looked her up, briefly: she was older than she looked, had risen from bondsperson to captain of a ship, and walked away at the height of her success because she'd found her calling in the law.

Not ideal – Dinh was older, but Minh Loan was more amenable.

Kim Thông smiled. 'I admire your passion, child. It's always been such a wonder to see it burn.' She turned, slightly, staring at the Fire Palace above them all – burning and fractured. The message was clear and unsubtle. 'But really, we should be asking ourselves how much we've earned by being *respectable*.'

'You mean by earning the weapons and support of the Đại Việt empire, and the greater wealth that came with that? By getting the space we needed?'

Respectable. It sounded, far too much, like the discourse her son had been spouting lately, and that *hurt*. How far did

Kim Thông's influence extend? Would proof she'd colluded with Censor Trúc to kill Huân even be enough to cause her downfall, or was her partnership with Xích Si pointless, dead before it had a chance to come to fruition?

It had to work. It was the only way.

'We have grown soft,' Kim Thông said, softly, slowly – spinning on the virtual rock floor, the stars in the crags lighting up as she did so. She was half-facing *Rice Fish*, and half-facing their audience – the ones she wanted to convince, because banner heads would have to take their members' needs into consideration. 'We left civilised company and its restrictions to build something different, and what did we achieve? We became the servants of another empire.'

Mulberry Sea, the Đại Việt envoy, was hovering by Hổ's side, her avatar relaxed – *Rice Fish* could see the casual stance of the bots. *Mulberry Sea* didn't seem particularly fussed. Where did she stand? *Rice Fish* knew that the Đại Việt empress was dying, but not which of her children she would name her successor in the hour of her death.

They'd only survived this far because of the Việt and their protection – and their wealth. And Kim Thông knew it. Why was she making this argument at all?

'This is a trial,' *Rice Fish* said, mildly. 'And the people on trial are here.'

She made a wide sweep with her arms, pointing to Chi Lan – who stood with her fists belligerently clenched – and the scavenger, Ái Nhân, whose face was pale, and who kept rubbing at her wrists. She'd been in restraints prior to the trial. Locked in a hold somewhere, when the pirates should have ensured she reached her destination safely. *Rice Fish* thought of Huân, and of corrupt militia – of the way Xích Si had tensed on their wedding night, expecting anger, and abasing herself before *Rice Fish*.

It wasn't fair. It wasn't *just*. How dare they take everything she and Huân had built, and make it as corrupt and as cruel as the world they'd left?

'Younger sister,' she said, sharply, to Minh Loan. 'What does the penal code say?'

How dare they?

Minh Loan was silent. Her virtual overlay was an elaborate thing: a scattering of dragon scales on her face, and the shadow of a ship behind her – a subtle suggestion of metal planes and sleekness whenever she moved. It was uncannily still now.

'This isn't about the code,' Kim Thông said.

This time Minh Loan didn't flinch, but the ship's shadow behind her did.

'This *tribunal* isn't about the code?' *Rice Fish* asked. She let the words hang in emptiness, the weight of them settle on the audience.

Kim Thông looked as though she wanted to argue, opened her mouth – and then thought better of it. She was cowed – for now. The sensible, merciful thing would be to leave it there, and hope that Minh Loan or the other elder would come to their senses.

Only *Rice Fish* hadn't got where she was by being merciful, or sensible.

'I'm grateful you're thinking about the future of piratehood,' she said, slowly, softly. 'I see you care about what we stand for, and what we can afford to gain or lose.'

'You know nothing,' Kim Thông's voice was sharp.

She certainly didn't know why Kim Thông was taking this stance. Outwardly, siding with Censor Trúc and with Hổ were two contradictory positions: one wanted to destroy piratehood; the other was chasing an illusory return to glory. Which was Kim Thông's true goal?

Minh Loan said, in the silence, 'The Red Consort is right.'

80

Ancestors, *Rice Fish* hated that title. But it wouldn't do to snap at Minh Loan. Instead, she leaned back, and smiled — slow and out of sync with any human movements, a gesture that would be unnerving to anyone unused to ships.

The other elder, Dinh, looked at Minh Loan. She spoke simply, furiously, to him.

'Article fourteen of chapter five — anyone who pays their dues is entitled to protection and an escort. Merchant ships use us as bodyguards to pass through the Twin Streams.'

She glared at both him and Kim Thông — though elders were meant to be unaffiliated to a banner, everyone knew it was a polite fiction, especially with only two of them in the room.

Dinh, as *Rice Fish* already knew, was weak. When Minh Loan kept glaring at him he finally grudgingly nodded.

Minh Loan said, 'This tribunal finds in favour of Ái Nhân. She is free to return to her family, and compensation will be paid into her indenture bond. Chi Lan will lose the captainship of *The Burning Pearl* and become a bondsperson again, and Linh of *The Peach-Sword Song*, who should have provided better guidance as Chi Lan's protector, will also lose her captainship and her status.'

Chi Lan's fists clenched.

'No,' she said, her face twisting into a scream.

She lunged towards Ái Nhân, and there was a knife in her hand — and Kim Thông, smiling, did nothing as …

Rice Fish breathed, and focused. Time, for her, matched the rhythm, not of the usual human reactions, but the rapid clock of her processors in the heartroom, blink-moment by blink-moment. Chi Lan's lunge became a set of movements so slow they lost meaning: the knife glinting; Chi Lan's bots immobile on her shoulders and chest; the inching forward of Chi Lan's body and hand …

Rice Fish moved. To her, it was much the same as walking,

leisurely and calmly, from below the dais with Kim Thông to where Ái Nhân stood frozen; to everyone human – and most ships, if they didn't bother to adjust their function rate – it looked as though she'd blinked out of existence and reappeared in the centre of the room. She grabbed Ái Nhân's hand – her bots moving beneath her avatar, gripping the scavenger's wrist and pushing her down. As she did so, she sent a voice-burst on Ái Nhân's private comms.

'Stay down, child.'

Ái Nhân tumbled like a planet-bound meteor. *Rice Fish* let go, and turned – keeping her thoughts deliberately empty – towards Chi Lan.

This time, when she grabbed her, it was with rather less delicacy – bones cracked audibly in the silence of the tribunal, with the same finality as metal plates bending and snapping, and the hiss of air as integrity was lost. Chi Lan screamed, high-pitched – she'd have recoiled in pain if *Rice Fish*'s bots hadn't had her in an iron grip. When she threw Chi Lan down, blood spattered on the floor; it washed across the stars shining in the crags, turning them the vermilion of official seals.

'You ...' Chi Lan tried to speak.

In the audience, a tall and stately pirate with billowing swathes of light around his avatar had risen, moving towards the centre – Linh, Chi Lan's protector, the one Minh Loan had stripped of her status. Her face was like thunder. *Rice Fish* stood, still synced to ship-clock – enjoying a moment of quiet before it all came crashing down.

'Get up,' Linh said to Chi Lan. 'You disgrace us all.' She glared at Kim Thông, and at Dinh – her face softening a fraction when she met *Rice Fish*'s impassive gaze. 'Elder aunt. Thank you for making sure my protegée stayed out of further trouble.'

Rice Fish bowed to Linh. It wasn't Linh she was worried

about, though it was good that the former captain stood by the tribunal's decision. Behind her, Ái Nhân was pulling herself to her feet, shaking and shivering, and looking at them with fear in her eyes — the expression hauntingly familiar. It was how Xích Si had looked before she'd thrown herself to the ground to beg for mercy — and *that* thought sparked an uncomfortable twist in her heartroom, a contraction that travelled up all the rooms of her body.

Kim Thông's smile was wolfish.

'Not everything is civilised, is it? Sometimes it's all down to blood and bones, if one must stop the sharks and tigers from encroaching on us all.'

Rice Fish put her hands together, rubbing them — it didn't really help, despite the sensation provided by the habitat. She could hear Chi Lan whimpering, and Ái Nhân's rapid breathing, and feel the mood of the pirates and bondspeople gathered in the room: some were content that justice had prevailed; some were indifferent; some bored; but far too many were leaning against the pews, smiling — and on their faces was sated bloodlust.

We've grown cruel for cruelty's sake, haven't we?

And she wasn't sure who she was asking, because Huân was dead, and what they'd built together seemed like any empire in the wake of a founder's death: as fragile as cracked celadon, and unable to withstand the stresses of the kiln's heat.

8

Fear

Xích Si watched *Rice Fish* walk into the tribunal.

She was still in her rooms. After *Rice Fish* had unexpectedly vanished mid-conversation, she'd somehow managed to continue making polite conversation. And saw them leave, and worried the entire time they would come back – appear in her rooms without needing any permission or accesses. The fear that, at any moment, they'd look at her and see prey, draw their guns and seize her the way the other pirates had when her ship had been broken, lurked at the back of her mind. She'd fingered her new bots, over and over, remembering the cracking sounds the old ones had made when they'd come apart.

She'd wanted to look for *Rice Fish* then – so desperately needed that companionship they'd had, the way that *Rice Fish* listened to her, *valued* her and her input, instead of dismissing her as worthless. She'd longed for connection, and maybe more . . . for that thrill she'd had when she realised she was touching *Rice Fish*, and that the ship could feel her to her core. That disconcerting and not altogether unwelcome spike of craving within her.

But she knew where she was. She knew what she was: a

scavenger held by pirates, and now wasn't the time to indulge in fantasies that would only harm her. Instead, she dealt with her fears and her longings by drowning herself in work: taking apart the information her delvers had returned on the Red Scholar's last battles. Bots and delvers could only do so much; Xích Si needed to dive into the processed data, and tease some sense from it all.

The only way the ships' behaviour at the battle made sense was if Censor Trúc had been listening to the conversations between the Red Scholar's banner ship and the smaller three-plates the Red Scholar had really been on – a precaution she'd taken to avoid giving away her position. Which meant bots with transmitters on both ships – and Censor Trúc knowing where the Red Scholar really was, and that she was trying to escape.

Which meant not only access, but that Censor Trúc could guess the Red Scholar's movements in advance of an unpredictable and highly charged space battle.

Unlikely, if not impossible.

Xích Si stared at the other battles. Was there anything to be gleaned from them? The Red Scholar's fleet had mostly been engaged against merchants – and not just any merchants, but the larger ships, the ones that could afford to bribe imperial officials for protection. Instead of defending the Jade Stream against the Đại Việt, soldiers and scholars would accompany their ships in exchange for space in the ships' holds – giving them a chance to make so much more profit than from a mere imperial salary. It was Palace season: the ships had dived into the ruins of the Fire Palace for Ashling artefacts, and headed out-system to sell, giving them the kind of money and reach that Xích Si would never have access to.

You're wrong, Ngà said, in her memories. *We can outfit a smaller ship. We wouldn't need much cargo to be profitable.*

I don't know ...

She'd seen the way merchants strode through the station as though they owned it, the way they took their crew and bondservants for granted – she wouldn't be like that, would she? She would just be ... wealthy. Secure enough to give Khanh a future.

Ngà's smile had been radiant. *Oh, child. Do you want to remain small and afraid all your life? This is your chance.*

But it hadn't been. Just a chance for Ngà to die – for Xích Si to escape, heaving and crying, as the ship burned; just a reminder that to reach out was to overreach.

Xích Si shook her head. She looked at the picture of Khanh she'd pinned above the console, shimmering in overlay: the small, determined face under the mourning band, the chubby cheeks smudged with oily dough. She breathed in, slow and even, feeling the emptiness of loss in her belly. The past was a dead weight, though. She couldn't afford to let it stop her.

There was nothing that struck her as being wrong with the fights between pirates and merchants. And yet ... something was off. Off in the way an Ashling fragment would look different from a normal asteroid, the way a piece of the Fire Palace would turn out to be radioactive or booby-trapped. There was something ...

She'd set her bots to look for anomalous patterns, but without knowing what she was looking for, it was a long, fruitless search. She had a mass of false alerts scrolling across her field of vision: an escort ship that wasn't quite following formation; a merchant open-the-void moving slightly too fast or engaging its long-haul drive slightly too late ...

Wait.

There.

And there.

And there.

The ships' behaviour was fine, but the messages themselves were off. And not even the messages, but their timestamps. During the very first fight that *Rice Fish* had given her – one near the middle of the raiding season, when the Red Scholar's fleet had been entangled with imperial cruisers – the average back and forth between ships was 3.5 blinks. The average back and forth in every subsequent fight – the four Xích Si had had, and the Red Scholar's final one – was 4.7.

She called up graphs, and stared at them for a while. Yes, there was a consistent delay on comms. So either the fleet had downgraded its comms or changed comms systems, or ...

Or someone was tampering with them. Best case, merely intercepting them; worst case, rewriting them. If Xích Si had to guess, they'd only started tampering massively on the final battle – they'd done trial runs first, perhaps enough to cause suspicion, and then caused the rout and killed the Red Scholar.

So someone was hacking the comms. How were they doing it, and how specific was it to the Red Banner? And, if this was part of the evidence *Rice Fish* needed, how could she prove it was the Green Scholar?

A belated and unwelcome thought bubbled up: whoever was keeping an eye on the ship-to-ship comms might also be listening in on the network traffic going in and out of the Citadel. Possibly even on what was happening within *Rice Fish*. Which meant *Rice Fish* had to be told.

But first she needed to find out how they were doing it, so she could suitably encrypt the communications of the Red Banner. And *then* she'd notify *Rice Fish*.

'Tiên?'

Tiên was some distance away, and her status set to *busy*. Xích Si hesitated, and raised *Crow's Words*, the head of her bannerpeople, instead.

'Yes?' The ship stood quietly to attention.

Xích Si took a deep breath. The ship was following her orders! She needn't feel afraid of it. But still ...

'I need you or your people to look for something.' She then sent the ship a detailed list to check for physical bypasses of the comms. 'Can you access other banners' space?'

A silence. *Crow's Words* seemed to be mulling on her words. Xích Si dug her nails into her palms and willed herself not to run away screaming. He was just thinking, not planning to raid her or grab her ...

'It depends what for.'

'To do the same checks.'

'Mm. ' Another silence. The ship's hazy and iridescent avatar pulsed, showing glimpses of his body in pieces – sun and starlight over the curve of a metal hull, wings banking in the darkness ...

'I have a contact in the Purple Banner. I'll see what I can do.'

After cutting off the comms, Xích Si stared, for a while, at the inside of her rooms, breathing hard. She got up from the console and went to the bed – would lying down help? But no, it just made her more jumpy. She'd tamped down the panic so many times today, and now she couldn't any more. Now all she could see was Ngà's splayed body and the sound her bots had made when they broke – and she was holding it together, but barely, because every passing moment the hollow in her stomach deepened, and it seemed to fill up her entire world.

She needed *Rice Fish*, and she needed her now.

But, when she reached out, what she got was a tribunal audience – and *Rice Fish* facing off with the smirking Green Scholar. That wasn't what she needed. She reached out to cut off the feed, because she didn't need pirate justice displayed on her screen, and then she saw what was going on.

They were fighting over a scavenger. Someone Xích Si

didn't know, though they might have passed each other, back in Triệu Hoà Port: Ái Nhân. Something in the way she stood – pale, and with her hands held in front of her as if still restrained – was all too familiar.

Pirates. Monsters. She'd almost been lulled into forgetting it – into forgetting what fuelled them and their Citadel.

But then *Rice Fish* started talking. Her voice was quiet and measured, and it boomed in the vast, cavernous space.

'You know the law. You know that dues afford not only safe passage, but an escort from pirate ships if deemed necessary.'

What?

Xích Si hadn't expected *Rice Fish* to *defend* Ái Nhân – hadn't expected her to argue for fairness and justice, and to not budge from that position even though it was an obviously losing one.

When Chi Lan struck with the knife in her hand – and when *Rice Fish* moved, lightning-fast, to protect Ái Nhân and send a bleeding Chi Lan to the floor, when *Rice Fish* faced all of them, the elders and Chi Lan's protectors and the fearful Ái Nhân – something sharp and uncomfortable fluttered in Xích Si's chest, an echo of the nausea and panic she'd felt earlier.

We're a safe space, Rice Fish had said, except that Xích Si hadn't believed her.

But it was true, wasn't it? Not everywhere, and not where the Green Scholar or Hổ held sway, but ...

The thought twisted in her chest, in that same place where she'd wanted to touch *Rice Fish*; to lay a hand on walls and *reach* her. That a pirate would stand up for a defenceless scavenger – that there were laws, that there were rules, and that *Rice Fish* believed in them ... Xích Si had heard the anger and passion in *her* voice when she'd spoken of the code.

She believed in them. She wanted to be fair. She wanted this place – this Citadel, those ships – to be a space where people like Xích Si had *rights*.

Xích Si felt as though she were dancing on the edge of a black hole — a horizon past which she would irreversibly be drawn towards ... something ...

Around her, the ship changed. Something in the quality of the air, in the firmness of the floors under her. She wasn't surprised when *Rice Fish* gently pinged her.

'May I come in?'

She should have said no, because it was a terrible idea. Because she was raw and vulnerable, and *Rice Fish* had just faced down the Green Scholar, and Heaven knew what kind of high she was riding ...

She should have said no, but she didn't want to.

'Yes.'

The door didn't so much open as fade into darkness. *Rice Fish* walked in, slowly; she wore peach-coloured robes with imprints of moons and banyan trees. Her long hair flowed into the floor, turning into the vast expanse of the sky halfway down her back; it looked as though she was dragging the heavens behind her, beautiful and terrible.

As she got halfway to the bed, something shifted — perhaps the room around her, perhaps *Rice Fish* herself — and Xích Si suddenly realised that the slowness wasn't to show off, but simply exhaustion, and the deliberateness was a sham to hide it. Her chest twisted again.

'May I?' *Rice Fish* pointed to the bed.

'Are you going to ask permission for everything?' Xích Si couldn't help the words, or the challenging way they came out — as if she was trying to see how far she could push *Rice Fish*.

'For the things that matter, yes,' *Rice Fish* said. 'Will you give me permission?'

Xích Si breathed out. 'Yes.'

It should have felt weird, sitting on the bed together, but it was no different from the console, was it? In essence, every-where she sat was next to *Rice Fish*.

'You're upset,' *Rice Fish* said.

Xích Si said, finally, 'I've had a long day.'

'Hmm.' A pause, then, 'Do you want to talk about it?'

'Do you want to talk about your day?'

A silence. Then, slowly, carefully, 'Is this about how I left you with Hồ?'

Was it? Xích Si considered it, for a while.

'No. I didn't ask for your help. Blaming you wouldn't be fair.'

'But we're not talking about what's fair, are we? So let me ask again. Is this about Hồ?'

'I don't know,' Xích Si said, finally, which at least was honest. 'It's about you, in a way.' About Aí Nhân, about Hồ, about the Green Banner. 'Maybe I hadn't understood what I'd let myself in for.'

She avoided looking at the picture of Khanh – at how it looked like something she'd put up on an ancestral altar with the other dead. She knew *Rice Fish* had seen it.

Another silence. Then a touch on her chin, and *Rice Fish* slowly nudging her face upwards, her touch faintly cold, faintly oily – that hint of deep spaces, of leaving normal time and space behind for the folded, intricate geometries of travel.

'You can still leave.'

'You need me. You said—'

'I know what I said.' A sigh. 'We're in this together, or we're not.' Another sigh. 'Maybe I was reminded of what it means to have no power today.'

'I saw what you did today,' Xích Si said, because these were the only words she had left. 'In the tribunal.'

'Did you?' A stillness that encompassed the whole room – the walls and the floor losing lustre and vibrancy and *life*.

91

Xích Si found herself aching to fill it again. 'We're a safe place. That's not empty words.'

'You're—'

'Pirates? Cruel? Kim Thông will be replaced, in time. We will change. We will become what we were always meant to be.'

'I didn't expect . . .' Xích Si started, and even before the room shifted and contracted under her, she realised what terrible words they were to say. What was she going to say? That she hadn't expected *Rice Fish* to be *decent*? Instead, she reached out with her hand and her bots – and slowly ran them down *Rice Fish*'s unbound hair. It felt like cold water under her fingers, like blunted regolith dust – smooth with just a hint of once cutting sharpness – and it parted like a river, showing stars in its depths. As the bots slid downwards, further than Xích Si's arms could reach, *Rice Fish* shivered – and laid her hand on Xích Si's lips, gently pressing with the delicacy of a kiss.

It was Xích Si's turn to inhale sharply as fire tightened her spine. *Rice Fish* withdrew her hand; laid it, gently, on the hand that was still touching her hair. They stared at each other; it felt very much like a held breath, the tension in the room unbearable.

Rice Fish's eyes were black, the colour of space without stars, of black holes without escape. Her skin shone, in the darkness of the room.

I go with my wife. A pirate consort – no, a pirate queen in her own domain, and she was beautiful and she was terrible and so, so vulnerable in that moment. The air trembled with a distant music, a distant heartbeat.

This was such a terrible idea.

'We should talk,' *Rice Fish* said.

Xích Si didn't move.

'Talk,' she said, flatly.

It hurt to speak, because every muscle wanted to continue combing *Rice Fish*'s hair — to follow it all the way down to the floor of the ship.

'Yes.' An inhale that was the purr of motors. 'Because you cannot want this.'

'Are you making my decisions for me again?'

A sigh. 'No. But you're on my body and surrounded by the banner. That's a recipe for disaster.'

'Because you think I don't know what I'm doing?'

'I don't know.' *Rice Fish* shivered, and it travelled through the entire room. At length she withdrew her hand, and held it out, palm up, to Xích Si. There was something in it, gleaming imperial vermilion: *Rice Fish*'s seal. 'Take this.'

Xích Si pressed her other hand — the one that wasn't in *Rice Fish*'s hair — to the palm. Something travelled from *Rice Fish* to her, burning as cold as ice moons.

'What is it?'

Rice Fish's voice was grim. 'An emergency override.'

'I don't understand.'

'If you want to leave, it won't matter where you are on the ship. All doors will open to you, even the heartroom. It won't matter whether—'

'Whether you agree? You could revoke it.'

'Not unless you relinquished it to me.'

'I don't understand,' Xích Si said, but she did. It wasn't a seal: it was a key. The key that turned this ship into just another room she could leave. It shifted the balance of power in her direction. She snorted. 'Do you think that changes everything?'

'I'm not sure it changes anything,' *Rice Fish* said.

They were still, facing each other. Within Xích Si, the seal burned and burned, its heat merging with the beating of her heart. She still had her hand in *Rice Fish*'s hair, feeling that

93

faint, cold sharpness under her fingers, the distant radiance of stars on her fingertips; the slow, steady beat of the ship all around her – silenced motors, the wash of starlight, and *Rice Fish* watching her – and in those dark, bottomless eyes Xích Si suddenly saw not reluctance but a deep-seated fear the same as her own. Not fear of what they'd do, but . . .

She remembered Hồ's words.

Not her lover. That's exactly what they were to each other.

Afraid that Xích Si would stop.

As if she was going to listen to an unpleasant, brattish pirate boy.

She brought her hand down, slowly and deliberately, combing hair all the way down the back – feeling it part under her fingers, the way that *Rice Fish*'s breath tightened in her chest, the way that her own quickened in response, the way something stretched and ached within her – and, with that same deliberate slowness, as if everything, stretched and heated, would just break if she pushed it too far, brought her lips against the ship's, and pressed.

She tasted like brine, like oil – a sharp tang on Xích Si's palate – the lips under her faintly oily, faintly pulsing with a beat too slow to be a human heart, tightening in response and pressing back, and Xích Si was afire now, breasts and belly aching.

She broke off, withdrawing, breathing hard, and they stared at each other. *Rice Fish* hadn't moved. She looked faintly shocked, but surely pirate mindships couldn't be shocked.

'That was . . . something,' she said.

Something good, or bad? But *Rice Fish* was smiling, uncertainly, as if she wasn't quite sure what was happening.

Xích Si had never been the kind to hide away on outer rings – to ignore or minimise danger in the Triệu Hoà Port habitats was a sure-fire way to get killed. Touchy subjects were best tackled head-on.

'You and Huân . . .?' she said.

Rice Fish's lips tightened. Xích Si was surprised to feel no fear, merely a ghostly, unreal twinge that soon faded. When had *Rice Fish* — a pirate, a mindship — become someone *safe*?

'Huân is dead,' she said at last.

'I know,' Xích Si said. 'What do you mean by that?'

Another tightening of the lips. 'What we had — whatever it was, however it was named — it's dead, too. Ghosts shouldn't walk with the living.'

It seemed to Xích Si that this ghost was not only very much alive, but was standing between them.

'I see,' she said. 'How would you name what you had?'

'Love,' *Rice Fish* said, simply.

But a very particular kind of love, wasn't it? A contract, Hổ had said. A partnership, perhaps. Xích Si had half a mind to march into Hổ's chambers — surely the Purple Banner had quarters in the Citadel — and demand answers he would probably refuse to give.

She said, finally, 'I'm not a stand-in for Huân.'

'I don't know what you want to be,' *Rice Fish* said, her voice as sharp as it had been at the tribunal. 'Or what we're meant to have.'

Neither did Xích Si, to be honest. Because if she let her brain have half a voice, it would not have let her run her hand down *Rice Fish*'s hair, or kiss her. It was one thing to make the best of a bad situation — to be civil with pirates and try to build relationships even though all she could see, most days, was Ngà's pale face; it was quite another to boldly go kissing the leader of a pirate banner.

But it had felt so good, and so right.

She said, finally, 'I think I know how she did it. The Green Scholar.'

Rice Fish's eyes narrowed. For a moment, Xích Si thought

95

she'd call her out on her deflection, but then she said, 'How she killed Huân?'

Xích Si felt a mixture of relief and disappointment that *Rice Fish* hadn't protested, and she wasn't sure which one was greater.

'I don't have proof,' Xích Si said. 'I sent my bannerpeople to get that. But I think she intercepted your comms. She did, or Censor Trúc, which works out to about the same thing.'

She outlined, briefly, her discovery and the evidence she was still working to uncover.

'Mmmm.' *Rice Fish* looked as though she'd swallowed something sour — with some of the initial weariness back in her voice.

'What's the matter?' Xích Si asked. 'I thought you'd be happier.'

A silence.

'You saw what happened at the tribunal.'

'Half of it. I saw you get your way. You . . . rescued Ái Nhân.'

'I did. But it cost me. Kim Thông had suborned two elders, at the least. And everyone in that room . . . they wanted blood, the same way she and Hổ do. The truth is . . .' Another silence. 'I'm not sure how deep her influence goes. Or what she wants, really.'

Ah.

'You think proof isn't going to be enough?'

'I think it's the only thing we have. Or don't have, at the moment.'

'I will find something,' Xích Si said.

'Why?'

'She's arrogant. People like that make mistakes. I've met her kind.'

An uncomfortably sharp look.

'Have you.'

'Magistrates, clerks, soldiers.' She shivered. 'They have power and they like it because they can hurt other people with it.' One of the clerks had kicked Khanh when she'd walked past, just because he knew no one would pay-stop him. 'But it makes them careless.'

The clerk had finally picked a target that was too large: the child of a small bot-handler whose brother was well connected on the First Planet. His subsequent fall and execution had been swift and messy.

'In other words, not that different from the monsters you think we are.'

'They're nothing alike!'

Another sharp, weighing gaze.

'If you say so.' An awkward silence that neither of them knew how to fill. 'Well, if that's all wrapped up, I'll take my leave. There are plenty of things that I need to deal with.'

She rose and walked to the door.

Xích Si watched her leave, digging her nails into the blankets to stop herself from calling her back.

9

Mother and Son

Xích Si was scarily efficient. Within hours of the trial, her banner mindship – *Crow's Words* – had got back to her, and Xích Si had forwarded the report and her subsequent discussions with *Crow's Words* to *Rice Fish*. Most of it was highly technical, but the gist was clear enough: there was no physical equipment, either aboard the ships, or aboard the Citadel, that would have relayed the fleet's messages to Censor Trúc. There was, however, a clever loophole: the comms protocol the banners used was unsecured against some authentications, and it appeared that all the imperial ships had, in essence, passed themselves off as the flagship of a pirate banner. It was deliberate, because they'd all been using a variant of the same identifications – just altered enough so that the comms' standard verification wouldn't see anything wrong.

They'd used the Green Banner's code.

Xích Si had also sent through detailed comparisons of authentication credentials and algorithms used. She hadn't, though, found evidence of who was using the codes, or how Censor Trúc had got hold of them.

It wasn't enough to incriminate Kim Thông, but Xích Si

seemed confident that further digging would uncover something useful. In the meantime, she'd suggested a change of protocols, which required *Rice Fish*'s permission. She also suggested it needed to be pushed to all banners, as they would be vulnerable to the loophole that had killed Huân. *Rice Fish* gave her permission for the upgrade, but pushing it to other banners ...

That required more thought. *Rice Fish*'s relationships with the rest of the council were strained. She was Huân's consort, first in line to become the Red Scholar, and many would respect that, but how many of them were suborned by Kim Thông? If the elders at the trial were any indication, more than she felt comfortable with. She would need to tread carefully.

Not that she could hide the upgrade from them.

In the end, she settled for notifying them that a chance was coming due to an inherent weaknesses in the protocols, without assigning any blame or revealing what she was thinking.

She'd expected some kind of reaction; what she didn't expect was a request for a private audience from Hồ – and not just through comms or with an avatar, but requesting permission to physically come aboard.

Why now? Why reach out? Because of Kim Thông? Rice Fish had told Xích Si she was sure of Hồ – that they might be estranged but he would never dare endanger the safety of the pirate alliance. But she had seen the easy way Kim Thông had suborned the elders and the sanctity of trial – she had seen both Hồ and *Mulberry Sea* in the audience – and, seeing Hồ's approving stance, and the joy in his gaze, she suddenly hadn't been sure where he stood at all.

She granted him permission to come aboard. After all, what could he do physically that he couldn't do remotely? Her core – the vulnerable part of her, the pulsing mass of flesh and optics wrapped around connectors – was in her heartroom in the centre of the ship, locked away behind metal doors. Now that Huân was dead and Hổ estranged from her, no one had access to it.

Except Xích Si.

That was an odd, unsettling thought. But they could not even begin to have a relationship – a partnership – until they were on an equal standing.

She'd assigned her private chambers to Xích Si, but there were others she could use for an audience: a small room, some distance from the heartroom, where they could both settle. It had the default overlay: scroll paintings, a longevity window opening on a faraway view of the Fire Palace and the Twin Streams, and a floor that looked like polished wood parquet but beneath which could be seen the purple-blue light of nebulas. She set her bots to prepare tea while Hổ boarded and approached. She could feel his tread, confident and quick; he'd been the kind of child who preferred to run, who viewed limits and setbacks as obstacles to be conquered. His heartbeat was slow and even, but his slightly dilated pupils and flush spoke to some strong emotion. Anger, probably.

When he sat down and lifted his teacup – when she felt his weight shift and rest on her floor, the slight way his centre of gravity moved when bending forward, the minute way holding the teacup changed his posture and weight distribution – she remembered him as a child, laughing as he tried to grab the stars on the floor, or when he'd wriggled against the walls or sat in the heartroom watching period vids, laughing at the ridiculous costumes – at the totally impractical long sleeves and trailing five-panel dresses that would only get caught between metal plates, the luxurious clothes that were the province of the extremely wealthy, the inner ring folks of Triệu Hoà Port.

After he'd left – after he became the head of the Purple Banner and became bitter and outspoken against her – she'd done the necessary thing, and revoked his access to her inner-most parts.

It had hurt, then, as much as it hurt seeing him physically here did – a clenching in her walls and corridors, a tremor on the edge of breaking in her heartroom.

'You wanted to see me?' *Rice Fish* said.

She sat cross-legged on a dais, framed by a huge chrysan-themum flower – not an overlay, something she'd had modded in during her marriage years.

'Yes.' Hồ set his cup down in his lap, looked at her. His bots were quiet – worn around his neck in a shimmering circle, and in a second ring around his belt. 'I'm surprised you accepted.'

'You're my son,' *Rice Fish* said. He was using 'elder aunt' to address her, a distant pronoun that he alternated with her formal title in the fleet. He hadn't called her Mother or Mom for *years*.

His lips thinned and his heartbeat quickened.

'You think I've come here for a reconciliation?'

'Of course not.' The hurt ran too deep. A *contract*, he'd said to Xích Si. *Shrivelled souls.* 'But it should still mean something.'

Again, a tightening of the lips. 'You overestimate what it means.'

'Mmm.' *Rice Fish* felt she was trying to outrun a much larger, much better outfitted ship, and every move she made took her further and further away from her destination. 'Why are you here?'

Hồ looked down into the teacup, and the last few drops glistening in it. *Rice Fish*'s bots were already brewing more tea – and in the background her crew was unloading Ashling artefacts, looted goods, and purchased supplies, each crate checked off in her mental inventory on a far, far away thread.

'You're fighting a losing war,' he said, using a plural pro-noun.

'Xích Si and I?'

'Ma and you ...' he paused. 'And yes, Xích Si and you.'

'A losing war?' *Rice Fish* calmly repeated his own words back at him, to draw him out.

Another silence.

Then, 'She's right. We're *pirates*. Not nurturers and authorities over the people.' He used the expression for a magistrate – the single official responsible for the well-being of the people in their jurisdiction – and it was abundantly clear who he was referring to. Any doubts *Rice Fish* had had about his allegiance died.

Not a reconciliation, then, but a drawing of lines. That ... It had hurt before, now she was just numb. He couldn't mean to. He couldn't possibly ...

'Fracturing the Fire Palace is easy,' *Rice Fish* said, mildly. 'But you don't build anything lasting beneath a smoking ruin.'

'We used to be feared. Our name used to mean something. Now it's all ...' He made an expansive gesture with his cup. 'Passes and clerks, and accountings. Bodyguards and escorts. We've become *bureaucrats*.'

'Like the ones many of us ran away from? You worry that we have become like our worst enemies.' *Rice Fish* hesitated, but she was too angry and hurt to keep it bottled up. 'That's not an unfair assessment. At the trial, I saw only the worst on display – rank corruption, privilege wielded like a cudgel, and the law broken to suit the powerful.'

'Mom!'

The word came out of him, resonating in the room like a ship's plates snapping. He got up – the shifting weight of his feet on her floors like two close punches – and stared at her, wild-eyed and dishevelled, his heartbeat rising faster and faster. She fought the urge to send bots to check in on him, because he was not her passenger, and she knew exactly the

102

nature of his distress. She wanted to hold him, to sing to him – to draw him into her heartroom and soothe him, now and forever.

She could afford none of those things. She held herself, quivering and shaking as much as he was – kept the lights and the overlay together with an effort of will, though the Fire Palace beyond the window blurred a fraction, and the nebulas dimmed. Nothing visible to human eyes.

'I can't be what you want me to,' she said, finally. 'Neither of us could be.'

'So now you start the cycle again with a prisoner you've rescued from the cells? What are you trying to prove?'

Xích Si isn't ...

She didn't know what Xích Si was any more, and that wasn't the point.

'What are *you* trying to prove?' *Rice Fish* said. 'That you're not my son? That you're different from Ma and me?'

He stared at her, an emotion she couldn't name in his eyes. She shouldn't have said that – because she was going to get an answer to a question she hadn't wanted to ask.

'You don't understand.'

'Then help me to.'

A pause. He was blinking fast – accessing the network, as he often did when confused or angry. He'd find some old vid or book and let it wash over him, ground him.

'We've gone soft. That's why the An O Empire is making such inroads with us. That's why Censor Trúc was able to ...' He couldn't quite bring himself to say the words.

'Kill your mother? Is that what Kim Thông is saying?'

Such a handy excuse, when she'd been the one to pass information to the censor. But she didn't have proof of that yet and couldn't afford to blurt it out, not even when angry.

'She knows we have to be feared. We have to avenge Ma!'

'Avenge her?' *Rice Fish* kept her voice cold – because how dare they? How dare Kim Thông pretend she wanted to avenge the woman she'd killed as surely as if she'd fired the ship's fragmenter-guns? She said, finally, as slowly as if she were still talking to a small child, 'The An O isn't making inroads with us because we've grown weak. It's because we've grown too big. Too bold.' She knew the truth of it as she said it. All of it – all of Hổ's raids, all of that bloodlust – only led to one thing: the anger of the Empress. The dispatching of Censor Trúc, the vow to end them all. 'We existed in a fragile equilibrium. Between the hunger of the Đại Việt, the disorganisation and corruption of the An O, the greed of the merchants scavenging in the Fire Palace. That's all gone now. The Đại Việt were withdrawing, and along with that came reduced protection. We're not weak. We're too strong.'

He looked at her as if she'd lost her sanity.

'We're going to stop raiding?'

'There's a balance,' *Rice Fish* said. She used *trung*, which simply meant 'middle'. 'Between survival and greed.'

'You're scared, aren't you? Like she is.'

He said it with the confidence and contempt of youth – he didn't quite know what it meant, to be scared to one's bones, to be clamped down to a dock and know that your captors would do as they wanted, and nothing and no one would protect you from their excesses ... And why should he? He'd grown up safe. That had been the point of everything she and Huân had built – of the alliance, of the tribunal, of the code.

'Kim Thông, scared?' Kim Thông wasn't scared. *Rice Fish* remembered the look she'd thrown her in the tribunal: naked anger and rage at being thwarted. Kim Thông carried grudges like Phổ Nhĩ tea, ageing and fermenting them and never letting go or forgiving. Defeat had made her nastier and vindictive, but it had been worth it. 'She's bitter.'

104

Power hadn't flown her way, and the vagaries of the pirate life hadn't satisfied her. It had all gone sour in her head.

'You don't know the first thing about her.'

'I know enough. You shouldn't let her get under your skin. You shouldn't trust her.'

'You think I'm under some kind of malign influence.'

'You're a *child*.'

A snort from Hổ. 'And that makes me incapable of reaching my own conclusions? It makes me weak and stupid? You always had a tendency to overprotect people. You're doing it to Xích Si, too. What do you think will happen, when she starts thinking for herself?'

That was unfair, and untrue.

'Leave Xích Si out of this.'

'She married you, she's already in this. It's too late, Mom.' The word was all withering sarcasm. His vitals were average now; he was still angry but it was burning cold. She'd dreamed of the day he'd use the proper pronouns again, but it was all turning bitter around her. 'You're outnumbered, and your time is passing. Ma is dead, and you cling to the past, to those wild dreams you had.'

'Fairness? Justice? You call them dreams?'

She'd raised him. She and Huân. How they had gone so, so deeply wrong?

'We're *pirates*.'

This was going nowhere — round and round in circles around the one fundamental disagreement they had.

'Pirates. Avenging the Red Scholar. You think raining fire and ice on the An O Empire is going to solve anything?'

'*You* think that depriving Kim Thông of power is going to solve anything?'

It would certainly remove the smooth-tongued tiger in their

105

midst. And then she remembered that Hổ's name meant 'tiger', too.

'I don't know why you're here.'

'Because I thought ...' His voice was shaking, his bots unsteady on his arms, his heartbeat quickening again. 'Because I thought you'd listen, for once. Because I thought you'd *care* for something beyond your ideals. But you haven't cared for such a long time, have you?'

'Because I wouldn't sleep with Ma to satisfy your image of a perfect family?'

'This isn't about sleeping with each other, this is about happiness! You're my parents! I watched you tear yourselves apart, grow more and more distant from each other, walk around some kind of gigantic black hole that just swallowed you up. I watched Ma collect her friends and lovers and never get the intimacy she craved. I saw the way it ate at her. I watched you become hollow at heart. '

'We made a decision,' *Rice Fish* said.

Huân had made a decision, but it would be unfair to let her carry the weight of it. He didn't need a window into her deepest shame.

'A decision? Contracts. Fairness. That's all you think there is to life, to marriage, to relationships. It's not going to change any time soon, is it?' He bent to put the teacup back on the table. 'I should have known. Goodbye, Mom.'

And then he was gone – she felt every one of his footsteps in her corridors, all the way to the docking bay airlock, the slight disturbance of air as he left and then his heartbeat and vitals were no longer hers to monitor – and all *Rice Fish* wanted to do was curl around the wound he'd left in her heart.

10

Teahouses

'Younger aunt?'

Xích Si, startled, looked up from the comms protocols she was deploying on board *Crow's Words*.

It was the pirates who'd been helping her: Tấm and Cám, the two sisters who she'd met at the same time as *Crow's Words*, and a mindship called *Plum and Peach*. They stood uncertainly in the corridor.

Xích Si let her bots finish rummaging into the innards of *Crow's Words*.

'Yes?'

Cám looked at Tấm. It was *Plum and Peach* who finally spoke, her avatar a deer with the shape of a ship caught in its antlers.

'We're going to get some tea. Do you want to come?'

'Tea.' Cám snorted. 'No. We're starting with tea, but then we're getting some rice wine. And getting seriously sozzled.'

Xích Si stared at them. 'I can't . . .' *Crow's Words* was silent; when she pinged him he simply said, 'I'm not much for drink, personally, but that's a good offer from good people. Go if you want.'

Tấm sighed, running a hand on her shaved head. She wore dark unornamented robes, and no bots — they were all in her sleeves, glinting when she moved.

'You've been working yourself to the bone trying to ensure we don't get killed like the Red Scholar. You need a break. We all need a break. Besides, have you seen the Citadel?'

'Kim Thông ...'

Rice Fish was still making inquiries, and there were more than a few Green Banner pirates who had come asking. But the idea — the thought she could go into a pirate citadel, all by herself — it was terrifying.

'She's scared,' Cám said, contemptuously.

'Li'l sis.' Tấm lifted a hand to stop Cám, and looked at Xích Si for a while. 'You are scared, but you're right to be scared. I remember what it was like, those first days in the fleet.' Her voice had changed slightly; the inflections and vocabulary were pure scavenger.

'You ...' Xích Si stopped. 'You were a captive?'

Tấm shrugged. 'A long time ago. I'm from Jade Mountains Ring, sector five, in Triệu Hoà Port.'

Not that far from where Xích Si and Khanh had lived.

'Jade Mountains Ring, sector seven.'

'I figured.' Tấm smiled. 'You have the accent.'

'You and your sister were both taken?'

Cám laughed. 'No. I came to join her.'

'Why ...?'

Why would one knowingly condemn themselves to death?

Tấm shrugged. 'Impressive filial piety, from younger sister to elder sister.'

'Hmmmf. I don't love you that much,' Cám said. In overlay, she had ghostly goby fishes swimming around her arms, and her ornate robes were studded with a persimmon and a loom — all images from the fairy tale she and her sister were named

108

after. The effect was not subtle. 'There wasn't much else for me. You know what it's like, the scavenger life. It wears you to a nub.'

Xích Si knew, all too well. Reaching out, again and again, and being denied, and being hurt. Pooling meagre resources with Aunt Vy, her friends Hoa and Vân and Ngọc Nữ. The comradeship between them did not change the fundamental injustice: that all their solidarity was nothing more than a thin bandage over a gaping wound; that all the sharing of food and time didn't change that there wasn't enough, because those who had the power and resources had hoarded it all, and blamed scavengers for wanting a fair life.

'Anyway.' Tấm looked embarrassed. She stroked the handle of a gun – in overlay it was inlaid with an intricate pattern of mother-of-pearl, with that particular sheen from Felicity Station, a costly design. 'I remember how hard it was, when I first came here. How alone you feel. You can't remain on board *Rice Fish* forever, and you're right that the Green Banner might be looking for trouble. But you should be safe with the three of us. Here.' She held out a similar gun to the one in her belt. 'You can have this, too. Though *Rice Fish* would also have a selection for you if you asked.'

'They'll have dumplings with the tea,' *Plum and Peach* said, inclining her head – the ship caught in the deer's antlers moved at the same time. 'The ones at the Hollow Bamboo are the best in the Twin Streams.'

A quick flash in overlay in front of her: steamed dumplings, turnip cake, rolled rice crêpes . . .

Xích Si pinged the network to look them up. *Plum and Peach* seemed to spend most of her time in the Citadel doing paperwork and administration. Tấm's last raid had been on a large merchant ship. The fight had been short and bloody, and afterwards she'd ransomed the merchants, the captain and the corrupt militia, but let the bodyguards and ship's crew go. She was married, with a wife, a husband and three grinning children. Cám was the most bloodthirsty of the three; she'd taken part in most of the same raids as the Red Scholar.

They all looked at her, seeming nothing so much as a group of friends intent on having a night out and getting a drink together, sharing their troubles over a cup of tea that later morphed into rice wine. They looked ... friendly. Concerned. It was hard to forget what they were. And tempting to, to just feel less isolated – and, on another level, to put some distance between her and *Rice Fish* and think on the kiss – or not think on it.

She guessed that if she was going to go out – and Tấm was right, she couldn't just keep hiding inside without having any idea of what was out there – then there were worse people to go out with.

'All right.' She reached out, taking the gun – feeling the weight and cold of it in her hands, slipping it into her belt and assigning a few bots to keep track of it. 'Let's go.'

The Citadel was nothing like what Xích Si had expected.

It was a riot of colours and sound, nothing like Triệu Hoà Port. The space was filled with corridors and compartments, but the overlay was different: the ceiling was invisible, replaced by a huge fractured image of the Fire Palace, the ruined planet that provided them all with their living, and the corridors had been tampered with to seem like the crevices of a canyon. Everything seemed vast and expansive, and Xích Si found herself taking in a deep breath under the unblinking light of stars.

Tấm was leading the way, weaving through a varied crowd of people that Xích Si couldn't place. People, ships, physically and virtually present – a dizzying array of avatars from animals to spaceships, of richly embroidered clothes and detailed overlays — and too much information from banner to indenture status to latest public raids, from previous avatars to personal preferences, broadcast like a spectacle.

'Skewer?' A merchant thrust one under Xích Si's nose.

Plum and Peach laughed, and her bots tossed something towards the merchant, and all of a sudden Xích Si was holding a skewer of meat redolent of grilled rice flour and peanut sauce. She bit into it, unthinking, and it was an explosion of flavours in her mouth, an unfamiliar and startling richness that dribbled down onto her lips.

'See? The best food,' *Plum and Peach* said happily. She expertly steered Xích Si away from a brawl — Xích Si only caught a glimpse of colourful clothes and ghostly avatars tangled together. 'Careful.'

Children were running, laughing and heedless of the noise, of the fights, of the life around them. Two of them — girls who couldn't have been much older than Khanh — came to stare at them, nudging each other. Xích Si stared back.

'Hello.'

'Hello,' the elder girl said. 'You're *new*.'

She was all wiry muscle, her cheeks plump and reddened, and she had a dab of peanut sauce clinging to her lips.

'I suppose so. Where are you from?'

'From here! Mama and Mommy are off getting some supplies before they head off for a last raid. Mama is about to pay off her indenture, you know. Mommy says if they can ransom a rich enough merchant, that should do it.'

The younger girl snorted. She was smaller and squatter, and overall quieter.

'Rich merchants are too hard. Too many bodyguards to get through.'

To kill, to wound, to capture. To kill like Ngà, to imprison

111

like Xích Si. It was casual and shocking — how could she say such adult, wounding things?

'I see,' Xích Si said. And, before she could stop herself, 'And what does your mama think of that? No, never mind, that's an unfair question.'

She was scared and angry, but she couldn't take that out on a child.

'Oh, it's you two.' Tấm had stopped and turned back.

'Auntie, Auntie!' the elder girl said. 'Are you back from the raid?'

Tấm laughed. 'Not for long, if I have anything to say about it.'

'They say the Red Scholar died,' the younger girl said.

'She did,' Tấm said. '*Rice Fish* has matters well in hand.'

'Oh, I'm not worried about *Rice Fish*,' the younger one said. 'But she must be so sad.'

'I guess. I'm not that kind of intimate with her.'

Tấm patted her pockets, finally found what she was looking for: a bauble she held up, tilting it so it caught the light of the Fire Palace above them, refracting the red highlights like a New Year's lantern. Tấm watched their faces for a while, and then threw the bauble. The younger girl caught it deftly.

'Tell your mama I have something else for her, too,' Tấm said. And, to Xích Si, 'These are Lệ Thu and Lệ Đông. Little demons in training.'

'We're not demons! We're *pirates*,' Thu said, resentfully. 'What's your name?'

'Xích Si.'

'Oh, you're an owl! I like it.'

Thu was brash and utterly without shame. Her sister Đông was quieter — she reminded Xích Si of Khanh, watching carefully and cradling the bauble between her fingers, spinning it so that the light from it merged with the blue light that surrounded her in overlay.

Xích Si felt a stab of pain, as if someone was twisting her innards. She missed Khanh so much – she missed *home* so much, she wanted to cry. She forced herself to set the feeling aside, knowing she'd pay for it later.

'Pleased to meet you both.'

'Us too!' Thu said, and Đông nodded. Thu pulled at her. 'Come on, let's go see the bot-fight!'

And they were off with only a brief goodbye.

'You all right?' Tấm asked.

Xích Si, startled, looked at her and saw a pirate with a gun in her belt.

'I . . .' She opened her mouth, and found words had dried up.

Xích Si couldn't read the expression in Tấm's eyes.

'Let's go to the teahouse.' She eyed the crowd, warily. 'There's too many Green Banner folks in here.'

'What do you have for her mama?' Xích Si asked.

Tấm looked sheepish, which was a whole look on a pirate with a gun in her belt.

'Never mind,' Xích Si said. 'I shouldn't . . .'

'It's nothing. A little something towards paying off her mama's indenture.' She must have seen Xích Si's face. 'We all go through it. It's not so bad. Every raid you take part in goes towards your freedom.'

Xích Si opened her mouth, closed it. It was unfair and monstrous. But she thought of Thu and Đông, the children she'd just seen – the bloodthirsty children, well fed, boisterous, unafraid of strangers. She thought of Khanh, thinner, quieter, already used to being silent and well behaved lest she be arrested by the militia or casually beaten by the tribunal's people. She remembered how she'd had to wait until Khanh was asleep to cry after Ngà's death, and the death of all her

113

hopes. So she held her peace, and merely followed Tấm back to the others.

Cám had a gun out by the time they came back.

'Big sis.'

'I know,' Tấm said. *Plum and Peach* was still, but something about them suggested coiled strength. 'We're being watched.'

'Can you show me?' Xích Si said. 'In overlay.'

'Sure.'

A nudge in Xích Si's overlay, and when she accepted it, people around her lit up. They were affiliated to the Green or the Purple Banner, but they mostly stood out by dint of being too casual, too unengaged in what they were doing.

'What do they want?' she asked.

'Nothing yet, I think,' *Plum and Peach* said.

'We should head back,' Cám said.

'Slink home like a mouse that's seen the tiger? No way,' Tấm said. 'Come on, let's get that drink.'

Xích Si watched their watchers, warily: a woman standing by the steamed-bun seller; a small group by the boisterous bot-fight in the virtual arena; a handful of ships' avatars who didn't seem interested in the teaware on display on trestles. She remembered how worried *Rice Fish* had been about Kim Thông's growing influence. *They'll make a mistake*, she'd told *Rice Fish*. And why would they be watching her, if they weren't worried about what she and *Rice Fish* could do?

'Yes,' she said, with a vicious satisfaction. 'Let's get a drink.'

There were more watchers on the way to the teahouse. By that point, Tấm no longer needed to point them out; Xích Si was tagging half of them through her bots' sensors. They were slick, but not that slick; Xích Si's bots could pick up on pretend disengagement, and on the way people's heads turned just a little too long to follow her.

They were headed away from the crowd, into more deserted alleyways with people in more discreet garb.

'Ah, not that way,' Cám said, one hand on Xích Si's upper arm.

Xích Si stared at her; the pirate appeared wary, and half-embarrassed.

'Isn't the teahouse down here?'

Ahead was a huge building with raucous noise, and some odd layers of filters on them; it felt as though half the noises were missing.

She reached out to lift the filters– and felt Cám's hand on her tighten.

'Leave it as it is,' Tấm said.

Cám tugged at her. 'Come on. The teahouse is that way.'

Why are they so skittish?

'Is it the Green Banner?'

None of the pirates spoke up. It was unnerving.

'I'm not moving until I get explanations,' Xích Si said.

At length, *Plum and Peach* spoke.

'It's the Redeeming House.'

Which made no sense to Xích Si.

'The market,' Cám said, curtly.

Somehow, it didn't sound like a place where one would buy rice or fish sauce.

'What are they selling?'

'Indentures.' Tấm's face was grim. 'Especially the hopeless ones.'

Indentures.

'You mean people.' It was like a dash of cold water across her face, after the conversation she'd had with Lệ Thu and Lệ Đông. 'What do you mean by "hopeless ones"? I thought it was fair. That everyone had a chance.'

A silence.

It was *Plum and Peach* who spoke, the ship looking down-right uncomfortable.

'You earn your freedom through your share of raids. Some captains don't let their bondspeople close enough to the action that they can earn anything. Or some people's indenture is just set high to start with, especially if they injured or killed pirates when they were taken.'

Taken. Such a euphemism for blood and violence – pirates bursting through the door, destroying every bot, dragging Xích Si out by her wrists and throwing her into a cell.

Xích Si stared at the building, at the light, at what she could hear through the filters. The raucousness of it, the laughter, the banter. The other things that didn't make it through: despair; abuses.

'*Rice Fish* said rape was forbidden in the banner. What of the other banners?'

Another studied silence, which was as good as an answer.

'There are rules,' *Plum and Peach* said. 'A few. No killing, no maiming of indentured people or prisoners. No indenture of children.'

And that was supposed to make it acceptable?

'You don't have to worry about that,' Cám said, which was possibly the worst thing she could have said at this point in time.

'Because of who I am? What of everyone else?'

Cám's grip was bruising. 'Do you think it's better in Triệu Hoà Port? In the outer rings, where people are worth less than meat?'

'That's not the point! The point is that it's supposed to be better *here*!'

She'd believed it. Ancestors, she'd almost believed it – almost swallowed whole what *Rice Fish* had told her, of a harsh but fair place.

'Please,' Tấm said. 'Let's go.'

Xích Si didn't move. She stared at the building, thinking of what it had been like inside her cell, waiting for the inevitable. Thinking of Ngà's corpse, pinned to the ruins of her ship – of how it had been so heartbreakingly obvious the pirates had toyed with her before jettisoning her into deep spaces. Of violence and exercise of power, and the way it underpinned everything in pirate society.

It could have been her in that market, but for the choice she'd been offered. The exit she'd taken.

Tấm's bots slid under her shoulders, and Cám's grip shifted, so that they were both marching her away from the jail.

'Let's go,' Tấm said. And, more gently, 'You can't change it, not now. Come on.'

No, she couldn't, not now and perhaps not ever. But that didn't mean she had to meekly accept it.

As they walked away, Xích Si could still feel the building, a dark, rancid thing at her back – a sour taste in her mouth that she couldn't bring herself to swallow away.

The teahouse was not a building, though they had to de-scend stairs to get into it. At the end of the stairs the space opened into a vast plain under starlight, dotted with tables. The overlay must have been a headache to sort out – how to extend perception like that – but it was smooth and utterly seamless, giving Xích Si the impression of a meadow or a plaza – something much, much larger than any space in Triệu Hoà Port, or at least the parts that Xích Si frequented. It was ... disconcerting. She kept expecting to bump into something, and having to readjust when she didn't.

When they sat down around a low table in the shelter of a rockfall, they could barely hear the other groups, thanks to the perception filters.

'There.' Cám leaned back, satisfied.

Tấm was watching Xích Si, carefully.

'You're still thinking about it.'

Xích Si took a deep, shaking breath, looking for words that would make sense.

'Do you expect me not to?'

Tấm's face was unreadable. 'I don't know what *Rice Fish* told you. But I'd expect some of it was about your not having any choice.'

Xích Si knew that, and it hurt.

'There's no perfect place,' Tấm said.

No. Clearly not. And this was a place where children could grow up well fed, bloodthirsty and unafraid – and where power was still used and abused. A glorious and terrible place all at once, and she wasn't sure what to make of it any more.

'You're right,' Xích Si said, finally. 'This isn't going to get solved tonight. Let's just ... have a drink.'

And she'd try and sort it out in her own mind later.

'Good.' Tấm looked relieved. She made a gesture, and the centre of the teahouse – which featured a drunk poet mindship loudly declaiming an epic battle, and an older woman playing the zither with a multi-choral augment – shimmered closer. Everyone she saw was armed with guns or knives. 'Time for poetry, then. She's very good, you'll see.'

Xích Si stared at her cup. It was a celadon blue shimmering with the light of the Fire Palace overhead. *Plum and Peach* and Cám opted for rice wine.

'Who?'

'The poet.'

It wasn't the kind of poetry Xích Si was used to. Poetry was quiet and contemplative and beautiful – this was bloody, and messy, and the zither's chords were just adding to the discordance. It felt as though someone was rifling through her entrails with the point of a blade. Yet it was strangely compelling – as

118

the poet talked of ships tearing at each other in the night, and the cold light of the stars running like tears on their hull, and blood binding them all together, she couldn't help but shiver.

'It's weird,' she said, finally.

'Ah.' Tấm nodded. 'Fair. Flower-poetry is a bit unusual in the Twin Streams, I'd guess. We have more ... traditional poets, too. Famous ones from the matter world.'

'Matter world?'

'Non-pirate society,' *Plum and Peach* said. 'We're the void.'

It made sense. It felt ... It felt as though Xích Si was looking at something large and bewildering – and, like the poem, it was strangely compelling.

'So what do you think the banner is going to do?' Tấm asked.

Xích Si looked up, startled, but Tấm was talking to Cám.

'Don't know,' Cám said. 'Council will say.'

Plum and Peach took a sip from her own cup.

'The council has its own issues.'

'Politics,' Tấm said. 'It'll work itself out.'

Except that Xích Si had seen at first hand, that it didn't.

'Did you see the trial?' she asked. 'Ái Nhân's?'

'Oh yeah.' Cám laughed. 'That's *Rice Fish* all over.' She sounded a little annoyed and a little wistful – reluctantly admiring. 'That's not how we're meant to work.'

Xích Si couldn't help it. 'The disregard for the laws, or what *Rice Fish* did?'

A sharp breath from Tấm. Xích Si braced herself for a nebulous blow – and was surprised at how fast she relaxed again, even though Tấm was still visibly angry. Xích Si had this faith that *Rice Fish* had been right: not just that *Rice Fish* would protect her, but that the banner would stand by her, too. When had that happened?

'The banner is fair,' Tấm said. 'I told you. We have laws.

And it's annoying that we have to sidestep them in order to insist they are respected. I don't know if I'd have done what *Rice Fish* did. But I don't think there were any other ways.' A sigh. 'We're not Triệu Hoà Port. Well, I hope we're not, though the Green Banner is certainly doing their best to make that happen.'

'Don't know what's happened to Kim Thông,' *Plum and Peach* said. 'She used to be decent.'

'Before my lifetime,' Tấm said. 'She's always been power-hungry.'

'Nothing wrong with being power-hungry,' *Plum and Peach* said.

Tấm threw her a look. 'We're all here because someone abused their power. Don't be so hasty to condone it. Kim Thông is overstepping, for sure.' She looked at their numerous Green Banner watchers. 'Whatever you and *Rice Fish* have on her, I hope you make it public soon.'

Soon. She'd make a mistake, and they could catch her. But then what? Change the banners, as *Rice Fish* had said? She didn't really know where Kim Thông's fall would leave her and *Rice Fish* — staring at each other over the literal void, the savagery of pirate society?

'So where did you learn all that bot-stuff?' Cám's bots descended to encircle her wine cup. 'Is that scavenging?'

'Yeah,' Xích Si said.

Tấm's gaze was uncomfortably sharp. 'Don't think so. Neither Cám nor I could have reinstalled an entire messaging protocol.'

'It's ...' Xích Si sighed. 'It made a difference, as a scavenger.' Being faster, being better ... it was a knife's edge between survival and death, and she'd had Khanh to think of. Khanh. Whom she couldn't see, couldn't contact — could just hope for in a world where hope made so little difference. 'Do you have any of that wine?'

'Feeling out of sorts?' Cám asked.

'Li'l sis.' Tấm's gaze was a warning.

She called up an overlay and ordered more rice wine, passing it around for everyone to pour what they wanted. Xích Si hesitated, and added yet more rice wine to the order.

Plum and Peach said, 'We all have those we left behind. It's hard.'

Tấm's bots pushed over the wine pitcher – one encircled by a ghostly tree whose colour echoed the light of the Fire Palace. The smell seared her nostrils. She tried not to think of Khanh, but it was too hard and she was crying.

She reached for her cup, drained it, set it back down on the table. A warm feeling spread in her stomach, but didn't fill the emptiness, or to make her miss her daughter less – all the little drawings Khanh had left strewn around the compartment, her habit of dragging her favourite turtle and sitting with it in her lap.

'I have a daughter,' she said.

'Shit,' Tấm said. 'You're going to need a lot more drink.'

'She doing fine?' Cám asked.

'Shut up.' Tấm's face didn't move, but she suddenly radiated menace.

'She'd like to talk about her child! She volunteered the info—'

Tấm punched Cám. It was smooth and so fast Xích Si barely saw it. One moment they were sitting side by side, and the next there was a crunch and Cám was reeling back, her hand going to her face – and her bots climbing up her arms, even as her other hand whipped out a knife.

'Whoa whoa whoa,' *Plum and Peach* said. 'Tone it down. Bar brawls are done with other banners. Not the people you go to drink with.'

'She hit me! Her own elder sister!' Cám was incensed.

121

'I warned you,' Tấm said. 'You deserved it.'

Xích Si drained her cup of wine, and then reached for the pitcher. Beyond her, Tấm and Cám were arguing – and moving further away from the table, the overlay taking over and doing some weird effect where they hadn't been gone for more than a blink, and yet seemed an entire measure away.

'You all right there?' *Plum and Peach* asked.

'No,' Xích Si said.

Her head was full of Khanh, and she felt as though she was going to sob. Or vomit. Or both.

'Hmmm.' *Plum and Peach* appeared to consider. 'Have another drink?'

It was a terrible idea, and Xích Si did it anyway.

They got Xích Si back to *Rice Fish* in more or less one piece, with the ever-present Green Banner and Purple Banner watchers trailing them. Tấm and Cám had got into some kind of brawl with the entire teahouse – Xích Si hadn't followed because she'd been busy drinking far too much wine. It had stung her nostrils and given her a general numb sensation at the back of her tongue. Now they were leaning against each other, drunkenly singing, Tấm sporting a black eye that her bots were already scurrying to treat, and Cám waving her gun as though she wanted to shoot everyone and everything around the Citadel.

Everyone was still abroad, everyone was still relentlessly cheerful and in Xích Si's face – skewers and smells and drinks. The deserted streets of Triệu Hoà Port just felt so far away, so different – no militia, no wealthy people with money to buy a blind eye to the curfew rules. And there was no running back, no running away. This was all she had now, now and forever – this raucous and terrible place which drank and sang and declaimed and sold people in a marketplace – and everything was unstable and sickening in the same way as her stomach and her heart, and she wanted to cry but couldn't.

She didn't know she was back on *Rice Fish* until her feet carried her up, and she felt something familiar and comforting – and realised it was the ship's attention turning her way.

'All right,' Tấm said through her comms. 'She has an eye on you now. We're off. See you tomorrow.'

Xích Si walked back to her room, unsteadily. The ship wobbled and changed around her, the corridors widening and receding out of sight, the overlays hurting her ears and eyes – and then they were being muted, one by one, as she walked past them, as if she were walking in a pool of silence. Bots scuttled past her – her own bots were busy tracing a path for her and she was following them, and she couldn't quite remember why she'd asked. Oh right, she'd had too much to drink. Way too much.

In her room, she sat down on the bed for a while, staring at the wall. She felt sadness and homesickness well up in her, like a huge wave clogging her stomach and lungs which swallowed up all the space within her.

'I know you're here,' she said.

'You're drunk,' *Rice Fish* said.

Her avatar hovered on the threshhold – not quite materialised yet, a faint shadow with bots under her.

'What does that have to do with anything?'

'That ...' *Rice Fish* hesitated. 'That means this isn't the best time for us to talk.'

'And when else are we going to talk?' Xích Si tried to breathe. It hurt.

'Tomorrow. Later. Go to bed.' *Rice Fish*'s voice was gentle.

She was beautiful and terrible, wavering in the lights overhead: her hair pooling into starlit darkness; nebulas wheeling in the red of her robes; the ornament on her topknot glinting

123

with the light of the Fire Palace; her eyes the colour of the void, inescapable black holes. Xích wanted to hold her so badly.

'Don't want to sleep. It hurts. Won't you come in?'

'You're drunk,' *Rice Fish* said, again. 'You're not in your right mind.'

'I didn't ask you to kiss me, did I?'

Rice Fish flinched. 'No. And I wouldn't even if you did.'

'Because you don't ... love me?'

A careful silence. The ship didn't move from her space by the door – watching her, tall and inscrutable and forever out of reach. The key to her heartroom was a weight somewhere in overlay space, burning like the wings of a vast bird.

'That's not the topic.'

'You ... I don't know where we stand. I don't know what we're supposed to do. I don't know ...' She was crying in great large sobs now, heaving out of her, uncontrollable wave after uncontrollable wave, the pirate children and the marketplace, the homesickness and thoughts and worries about Khanh and everyone and everything she'd left behind overwhelming her. She wasn't going back. She wasn't ever going home. It was all dead to her. She was a consort and a pirate and that was the sum of her life, and even if they dealt with Kim Thông she didn't see anything other than a tightly circumscribed circle where she would live and die ...

Coolness, on her. *Rice Fish* had crossed the threshold, was gently holding her.

'Ssh,' she said. 'Ssh, li'l sis. I have you.'

Cold and sharpness wrapped around her. Bots scuttling in the room.

'You don't have much of anything, do you?' Ancestors, she was such an ugly mess of a drunk. 'I apologise for the mess.'

'I have enough. And I thought we had said no apologies.'

There was fondness in *Rice Fish*'s voice. 'Come on. Let's get you to bed.'

The warmth moved, changed — she was being picked up and carried, bots beneath the avatar at work, the sharpness of *Rice Fish*'s touch — and it lasted too long, not long enough, before she was back on the bed, lying down and staring at the wavering ceiling, trying to blink away something that felt like tears, except she felt all wrung out inside and the headache was climbing up from her eyes to her forehead.

'I've left you something to drink and some food,' *Rice Fish* said. 'Good for hangovers.'

Xích Si thought about sleep; and about that boisterous and alien place, just beyond *Rice Fish*, where there were children laughing and smiling, and there were brawls in teahouses; and about silence and the ship's ever-present watchfulness, except, of course, she didn't watch in Xích Si's room.

'How do you do it?'

'Do what?'

'Keep moving and smiling when you've lost so much.'

'Ah, grief.' A silence. 'Because it's necessary. Because grief isn't the whole of who I am. Because I have people to think of.'

'They're not ...' Xích Si thought of Tấm, punching Cám when Cám had upset Xích Si ; of *Plum and Peach*, walking her back; of Lệ Thu and Lệ Đông, looking up at her with that utter certainty, their faces blurring to become Khanh's.

There are rules of indenture, *Plum and Peach* had said. *No children.*

And they were right: in Triệu Hoà Port, there were no rules, no protection for the likes of Xích Si or Khanh.

'They're not my people.'

'I know.' Fond amusement in the ship's voice. 'But they might be, given time.'

And then she was gone.

11

Warnings

A knock, on the door.

Xích Si, startled, looked up from the ship's schematics she was trying to untangle. A spike of pain went through her head – she'd woken up from her night of drinking with a splitting headache and a very strong sense of dissatisfaction at the way things had played out when *Rice Fish* had put her to bed.

'Yes?' she said.

If it was *Crow's Words* looking for gossip . . .

The door opened, revealing *Rice Fish*, and a group of bots carrying a tray of tea that smelled like damp fungus.

'Here,' she said. 'I've brought you something for the head-ache.'

She . . .

She'd come back. Xích Si stared at *Rice Fish*. Words seemed to have fled altogether, leaving her exceedingly awkward and slow.

'Come in,' she said. She shrunk the schematics on the con-sole, and had her bots drag out the small table she used for her tea. 'I'm sorry, it's a bit of a mess. I was working—'

'It's all right,' *Rice Fish* said.

Her bots ran up, legs skittering on the floor, to join Xích Si's. For a moment they stood side by side, watching the bots work.

'Thank you,' Xích Si said. 'For yesterday.'

Laughter from *Rice Fish*. 'No need to thank me.'

She stared, hard, at Xích Si as if drinking all of her up, dark eyes wide, showing the vast expanse of space – and something snapped in Xích Si, and she bent down and kissed *Rice Fish*.

The lips under her were as sharp as moon dust. She swallowed something that tasted like salt and made her feel giddy with an unfamiliar feeling. The entire room under her convulsed.

Rice Fish broke off the kiss.

'You told me to wait until I wasn't drunk,' Xích Si said. The headache had receded. 'I'm not any more.'

Rice Fish was breathing, hard, the bots and the room completely still.

'I believe what I said was that we would *talk* when you weren't drunk.'

'We can do both.'

'Demonstrably so.' *Rice Fish* raised a hand to her lips, rubbing it against them. Her skin sheened, matching the colour of the walls for a bare moment. She looked as though she was going to say something else, but settled for, 'Have some tea.'

Xích Si sat down in a chair, sipping the tea. *Rice Fish* sat down as well, sipping from an overlay cup. Her face was frozen in a peculiar expression Xích Si had never seen on her: utterly relaxed and at ease, her entire body language subtly changed.

Xích Si wanted to talk about the Redeeming House – about the indentures and the unfairness that underpinned everything – but . . . it would all still be there tomorrow, and she was here, with the tea, with the dumplings and that unfamiliar warmth in her stomach. She was *happy*, and it was horrible and selfish, but she wanted to take a moment to enjoy it.

Tomorrow. She'd talk about it tomorrow.

'Does it help?' *Rice Fish* asked. 'The tea?' She gestured. 'I brought some soup and dumplings as well.'

Xích Si eyed the dumplings. 'What are you getting out of drinking the tea?' she asked, finally. 'You don't eat, do you?'

Amused laughter from *Rice Fish*. Xích Si could have listened to it all day long.

'No. It brings back memories for me. Did you have a favourite dish when you were a child? Something that, even now, brings back the memories of how happy you were? That's what eating is like, for me.'

Memories. All kinds of memories. Xích Si sipped the tea – it tasted like fungi, like the greenhouses after the watering cycle, muddy and damp and unexpectedly sour. She was relaxed and simply enjoying the moment, reassured by *Rice Fish*'s presence at her side, utterly safe – giddy with a happiness she was unwilling to let go of.

'Talk,' she said, finally.

A sigh from *Rice Fish*. 'I don't know what you want to talk about.'

Xích Si wasn't sure, either. She settled for, 'I don't know where we stand. Where it's all going.' She raised a hand. 'Don't say anything about deploying a comms protocol, please.'

'I wasn't going to.' *Rice Fish* didn't speak for a while. 'I don't know, either. We had an arrangement. A contract.'

Something that Xích Si now realised wasn't just for her physical safety, but was deeply meaningful to *Rice Fish*. A safeguard against ... what? Taking advantage of her?

'We're a bit beyond business, aren't we?'

Another sigh. *Rice Fish*'s hair was turning blue and red, the colour of nebulae, gently pulsing; the pattern was showing under the skin of her face as well.

'Demonstrably so.'

'And . . .?'

'Li'l sis . . .' A silence. 'What do you want this to be?'

Oh, no, she wasn't getting away with this.

'What do you want?'

Rice Fish froze. The expression on her face shifted. Fear. Panic. *Why?*

Xích Si said, slowly and carefully, 'Perhaps, for now, what I want is this.'

'Tea and dumplings?'

'You know what I mean. For us both to admit that our relationship is changing. And that it goes beyond the terms of a contract. Beyond articles and paragraphs and things that can be weighed and measured.'

Rice Fish looked as though she was going to vanish out of the room, which was an unusual and fairly disturbing dynamic, considering that Xích Si was usually the scared one. She took one, two breaths. Xích Si rose, laying a hand on her shoulder – slowly, carefully wrapping herself behind *Rice Fish*'s avatar, feeling the perception layers kick in and the touch of faintly warm skin under her touch.

'It's all right,' she said.

She thought – now, of all times – of the mindship with the six arms she'd seen, the first time she'd come out of her cabin. Of how they'd left her space to say what she wanted, and how it hadn't mattered if the answer wasn't the one they'd sought– how they had projected that utter certainty that they would respect Xích Si's answer.

'You don't have to answer now. And it can be yes or no, or that you don't know yet.'

She felt *Rice Fish* slowly relax under her, the feeling of tension in the room and in the walls draining away.

'It *has* changed,' the ship said, finally. Nebulas wheeled, on the overlay on the floor of the room, in *Rice Fish*'s pooled hair.

'What we are to each other. What we ...' She stopped, and gazed up, towards Xích Si, and her dark gaze wasn't terrible and distant, but more terrifying yet – profoundly vulnerable. 'What we feel for each other. I ... I care about you.'

Beyond contracts, beyond fairness.

Xích Si opened her mouth, felt burning words rise in answer, swallowed half of them.

'I do, too.'

They stared at each other: *Rice Fish*'s face, upturned – the ship, for once, not towering or distant, but looking as though a word, dropped from Xích Si's lips, could break her in half; Xích Si, breathing hard, her bots frozen in place, feeling her heart three sizes too large for her chest.

Happiness.

And it seemed such an edged, fragile thing that Xích Si wasn't sure what to do with any of it.

Rice Fish walked out of Xích Si's cabin feeling absurdly small, and absurdly large.

So many things were requiring her attention. A lot of the pirates who usually berthed with her – the ones whose ships were in her hangars – had disembarked, going back to their compartments outside of holding seasons; those who had remained were rowdier than usual, and tense – they knew the mood wasn't entirely conducive to celebration; Hồ, who was busy undermining her.

I care about you.

As *Rice Fish* had said it, she'd felt the truth of it – the weight of it, and the sheer terror that came with it, the vulnerability she was admitting to. She'd waited, holding everything – bots, motors, sensors – utterly still, bracing herself for Xích Si to look sadly at her and tell her that it wasn't possible, that they couldn't jeopardise the partnership they'd had. That love burned bright, nova-like and swallowed up everything in its destructive wake, spending itself in the ashes of the lives it had wrecked. Hers and Huân's. Hers and Hồ's.

And it hadn't come.

Instead . . .

Instead, she'd been given a gift.

Xích Si's gift. A fragile, weightless, infinitely precious thing like cracked celadon, that she wasn't sure how to hold without breaking.

I want us both to admit that our relationship is changing. That it goes beyond the terms of a contract. Beyond things that can be weighed and measured.

She didn't know where it was going. Where it would stop. And she was braced always for it to stop – for things to go wrong, for a sad look and a heart-to-heart talk.

But, while it lasted, she could just breathe all of it in and treasure it, holding it close: something that made her giddy and young and hopeful in a way she'd never been before.

Xích Si was overseeing the deployment of the new comms protocols with Tiên when *Crow's Words*, the mindship under her orders, pinged her.

'Younger aunt? Do you have a moment? In avatar space?'

He sounded embarrassed and diffident, which was . . . not something she'd expect of a banner's ship. What was happening?

'For sure,' she said. And, to Tiên: 'Can you take over from me for a moment?'

'It shouldn't be a problem,' Tiên said.

They were both in avatar on one of the Red Banner's ships – not a mindship, an old planet-hopper with a system that was so out of date it was a flying security menace all by itself, even prior to the insecure protocols. Xích Si had pushed to install all

131

the newer upgrades, and now all the piloting and maintenance bots were in their berths being updated – she'd had to tinker with some of them, despairing she'd ever make them work.

'I'll write you a report. If anything major occurs . . .?'

Tiên looked to Xích Si for guidance – giving her an odd and unsettling feeling, because in Xích Si's mind, she was still the bodyguard who'd stood behind *Rice Fish* in the threshold of her cell. But Xích Si was in her element and knew exactly what to do.

Xích Si hesitated. 'Just pause and let me know. I'll handle it.' The planet-hopper was a terrible place to have any privacy so she repatriated her avatar to her quarters on *Rice Fish*, and invited *Crow's Words* there. The ship stood, awkwardly, on the threshold, his iridescent human-shaped avatar shimmering in and out of existence. 'What is it?'

Crow's Words held out both hands in front of him, as if presenting some kind of imperial decree. His entire stance suggested he'd have dropped to one knee if he could have.

'Here. I think you should see this, elder aunt. Please . . . let me know what you want to do about it.'

'I don't understand,' Xích Si said.

The ship looked as though he wanted to bolt back out of avatar space, but he held himself still with an effort, watching her.

'You trusted me,' *Crow's Words* said. 'With the Purple Banner.'

'Oh,' Xích Si said. 'Of course.'

And then she thought of Hố, and the tense relationship he had with *Rice Fish*. He was head of the Purple Banner, and anyone else in the Red Banner might have been more diffident than him about trusting a ship that openly admitted to having ties with them; but it hadn't occurred to her. When scavenging, one could seldom afford to be hung up on propriety – not

132

that said propriety protected them against the exactions of officials.

'All right.'

What could be making him so uneasy? She'd checked his record, and it was a long stream of attacks on merchant ships, most of them frenzied – though he didn't kill, preferring to single out the wealthiest for ransom. She supposed that was morality, insofar as pirates went.

She took what he proffered: a handful of data files that he could have forwarded to her. He had clearly wanted to be present when she opened them.

And then her heart stopped in her throat, because they were vids of Khanh.

Her daughter didn't look happy any more: she looked pale, and haunted, and the stiff way she moved tore Xích Si's heart out. What had they done to her little girl? She opened the other files: it was a listing – she saw only the first words: 'six-year-old offered for indenture . . .' and then everything blurred together as her world contracted to black.

How dare they? How . . .? She'd left her with Aunt Vy and her partner. She'd trusted them. She . . .

She couldn't breathe. She couldn't focus – all she could see was the multitude of uses a six-year-old could be put to. The least worst case was back-breaking, lung-choking labour gathering Ashling artefacts in narrow corridors, and from there her fears jumped to so many unsavoury other things, so many twisted reasons people would want to buy a scavenger child . . .

Breathe. Breathe. She needed to . . .

How dare they?

'Elder aunt?'

Crow's Words was waiting for her in the doorway. He looked concerned – she must look a terrible mess – and wasn't it an irony that pirates would be kinder and more generous than port-siders?

'Thank you,' Xích Si said, forcing herself to breathe, to smile through a mouth that felt stuffed with sharp dust. 'Does *Rice Fish* know?'

A hesitation. 'Do you *want* her to know?'

She measured what he offered: a shift of loyalties, and such a terrible foundation on which to build anything.

'Yes,' she said. 'You can't hope to keep that hidden.'

But she needed space to think, and she didn't know when she was going to get it.

'Here.' *Crow's Words* moved something that looked more like an aileron than a hand. 'It's on a time delay. She'll be notified in a couple of centidays.'

She couldn't read his expression, but the pity in his voice was unmistakable.

'Thank you,' she said, because she hadn't asked him for the kindness and he had done it anyway. He had given her a chance to think. 'Do you have children?'

'Two piblings in the banner. And ...' This time the expression on his face, between glimpses of metal plates and exhaust holes, was clearly a grimace. 'A sister and another pibling in Triệu Hoà Port.'

'Ah. How long ...?'

'Decades.' A dry laugh. 'They might be dead, for all I know.' Xích Si moved, slowly, too slowly — she wasn't even sure what she was intending — to embrace him, somehow, but he'd already stepped back out of her rooms, his avatar slowly fading. 'I'll leave you, elder aunt. It's not easy, that grief. Or longings for the matter world.'

The way he said that last — it was a pirate idiom.

And then it was just her and the vids of Khanh, and it hurt so much.

She walked back to her console, stared at the picture of Khanh – slowly erased it with a sweep of her fingers, and replaced it with a still from the vid, a frozen fearful face. Her bots came down, crawling over it, running around and around in circles, seeking a solace, or a pathway to it, that she couldn't find.

It had been one thing to leave Khanh. It had not been easy, but there had been a measure of comfort in it – an assurance that she was sacrificing herself for the good of her daughter. That no mother could pass a death sentence on to a child. But now it was different. Now Khanh was in danger, and she didn't know what to do.

Now . . .

Absurdly, irrationally, she thought of *Rice Fish*. Of sitting together on the bed – of being comforted. Of being given the override and the key to the heartroom, a freedom she had never expected. Of being told she shouldn't have to abase herself to anyone.

Before she could change her mind, she called the ship.

'Yes?' *Rice Fish*'s voice echoed under the ceiling of Xích Si's room. 'What is . . .? Oh.' A silence. 'Your heartbeat has gone up significantly, and you're breathing *very* fast and sweating profusely.' Another pause. 'Adrenaline spike? What's going on?'

The words were out of Xích Si's mouth before she could think. 'I need help. Please.'

A clicking noise: bots coming from the ceiling and from behind the walls. Even as *Rice Fish*'s avatar materialised behind the console, hair glinting in the darkness, she'd lowered the lighting, and the void in her eyes was growing and growing, her skin taking on the stark shadows cast by some faraway sun.

'I'm here.'

A heartbeat, slow and stretched to an eternity – and then she'd blinked out of existence and rematerialised behind Xích Si, and her arms encircled Xích Si's chest, slowly and carefully, a press of fingers on shoulders so firm Xích Si could feel each of them. She said nothing, merely held Xích Si – warmth slowly rising until it seemed lodged in Xích Si's throat. Behind her, more clicking, more dragging.

'I'm making you some tea,' *Rice Fish* said, her voice slow and even. She withdrew from the embrace calmly and deliberately, leaving Xích Si feeling as winded as if she'd run a marathon. 'I'm here when you're ready. Take the time you need. It's all right.'

She must have done something more than make tea. She must have tweaked the ambience, because the smell that rose in the room – a mixture of motor oils, scrubbed air and sharp, grassy tea – was like the corridors of Triệu Hoà Port, a slow gut-punch of comfort and nostalgia all mingled in one.

Xích Si forced herself to breathe.

'It's Khanh,' she said. 'My daughter.'

She played the vid with a wave of her fingers – it was short, and without sound. She dared not turn around to see *Rice Fish*'s face. She was *scared* of what the ship would say, how deeply it would cut to be told, again, to forget her daughter, how many more unfair sacrifices she'd be expected to make because of corruption and greed and unjust laws – and there was no one she could point out or be angry at except tens of thousands of years of the world always being that way.

'They're selling her for indenture.'

A silence filled the room – the darkness taut and becoming tauter still. Anger from the ship.

'So much for the solidarity of scavengers.'

'Don't ...' Xích Si exhaled. 'Pirates ...'

'Aren't standing with each other either? We try to.'

'So do we!'

Xích Si turned, then, trying to still the frantic beating of her heart – her bots tight around her fingers and pulling on her hair, her entire body too small and too taut for her skin.

Rice Fish was sitting cross-legged behind a table – her long hair had spread, becoming the surface of the table – and on the black sweep were two cups of tea, and a plate of translucent dumplings, surrounded by a loose circle of bots. The steam rose, making her waver in Xích Si's eyesight – her gaze was dark and bottomless, her face utterly calm.

She was infuriating.

'You have no moral high ground,' Xích Si said. 'I saw the Redeeming House!'

A silence.

'We're fair.'

'You're not! You exist because you kill, you sell people when they're no longer useful . . .'

Rice Fish didn't move. Around Xích Si, silence was spreading, as if she'd thrown a rock into a pond and was watching its ripples grow larger and larger.

'We don't indenture children. You know that. And . . .' *Rice Fish* made a movement with her hands, and all the air seemed to rush in – and out again, a sharp, whistling noise past Xích Si's ears. An exhalation. 'I get you're upset, and angry. But is this really the conversation you want to be having now?'

A deep, shaking breath.

No indenture of children.

Xích Si thought of Lệ Thu and Lệ Đông, of how well fed, how carefree they had been.

'I . . .' She stopped, because the smell of the tea was in her nostrils, and *Rice Fish*'s look was concerned and she was undone.

Rice Fish said, 'Tell me about your daughter.'

137

What was there to tell? Xích Si tried to speak, found herself choking on words. *Rice Fish*'s bots scuttled towards her, dragging a cup of tea and leaving it on the floor. She kneeled, feeling the coolness of the ship's floors under her – the way she rested her entire weight on *Rice Fish*'s body. The teacup was smooth and warm – she gulped its contents without realising what she was drinking.

'She's six,' she said, finally, managing to kneel on the floor and look up at *Rice Fish*. 'She wants cuddles and kisses and too many sweet dumplings, and not … this.'

'I know.' *Rice Fish*'s voice was dark. 'But that's not what I meant. What I meant is, what are you going to do about it?'

She didn't know. Pay the indenture? Could she?

'What can I do about it?'

Rice Fish's gaze was calm and steady. 'You tell me.'

'I'm not the banner leader.'

'You're my wife.' *Rice Fish*'s voice was steady. 'What I'm trying to say is that I will support you in whatever action you want, but you have to figure out what it is, first.'

What she wanted. It was terrifying.

'The last person who asked me that died. In a pirate attack.'

Rice Fish still didn't move.

'I'm sorry,' she said. 'No wonder you're so scared. I don't have anything more to offer but my word that I am a safe place, but as you have seen, we are ringed by tigers and sharks until we can expunge Kim Thông's influence. How long ago was it?'

'Four years.'

She thought of Khanh after the pirate attack – of the way she'd stumbled back into Aunt Vy's compartment with the militia's insistent questions in her ears, and the way the little girl's face had lit up on seeing her. How she'd launched herself, screaming 'Mommy!', and clinging to Xích Si's leg with both pudgy hands wrapped around her calf. 'Mommy,

Mommy, you're back! Mommy!' She thought of the way she'd smiled and tried to pretend everything was all right, setting aside the grief and the fear of her near escape, and the militia's subsequent dark hints that she'd only survived because she was their accomplice, carrying the guilt of living.

'I survived, but my crew-mates didn't. The person who asked me what I wanted – they died, and they didn't die well.'

'Ah.' A silence. 'Four years isn't such a long time. I could probably find out who did it.'

'No!' It was a panicked scream. 'I don't want justice. This is about Khanh. This is about what I want for Khanh – this is about ...'

She stopped, then, because she didn't entirely know what it was about; because it was too much again; because there was no time; because she'd failed her daughter.

A clink on the floor, and small imprints on her legs. *Rice Fish*'s bots were scurrying upwards – up her legs and then up her spine – pressing down gently and insistently until the obstruction in her chest lifted.

'What do you want?'

Rice Fish got up, and walked towards Xích Si – her hair lengthened as she did so, her face and body narrowing until she seemed to be merely an extension of the room, her skin the same colour as the floor, her face dotted with stars and galaxies slowly whirling on her clothes and hands. She stopped, her face a mere knuckle-width from Xích Si – Xích Si could feel her in the air, the way the entire ship weighed around her, the arch of the room's ceiling, the warm floor under her, the motionless bots on her spine.

'What do you want?'

Her eyes were two black holes into which Xích Si spiralled, and there was no end to her fall.

Buy the indenture. Give Aunt Vy enough money so she could

raise Khanh. Give Khanh a safe place to grow up in. Give ...

But Aunt Vy had made the decision to sell Khanh. She might be desperate and hounded, but ...

But you would have died before letting it come to this. It was a colder and more merciless part of her speaking. One who had seen *Rice Fish* move to protect a scavenger – one who knew, deep, deep down, that Triệu Hoà Port was not safe. Would never be safe for a scavenger or their child.

Which left ...

Rice Fish's eyes held her, unwavering.

What do you want?

I am in a safe place. Ringed by tigers and sharks. And not just Kim Thông, but the deeper injustices – all their freedoms and ebullience built on deaths, on servitude, on the blood and toil of others.

And yet ...

She remembered Chi Lan's blood, spattering across the tiled floor. Ái Nhân's face as that happened, frozen in slow incredulity – the utter conviction in *Rice Fish*'s voice as she reminded them of the code. Her night out with Tấm and Cám and *Plum and Peach*, the crowded streets with so much exuberant and bloodthirsty life in them – and the fondness in Tấm's eyes as she threw Lệ Đông a bauble.

There are rules. No indenture of children.

Safe.

'I want my daughter to come here,' she said.

And, quivering and struggling to breathe, she reached out and took *Rice Fish*'s silently proffered hand, and held on to the familiar oily warmth like a lifeline in the void.

12

Openings

On the evening before Xích Si and her crew's departure for Triệu Hoà Port, *Mulberry Sea* asked if *Rice Fish* would visit her.

Mulberry Sea's body was docked in the central part of the Citadel — a dock that belonged to no banner and that no banner could enter without permission, a little piece of the Đại Việt Empire in the midst of pirate space. *Rice Fish* had been given embodiment privileges, but still chose to walk in avatar shape from the dock onto *Mulberry Sea*, because it quieted her restlessness. She missed space and the sensation of always moving — here there was no starlight and no solar winds, just the slightly too wet environment of the dock against her hull. The quiet season was always hard, but there was no way she could afford to miss council sessions.

It was quiet on the docks. As she walked away from banner space the corridors subtly changed, becoming larger, objects becoming subtly unmoored. The people changed, too, the An O chatter becoming Việt, and their gestures smaller and more contained — they were used to the lighter gravity of the habitat, and everything here was too compressed, too heavy for them.

Rice Fish had opted out of the sensation of gravity for her avatar; to her, the change of space made little difference, and the only things she felt were the floor — cold metal under her bare feet and under the sweep of her hair — and the prickle of air against her skin, both the interface-relayed one for her avatar, and the one pressing against her hull, slightly too clammy and slightly too pressurised.

The airlock was open, bots crawling around it — at a glance, *Mulberry Sea* had diverted most of her available defence bots to the outside. *Rice Fish* came on, held a hand on the frame — feeling the distant heartbeat of the other ship.

'Are you afraid I'm going to invade you?' she said.

Mulberry Sea laughed. 'Of course not.'

She didn't bother to manifest an avatar. Instead, she guided *Rice Fish* to an empty room with visual and tactile prompts.

Its floors were unadorned, its walls likewise: just bare metal with the faint oily sheen characteristic of mindships. There was a single table with a plate of dumplings, smelling of cabbage and meat, with the sharp tang of black vinegar sauce, and a very conspicuous gap where *Mulberry Sea* had consumed one. *Rice Fish* sat cross-legged in front of the table, picked up a dumpling, and ate it.

It was a virtual one, of course — and as it slid inside her mouth the black vinegar spiked sharply against *Rice Fish*'s virtual palate, and she was young again, watching her baby sibling dribble sauce all over her own floors — hearing her mother sharply call their name. 'Thanh, don't bother your sister!' And the baby just laughed and laughed, running their fingers through the sauce, the sharpness of it spread all over *Rice Fish*'s floor, a barely perceptible weight, a smell she didn't yet know, a laughter that was loud and carefree and made the air shake with its wonder.

'It's been a while,' she said, finally.

'Yes.' *Mulberry Sea*'s voice came from all around her, faster than human words.

There were rules among ships, and even more around nations. Food had been offered and shared. *Rice Fish* had come aboard, where she was vulnerable – but the space she ruled, although beset and shrinking, encompassed the one around *Mulberry Sea*.

Rice Fish shifted to low-ship-speech – faster and more simultaneous than human speech, multiple process-threads thrown at each other, answered – and the space around them lit up with code and images and sounds.

[Mulberry Sea] The Empress is dying and her successor believes in propriety ...

[Rice Fish] The An O Empire presses you harder, doesn't it? Your mistress wants results before she dies.

[Mulberry Sea] Pirates are weak and an embarrassment ... Do you believe your wife's death to be an unfortunate accident?

[Rice Fish] The bots on your door aren't to defend against me. You're afraid of the other pirates – the ones who think we shouldn't ally with official powers. Of Kim Thông.

[Mulberry Sea] I like you but I cannot afford to support you. My empress needs a strong claim and a stronger fleet ...

[Rice Fish] My wife's death was not random. You know who killed Huân. You know it started here in the Citadel.

[Mulberry Sea] Can you hold the other pirates, pirate consort?

[Mulberry Sea] Can you take what is yours?

[Rice Fish] The pirate alliance is not weak. Don't count us dead yet ...

[Mulberry Sea] I can guess who killed your wife, but it doesn't matter much.

[Rice Fish] We are a place where justice means something.

[Mulberry Sea] Are you?

[Mulberry Sea] A warning, younger aunt. A fragile pot should not go near the fire.

[Rice Fish] I don't understand. You, or your position?

[Mulberry Sea] You are hard-pressed. Your position on the council is fragile.

[Mulberry Sea] Your new wife is a liability. The expedition you blessed for her – a raid out of raiding season, which exposes the banner – it's your fire, and your wife is the crack.

[Mulberry Sea] Don't expect your son to go easy on you.

[Rice Fish] Does Kim Thông's influence extend so far, then? To everyone on the council?

[Mulberry Sea] You misunderstand Kim Thông and what she's willing to sacrifice.

[Mulberry Sea] You haven't asked why we are withdrawing.

[Rice Fish] Kim Thông wants power.

[Rice Fish] I stand by my wife.

[Rice Fish] The Việt empress is dying—

[Mulberry Sea] That's sweet, if impractical.

[Rice Fish] And will you go easy on me, if my son doesn't?

[Mulberry Sea] You know my position.

[Mulberry Sea] This isn't just about our empress. Your position is weaker than you think. This isn't about a difference in ideology between you and Kim Thông. The raids are the point. The enmity of the An O Empire is the point. Kim Thông doesn't want you to become bolder or stronger. She doesn't want to become more powerful. She wants out – and she'd rather

	put everything to the torch rather than let others enjoy what she doesn't have.
[Rice Fish]	Why—?
[Rice Fish]	The amnesty.
[Mulberry Sea]	She'll sell you to the censor to save her skin, and start a new life in the An O Empire.

It stopped, then. The room was a mass of flickering lights and exposed machine code, threads shimmering between almost every point: a map of the Đại Việt; a vid of Hồ; a determined Xích Si arguing with *Crow's Words*; a replay of the trial in which *Rice Fish* had intervened – the faces of the counsellors; an overlay of Triệu Hoà Port with every militia post outlined in black, the Fire Palace looming over them all; the bamboo flute flag of Censor Trúc over a background of exploding ships, all labelled with names and victims ...

'Warnings,' *Rice Fish* said, aloud. 'Is that what I'm here for?'
She wants out.

Kim Thông wanted power and stability, and that didn't lie with the pirates any more. Kim Thông wanted to kill them all rather than let them enjoy anything – and buy herself the censor's good graces in doing so. No wonder these two were working together.

The mass of data contracted, became more sharply defined.

'You have the information?'

'I do. I don't understand ...' But she did, because it had been part of the information; she and *Mulberry Sea* went back – way back. 'You want me to stop Kim Thông.'

Mulberry Sea said nothing.

Rice Fish heard the words she wasn't saying. *Mulberry Sea* didn't trust *Rice Fish* to stop Kim Thông, or to protect her any more. That hurt: that one day it was *Mulberry Sea* she was no longer able to protect, and the next day it would be the

145

indentured in the banner, and then her own bannerpeople ...
and then Xích Si and her daughter?

It *hurt*. No. That wasn't it. It made her unspeakably, un-
believably angry.

How dare she? How dare Hồ?

'You think I'm done for.'

'Not yet.' *Mulberry Sea*'s voice was thoughtful. 'Can you get
Kim Thông off the council?'

Rice Fish's heart sank. 'You know I can't. I need evidence.
You could tell Hồ ...'

Mulberry Sea's voice was pitying. 'You think I didn't?'

And he had not believed her. Of course he hadn't. He didn't
want to hear anything that contradicted his own vision.

'You must have something—'

A laugh from *Mulberry Sea*. 'Even if I did, what difference
would it make? Evidence isn't going to be enough, younger
aunt.'

'What do you mean?'

'You know what I mean. The truth rings out as loud as a
pagoda bell, but it's not always heard in the world, is it?'

'I'll make sure it is.'

But she knew, deep down, that it might be too late already.
She remembered the pirates at the trial, the way they'd waited
for blood to be spilled. She remembered the elders – the easy
way Kim Thông had inserted herself into the proceedings as
though she belonged there. A rot that went deep – and she was
alone and vulnerable, because Huân was dead, because Xích
Si needed protection *Rice Fish* wasn't sure she could provide
any more. And, in this vulnerable position, she had agreed to
something more dangerous and chancy still: a personal rescue
which took Xích Si into enemy territory.

'Do you expect me to say no? To rescuing a child?'

Soft laughter from *Mulberry Sea*. 'I've known you for a

while now, haven't I? You could no more say no to this than you could stop breathing. But was it wise? Of course not. If Xích Si goes ahead, and it goes wrong in any fashion ...'

Rice Fish picked a thread from the shimmering mass — of pirates being outnumbered by the imperial navy — and wrapped the fingers of her avatar around it until it was nothing more than a mote of light underneath her skin.

'Then we'll make sure it doesn't go wrong, won't we? Thank you for the warning.'

Going back to Triệu Hoà Port was a wrench in so many ways.

Xích Si couldn't go back under her own name, and *Crow's Words*, the ship she was on, was a known pirate associate and therefore unable to dock under his real name. Instead, he faked credentials as an out-system merchant, and was assigned a docking bay far away from the main ones. He had offered to bribe officials to get a closer one, but Xích Si had vetoed it.

'We'll be spotted,' she'd said, but the truth was that she'd seen too many people exchanging too many bribes for petty, hurtful things, and she couldn't bear to do the same.

She'd taken only a small crew with her: *Crow's Words*, and Tấm and Cám, who had volunteered. Tấm had cursed under her breath when Xích Si had finally told her over a drink at the teahouse, and simply held out her gun to her. Cám had grimaced, and followed.

'Name and business?'

The customs official appeared bored — and then something must have caught her eye, because she bent and stared at Xích Si full in the face, and Xích Si found herself wilting.

I'm a pirate, here to get my daughter. I can't say that, I can't say that ...

'We're from the Twenty-Third Planet. There to unload some rice wine.'

The words seemed to come from some far-off place, even as the ship's manifest appeared in front of the official.

The official's bots were all over her face and her hands: they crawled on the manifest itself as if they could take it apart. Her hand clenched and unclenched.

'Long way to come for rice wine,' she said. 'I take it you expect big profits.'

Oh.

Of course. She wanted a cut of said profits. Xích Si opened her mouth to protest, but *Crow's Words* got there first.

'Our sponsor on the Twenty-Third Planet, Magistrate Minh Đức, certainly expects so.'

The official's face turned sour. The magistrate was one of the Three Hollow Ones – scholars known for their devotion to duty and incorruptibility.

'Hmmf,' she said. Her bots clicked, stamping the entrance form. 'Make sure you pay your exit fees on the way out. And no cheating.'

Once they were into the corridors of the habitat, Xích Si finally allowed herself to breathe.

'I hope that was all right.' *Crow's Words* sounded preoccupied.

Their avatar kept pulsing between the featureless human shape and the larger suggestion of a ship, in a way that was quite dizzying. It seemed he was opening up the habitat to space as he walked, and every time she looked at him, Xích Si fought her own instincts to jump for the nearest suit – he looked like a walking habitat breach.

'That was well done. Can you tone down the pulsing? Please?'

She was short of breath, with a panicked knot in her belly. They were going to arrive too late to rescue Khanh. They were going to get caught. The official had already flagged them for their refusal to bribe her. They stood out in the busy crowd because they were too unusual, too ill at ease. All the myriad ways that this could go wrong ran through her mind in an endless unpleasant loop.

They . . .

Focus.

She took a deep, shaking breath. She'd faced *Rice Fish* on her wedding night – how was this a greater challenge?

Focus.

She dug her fingers into her palms, brought her consciousness back from her fears and focused it just on herself, on her breathing, on the bots on her fingers which were an extension of her will, shifting with every breath. Focused on *Crow's Words* by her side – who was not *Rice Fish*, and who would never be *Rice Fish*.

That was what she had, and by Heaven, it was going to be enough.

'*Crow's Words*? Tấm? Cám?'

'Yes?'

'Let's go,' she said.

She'd thought the habitat wouldn't have changed, but it had: it was small and dingy and cramped, and even the myriad virtual overlays could not disguise that fact. The decorations were faded and uninspiring, the songs exhausted and sad – and the people they passed, the other scavengers, gave them a wide berth.

'Do they know what we are?' she asked, as they stopped at an intersection: a mere crossing of corridors with a diminutive fountain in the centre. She didn't vocalise it, merely let the conversation happen in their own private layer.

'I don't think so,' Tấm said. 'They're just scared of anything and anyone unusual.'

'Scared,' she repeated.

As they went down one more corridor, Xích Si realised that

had been her, once upon a time. That she'd kept her head down and not dared to dream large, because she knew she would always get kicked in the teeth.

It wasn't the habitat that was smaller. It was that she had outgrown it.

'Yeah,' Tấm said. 'I don't miss that life.'

'You're a pirate now.' She was the one who killed people, who took captives. 'One of the masters.'

A shrug from Tấm. 'No, we're something else. We're fair. Or at least I try to be.'

Xích Si wanted to hate her, to hate the whole system. And she did. But she had *Rice Fish*'s voice in her head, asking if it was truly worse than the system that was selling her daughter?

And she knew the answer – that it was equally unfair, but that at least she had hope that she and *Rice Fish* could work towards changing it.

As they walked, her bots were tracking information: the listing for Khanh was still up, and the address given was Aunt Vy's house.

'What now?' *Crow's Words* asked.

Xích Si wanted to charge in and confront Aunt Vy, but she'd had time to think on how reckless and counter-productive that would be.

'You are going to go in and negotiate to buy the indenture.' She looked at Cám, who grinned.

'We usually negotiate with our guns,' the pirate said. 'Or with very well-armed spaceships.'

Before Xích Si had time to tense, her elder sister laid a hand on her shoulder.

'Not with this, li'l sis,' Tấm said. 'And this isn't the time for jokes.' She turned to Xích Si, and pulled off something very close to a militia acknowledgement. 'We'll do it. Will you be listening in?'

Xích Si weighed the idea for a fraction of a second. The knot of tension in her belly was getting worse and worse, tightening around her, and every single one of her bots' feeds was close to overwhelming her.

'Yes. The stakes are too high.'

'All right.' Cám stared at *Crow's Words*. 'You stay back. We don't want to get too distinctive.'

And, just like that, they were gone.

13

The Matter World

Xích Si found a nearby teahouse where she and *Crow's Words* sat down. It was unusual in having five floors — and it made itself seem larger still through some very careful perception filters, the kind that must have taken a special permit to get. They sat facing each other on the first floor, which had a wide balcony overlooking the plaza — the perspective tweaked, so that the small area between two compartments appeared a long way off.

'They know what they're doing,' *Crow's Words* said.

He sounded relaxed, which didn't reassure Xích Si at all. Tấm and Cám had vanished inside Aunt Vy's house and all Xích Si could hear was distant, featureless chatter — meaningless words, greetings exchanged; she couldn't focus on anything. Aunt Vy would be smiling, offering up Khanh as if she were some prized object — see this pretty, obedient child, see how much she would be of value … How could she …? How …?

She drew in a deep, shaking breath. *Focus*. She was getting nowhere. No, worse, she was actively hindering the rescue. To *Crow's Words*, she said, 'I need you to take over. I can't …'

The ship looked at her, translucent face inexpressive. She

braced herself for flippancy – or pity, which would have been worse. But he simply nodded, setting aside his chopsticks and bending forward intently, the bots he'd brought onto the habitat clustering around his bowl of noodle soup.

Xích Si let the conversation wash over her, so low now that words were inaudible. She tried to eat her dumplings at the same time, listlessly chewing on them; the thick dough tasted like cardboard. It should have been familiar and comforting, the dumplings of the scavengers' quarters she'd eaten her whole childhood, but instead it tasted bland – too much dough, not enough meat, and too roughly shaped. Pirate food hadn't seemed that different, and yet ...

There was a higher-pitched voice that had to be Khanh, in a tone she couldn't quite make out; how much had her daughter been told? She'd tried to shelter Khanh as much as she could – to smooth out the hardships of scavenger life, the shock of losing Ngà, the scars of the militia's interrogation. But ... she was Khanh's mother and she'd vanished, and that would have taken its toll.

The voices were faster now, getting more agitated. And there were others, high-pitched and faster still, and they sounded angry. Demanding. Unused to being told no. Neither of them could belong to the sisters.

'*Crow's Words*?'

He was listening, transfixed, his eyes not on her, his bots in an unmoving, uncannily still circle – not a single metal leg even so much as quivering.

Something was wrong. Xích Si looked up from the table. The plaza was deserted now, but tapping into her bots' recorded feedback showed her two other people walking into Aunt Vy's home – one of them walking with the slow and ponderous gait characteristic of a tribunal clerk.

No no no.

'*Crow's Words*!' There was no time, so she reached out and dragged the ship. It felt like grasping air for a few agonising blink-moments – until the overlays of physical perceptions kicked in and she belatedly grabbed what felt like a shoulder, but was far too pliant and as cold and as oily as ship's metal. 'What's going on?'

The ship shook himself, gaining substance as he did so – the shadow of his body receding to leave only the shape of the avatar.

'I don't know. The feed suddenly went blank . . .'

Khanh.

Xích Si's world shrunk down to the frantic beating of her heart – the painful hammering in her chest. She stood up and ran, without listening to the rest of what *Crow's Words* was saying. As she left the teahouse, the perception filters peeled away; the distant plaza abruptly became a small and cramped space she easily crossed, and before she realised it she was at Aunt Vy's door. It was closed, but it opened for her when she laid her hand across the sensor – it looked as though Aunt Vy had never revoked her authorisations – and found herself, out of breath, in the middle of a packed compartment.

Tấm and Cám were facing Aunt Vy, and the two people Xích Si had seen – the clerk and what looked like an aide – stood in a third corner, watching them both and looking for all the world as if they were going to march everyone back to the tribunal.

Xích Si barely had time to catch her breath before something large and heavy barrelled into her.

'Mommy! Mommy you're here Mommy Mommy . . .'

Khanh was clinging to her, both arms obstinately wrapped around her, face held against Xích Si's tunic.

Some emotion, long held, coalesced into hard steel.

'I'm here, child. And I'm not leaving without you.'

154

She had nothing but ice left in her as she turned to face Aunt Vy. The older scavenger was pale, breathing hard, her bots clustered on the floor and walls – half-watching the clerks, half-watching Tấm and Cám. Which left nothing between Aunt Vy and Xích Si.

Xích Si kept her voice calm, even.

'I'll be redeeming the indenture.' A statement of how things would be, rather than a question.

She kept her arms around Khanh, her feet firmly rooted on the floor of the compartment – the overlay was a white surface with a mingle of calligraphy, excerpts of poems neither she nor Aunt Vy could ever hope to understand.

'You left.' Aunt Vy's breath came slow and fast. 'You abandoned her.'

'So you decided to *sell* her?'

She was angry. It wasn't a smart thing to say.

'You left,' Aunt Vy said, again. 'You just walked out like it was no big thing, never gave us any news, and trusted us to do the right thing?'

How dare she? It wasn't as though she'd *chosen* any of it.

'I . . .' Xích Si opened her mouth, closed it – forced herself to focus on the wider picture.

'What went wrong?' she asked Tấm and Cám.

'They were not interested in the offer,' Cám said.

Tấm's subvocalisation on the comms was sharper. 'They were stalling us. Waiting for a higher bidder.'

A higher bidder. For a child. For her *child.* Xích Si's entire world flashed red.

'How could you?' she asked Aunt Vy. And, to the clerk, who had not moved, 'You think buying a child is a morally defensible choice?'

'It's not,' the clerk said. She sounded utterly serious.

There was nothing extraordinary about her: a middle-aged

155

woman with grey in her hair – more than there should have been. Probably an aesthetic choice, especially for a woman with a tunic like that, with carefully designed overlays of bamboos and orchids overlapping each other. It was a painstaking work of what was clearly artistry, rather than mass production – she could easily have afforded a high-quality rejuv. Her eyes were piercing; her mouth was thin and looked as though it rarely stretched into a smile. She looked like she'd benefited from corruption in a larger way than mere paper-pushers – used to power and all it entailed – and Xích Si had just yelled at her and somehow expected it to work out in her favour.

She would have Xích Si beaten up. Or arrested and beaten up, which would be worse because there were no witnesses or controls in the tribunal's jails.

Xích Si opened her mouth to apologise, and then realised she was finished with apologies she didn't believe in.

Enough forgiving the unforgivable. Enough condoning the un-savouriness of Triệu Hoà port.

She stared at the clerk.

'Mommy . . .'

'Not now, sweetheart.' She kept her hand on Khanh – felt her child shiver beneath her. Any moment now, the tension in the room was going to be unbearable for Khanh, and she was going to snap and run screaming, towards Aunt Vy – or worse, the clerk. 'I've got you. You're safe.'

'Give her back,' Aunt Vy said.

'Now now,' Tấm said, with an edged smile, and a hand in her jacket that suggested she was about to pull a knife on-station – one of the gravest of offences, a danger to the integrity of the habitat. 'How about we sort this out like civilised people?'

It was the clerk who spoke, then. 'But you're not civilised, are you? You're pirates.'

No.

No. It wasn't possible. They were here incognito. They could not afford to be caught. They could not afford to be seen for what they were. They ...

And where was *Crow's Words*?

'In the teahouse,' Crow's Words' voice, low and even, said over her comms. 'Trying to think of a way out of this.'

The implication was clear: he wasn't finding any.

Xích Si said, slowly and carefully, 'You're not here for the child.'

The clerk smiled. It was as cold as the depths of space.

'No. I'm here because someone made a report about illegal goings-on here, which we corroborated with bots and surveillance camera evidence.'

She made a gesture, and everything slowed down and froze – and all of a sudden Xích Si couldn't move any more, couldn't hear *Crow's Words* any more, or the sisters. Her bots fell away from her, deactivated – but they made no sound as they fell, because the clerk had thrown a muffler over the entire overlay. Her movements were slow, the air seeming to turn to tar around her – she'd also affected the air around Xích Si, hardening it into a small bubble in which she could barely move.

No no no.

She clung, tightly, to Khanh.

'Stay with me, child. Stay with me.'

A scared whimper from Khanh.

The clerk walked to face Aunt Vy, her words echoing in the small compartment – another overlay.

'Nguyễn Thị Diệp Vy, you are under arrest for the use of counterfeit money and consorting with pirates.'

She sounded not just annoyed, but utterly disgusted. And no clerk should have had the privileges she had over the habitat.

'You're not a clerk,' Xích Si said. Because of the muffler, her voice came out tinny, but she heard her all the same.

157

'My name is Ngọc Trúc,' the clerk said, and oh Heaven she wasn't a clerk at all, how had Xích Si ever mistaken her for one?

'The censor. *You're* the censor.'

The one whose troops had killed the Red Scholar.

Censor Trúc turned, briefly, to look at Xích Si. Her militia aide was arresting Aunt Vy, who was putting up a doomed fight against the restraints.

'I have that honour, yes.'

Tấm and Cám were clustered against each other in the same slow bubble – back to back, Tấm still with her hand inside her jacket. Cám's hands were slack, but all her bots were on her palms and on her fingers.

'I wouldn't,' Trúc said. 'You're outnumbered.'

Cám snarled. 'So you think we'll come quietly, to be tortured and executed?'

She frowned. 'I don't hold with torture. And in your case, while you are pirates, I can't actually hold it against you. Sneaking into the habitat on false pretences, perhaps.' She sounded thoughtful.

'Piracy is death,' Xích Si said.

Censor Trúc wasn't what she'd expected at all – though now she wasn't sure what she had expected. Some kind of corrupt monster delighting in their pain?

'Sometimes it is, indeed,' Censor Trúc said.

More militia had arrived; two of them dragged Aunt Vy away, and the rest warily surrounded Tấm and Cám, guns out.

Censor Trúc held up a hand. 'Hold. They're armed with irregular weapons,' she said. And, to the sisters. 'It really would be best if you surrendered.'

'Mommy ...'

Desperation made Xích Si bold. She said, 'You aren't here for us.'

158

Censor Trúc turned to look at her. Her tunic moved and stretched for a brief moment, the bamboo and orchids pulsing larger. Her gaze moved down, to Khanh.

'No,' she said. Her voice was quiet. 'But I'd be failing in my duty if I didn't take advantage of Heaven's unexpected blessings.'

It was over. Xích Si shouldn't have taken such a risk, shouldn't have reached so high. Why had she thought she could get more than she had? Why had she stretched her luck until it broke?

Khanh's body was warm against hers, and she remembered why. There had been no other decision to make. The serious way in which Censor Trúc had answered when she'd challenged her about the indenture — her entire demeanour and behaviour, her disgust at torture.

'You said we hadn't comitted piracy.'

'Pirates aren't allowed on the habitats.' She moved closer to her. Khanh buried her head into Xích Si's midriff. She could feel the quivering tears on her flesh, each of them a small, hurtful burn. 'And three fewer pirates to plague us would be a blessing, wouldn't it.'

She'd killed the Red Scholar. It was hard, looking at her — at her mild-mannered eyes, the plain, unadorned bots on her shoulders, the gentle strength of her pose — to remember that. She'd killed the Red Scholar, not out of spite or out of corruption, but because she genuinely believed she was making the habitats a better place.

'Please,' Xích Si said. 'I know we're meant to stay away, but I came for her. Because they ...' She swallowed. 'Because Aunt Vy put her up for indenture, and it was my fault.'

'Indeed.'

A silence. Censor Trúc was watching her, eyes unreadable.

'Please.'

'Are you suggesting I let you go? You have nothing to bargain with.'

'I'm not bargaining,' Xích Si said.

'Demonstrably not.'

Xích Si thought, ironically, of *Rice Fish*. Of the way she'd sounded when speaking of her dead wife, of what she and the Red Scholar had tried to build. Of what they stood for and the inner fire that moved them — the utter belief that society was rotten and that they were building a better one. She'd heard that same passion in the censor's voice.

'She's six years old. She was for sale for anyone to do what they wanted with her.'

Silence.

'I know that it's not illegal. But is it right?' She used *nhân*, the scholarly word for benevolence and virtue.

Censor Trúc's eyes weren't dark the way *Rice Fish*'s were, because she was human, but they were like black holes nevertheless, taking in everything and reflecting nothing back. She was weighing her — appraising her, the way she'd so often been appraised, and found wanting.

'You can't correct one wrong with another,' Censor Trúc said.

'Then tell me how I am supposed to do the right thing.'

'By not turning to piracy!' Her eyes blazed.

Xích Si braced herself for the militia's dragging her away, as they'd taken Aunt Vy.

'Khanh has done nothing. Please. Help her, if you won't help me.'

More silence. She tried to reach for *Crow's Words*, but the ship was not on her comms any more. When she moved a fraction, her feet hit the deactivated bots lying on the floor. All she could hear was her frantic heartbeat, the rhythm of her desperate prayer to her ancestors.

Please. Please let her remember what it means to be compassionate. What it means to do the right thing. Please let her have mercy. Please please please.

At length, Censor Trúc sighed. She made a gesture, and the muffler dropped away, as did the strictures that had been hindering Xích Si's movements. Her bots clicked awake – clustering together as they rebooted.

'Just this once,' Censor Trúc said. 'And not for you, but for her.' She reached out and ruffled Khanh's hair, slowly and so gently, as if she was afraid she would break something irreplaceable. Khanh didn't move, didn't turn to face her – she clung to Xích Si, too silent, too still. Scared half to death. 'Go, before I change my mind.'

Xích Si was halfway to the door, followed by a chastened Tấm and Cám, when she heard Censor Trúc's voice again.

'Younger aunt?'

'Yes?' Khanh's hand was warm in hers.

'You owe me. Like for like. And I'll collect what's due in good time.'

She thought about Censor Trúc's words all the way to the ship – as *Crow's Words* tried to get Tấm and Cám to explain what had happened, as she held Khanh, keeping her exhausted daughter close to her. They went away for a moment as she put Khanh to sleep in one of the berths on *Crow's Words* – really little more than an extrusion of metal that Khanh huddled against, warily watching her.

'Mommy?'

'Yes?' she said.

Her bots were running check-up cycles after their deactivation. Khanh was clutching Thanh Quy Quy, her favourite plush toy, a much-battered turtle; they'd grabbed it as they left, under Censor Trúc's burning gaze.

'What's going to happen to Auntie Vy?'

'I don't know,' Xích Si said. 'She did some very bad things.'

Khanh's mouth puckered, and Xích Si held her tight.

'To you, too, little fish?'

A silence. Khanh was breathing faster and faster, clinging tighter to the plush turtle. Xích Si's heart tore.

'We can talk about it later. Just sleep. You're safe here.'

Khanh snuggled against her. She said, finally, 'I was bad. I stopped believing. I thought you wouldn't come back.'

'Oh, sweetie. You were very brave.'

'I wasn't!' Khanh grimaced. 'I was scared the entire time.'

'That's what being brave is about,' Xích Si said. 'Being scared and doing the right thing anyway.'

Khanh's gaze was distant. 'I was scared. There were so many people. Poking and prodding and hurting me. Because I've been a bad child. Because I've been ungrateful. Because it's all for my own good.'

Ancestors. Xích Si closed her eyes, tried to breathe through lungs that seemed to have turned to tar. Around her, the alcove grew dark, and the sounds of Tấm and Cám receded – *Crow's Words*, turning this cramped space into an impenetrable room. Stars winked over their heads, gently wheeling in the sky.

'It's not right,' she said, finally. 'Adults don't hurt children. Ever. No one.'

A silence.

'Then why were they doing it?'

'I don't know.' Xích Si was crying now, and it was good that it was dark, that Khanh wouldn't see it. 'But I'm here now. It's over. We're going somewhere you'll be safe.'

'Where?'

'A city of wonders,' Xích Si said. She thought of *Rice Fish*, and of the banners, and of the way their safety was burning up faster than they could build it. 'I'll introduce someone to you. A good friend.'

If that was what *Rice Fish* still was to her.

'A good friend. That's good,' Khanh said. 'I didn't have any friends. They all left. All got taken by the bad people. I was so unhappy, Mommy . . .'

As they entered deep spaces, Khanh finally fell asleep, shuddering and clinging to Xích Si, her body slowly and steadily relaxing until her head lolled back and her grip slackened. Xích Si stared ahead still, tears streaking down her face, her heart torn to ribbons.

'We'll be at the Citadel in a couple of days,' *Crow's Words* said. Oh. Sorry. I'll go.'

'No, it's all right,' Xích Si said, but it wasn't.

She felt wrung out, as if she'd been blasted into space without a suit and had had to hold her breath for those precious few seconds until she could be rescued.

Crow's Words said, 'I'm sorry, earlier, for not being of any use.'

'Don't be,' Xích Si said. 'What could you have done?'

A silence. She could feel the steady hum of the ship's motors under her, like a breath underlying her own.

'I did try a few things. And . . . I may have something.'

'Something?'

The ship's avatar grinned. 'Something from the censor. But I need to decrypt it first. It's going to take a few days.'

'You *hacked* the censor?' It was Tấm. The younger pirate looked begrudgingly impressed. 'Now *that'd* be something worth boasting about.'

'She was a little busy with you,' *Crow's Words* pointed out. 'That helped. And for all I know, I just got the equivalent of the book she was reading.' He made a face superimposed over a glimmer of oily metal. 'Though it'd be funny if she turned out to be a fan of trashy historicals.'

Xích Si lay back, winded and exhausted, and let their chatter

163

wash over her. She held Khanh and tried to stop crying in the dark — not that it helped.

Pirates. The Citadel. The Green Scholar. Censor Trúc.

You owe me, the censor had said. Xích Si felt small and scared, and ashamed: her first time out in the matter world without *Rice Fish*, and this had happened. A complete mess that had only turned to success through sheer chance. The others would tell *Rice Fish* as soon as they arrived, and the thought of dealing with *Rice Fish*'s disregard ... No, worse than that: her disappointment. It was making Xích Si sick to her stomach.

Not now. It doesn't have to be now.

'*Crow's Words*?'

'Yes?' the ship asked.

'Can I be the one to tell *Rice Fish* how it went? With the censor?'

A silence.

'Are you afraid of her?'

'The censor?'

Crow's Words' voice was gentle. 'You know that's not the question I'm asking.'

She wasn't afraid of *Rice Fish*, but she knew *Rice Fish* had far too many things on her mind, and far too little time in which to treat them. The censor was far away, and surely she would never have a chance to collect on anything; her word and law had no value within the Citadel. She'd tell *Rice Fish* — of course she would. But right now she was exhausted and scared and she couldn't bear the thought of disappointing *Rice Fish*.

'I just want time to think it through.'

Cám said, '*Rice Fish* is our banner head. We really should tell her.'

Crow's Words sighed. There was pity in his voice. 'Xích Si is right. It doesn't need to be right now.'

164

Tấm looked at Xích Si for a while, her bots tapping on the table.

'Give her a break, big sis,' she said to Cám. 'She's gone through ten hells and back. There's no urgency.'

'You're her wife,' *Crow's Words* said. 'You can tell her. In your own time. When you feel better.'

'Thank you,' Xích Si said.

'Oh, don't mention it,' *Crow's Words* said. 'And Tấm is right. There's no urgency.'

No, none. It could wait until she'd rested. There was no urgency. She needed to focus on what mattered now: getting away from Triệu Hoà Port. Settling her daughter in. And trying to forget the pit of dread in her stomach, the one that wouldn't close no matter the distance between her and Triệu Hoà Port.

I'll collect in good time.

Rice Fish had forgotten how small children were: how lightly they weighed on her floors; how high-pitched and piercing their laughter was; how all-encompassing their exhaustion could be, when it finally struck.

At the moment, Khanh was exhausted but trying very hard to stay awake, which made her irritable.

'So you're Mommy's friend?'

The six-year-old's gaze was sharp. *Rice Fish* had put together a bedroom for a child based on what Xích Si had told her: an overlay of colourful characters from *Return to Dragon Station* and from *Vermilion Moon* – Hoa Phông with her companion mindship, *The Azure Dragon in Sunless Woods*, and the steel fans she used as weapons, and Hoàng Hoàng, the space-travelling phoenix, with wings slowly spreading to encompass entire planets. Khanh had stopped, transfixed, to look at the phoenix, clinging to her turtle plushie. *Rice Fish* suspected the spaceships and other animals she'd furnished the room with were going to remain untouched for a while.

'She's Mommy's wife, little fish,' Xích Si said. She was leaning against the wall of Khanh's bedroom, her face pale and her vitals – from heartbeat to reflexes – suggesting extreme fatigue. 'We're married.'

'Oh.' Khanh stared at *Rice Fish* – not at the avatar *Rice Fish* had manifested, but through the walls and the overlay. On the floor, planets and stars wheeled, slowly – the same rhythm as the ones outside. 'Does that mean you're my mommy, too?'

It was a good thing that *Rice Fish*'s reflexes were faster than humans, because she was only just in time to prevent herself from choking on her own breath. *Her mommy*. She blinked – a slow ponderous motion that tightened the air in all her cabins – remembering another small, preternaturally serious child sitting in bed, waiting for his bedtime story. *I want another story, Mommy. Please? Pretty please'*. And that same child, years later, standing in a room where she felt every sign of his anger like a blow: *I thought you'd care. But you haven't cared for such a long time, have you?*

She felt like she was choking on tears.

'If you want me to be, yes,' *Rice Fish* said. 'Do you like the room?'

'It's so cool,' Khanh said, her diffidence falling away like a discarded coat. 'I've never had Hoàng Hoàng on my walls! Can you do Thanh Quy Quy?'

Her turtle.

Rice Fish smiled. She focused for a moment, and the overlay slowly changed: a giant azure turtle swam in between two of the planets in the corner, all in translucent swathes of lights, mouth open to swallow stars, and the same stars dancing on the vastness of her shell. Khanh clapped in delight.

'Oh! Oh!' And then, to Xích Si, 'I like it here, Mommy.'

166

Xích Si's smile was terrible: a stretching of lips over unending bleakness.

'I'm glad,' she said — and before Khanh could work out that she didn't mean those words, *Rice Fish* sat on the bed by her side, drawing her into her embrace — the warm flesh resting against her, the frantic heartbeat slowly quietening.

'Would you like to hear a story? One your brother —' the words hurt, like jagged wreck-metal '— loved when he was very young?'

'Brother?' Khanh tensed. She was going to have to share this wonderful space with a child she didn't know. 'I don't want a brother.'

'Child!' Xích Si said, her voice sharp.

Rice Fish waved her away, widening her eyes to let Xích Si know now wasn't the time.

'Your brother is very busy,' *Rice Fish* lied. 'You may never see him at all.'

She made the room light up with stars, and the phoenix beat her wings over the planets — and she settled down to tell the story of the banyan tree in the moon of Old Earth, telling herself, over and over, that Hồ's rejection no longer hurt.

What a nice story that was. What a nice lie.

'Thank you,' Xích Si said. She was sitting in her rooms, the picture of Khanh over her console replaced with a feed into her child's room — blurred and fuzzy, it just showed her sleeping. She was going to need to leave Khanh space to be herself, later — to think about education and age-mates and all the other questions; to think about healing. But right now she was sitting on the bed, and she didn't have the strength to get up.

Rice Fish sat in the chair by the console, sipping a cup of tea Xích Si's bots had prepared for her. Her black-on-black eyes were wide open, her face slack — the length of her hair

167

merging into the floor in a wide sweep of night sky. She looked as exhausted as Xích Si felt.

'It's nothing,' she said. 'I'm your partner.'

Xích Si hesitated, and then, 'You look like you've been having a terrible time of it.'

She glanced at her messages – the usual banner updates – but she saw that *Crow's Words* had sent her a block of data, accompanied by a note that he'd decrypted it and found mostly meaningless messages. She could hear the ship's disappointment dripping from every word.

Rice Fish's bots clicked, briefly, on the floor.

'Nothing,' she said. 'Politics.'

'How bad is it?' Xích Si said.

'Desperate,' *Rice Fish* said, with a low, short laugh. Xích Si hadn't expected that to hurt.

'I'm sorry.'

'That's not your business.' *Rice Fish* drank her tea. 'You need to rest, first and foremost. You look like you're about to collapse.'

Xích Si was, but she was also too wound up to let go.

'It is my business. As you say – we're partners.'

Rice Fish's face went through a series of complicated emotions. She looked like she was about to cry, which was scary in and of itself.

'Partners.'

And something more, weren't they? But the words wouldn't come to Xích Si's lips.

'Always.'

'Partners,' *Rice Fish* said again, as if repeating the word would somehow make it real. 'Well, that's a partner's job. Let me take care of the politics?'

A ping, from Xích Si's mailbox. Multiple messages from *Crow's Words*, with a strongly worded header about how these weren't urgent and she could look at them in the morning. She ignored him. If there was any chance she could alleviate *Rice Fish*'s distress …

It looked as though he'd found the equivalent of Censor Trúc's flirty vids and texts: unexpectedly suggestive and so completely at odds with the censor as Xích Si remembered her – tall and unmovable, and taking away air and motion with a gesture – that it gave her whiplash.

Wait.

'Hang on,' she said to *Rice Fish*. 'I want to check something.'

Not that uninteresting. Something about the rhythm of the words, about the shortness of the syllables used – it looked like poetry, but it was all wrong. It was …

She called up the network comms she'd studied earlier – the ones from the earlier battles – and ran her bots on it for a fraction of a moment, comparing notes.

There.

They weren't flirty messages at all. They were authentication codes, passed back and forth. The same codes the imperial fleet had used to pass itself off as a banner's flagship. And the sender …

She said, slowly, to *Rice Fish*, 'Do you have any messages sent to you by Kim Thông, and can you forward them to me?'

Rice Fish's voice was puzzled. 'Yes, of course, but is this really the time—?'

'Yes,' Xích Si said. 'Now.'

She was exhausted and she was going to pay for this later, but she knew a trail when she saw one. She stared at the messages *Rice Fish* had sent her. They weren't the same sender ID, of course, but … She sent her bots to take them apart – waited, with bated breath, for the results.

There.

'She sent them,' she said to *Rice Fish*. 'Kim Thông.'

'Sent what?'

Rice Fish had risen, more sharply defined, the chair falling away from her and her hair becoming individual strands again.

'The codes. The ones Censor Trúc used to pass her fleet off as part of the alliance.'

'She what? Surely ...'

'I told you,' Xích Si said. 'She's arrogant. They always think no one can catch them – it starts with small things and then they grow bolder and bolder. Here.' She sent *Rice Fish* the entire message thread. 'She passed them off as messages about something else entirely, but you can see they're not quite right.'

'I can ...' *Rice Fish*'s eyes were the dark between the stars. 'How did you get this?'

'We ran into the censor in Triệu Hoà Port.'

'You ...' *Rice Fish*'s eyes blazed.

'It's all right,' Xích Si said with an ease she didn't feel, because the very thought of Censor Trúc made her nauseous. 'We got away.' She thought of the debt, but the thought of discussing it exhausted her. It was just going to needlessly worry *Rice Fish*. Later. She'd said she was going to mention it later. 'She was ... scary.'

'Scary.' *Rice Fish* breathed slowly, evenly. 'You're lucky to be here. I'm sorry.'

'What for?'

'I couldn't be there to protect you.'

That wasn't what she'd expected of *Rice Fish*, though, was it?

'It's all right.'

Xích Si closed her eyes; a wave of fatigue was rising in her – it would be so good to let go, to lie down and let the world fall away ... And then she must have blinked, because the ship's arms were around her, and she was slowly falling backwards

170

into the mattress, *Rice Fish*'s arms gently cushioning her fall onto the pillow.

'Big sis ...' she said, and *Rice Fish* – who had pulled back and now loomed over her, blurring into the room's walls and floors – laid a hand on her lips, the chilled sharpness of her skin spreading to Xích Si's entire face.

'You need to sleep,' *Rice Fish* said.

'I'm supposed to help you.'

Each word felt like a stone in her mouth. *Rice Fish* had not removed her finger; it felt as though she was catching them all.

'You already have. Sleep,' *Rice Fish* said – and, bending down, kissed her gently and slowly on the lips. 'I'll be back. I promise.'

And then there was only darkness.

14

Connections

Xích Si woke up. It was still dark. A quick check on Khanh showed her daughter still sleeping – but she went to Khanh's room all the same, because she had to be sure, because it didn't feel real that her daughter was here with her, in the Citadel. The ship's corridors were empty, and all she could hear was the sound of her own footsteps – *Rice Fish*'s attention was elsewhere, and the bots that scurried past her did so without any particular intent.

Khanh was curled around her plush turtle. At some point she'd emptied all the other toys onto the bed, and she was sleeping in the middle of a fortress of cute animals and holograms that provided low-key, relaxing music. Whenever she moved, one of them would start a slow, reassuring melody, and Khanh would relax, though she still clung to the turtle as if it were a lifeline.

Xích Si bent down, stroked her hair.

'I have you, sweetie,' she whispered. 'We're here. We're safe. No one is ever going to hurt you again.'

She sat, for a while, in the dark, staring at Khanh, her bots gently pulsing on her fingers. It felt right in so many ways

– and so strange in others. She'd left Triệu Hoà Port behind, and would not go back. There was her debt to Censor Trúc, but she didn't want to think about that. Not here, not now.

'I thought I'd find you here.' It was *Rice Fish*. She was standing at the doorway of the room, framed in the perfect circle of its entrance. Her hair shone; she'd tied it in a loose topknot, the rest of it falling down her back, moving like a sea of black glass as she came into the room. 'How is she?'

'Restless,' Xích Si said.

'It's early days.' *Rice Fish* sighed. 'Come. You need tea, and food.'

After a last glance at Khanh, Xích Si got up, following *Rice Fish* down the corridors. The route they were taking – past alcoves with scuttling bots, more and more of them, and sleeker models she'd never seen before – was utterly unfamiliar.

'This isn't the way to my rooms.'

'I know,' *Rice Fish* said. 'We're going to mine.'

Xích Si thought that just meant *Rice Fish* would go to her own quarters. But as the overlays became more and more fragmentary – the images and holograms and vids giving way to long strings of verses, going from modern calligraphy script to something more archaic, closer to the Old Earth alphabet – and as the number of bots increased until she had a clicking, metallic escort around her, both on the floor and on the walls, she realised what *Rice Fish* had meant.

'We can't—'

'Ssh.'

Ahead, *Rice Fish* had stopped at an octagonal crossroads in the corridors. There was a single water basin: a physical one, not an overlay, though the myriad silver fish swimming in it were virtual – rice fish, like the ship's name, no larger than the palm of Xích Si's hand. Six of the accesses were in absolute darkness, with no overlays or ornaments. The seventh was the one they'd come along, and the eighth … The eighth flared out as *Rice Fish* walked, becoming the faint shadow of a square arch with a roof, like the entrance to a Temple of Literature. The ship's avatar was … not fading, but somehow growing larger and larger without moving – as if for the first time Xích Si could really *see* that the avatar was the ship and the ship was the avatar, and they were inextricably bound together.

Under the arch were faint lights like ten thousand butterflies set alight – they were bots, but so light and small they floated in the air.

It smelled of motor oil and brine and a faint aftertaste of something sharp and chemical, something that reminded Xích Si of hospitals and apothecaries. She paused on the threshold, breathing in the room. The ship's heartroom. It felt … the opposite of unreal. It was heavy and meaningful and undeniable.

It was a large, octagonal room, with pillars of scrolling text dotted at regular intervals in the middle. And behind the pillars, faintly visible, cables and masses of components she couldn't quite identify, crawling with bots. The butterfly ones danced in the air as Xích Si made her way to the centre of the room, breathing harder and harder.

Rice Fish was waiting for her in the centre; behind her was something that looked like a throne that had erupted with spikes and thorns, and impaled on it were a softly pulsing series of globes of glistening flesh with shining metal inserts.

This was *Rice Fish*. The Mind at the heart of the ship. The will and consciousness that drove her body – and her avatar stood in front of it, hair lifted in an invisible wind and shining as bright, and as fragile, as jade, her tunic merging into the endless flow of letters around them. That flow of letters was on the globes and on the throne, too – and both the mind on the throne and the avatar were her, and they were both wholly, heartbreakingly beautiful.

Xích Si's throat was dry. She couldn't imagine many people coming here. The Red Scholar. Hồ? Technically she'd been given access, but she would never have dared on her own . . .

'You trusted me with your daughter, and your future,' *Rich Fish* said quietly. 'The least I can do is trust you in return.'

Xích Si's heart felt constricted, beating madly against a cage of ribs that had grown too small to contain it, reverberating into her bones.

'May I . . .?'

Rice Fish moved aside, slightly. Xích Si walked to the throne, trailed by the butterfly bots – lifted a hand on which shone her own bots, and gently trailed it across the Mind's surface. It pulsed, slightly, and *Rice Fish* drew an audible breath that contracted the walls of the heartroom around them.

'You're beautiful,' Xích Si said, struggling to breathe.

Rice Fish's face stretched into a smile that illuminated it.

'You're very kind.'

'Not kind. Truthful.' Xích Si couldn't bear to remove her hand – to grow distant from *Rice Fish* again. 'I've never seen anyone . . . quite like you.'

Rice Fish looked as though Xích Si had stabbed her.

'I'm sorry. I didn't mean to—'

'It's all right.'

But it wasn't, was it? Xích Si thought of Hồ and what he'd said. Shrivelled loves and pleasures taken outside the marriage. The shadow of the Red Scholar and whatever had gone wrong. There was nothing wrong with not wanting sex as part of a relationship – but *Rice Fish* had wanted it, hadn't she? So strongly and so desperately.

She said, finally, 'You should know I only say what's on my mind. I'm not being kind or polite. You are beautiful, and—' she ran her hand, slowly and gently, over the Mind's skin

'—there are so many things I'd like to do with you, if you would allow me.'

Under her touch, *Rice Fish* contracted, and the thrumming of the room grew faster and faster.

'What kind of things?'

Her avatar was now standing a hand's breadth from Xích Si – and everything in the room was saturated with her presence.

Xích Si grabbed her with one hand, and kissed her, leaving the other hand resting where it was, her rising heartbeat echoed by *Rice Fish*'s. She tasted of oil and brine, her lips cold and sharp, and Xích Si's chest tightened in response. She drew slow, wide circles on *Rice Fish*'s skin, feeling it contract under her with every one of them.

'Are you sure?' *Rice Fish* asked, her voice grave, her eyes black on black – but beneath her Xích Si felt the floor shiver.

'Oh, big sis.' She laughed, and it hurt, because she wanted to be held, she wanted to be filled – she wanted ... 'We're past that, aren't we?'

She kissed *Rice Fish* again, while her bots ran down that impossible length of hair, slowly pulling out hairpins until they clattered to the floor – and then her own hands followed them, losing themselves stroke after stroke in that cold sharp mass that parted strand by strand under her fingers, and it hurt to breathe again, ribs and skin afire.

Rice Fish blurred, for a fraction of a second. Her robes didn't vanish so much as recede, the golden orchids and half-bitten peaches becoming moles and blotches on her skin, and even that fading in turn. Her skin was dark and weathered, with a slightly metallic gleam.

'Go on, then, li'l sis,' she said, and her smile was the stars and the Fire Palace all jumbled together. 'Show me.'

The butterfly bots coalesced around Xích Si – a diffuse and distant touch that grew closer and closer, a gentle shivering pressure that went from aimless to deliberate. Clasp after clasp undone on her clothes, and the tunic and trousers and under-wear she'd been wearing falling away, pooling around her like water.

She stood there, admiring *Rice Fish*'s avatar. Both of them naked. Exposed. Vulnerable. Her heart pulsed in her chest.

'Please,' she said, giddy with need. 'Don't stop.'

The butterfly bots started again, strokes on the inside of her legs – soft tingles, maddeningly slow, edging upwards bit by bit. She drew in a sharp, shaking breath, kept one hand and her bots in *Rice Fish*'s hair, and let the other one trail over the Mind's exposed skin, alternating circles and pressing down, stepping up the rhythm as *Rice Fish* gasped – and whenever she did so the cloud of butterfly bots around Xích Si would contract, holding her still as if utterly bound.

'Big sis.'

She ran her fingers down *Rice Fish*'s chest, feeling her breasts tighten under her touch – gently pressing down again and again, feeling the slight yield, watching those black on black eyes dilate, hearing *Rice Fish*'s breath hitch in her chest, seeing her so swept up she barely blinked any more. Her other hand remained on the Mind, pushing harder, sinking into warm flesh.

'Yes . . .'

Rice Fish's voice was a hiss, echoing in the heartroom – the scrolling characters all faded now, only darkness remaining, the tension in the air rising and rising, swirling around her like the onset of the monsoon.

Xích Si reached out, putting a finger over *Rice Fish*'s lips – and then slipping it inside, pushing back and forth between slick lips.

Her bots were on the throne now, drawing on the Mind's exposed surfaces with the same alternating of slow circles and pushing, and shudders racked the room around her. She withdrew from *Rice Fish*'s mouth, ignoring the ship's slight whine of frustration, and started stroking her flesh again.

The butterfly bots around Xích Si had pushed her back, into the Mind's embrace – the slight give of the globes' flesh on her exposed back, the sharper touch of the metal inserts, the shuddering and contracting, and the answering waves of need within her, clenching and unclenching. It felt as though the air itself held her – stroking, maddeningly slow – again and again until she was incoherent.

'Please . . .'

Rice Fish laughed, or tried to, because she was moaning, too. Her flesh circled around Xích Si, pinning her wrists to the throne, and *Rice Fish*'s bots were still stroking her – her entire vision wavering and narrowing, her body contracting to a single narrow point of pleasure – until it swept outwards through her and *wrecked* her and she screamed.

She would have collapsed, boneless and drained – but the bots had not stopped between her legs, had not stopped inching upwards, and the pressure and the need built up again and swept through her again, wringing her like a rag, and she drew a burning breath and screamed again, wordless as the ship buckled and shuddered around her, and *Rice Fish*'s avatar grew fainter and larger and she moaned and moaned, breath quickening, her skin becoming harder and harder under Xích Si's bots, until she convulsed, too, the floor tightening under Xích Si's soles in waves – and it wasn't a scream *Rice Fish* let out, but something larger and more primal that made the entire room, the entire ship shake.

And then it was over, and they lay in each other's embrace in the heartroom, utterly spent.

*

178

Rice Fish didn't sleep, per se – but she did rest. At the moment, she was doing just that: her avatar in the heartroom, sitting with Xích Si cradled on her knees – feeling the weight of her wife, the warmth of her skin on hers. Her bots were monitoring vitals: the relaxation of all her muscles, the way her skin rippled in subtle patterns of heat, the even heartbeat. Nothing else – the passengers on board, the distant hold of the Citadel keeping her docked, the bots cycling through her corridors, the distant hum of space, the unceasing chatter of comms – mattered.

Presently, Xích Si stirred, and opened her eyes – and relaxed, seeing her.

'Big sis.'

She said nothing more, merely relaxed into *Rice Fish*'s grip. *Rice Fish* stroked her cheek, gently. She felt happy. She shouldn't have – so many things to worry about, the Council and Kim Thông and their precarious future – but it just ... felt good. It felt right, in the same way that rescuing Khanh had. As inevitable as the light of suns, as gravity.

It shouldn't have.

Marriages weren't meant to contain this. She wasn't meant to hold her wife and feel like everything was bursting within her.

'There is tea,' *Rice Fish* said, because her bots had prepared it and it was a less weighty conversation than everything else she wanted to say. 'If you want.' She checked, briefly, outside the heartroom. 'And then we can go check in on your daughter.'

Xích Si said nothing for a while. Her eyes were unfocused; she half-looked as though she was going to fall asleep. *Rice Fish* knew the feeling: not ready to face the world yet. They were both in a bubble – thin and fragile, and only lasting a moment – though they wanted that languorous moment of stretched happiness to last forever.

179

Xích Si stretched, and sat, holding a cup of tea, wedged between *Rice Fish* and the throne. She was warm and smelled faintly of jasmine, and the weight of her presence in the heart-room changed it — it was still *Rice Fish*'s inner sanctum, the place in which she found refuge, but Xích Si was there. She *belonged* there. She picked up her overlay cup with the ava-tar's hands, breathed in the aroma — she was a child on one of the numbered planets, and her long-dead sibling Thanh was reading a story to her. Other memories, too — of Hổ as a child, and of Huân — and these ones hurt and she didn't want to dwell too much on them.

'It was wonderful,' Xích Si said.

Rice Fish laughed. 'I could say the same.'

But not expected. Not deserved. Not right. She pushed the doubts back into the deepest of her processing threads.

'What ... what now?' Xích Si asked.

Rice Fish's comms had been blinking at her for a while, a high-priority thread in her. She'd been steadily ignoring it, but she knew it was Tiên. Her voice hardened, every single connector clenching on the throne.

'I go to the council with the evidence you've given me, and make Kim Thông fall.'

Xích Si was too polite to question her, but *Rice Fish*'s bots nevertheless felt her unease, the slight clench of her hands, the thin film of sweat.

'About the censor ...' Xích Si said, slowly.

'What is it?'

Xích Si looked small, struggling for words.

'She scares me. She ... She threatened me, in Triệu Hoà Port. And ...' She stopped, again, breathing hard.

Scared and small, the way she'd been, in the very beginning. Going back to everything that *Rice Fish* had thought gone.

Xích Si had blossomed here in the Citadel, and the censor, with a few well-placed words, dared to take this away?

'Don't worry about this,' *Rice Fish* said, coldly. 'The censor won't come here. She can't touch you.'

'But—'

'Trust me,' *Rice Fish* said, with a confidence she didn't feel but projected on all her manifestations – from throne to avatar to bots – until the room rang like sharpened steel. 'I handle the politics, and I've got this. And meanwhile, you need to take care of Khanh.'

Rice Fish remembered, all too well, *Mulberry Sea*'s warning, Hồ's warning. The waiting audience silently hungering for blood at the trial. It was not going to be easy, or trivial, to do. But she couldn't afford doubts. She was the elder in this partnership – the strong one, the one who could make space for Xích Si. What she did not, could not afford, was her own vulnerability.

'Big sis . . .' Xích Si started, stopped.

Rice Fish bent, and laid a finger on Xích Si's lips, feeling gently pulsing warmth under her avatar's touch.

'I've told you. I've got this, li'l sis. Now go, before your daughter wakes up alone in a deserted room in a place she doesn't know.'

15

The Council

Tiên was waiting for her in the central plaza. Her clothes were ornate and colourful – a riot of embroidery, of shadowed orchids and mạt chược tiles, of bitten-into peaches, golden vases and other explicit references. Her face, though, was utterly serious. She didn't need to speak: she'd already sent *Rice Fish* everything through the network. She just raised an arm, sleeve billowing in the wind, and pointed to the central depression – the downwards slope of scree leading to the administrative zone. In the maze of corridors extended by perception filters, she was not heading to the wide open area of the tribunal, but a smaller room: the council's private deliberation chambers.

Rice Fish could have projected straight in front of it, but she needed the time. She needed to collect herself: to go from the lover who'd woken up with Xích Si pillowed on her steps – feeling the warmth of a body and the languorous relaxation of limbs against her – to the pirate consort. She was walking as fast as was permitted to avatars – flickering and projecting faster than embodied humans. In her mind she saw the corridors of a ship instants before pirates rushed on board. She heard steel on steel and the clamour of battle – hung silent in space in the instant after she'd fired shots, watching the inexorable way they'd curve towards the other ship, too late for a last-minute dodge.

The corridors were all but deserted, which was odd. This time of day they should have been full — and the deeper she went, the more they opened up through the perception filter, becoming canyons, the Fire Palace hanging closer and closer until the air was roiling with its presence, a feeling that was all the more disturbing as the heightened temperature was damped down by the perception filters. *Rice Fish* was left with a strong sense of threat that wouldn't dissipate as her activated bots joined her, clustering in the shadow of her avatar.

The doors to the council room were open, and the guards outside were White and Black Banner. They gave *Rice Fish* a curt nod as she came in, Tiên behind her. Tiên had drawn an arc-blade. *Rice Fish* knew the value of theatrics, and appreciated Tiên's.

The ceiling wasn't stars as in the tribunal, but Ashling characters silhouetted against the looming ruin of the Fire Palace. The fractured planet and its equally fractured rings were seemingly held at bay by a ring of bluish characters that *Rice Fish*, not being a scholar, couldn't quite identify — was that 'duty' somewhere, and 'protection', or possibly 'war'?

In the shadow of the planet was the speaking circle, and surrounding it the lacquered pews — the same as in the tribunal. Filling each pew were the council members.

Hồ of the Purple Banner, his face unreadable. Kim Thông, the Green Scholar, smiling broadly. The White and Black Scholars, Châu and Anh Thảo — and next to them *Mulberry Sea*, who sent *Rice Fish* a curt acknowledgement through the network, ship to ship. Of them all, the White Scholar and Hồ were physically present; everyone else was in avatar. It was particularly visible with the Black Scholar, who had the antlers and the elongated serpentine spine of a dragon, but her physical face.

Mulberry Sea spoke first, as *Rice Fish* took her place. It was ice-cold in the perception layer.

'Younger aunt, I believe you wished to bring something to the council's attention?'

The air, stilling, becoming as sharp and as stinging as atmosphere on her hull. Everything slowing down – the bots at Kim Thông's feet frozen in place, the careful masks on the White and Black Scholars' faces, the uncanny stillness of *Mulberry Sea*'s avatar.

'Yes,' *Rice Fish* said.

She sent through all the evidence she and Xích Si had gathered – but didn't leave her space. The message was clear: she was letting her data speak for itself.

There was silence. It was *Mulberry Sea* who broke it.

'Interesting,' she said.

'Lies,' Hổ said, a fraction of a second later. 'Come into the circle.'

Rice Fish didn't move. Instead, she sent a single message from Kim Thông to Censor Trúc into the circle, letting it shimmer over the five-petalled flower of the Pirate Alliance.

The White Scholar glanced at the Black Scholar; something crossed between them, something *Rice Fish* couldn't quite read.

'These are very serious accusations.'

'I know.' She had to remain quiet. She had to leave her fury out of this – her grief, her anger at Huân's senseless death, at all the things that it left forever unsaid between them. Her anger at Kim Thông and the casual way she was sacrificing them all for her own gain. She was here as the de facto head of the Red Banner, not as a grieving, hysterical consort. If she showed anger, rage or uncertainty, they would tear her to

184

pieces. 'I do not make them lightly. And I want answers, as I believe you will.'

Hồ spat, 'Answers! As if your fabrications—'

'Younger brother.' Kim Thông held up a hand – and *Rice Fish* could have sworn that, before she checked herself, Kim Thông had been about to use 'child' for Hồ – an utterly inappropriate title. Even *Rice Fish* would address him as 'younger brother' in the context of council deliberations. 'Serious accusations deserve a serious answer.'

Her avatar flickered – crossing the space into the speaking circle in a few blinks. She stood next to the message, staring at it for a while.

The White Scholar looked up from the data. She was a middle-aged woman, ten years older than Hồ; but her voice was quiet.

'Elder sister,' she said to Kim Thông. 'These are communications between you and the censor. How do you explain them?'

'They're not hers,' Hồ spluttered.

'I don't think that's true. They're very clearly coming from your personal comms. And equally clearly being sent to the An O Empire. Well?'

Kim Thông hesitated. Was she going to deny it? What lie could she come up with, that would save her?

'Sometimes it's necessary to talk to our enemies. To lead them astray.'

'Astray?' The Black Scholar's voice was incredulous. 'Are you saying you provided false information to the censor?'

'Yes,' Kim Thông said. 'I acted for the sake of our survival. We all know –' her hand swept out, encompassing the council room, the five-petalled flower, the Fire Palace looming over them '– that we teeter here on the event horizon of black holes. One mistake, and we'll all be sucked into a spiral from where there is no return.'

It might have worked, once. Fear might have thrown the council off course. But *Rice Fish* saw the grim lines of the White and Black Scholars' lips. It wasn't quite enough, as blusters went.

'These are our authentication codes for a ship of our banners,' *Rice Fish* said, mildly. And, to the White and Black Scholars: 'You can check them, if you wish.'

'We have,' the White Scholar said. 'Elder sister, how exactly are you providing false information?'

Kim Thông looked taken aback. She looked at Hồ for a blink, and must have decided that she couldn't trust him to be of any help.

'Sometimes it's necessary to mix in the true with the false.' Her voice barely shook, but the bots on her wrists did.

'It is,' the Black Scholar said, after a pause. 'So you are gaining her trust and waiting for a moment to betray her?'

No. That wasn't where it was supposed to go. But *Rice Fish* wasn't quite done yet. There was more data.

'Younger sisters,' she said to the White and Black Scholars. 'Younger brother. You haven't looked at everything I sent.'

'I see a mass of logs,' the White Scholar said. 'What of it?'

'These are the logs from the battle where the Red Scholar died,' *Rice Fish* said. She said it quietly, softly, with as much determination as she'd have used for slipping a knife between an enemy's ribs. Which, in a very real sense, she was doing. She was almost there. Just a little further to go, and they would see. They would have to acknowledge the evidence in front of their faces. 'Look at them. Look at the codes used by the imperial ships when they attacked us.'

'These are lies!' Kim Thông's voice was sharp. 'Logs you and your pretty new wife have made up out of whole cloth.' And to the other scholars: 'You cannot possibly believe her. She's running desperate because she's lost influence after the Red

Scholar's death. It's nothing more than private grievances.'

A silence, spreading like that after a mindship's death wound – in that moment when everything still seemed normal, right before blood spurted out through thrusters and fins and heartroom.

At length, the White Scholar said, 'We will, of course, request the originals and see if they have been tampered with. I will say, though, that if it's been invented, it's remarkably consistent and coherent.'

'You cannot ...' Kim Thông was trying to control herself, and failing.

It was almost over. She'd won. She hadn't thought she could sway the council.

But then, in that silence, Hổ spoke up.

'Where did you get this evidence, elder aunt?'

Rice Fish saw, a fraction of a second too late, where this was headed – that instant of stillness before a ship dived into deep spaces, or before the scalpel was driven in.

Hổ went on, 'The timestamps on this message are clear, aren't they? You did not get these from the Green Scholar, but from the censor.'

Every pair of eyes and every avatar turned towards *Rice Fish*, as if she was now the one in the circle. She weighed and discarded too many answers, and went, in the end, for the direct confrontation.

'The Green Scholar sent the codes. To an imperial fleet. One that killed the Red Scholar. Why would she do this? For the sake of our survival, really?'

Kim Thông stared back at *Rice Fish* levelly, her mouth a thin line in the wrinkled oval of her face. And in that instant of silence it was the White Scholar who spoke.

'Perhaps. Perhaps not. But I would like to know,' she said, 'how you got hold of this message, elder sister.'

The Black Scholar watched, but said nothing. It was Hồ who moved, throwing something into the centre of the circle – a small speck that looked like a grain of rice, twisting and tumbling, until it hit the ground and blossomed like a twisted flower.

The vid was short, but unambiguous. It showed Xích Si facing off against the censor, holding Khanh against her. The sound was pitched low, almost inaudible – only bits and pieces floated up, about pirates and sales and children.

Xích Si.

Xích Si had said something about the censor threatening her. *Rice Fish* had assumed they'd fought, and barely got away, and Xích Si had never, ever corrected or denied that assumption. She'd never, ever said that she'd been on the verge of getting arrested by the censor.

'An unauthorised and risky raid into An O Space.' Hồ's voice was quiet, as devastating as a scalpel slowly drawn across flesh. *How could he?* They were never going to love each other, they were never going to even care for each other, but she'd hoped, all the same, that he would ... That he would have *standards*.

'There was a *child* at stake,' *Rice Fish* said.

'A personal mission.'

'So you'd have let a child be abused? Is that what I should have done?'

She was angry now, because it wasn't just Hồ. It was Kim Thông, and the ruin of everything she and Huân had worked to build, the chains of brutality and injustice they had striven to break with every new person that joined them. They'd built a world away from the savagery of the civilisations they had left behind, a refuge where everyone had what they needed and deserved. All that painstaking, thoughtful, caring work, so that Kim Thông could parcel it up, break it, and offer its ten thousand pieces in return for amnesty. So that her own son, who had grown up in what they'd built, could hunger for adventure and cruelty, and deem the pain of a child fair payment for indulging both urges.

'I don't know what I would have done.' Hồ wouldn't look at her. A properly respectful look from a son to a mother. As if he was ashamed. 'But I know what happened.' On the vid, Xích Si had stopped moving, the air shimmering with the faint translucence of a slow bubble. She was being arrested by the censor. 'What I don't know is how she came back.'

'You dare—'

'Look at it,' Hồ said. The censor made a gesture, and the bubble popped. She had a brief talk with Xích Si, before turning away and leaving with two prisoners in tow. 'Look, Mom! And tell me how your *wife* came back. Tell me how a pirate was arrested and isn't dead! Tell me what kind of bargain that requires!'

What kind of bargain? How dare Xích Si? How could she? How could she not mention this – any of this? How could she let Rice Fish *walk straight into the council with this massive liability, left in her opponents's hands?*

How could she?

Rice Fish looked at the other members of the council – at the minute creases under the Black Scholar's eyes, at the way the White Scholar bit her lip. At *Mulberry Sea* and the careful way her avatar was positioned, nose inclined, body away from her own council chair.

'I call for a vote,' Kim Thông said, in the silence, and her voice had the sharpness and focus of a laser. 'On a matter of utmost security to all of us. I call for a vote on the right to a seat at this council table.'

Even before the votes were cast, *Rice Fish* knew which way they were going to fall.

189

Xích Si was reading a book to Khanh when her comms pinged. At first, she thought it was *Crow's Words*, or *Tấm and Cám*, and her hand came up to dismiss the notification, but then she saw that the seal associated with the comms was blank. What was that? She held up her hand, hesitating, and in that moment the seal shifted, and became the outline of a bamboo branch with frost on its leaves.

A personal seal. Frosted bamboo, in the decline of old age. She knew who that had to belong to.

Censor Trúc. On her own private comms line, in the heart of the Citadel. On *Rice Fish*'s own body.

Impossible.

The seal shimmered, the comms pinging her insistently — the impatience clear.

You owe me. For life.

Xích Si kept her voice slow and even, as she sent through a request to delay the call for a few minutes.

'Sweetie?' she said to Khanh. 'Let's finish this. Mommy has work to do afterwards.'

The censor acknowledged her request for delay, but her seal did not vanish; she was still calling. The message was clear: delay was barely tolerated.

Somehow, Xích Si got through the story. Somehow, Thanh Quy Quy and her friend the phoenix saved the named planets, with the seal blinking in her overlay the entire time. Somehow, the ships they were protecting made it safely to harbour. Somehow, the children on board were reunited with their parents.

Khanh clapped when it was done, and the holos of the turtle and the phoenix remained on the wall, smiling at her. She was holding her plush turtle and sucking her thumb, leaning against Xích Si. Xích Si wanted to hold her and never let her go, but she couldn't.

'I have to go,' Xích Si said. 'Something came up.'

Khanh looked up at her with a shrewdness belying her age.

'Mommy? Why are you upset?'

'It's all right,' Xích Si lied, and fled the room with the comms still blinking in overlay.

She went to her own rooms, where she engaged the privacy filters. Sat on the bed, clinging to one of her bots, trying to breathe, before she let the seal bloom in her field of vision.

'Yes?'

'Child.'

Censor Trúc was sitting in what looked like a private study. It spread as Xích Si watched, taking up half of her rooms, its overlay representation covering the console where she'd sat with *Rice Fish*: it was a study of scrolls and tasteful holos of starscapes, and a garden with elegantly scattered rocks by lotus-covered ponds, and a pavilion. An exquisite and expensive overlay designed by a master, a reminder of where the censor came from and what means she wielded.

'I told you we'd see each other again.'

Xích Si struggled to breathe. 'And with such haste,' she said finally.

Censor Trúc smiled. It didn't reach her eyes. She had bots on her shoulders and on her hands — not the usual many-legged contraptions so present in the belt, but small and serpentine ones with shimmering manes: the dragons of the throne that she'd been sworn to defend. A host of them clung to her topknot, which wasn't a traditional scholar's knot but had long hair streaming away from it, streaked with grey.

'Piracy is always a matter of urgency.'

'What do you want?' Xích Si asked.

Censor Trúc's eyes crinkled a fraction. She thought Xích Si uncouth for getting to the point — as if scavengers had time and leisure to mince words — and was too polite to say it.

Xích Si was not. 'You despise us. You think us vulgar.'

'Scavengers? No,' Censor Trúc said. 'I think you *vulnerable*.'

'So you patronise us?'

Censor Trúc smiled, and it was edged. Her voice, when she spoke again, was sad.

'Tell me — could you have rescued your daughter yourself, without any intervention?'

'If you hadn't been there, I would have!' Xích Si thought of Khanh and of the lines putting her on offer — begging any stranger to pay coin for her, for the right to own her and hurt her. 'You're just defending this, aren't you? The ability of the strongest to do what they want to the weakest. Your law is nothing but a shield for the cruel.'

'And you kill people. You pillage ships and torture crews to find money to subsist on.'

Xích Si thought of Ngà, of the body she'd found. Of *Rice Fish*, frowning and telling her she could find and punish those who'd done it. Of the trial, and *Rice Fish* harming Chi Lan rather than see Ái Nhân harmed, even though Ái Nhân was a scavenger.

'There are rules. We're not lawless.'

'Rules don't change the nature of what you're doing. Let's not compare wrongs.'

'I haven't killed anyone.'

'Not yet.' Censor Trúc's voice was even, but it sounded sad, which was infuriating. She — who hadn't known hardship and had never feared for the safety of her children — had no right to judge. 'Now, I want the Citadel.'

'No.' It was reflex, welling out of Xích Si like breath after a gut punch. 'It's a place of safety. It's my *child*'s place of safety.'

'You'll find you don't have a choice.'

'Because I owe you a debt?'

'Because I'll take it another way, if not through you.' Censor

Trúc stared at her. 'And if you're the one who gives me access, then I'll give you something else in return.'

A silence.

Of course that is her angle.

'You already have Kim Thông, you don't need me.'

'I dislike Kim Thông. Traitors can't really be trusted.'

'But you're asking me to betray. Isn't that a conundrum?'

'I dislike Kim Thông because she's doing it for personal gain. She wants to be wealthy and safe, above her former comrades – even, and especially, if it means burning it all to the ground. But you're different, aren't you?'

'I told you. Don't patronise me.'

'You misunderstand me. I'm not patronising you. I'm admiring. It was a big risk to come back into the habitats, knowing it meant the slow death if you were caught, and you did it anyway.'

'Do you have children?'

A silence.

'Yes. Adopted. Neither my spouse nor I have any interest in physical relationships.'

'Then you'd understand coming back wasn't really a choice.'

'You think so. But I can assure you, as a censor, I've seen many parents who would not only consider remaining safe a viable choice, but would pride themselves on making it.' Her lips were a thin line, like the edge of a vacuum blade. 'They would *boast* about it, saying it was for the child's own good.'

'I only did what was right,' Xích Si said. She felt winded, as if she'd run through the entire Outer Rings and was now teetering on the edge of some black hole large enough to swallow everything she cared about. 'This isn't about me.'

'No.' Censor Trúc was silent for a while. Then she made a gesture, and the overlay of bookshelves and starscapes and garden receded, leaving just her own avatar facing the console, with

193

the dragon bots in her hair. 'This is about what's right. This is about building a fairer world.' Her face was softer now, her voice barely audible, but still with that core of steel in it. 'The civil service is rife with corruption. Void gifts pay for drugs like Hell Bridge, and Lantern Poppy. Triệu Hoà Port has become a place for the worst excesses of the empire – as you say, the law as a shield for cruelty, and a spear for hurting the weakest. I've come to clean up all that, but that has to start somewhere.'

'So you're saying we're responsible for civil servants taking bribes.'

'That's not what I'm saying. I'm saying that piracy is part of a system that's doomed to end. And the sooner you realise it, the better.'

'So you can put us all to a slow death?'

A gentle snort. 'The empress's policy of death for the first pirate offence drives pirates to remain pirates. Worse – it drives recruitment. People like you – you would never have become a pirate if you could have slunk home and picked up the threads of your old life again.'

'I ...' Xích Si opened her mouth, and didn't have a reply. If she could have escaped, if there had been an escape ... But even if there had, they'd have come to the same place in the end: to that slowly shrinking life with no hope of change, those ever-narrowing circles that had led to Khanh being put up for indenture. Xích Si's departure had just accelerated the inevitable. And if she had left, then she'd never have met *Rice Fish*. 'I don't know.'

'Honesty. That's refreshing. As I said—' Censor Trúc reached out for a bot, and gently smoothed its mane '— I have been given powers to change some things. To grant some amnesties.'

'You ...?'

'You were ready to sacrifice everything for your family's safety. Safety is what I'm offering.'

'But you're asking me to sacrifice everything again.'

'Not everything. Within your family I would, of course, include your wife.'

'She'll never be willing—'

'She'll have no choice, when the Citadel is ashes. She can die a pirate – and I can assure you that if she doesn't fall in battle, her death will be a slow one, by ten thousand cuts, in an example the Twin Streams will remember for generations – or she can live within the Four Occupations and within the harmony of the Heavenly Mandate.'

Rice Fish, a scholar? Or a craftsman? Xích Si couldn't imagine either of those things.

'I don't have to trust you.'

'No. As I said ... I'll get the Citadel, one way or another. The question is whether you can benefit on the way.'

'You said I had a debt towards you. That you'd collect it.'

'I did. That may not have been the entire truth.' Censor Trúc smiled, and said nothing, for a while. And then, finally: 'You risked everything for your child. I'm loath to see that kind of loyalty go to waste in penal servitude or on the execution grounds. Think about it?'

The comms ended: she slowly faded, until only her seal remained, and then that, too, faded. And then there was just Xích Si, staring at the console for a full, desperate heartbeat before she dropped the privacy shields and pinged *Rice Fish*, repeatedly and desperately – to no avail.

I'll get the Citadel, one way or another.

16
Wounds

Rice Fish didn't remember how she came back.

She must have walked, but then where was Tiên? She was ... She was in the Citadel, and then she was back in her body — in the heartroom, sitting on the steps before the throne and her organic core, desperately trying to focus, the bots around her scattered like the corpses of slaughtered birds, feebly twitching. She was shivering and shaking — every single sensor input merging together: the coldness of space on her hulls; the footsteps in the corridors; the voices in the rooms; the smell of steamed buns; the chatter of comms and other ships; the awareness of being docked, gently held by the magnets tying her to the Citadel. It was all too much at once, and she couldn't deal ...

And yet, if she stopped to sort out those inputs, the moment they started falling away, she'd remember it all, with merciless clarity: the council room, the expression on their faces. The voting tokens, revealed in one sweep of the Black Scholar's hand. Kim Thông, gloating. The Black and White Scholars, regretful but united. *Mulberry Sea*, neutral, diplomatic, but then she'd always been honest about what this entailed, had always told *Rice Fish* where she stood. And Hồ, looking at her with pity in his eyes. As though she was some scholar whose time of imperial favour had come and gone, and she didn't have the intelligence to realise it.

As though she was nothing, any more.

She was once more at the Citadel's docks, hanging motionless and powerless to affect anything − her thoughts racing around in circles, and nothing and no one was going to help her. Huân wouldn't come for her, wouldn't save her ...

How could they?

How could Xích Si?

She felt, more than heard, the door to the heartroom slide − a tearing open deep within her as the door opened, and footsteps on the floor, their touch on her floors lighter and lighter as they started to run.

'Big sis? Big sis!'

Bots on her avatar, holding her, and Xích Si running up the steps, and laying her hands on *Rice Fish*'s organic core − the warmth of her skin like a shock, her voice saying, 'it's all right, it's all right', over and over again − until the shaking abated, until her avatar stopped slipping out of her control, and she could look up out of a face that wasn't melting off or shimmering into oily nothingness every few blinks.

'Li'l sis.' Her voice felt clogged.

'Ssh.' Xích Si's hands were still wrapped around *Rice Fish*'s organic core. She was shaking, too. Pupils dilated, and adrenaline throughout her body. 'It's going to be all right.'

It wasn't all right. She was a mess. So much of one she'd made her usually composed and timid wife run across the ship to comfort her.

Her composed, timid wife who'd just been instrumental to her downfall.

'No,' *Rice Fish* said. 'It's not.' She drew in a deep, shaking breath, felt it echo around the room, felt the sharpness of connectors against her, everything of hers gathered into this small space, this small here and now. 'They threw me out, li'l sis.'

'I . . . I don't understand.'

'They voted me out! The council. They said I'd recklessly endangered the Citadel and everyone within.'

'By trying to figure out who killed Huân?'

It was all coming boiling up, and she was close to losing all control.

'Because you didn't tell me about the censor! How could you?'

Xích Si withdrew her hands as if scalded. 'I don't understand.'

'She arrested you. Didn't you think that was going to matter? Where the evidence came from?'

Xích Si stared at her. 'I tried telling you! You told me to trust you. That it didn't matter. That she couldn't touch us.' She was shaking. 'I thought you'd understood!'

'You're the one who doesn't understand. How could you let me walk in there with this at my back? You might as well . . .' *Rice Fish* tried to breathe, but there were too many cables and connectors in the way, and it didn't feel like anything reached her. 'You might as well have voted with them.'

It was such a betrayal; and made worse by the fact she hadn't expected it at all.

Xích Si breathed, hard and fast, her heartbeat frantic.

'Politics,' she said. 'I don't understand how it can make such a difference!'

No, she hadn't, had she. And that made it so much worse, because she couldn't see it. Maybe she'd never see it. *Rice Fish* had thought they had an understanding – that Xích Si could have a sense of what mattered to her. But perhaps they'd never really had that.

'Who has the Red Banner now?'

'Does it matter? They'll nominate someone. A sycophant of Kim Thông, no doubt.' She was still focusing on the wrong things. On the wrong priorities. 'This isn't what you should be worrying about.'

'I'm not a child!' Xích Si's voice was hard, her bots glinting on her fingers as she clenched her fists. 'You didn't listen to me when I tried to warn you. And you're not listening to me now.' There was something in her voice, something shaking and shivering, some weakness and vulnerability that hadn't been there before.

'You're afraid.'

'And why wouldn't I be? You're no longer on the council. As you said – you can no longer protect me.'

That hurt. They'd moved quickly to strip her of her banner-people – cut off her privileged accesses to the Red Banner. Word was spreading, as fast as strands of starlight. She could, perhaps, call on Tiên and a few bannerpeople as a personal favour, but beyond that ...

'You'll have lost your own bannerpeople in the wake of my fall.'

'It's not about the bannerpeople!'

Rice Fish raised her eyes, looked at Xích Si – dishevelled, breathing hard, her bots trembling on her hands. She called up her own scattered bots – a considerable effort – and scanned her. She'd run through the entire ship to find *Rice Fish*, but the adrenaline rate was still too high. Her agitation had predated the run. And there were multiple missed comms attempts to *Rice Fish*.

'What happened to *you*?'

'The censor happened.' Xích Si breathed in, hard.

'She can't reach you here.' *Rice Fish* saw Xích Si's sharp intake of breath, reverberating under the ribbed ceiling of the room. She remembered the vid she'd seen, the one Hổ had showed her. 'She let you go, didn't she. What did you do?'

'I did *nothing*!' Xích Si's voice was tight. 'She let me go because it suited her.'

'Because she wanted something from you.'

'You're still not listening! This isn't what we should be talking about now.'

'Then *talk.*' *Rice Fish* couldn't keep the anger out of her voice, or out of the heartroom; it was making the floor contract and vibrate.

'I tracked that transmission the censor made to me. It's not coming from the port.' She gestured, and something shimmered into overlay: a position halfway between Triệu Hoà Port and the Citadel. 'I can't track it more precisely right now because it's encrypted and we're too far away, but she's moving at about the pace one would expect for an open-the-void.' *Rice Fish* could feel the panic coming off Xích Si: sweat glistening beneath the clothes, her bots' unco-ordinated movements, her eyes blinking faster than usual. 'At this rate, they'll be here in three days. Assuming they don't have a mindship.'

'The censor doesn't have an invasion fleet,' *Rice Fish* said, with a confidence she didn't feel. 'If she did, she'd never be acting through Kim Thông.'

'I think she's been given enough.'

Rice Fish started to speak, stopped again. Ships needed navigation subroutines to get through the clusters of asteroids that made up the Citadel, but the censor couldn't have that, could she?

'We're safe from her here. Now tell me what she wanted from you.'

Except that Kim Thông had those subroutines, and Kim Thông didn't mind if they all burned.

'Stop lying. To me. To yourself! We're not safe. Perhaps we

200

never were, not from the moment I came on board.' Xích Si was breathing too hard, each hitch in her breathing magnified by the sensors. 'You're not in control any more. You're not ...' She stopped, then.

'We have to tell the council,' *Rice Fish* said.

'The council who just threw you out?'

She'd forgotten — and then she remembered and it hurt all over again, and it made her angry.

'Because of what you didn't tell me!'

Xích Si's hand rested, lightly, on *Rice Fish* — not on her avatar, but on her organic core, on the throne. It felt too cold and too heavy.

'Think. This is exactly the way you got thrown out of the council — based on evidence brought by comms with the censor. They won't believe you. Or Tiên. Or me. They won't want to send a costly scouting fleet just to check. They believe themselves impregnable.'

'You think we're going to lose. Not now maybe, but later. You think we're doomed.' It suddenly came to *Rice Fish*, as merciless as enlightenment — utter clarity about what Xích Si was really saying. 'That's why the censor let you go. That's what she wants from you. Our lives in return for helping her.'

And Khanh's life, of course — which would no doubt matter most to Xích Si.

'Yes.' Xích Si's eyes were feverish.

'And you're tempted.'

How could she be? But of course, she'd been a pirate for less than a month. The Citadel didn't mean to her what it did to *Rice Fish*, or had to Huân.

'I wasn't! Not until I found out that you've been cast out.'

'That changes nothing,' *Rice Fish* said, trying to ignore the way the words made her feel short of breath and disconnected from the reassuring vastness of her body.

201

'True. Because it's too late. If they'd rather listen to Kim Thông than you, with the evidence that's been presented to them — if they'd rather cast you out on a technicality rather than avenge the Red Scholar, then we've already lost. It's already undone.'

She was turning her back on them, on all of them, so easily.

'We built something here,' *Rice Fish* said. 'After years and years of careful planning. A place where people like Khanh could be safe. And you just want to cut and run, like a thief?'

'Like a pirate.' Xích Si's voice was bitter. 'I thought we could change the banners, like you said. That there was time to create something else, away from Kim Thông's shadow. But we don't have that time. So it's time to leave, yes. I'm a scavenger. That's what we do, when it gets too hot. Run away before we die!'

'No. You're a pirate,' *Rice Fish* said. 'You married one. You *chose* to marry one. And you keep thinking small. You keep running away. You've spent your entire life being small and insignificant, and hoping you go unnoticed. How did that work out, when Khanh was in danger?'

'Don't you dare—'

'You're *afraid*. Afraid to reach out, because the world might burn you. It'll burn you anyway, because it's not fair. It's high time you accepted that you have responsibilities. That you *can* change things. That you *must* change things.'

'You're just ...' Xích Si made a small, stabbing gesture with her hands, one that resonated under *Rice Fish*'s ceiling. 'You're obsessed with that place, but it's been dead for a long time. Kim Thông hollowed it out right under you. And before that — how can you say it's a place of freedom, when you pillage and take captives? When you indenture servants? When you kill ...' She stopped, then. 'Your rules are just a lacquer over the law of the strongest.'

'That's not true. Huân—'

'Stop talking about Huân! Stop worshipping her like she's a living ancestor!'

'She was my wife. You didn't *know* her. You have no idea what you're talking about.'

Rice Fish couldn't breathe. Because the mere mention of Huân constricted her – made her painfully aware that she was just a Mind on a throne, locked in the middle of a too large, too ungainly ship.

'I don't need to know her, because she's here. She's everywhere, big sis. You're so obsessed with what you built together, with the perfection and pristineness of it. If she was such a paragon of virtue, then tell me – why did she teach you to be so unhappy?'

It was like a dash of cold water thrown over naked wires: cold one blink and stinging, numbing, the next.

'She did not—'

'Didn't she? When we kissed, here. When we made love. When you thought you were unworthy of being *desired*. Who taught you that, big sis?'

Rice Fish tried to speak, found only scattered processes – disintegrating and contradictory stimuli, bots and Mind and rooms, and corridors her consciousness was retreating from.

'Go,' she said. It was the only word she could think of. 'Go and deal with the censor, then, if you think so much of her chances. *Child.*'

Xích Si withdrew her hand and stared at *Rice Fish* – left to right, from avatar to organic core. Her face was pale, her entire being lit from within by light – so that *Rice Fish* could see the bones beneath her skin, and her heart, beating hard against translucent ribs.

'I'm not a child.' She breathed, hard, vapour hanging in the air.

Rice Fish kept her voice cold and emotionless.

'Go.'

For a moment more – a blink that stretched, inchoate, until it felt like a lifetime – Xích Si remained where she was. There were tears in her eyes. And then she turned on her heels and ran, until *Rice Fish* could no longer feel her footsteps on the floor of her heartroom.

Xích Si hadn't meant for everything to turn into an utter, unmitigated disaster, but once it had it was hard to pull back.

'Are you all right?' *Crow's Words* asked.

It was the third time the ship had asked since she'd moved her and Khanh's things on board – she hated it, but being on board *Rice Fish* at the Citadel, in the midst of people who had just proved how untrustworthy they were, was an even worse choice. It was just for a short while, anyway, while she worked things out.

If she worked anything out before the censor arrived.

She'd told *Crow's Words* that she and *Rice Fish* had had a fight, and it was true. He'd immediately assumed it was in the wake of *Rice Fish*'s dismissal from the council – that it was something to do with *Rice Fish* being too proud and too unbending to move, and Xích Si being scared for herself and Khanh. It . . . had had some relation with the truth. But Xích Si hadn't told him about the censor. About the fleet on its way to them. About the fact that the Citadel and everyone on board, including him, was in mortal danger.

She'd told herself that he wouldn't listen to her anyway. That, like *Rice Fish*, he would choose to stay and fight, and die.

But, deep down, she was afraid. Afraid he'd judge her for choosing to run away. For being willing to sell out the Citadel to the censor, if it saved *Rice Fish*'s life.

His rooms were smaller than *Rice Fish*'s, and the decorations slightly different: he favoured more modern art pieces, and half of them were physical rather than overlay. His bots were visible everywhere, though Xích Si couldn't say if that was normal or because he wanted to keep an eye on her. In the middle of the room was a table with some food, and sitting spaces marked out in concentric rings, like the ripples of a pebble in water, except the lines kept changing colour and wavering.

'I'll be fine,' Xích Si said. 'I don't think I'll stay long. Khanh and I should really be getting back ...' she paused, then. *Three days.*

'Back?'

'There's not really any place for us here.' Xích Si exhaled, feeling as though she was breathing out regolith dust, and its sharpness cut her everywhere. 'And with Kim Thông looking for revenge ...'

Silence. She hurt for lack of words.

'Yeah,' *Crow's Words* said, finally. 'You both need to be careful. There are rumours that Kim Thông wants to finish the job she started by getting *Rice Fish* kicked off the council.'

'Finish. You mean kill her?' Like she'd killed Huân. Kill Xích Si. '*Rice Fish* knows?'

'Of course she does,' he said. 'Her wife was the Red Banner's Scholar. It's a common enough thing. Pirates don't die in their beds.'

'I guess,' Xích Si said. She shouldn't have cared, but of course she did. She loved *Rice Fish* — but love wasn't enough to build something lasting. Not enough to close the chasm between them. 'You needn't worry about me. I'll be leaving.'

Crow's Words stared at her, for a while, his iridescent face blurring away to reveal portholes and navigation screens.

'If you need to go somewhere within the Twin Streams, I'm

happy to take you.' A shrug which dragged ghostly starlight into existence. 'The banner is in enough of a disarray that no one will notice.'

'You ...' She hadn't expected his kindness.

You're afraid. Afraid to reach out, because the world might burn you. He was going to die. They were all going to die, and she hadn't told him. She'd lied to him, and now she didn't know what to tell him that wouldn't make this worse.

He was crouching, his avatar glowing on the floor of his own body – his bots, silent and sharing his iridescence, standing guard. His eyes were stars reflected on his hull.

'It's all right.' He gestured to the table, where his bots had set out steamed dumplings and an assortment of sauces and tea, the smell of fish, vinegar and coriander sharp in the air. 'You can eat and decide. There's no hurry.'

'Oooh, dumplings!' Khanh said. 'Can we, Mommy?'

She'd come when Xích Si had asked her to – Xích Si had told her that they had to change houses because she and *Rice Fish* had argued, and they could no longer stay in the Citadel. Khanh had said nothing, but Xích Si knew that her daughter would not let the matter lie.

'Of course,' Xích Si said.

She watched Khanh lift the lids on the steamer and try all the sauces, making small delighted noises.

'You should eat, too,' *Crow's Words* said – he was younger than her but clearly determined to go full uncle on her. 'Eating won't solve any of the problems under Heaven, but at least you'll face them with a full stomach.'

Xích Si said, finally, 'You haven't asked—'

'What happened?' His eyes were metal again, molten silver. 'If you want to tell me, you can. But you don't need to.'

'She's your banner head!'

'Not any more.' *Crow's Words*' voice was bleak.

What about loyalty? What about duty? Xích Si wanted to ask, but the air around her was tight, a piece of steel before it snapped. Of course. She was so engrossed in her own misery that she'd never noticed his.

'You're not happy.'

'It's the way the wind blows. I don't have to be happy or unhappy. Just to follow where the storms go.' He used a word that could mean storms or war, or violence. And, finally, after a hesitation that made the floor under her shake: 'I know it's not your home. Not in the way it is for me.'

'Were you born here?' She'd never even asked.

Crow's Words laughed. 'Mindships are empire-made. No, I wasn't. But I came here when I was very young. With my mother.' A silence. 'It was ... bad, where we were.'

His mother. She could only guess at what had driven her to seek refuge here, at how serious it must have been. Or did it have to be? It wasn't even the large things, on the habitats — just a long slow process of attrition.

'Anyway,' *Crow's Words* sounded embarrassed, looking away, and even his bots scuttling back. 'I understand you've not got a whole lot tying you to here, and I can see why you'd want to head another way. Back to the port and somewhere the empire can't arrest you for piracy.'

The thought of Triệu Hoà Port was a blade in her mind. What was she going to do anyway? Where would she go?

'Are we leaving?' Khanh asked, mouth so full of dumplings she looked like a star-eater. 'I like it here.'

'We're ... We're not safe here any more, sweetie.'

Rice Fish's voice, in her memory: *You keep thinking small. You keep running away.*

A frown, from Khanh. 'Mama said she'd protect us.'

Xích Si opened her mouth to say that *Rice Fish* wasn't her mama, and then closed it. She really wasn't ready to have

207

that conversation, and it would have been massively unfair to Khanh – who was going through enough upheaval as it was. They could sort that one out later.

'We quarrelled.'

Khanh eye-rolled. 'And you think she'd stop protecting us? Mommy. Really. She's not that kind of person.'

But that wasn't the issue, was it? The issue was that if she stayed, they were all going to die alongside the pirates. Including *Crow's Words*.

She wasn't being fair, or kind.

'We can't stay,' she said. 'It's ... sometimes people need their own space, and this is one of those times.'

'I don't want to go!' Khanh looked as though she was about to cry.

'It's a lot and you're unhappy. That's fair.'

Xích Si kneeled, and hugged Khanh, holding her fast – trying to focus on the here and now, not on the uncertain and frightening future.

Khanh looked at her, sniffing. She finally stopped, and sighed, with a disturbingly adult expression.

'Can we still talk to her?'

'Maybe,' Xích Si said.

'Mommy!'

'Yes.' *No lies.* 'Not now, but perhaps later, but I can't promise ...' She stopped, then. 'Mommy's relationship to Mama doesn't affect yours to Mama. You can call her later, and she can make her own decisions.'

'She'll talk to me.' Khanh sounded very certain now. Xích Si wished she had Khanh's iron-clad resilience.

'That sounds fair. Child, can you go watch some *Vermilion Moon*?'

A pout. 'You want to have an adult conversation.'

208

'Yes.' Xích Si sent her bots, scuttling, to get some dumplings. 'You can take some of the há cảo.'

Khanh glared at her. 'I'm not that corruptible.'

Xích Si didn't move, or speak, and Khanh finally moved away, grumbling – into the corner of the room that was her bed. She fired up *Vermilion Moon – Crow's Words* gestured, and there was the familiar shimmering of a sound filter going up, cutting Khanh off from their talk.

'What is it?' He sounded concerned. Worried. About the wrong things altogether, she'd guess.

She said, finally, 'The censor is going to take the Citadel. Her fleet is on the way.'

'The censor—'

'She wanted me to betray the Citadel. I won't.'

'I didn't think you would.' His voice was grave. It hurt her more than it should have, his trust – because she'd been tempted. Because *Rice Fish* had seen how very much she'd been tempted.

She missed *Rice Fish*, so much – except that *Rice Fish* was a mess of barbs and hurtful repartee, and Xích Si still couldn't forget how much her words had torn at her, opening up wound after wound, heedless of Xích Si's pain. Laying her bare like a flayed body, gasping and struggling to move, every last bloodied bit of her exposed to wounding, burning air.

You just want to cut and run, like a thief?

How dare she? Running away was the sensible thing. The *only* sensible thing. They were outgunned and outnumbered, and the censor wouldn't let anyone go this time. And there was Khanh to think of. The crimes of parents fell on to children, and that included piracy.

No, she couldn't afford to be caught. She had to run. She'd sacrificed so much, and it was the only way.

Run run run.

Crow's Words said, 'You're safe from the censor here. No one has ever taken the Citadel.'

Exactly what *Rice Fish* had said to her – the Red Banner dogma. The lies they could no longer afford.

'You don't understand. She'll get there, and it doesn't matter that I'm going to refuse her. Because she has Kim Thông.'

'Kim Thông wouldn't ...' *Crow's Words* started, and stopped. 'Is *this* what you quarrelled about?'

'Not exactly,' Xích Si said.

His eyes narrowed. The air trembled, for a while.

'You could have told me.'

'I just did.'

'You did.' He stared at her, for a while.

She didn't know what compelled her to go on. The silence? Her previous lack of honesty? She owed him, for taking risks for Khanh. All of these reasons. None of these reasons.

'The council voted *Rice Fish* out because we got entangled with the censor in Triệu Hoà Port. They won't listen to me or her, and the information I have on the invasion fleet is from the censor. They won't consider it reliable.'

'Surely they ...' *Crow's Words*' iridescence dimmed, like a hurt child.

'They won't,' Xích Si said, firmly. 'Even *Rice Fish* knows this.'

He looked at her for what felt like ten thousand years. His bots were slowly converging back towards the doorway from the ceiling of the room and the table, and Khanh's bed – drawn to him as a comfort.

Finally *Crow's Words* sighed. 'I suppose it's true. I'm not surprised. People like me don't have a whole lot of say in this kind of thing.'

'It's your home!'

What did it matter to her ...? But of course it did matter. It wasn't that she didn't care about the pirates – about Tiên,

210

about *Crow's Words*, about Tấm and Cám, even about *Mulberry Sea*. It was just that nothing they'd do would save the Citadel.

'Yes, it is. Normally I'd ask and count on *Rice Fish* to defend us. Now ...' He spread his hands. 'I don't know. Not any more.' He took a deep, shaking breath. 'If you'll excuse me, I need a moment to digest this.'

His avatar started shimmering out of existence, becoming a barely visible outline against the cabin's door.

It was the lack of anger. It was the resignation. The deep-seated belief that he had no idea and held no hope.

'Wait,' she said. 'Wait!'

'What's the point of waiting? It's going to happen, isn't it? With *Rice Fish* gone, and Kim Thông dominant in the council. What's it going to change?'

He was still in outline, but she could feel him now, the blazing fury shaking in the floors and walls and tightening the air around her.

'I ...' She didn't know what to say.

'There's no other choice, is there? Just running. Or futilely trying to convince the council in the little time we've got left – time in which there's barely anything we can do anyway.'

You keep thinking small. You keep running away from everything.

She wasn't ... She ...

She couldn't breathe, any more; couldn't think, with everything coming to a head – with her bots tight on her fingers, their useless weight ... *Crow's Words'* anger, Khanh's silent resentment and incomprehension ... and before she could think, she'd called *Rice Fish*.

'Big sis?'

Silence. Of course. They weren't talking to each other any more. Of course she wouldn't want to listen to anything Xích Si had to say. They'd hurt each other too much ...

211

Wait.

That wasn't the silence of someone not responding. It was another kind.

'She's out of reach,' Xích Si said, aloud. *'Rice Fish?'*

'That's not possible.' *Crow's Words* said. Sharp and still angry, but Xích Si didn't care about that any more. 'She has her own comms array. She could be in the middle of space and still communicate with us.'

She was, in fact, in the middle of space: her last known position had been heading out of the Citadel on an intercept vector with the censor's fleet. She had gone to get more evidence. The kind that she hoped against all hope would be believed. Typical. And then . . .

A flare. A jumbled distress call — so badly mangled it gave no precise location — and then silence.

Xích Si took a deep, shaking breath — forced herself to *focus*. She couldn't afford the sick feeling of panic which was twisting her insides with nightmarish and useless ideas of what might have happened.

'Two main hypotheses — she's either lost comms because she's been captured, or because she's been damaged.'

Crow's Words didn't move for the longest while. He looked like he'd been dealt a mortal blow and hadn't yet worked it out.

'She what?'

'Captured.' Xích Si said, firmly. 'Or damaged. She had time to send a distress signal, so I think damaged is the most likely.'

Or dead, but she didn't want to think about that. She took in a deep breath, held it until she finally stopped shaking.

'What now?'

'I don't know.' Xích Si raised a hand to forestall his panicked objection, the bots on the back of her fingers turned towards him, like unprimed weapons. 'Yet.'

17

Fire and Darkness

It had seemed like a good idea at the time to *Rice Fish* — which were words generally reserved for ideas hatched in the dead of night, or under the influence of way too much rice wine.

Still smarting from her fight with Xích Si — and with the odd, unnerving pain of watching Xích Si pack her things and go, with Khanh throwing one last, piercingly perceptive look at her as she stepped off the gangway — *Rice Fish* had made a decision.

She needed irrefutable evidence of the invasion fleet, untainted by the censor. Which meant someone going and seeing it for themselves. With the Red Banner stripped from her — a loss that stung, all her authorisations removed and her unable to access so much as the comms-channels — she had no one to send. So she sent herself. She existed in an odd, liminal space where she was no longer the head of the Red Banner, but no longer a simple member of the banner herself. Pirate society had no provisions for this to happen: she should be imprisoned, or dead. Or in exile.

Kim Thông probably didn't want her to go into exile. It would certainly be convenient, but it would be bloodless — and remembering Kim Thông's face as *Rice Fish* humiliated her in front of the tribunal, *Rice Fish* knew she wanted payback for this.

She'd evacuated her passengers. Not that she'd had to work very hard at it, because most of them had been leaving already. Word of her dismissal from the council had spread fast, and many in the Red Banner had been afraid, or wanted to go where the shadow of favour fell, or both. Some she'd had to argue with more strenuously, but even in the midst of terrible ideas, *Rice Fish* had been adamant that she wasn't going to endanger more people than necessary.

So here she was. With Tiên.

'I'm sorry I got you into this,' *Rice Fish* said, not for the first time.

'Don't even think of leaving me behind.' Tiên was sitting in her usual cabin, cross-legged on the bed – her weight was a distant thing, like an ache. *Rice Fish* was standing by the bed in avatar shape, her long hair sweeping the floor and creating a shimmering pool of stars. Tiên said, 'Besides, it's a lot more entertaining than watching Red Banner politics currently.'

Ouch. Rice Fish winced.

'I felt that,' Tiên said.

The tremor must have gone straight to the cabin walls.

'Anyway,' Tiên said, with a sigh, 'are you sure it's the right place?' She'd called up an overlay – she was lying on her belly on the lavishly embroidered coverlet, her own clothes as or more extravagant – shimmering phoenixes in flights on the back of her tunic, and the five panels of her dress in five different and equally vivid colours, each with a matching set of bots hanging from her shoulders and ears. A final and larger bot was circling her neck and running along her spine, shimmering with oily iridescence. At the moment it was the only one moving, its appearance rippling and changing as it digested data. 'Can't see anything in all this empty space.'

Rice Fish called up the co-ordinates *Crow's Words* had sent again, staring at her own overlay.

'Yes. More or less.'

'More, or less?' Tiên's legs beat against the air, thoughtfully.

They weren't *on* the spot, obviously: *Rice Fish* was in space, in a pocket between a bunch of asteroids that had required a few manoeuvres to get past — she had a few scrapes where one of the smaller rocks had rubbed against the bottom quadrant of her hull, and she'd had to fold all her ailerons to get past. The familiar cold of the vacuum — the slight press of the solar wind, the awareness of the slow, intricate movement of the asteroids around her — soothed her. This was where she was meant to be. Away from the Citadel. Away from the painful, vivid memories of votes being cast one after the other, cementing her failure. Away from Xích Si.

It was also, quite obviously, empty of anything remotely resembling a ship. Just asteroid after asteroid, tumbling across her field of vision; a slow dance that her bots plotted for her, thread after thread of data sent to her so she could process how to move — how she, too, could dance and avoid them.

'Maybe the censor was lying,' Tiên said. 'After all, she's hardly a reliable source.'

'Xích Si seemed convinced,' *Rice Fish* said, before she could stop herself.

Tiên's look was pitying. *Oh, that's how it is, is it?*

'Point taken,' she said, her voice carefully neutral.

Her bots were busy; *Rice Fish* could distantly feel the requests they were making for her sensors' data.

'Need help?' *Rice Fish* asked.

'Mmm. Two can work better than one.'

Rice Fish linked up her bots and sensors with Tiên's — a parallel network of threads all combing through temperature and data from various wavelengths, trying to locate patterns that might be comms, that might be the shadow of ships. She found herself, absurdly, thinking of Xích Si — of sitting next to her by the console of her room, looking at Huân's last battle — feeling her closeness, the taut concentration in the way she held herself, like two spears thrown together towards the Heavens, perfectly matched ...

Your rules are just a lacquer over the law of the strongest.

'So you're done with her, then?' Tiên's voice broke her concentration.

Rice Fish startled. 'I don't know what you mean.'

'You do.'

'Yes, and maybe I don't want to talk about it.'

They were past the point of no return, weren't they? They'd both said and heard unforgivable things ...

'Mmm. I feel maybe you do need to talk about it. You're still married.'

'Divorce is a thing.'

The moment she said the word — the moment she felt the finality of it, considered the *idea* that she might lose Xích Si the way she'd lost Huân — she felt the hollow open in her heart-room, quickening the beat of her thoughts.

'Is it?' Tiên's voice was neutral.

'Yes.'

Rice Fish breathed in, hard, trying to steady herself. She'd not felt this panicked for a long time, her bots on the verge of escaping her unconscious control, her processing threads running amok through her entire body, from corridors to hull and from ailerons to cargo holds.

If your wife was such a paragon of virtue, then tell me — why did she teach you to be so unhappy?

216

'As you wish,' Tiên said. And then, finally, 'Do you want my opinion? As a friend?'

She wasn't sure she did. Tiên waited, all the same, and the uncertainty of it – no, not the uncertainty; the half-knowing and half-suspecting, the unbearable feeling she could predict the words but couldn't hear them yet ...

'Say it,' she said, hoping for the abscess to burst.

Tiên was still staring at the screen.

'It seems to me,' she said, finally, 'that you both got to the point where you loved each other deeply enough to hurt each other deeply.'

'You don't know what she said. What she did.'

'No. Or what you said, either. I'm not here to judge. Just that–' she shrugged '– she was good for you. And you for her. And sometimes things will rupture, won't they? But it's always about how it can be fixed and on what terms.'

'On what terms. What if I don't want it to get fixed?'

'Then that's what you want.' Another shrug. 'But you don't sound like someone who's walked away with no regrets.'

It didn't mean anything. Things could hurt and be untrue. Fights didn't have to be patched up. Wounds didn't have to be healed. Words didn't have to be taken back ...

'Here,' Tiên said, just as *Rice Fish*'s bots pinged – and the entire network of information lit up like New Year's lanterns. 'Oh, hello.'

Oh, Heaven.

Not just a small fleet, a few heavily armed merchants; not just an unofficial escort with void-gifts and other bribes; not even just a censor's accompanying bodyguards. This was an army – *Rice Fish*'s low-level algorithms were sorting out shapes as the sensors' data shifted, counting the different ships. It was hard, because they kept moving, kept dodging, and the image wasn't good – they were at the upper limit of the sensors' resolution.

Too many. Too many moving, too many shielded. Too many troop transports. The word that came to her then, was *vạn*. *Myriad*. Ten thousand, thousand ships – an army that seemed endless.

'They're halfway to the Citadel already.' Tiên's voice was flat. 'And they've disabled the sentinels, which means they know where they are.'

Which meant Kim Thông had provided them with more than just the guiding algorithms – some kind of modified version, as they were weaving their way quite slowly – or maybe the censor was just expecting treachery. Which would be smart, since their information came from Kim Thông.

'We have to warn the council,' *Rice Fish* said.

She was going to need some kind of amplifier; this far out in the asteroid field, with the sentinels' relays taken out, she could only send the barest of position acknowledgements. Maybe if she bounced a message off the invading ships themselves? That was a dangerous undertaking ...

'Elder aunt?' Tiên's voice cut through the morass of her thoughts.

'Yes.'

She was busy looking for an antenna, or something similar. A mirror that she could use to bounce off.

'There's something off—'

'Not now.'

'No, I mean here. On you.'

'I don't understand—'

A noise, like glass shattering. Blistering heat that spread like a storm of firebirds breaking free of her holds, all sharpened beaks and claws, every hit magnified by the previous one, an unending scream in her thoughts, her processes scattering and breaking away – all of it going up and outwards and sucking everything in its wake – walls torn like rice paper, corridors bulging and then bursting apart from the shock wave – it hurt, it hurt so much, what was happening, oh Heaven it hurt so much . . .

A bomb, she had time to think, in the blink before everything fuzzed and went searingly white – and then she was falling, and darkness spread and took her whole.

Xích Si tried to breathe. It was hard.

'I don't know where she is,' *Crow's Words* was saying. 'We could enquire, but . . .'

But they'd have to do so carefully, because they didn't know who was involved in whatever had happened.

Crow's Words froze, his avatar locked into place – the stars within their outline still slowly moving in a way that made Xích Si's eyes ache.

'There's someone . . .' he said. 'For you.'

And then he closed his eyes, and faded – his outline remaining there, visible if Xích Si focused.

It was *Mulberry Sea*. The ship appeared in the middle of the room, turning left and right as if she were banking within space – taking in everything with what looked like good-hearted curiosity.

Xích Si wasn't in the mood for any of that.

'What do you want?'

'Why, no welcome or honorifics?'

Mulberry Sea chuckled. It had an edge to it, something that suggested danger to Xích Si – a tone she'd heard from other scavengers, seconds before an innocuous-looking asteroid burst apart, or before debris punctured oxygen lines.

'What. Do. You. Want?'

Mulberry Sea was looking at Khanh – who had finished watching *Vermilion Moon* and clambered down, *Crow's Words*' filters lowering as she did.

'You're leaving, aren't you?'

Before Xích Si could answer, Khanh said, 'Mommy said it was no longer safe here.'

'Your mommy is right.' *Mulberry Sea*'s voice was grave. 'It's not safe here any more. I'm leaving, too.'

'Wait,' Xích Si said. 'You—'

'I know when to cut and run,' *Mulberry Sea* said. Her voice was emotionless.

The bots on Xích Si's hands tingled. 'So you're here to warn us. You think we don't know.'

'No,' *Mulberry Sea* said. 'I'm here to tell you that Kim Thông has taken the elite ships of the Green Banner, and left the Citadel.'

Xích Si stared at her, the small ship's avatar in the centre of that alien cabin, with the food hastily put together for her — small comforts on the edge of the oncoming storm.

'I don't see how that is my business.'

Mulberry Sea's voice was serene. 'You asked why I was here. As a friend.'

'To us?'

'Mmm. Not specifically.'

And not to *Crow's Words*.

'You know where *Rice Fish* is.'

'Not in detail,' *Mulberry Sea* said. 'And I know that Kim Thông planted a bomb on board, but that it didn't kill her.'

'You knew and didn't tell her?'

'I only found out after it exploded.' *Mulberry Sea*'s avatar was very still, towering over them all. 'But that's not the point. Kim Thông is going to try and kill her.'

'With ships from the Green Banner?'

It still made little sense.

A twist, in the air, like a quirking up of the lips.

'The censor's fleet will not kill *Rice Fish*, if they capture her.'

220

No. Of course not. She didn't like Kim Thông. She'd offer amnesty to *Rice Fish*, first. Not that the stubborn ship would listen to *that* offer, but the censor was still unlikely to execute her on the spot. She believed in justice. In fairness. There wasn't that much, really, that separated both of them — and wasn't that a sobering and scary thought?

'And Kim Thông wants her dead.'

'You saw it.'

'Because of the trial.'

'She humiliated Kim Thông in front of half the banners. There was only ever going to be one outcome of this.'

'And she just gathers the most deadly ships in the banner and leaves ...'

Xích Si opened her mouth, closed it. Of course Kim Thông would want those ships with her, just in case the censor double-crossed her the same way Kim Thông had double-crossed so many others. Of course she'd want to be away from the Citadel at a time when it was going to be invaded. And if she was caught, what did it matter? Kim Thông *owned* the council anyway.

'I don't see how any of that is my concern.'

'Is it not?' A dip, from *Mulberry Sea*'s prow.

Khanh was watching them both, eyes wide. 'Mommy ...'

She didn't know where *Rice Fish* was, exactly. But she was alone. She'd only taken Tiên and maybe a few bannerpeople, and that was it. She'd gone off somewhere — presumably to look at the invading fleet, to desperately get some evidence to the council, not understanding that the people she was trying to convince didn't care. They'd already chosen their sides. Picked lies to believe in. It was too late, and *Rice Fish* was alone, with a choice of being caught by treacherous pirates, or by the censor — and it said a lot that right now, the censor was her best option.

Mulberry Sea's smile was felt in the tightening of the air, in the upturning of her prow.

'You'll let her die, then.'

No, of course not. 'We *quarrelled*. We didn't swear eternal enmity. Of course I don't want her to die! But I don't have anything. I don't have anyone. You're asking me to go up against an invading fleet and half a banner! Unless—'

'You're asking me for help?' *Mulberry Sea*'s tone suggested her answer before she gave it. 'I would, if I could. But I don't have people within the Citadel.'

Then who?

'The Red Banner. *Crow's Words?*'

Crow's Words' outline shivered. 'The banner won't follow you.'

'Not even to rescue *her?*'

'Not into the jaws of an imperial invasion fleet. Or against their own siblings. *Rice Fish* could possibly have asked ...'

But she wasn't *Rice Fish*. And she didn't want to be. That was the whole point, wasn't it? That she just couldn't make the same decisions *Rice Fish* had – that she couldn't see the Citadel or the pirates the same way *Rice Fish* did.

She stared, for a while, at the carvings. At the bots on her fingers and in her hair – the gifts *Rice Fish* had made her on her wedding night. They felt impossibly light and inconsequential.

Xích Si had a pirate mindship, an ambassador with no troops, a child of six, and bots. It was nothing. Perhaps, if they found *Rice Fish* fast enough, if they could somehow avoid half a banner and the censor's fleet ...

No. That was daydreaming, and daydreaming had never got scavengers anywhere.

'I can't do anything!' she said. Again and again, she crashed on the same inescapable facts: she was nothing, and reaching out brought her nothing but failure. 'I just ...'

Breathe.

Breathe.

Slowly, carefully – gradually – putting it all together, getting it all under control. *In, out. In, out.*

Think.

Rice Fish *could have asked.*

You'll let her die, then.

We didn't swear eternal enmity. Of course I don't want her to die.

Of course.

She took a last, shaking breath – raised her hand, the bot on the back of it angling so it caught the light, dazzling like the heart of a star. There was a solution to this.

'Let's go,' she said, ignoring Khanh's startled gaze.

There was someone she needed to give a very stern talking-to.

Rice Fish woke up, and everything hurt. Space around her was a tessellation of stars and asteroids, distant and blurred and . . . no, not just distant – inaccessible. She could see them, but the familiar lull of their song and pressure was dampened, and . . .

It hurt. Everything hurt. *Ancestors.* Holes in her corridors, burst pipes, bots that wouldn't answer to her any more – she was in the heartroom and even that was covered in debris and she wasn't sure she could still breathe through the incessant ringing that filled her.

Tiên.

She couldn't hear, or feel, Tiên any more – not even as a weight on her floors.

'Child? Child!'

A few bots limped to life in the farthest reaches of her perception – she knew where they were but they felt so distant, so disconnected – and they slipped, time and time again, from her control. *Focus.* She needed to focus, but she hurt so much, and the air on board tasted of shrapnel and debris, cutting into her exposed surfaces.

Everything was sideways and wrong. Her leftmost rear motors were gone – the blast doors had fallen and her faltering sensors could no longer cover that section, but she still *felt* them as if they were still there, pressing against the cold of space. In the heartroom, butterfly bots were scattered on the floor, faintly thrashing, every one of their movements a pinpoint of pain. She tried to steady herself – to move – but it wasn't just the leftmost rear motors. No motor worked. She was drifting in the vacuum of space, the intricate interlocking gravity fields controlling her movements. Her oxygen levels looked fine, though lights flickered on and off, and the ambient holos were fading in and out – it took too much energy to maintain them and she could barely summon bots to do her bidding.

Rice Fish tried to speak, but the external comms were dead, too; just the ship-wide ones were left to her. She was mute. No way to signal Xích Si or anyone in the Citadel. She could send a distress signal ... no, these were gone, too, blasted away in the explosion. And even if she did, the most likely person to find her now was the censor and the imperial fleet.

'Child!'

Her voice echoed under the vastness of her body, and there was no answer – just the distant sound of more debris falling. Where was Tiên?

Ancestors, please let her be fine. Please please please. She didn't know if Huân was listening – if she was inclined to grant *Rice Fish* anything ... but. *Please please. Let her be fine. Let her be alive.*

Bomb. There'd been a bomb somewhere in the cargo holds. In the rear, where she'd lost everything. She was lucky to be alive. She ...

The bots found Tiên. She wasn't in her cabin, but she hadn't gone far — just out in the corridor, a forearm-length away from the blast door. *Rice Fish* could barely feel the weight of her through the haze of other signals, the ones she couldn't filter out, all the urgent ones about scored walls, gaping holes in ceilings, torn alcoves, fountains leaking oil and blood, and bots scattered and dying all over her.

Slowly, haltingly, she waited for the bots' data to come in. Tiên was breathing slowly, but deeply. She was unconscious, and bleeding, her vitals scattering all over the place. *Rice Fish* applied first aid as much as she could through the bots.

'Child,' she said, again. Tiên stirred, but didn't wake up. She wasn't likely to. *Rice Fish* wasn't even sure if she'd stabilised her enough to survive. 'Child.'

It was just the two of them in the middle of space — wounded and powerless, drifting between asteroids with no means to call for help or defend themselves.

Child.

How were they ever going to get out of this?

18

Banner

Xích Si found Hổ in his quarters in the Citadel – not aboard a mindship, but in a wide airy room, the window of which opened on the overlay of the Fire Palace. He sat in the centre of a wide circle of carved stone, surrounded by his bots, inhaling a cup of tea from a cracked celadon cup – looking more like a gentleman-scholar from the First Planet than a pirate – though the window of the room revealed the ruined mass of the Fire Palace, the carvings and the metallic walls behind him were more reminiscent of a ship's streamlined cabin, and he carried an overlay sword on his back.

He didn't rise when she and *Mulberry Sea* came in, followed by a posse of guards, but his gaze turned jewel-hard, the tigers on his robes slowly uncurling, the bots encircling his wrists slowly unfolding.

'You're here physically.'

Mulberry Sea, of course, wasn't. Xích Si glared at him. Her adrenaline was still high – the moment it wore off, she was going to remember what terrible threads of terrible ideas had got her there.

'So you don't cut this conversation short.'

'I still can.' He smiled, gesturing at the guards behind him. Ghostly ships spun around the metal flame ornament of his topknot. 'Just have you dragged away. And really, walking into enemy territory?'

'You tell me.' Xích Si glared at him. *No more being scared of him. No more tiptoeing around a brattish pirate boy.* 'Where is *Rice Fish*?'

'How should I know?'

It was *Mulberry Sea* who spoke.

'She's alone and wounded. And Kim Thông has gone after her. Ahead of an An O invasion fleet.'

Hồ stared at them both. He rose, finally — the tigers on his robes fanning out their tails as if they were foxes, beguiling predators, all deadly grace and coiled power — and behind him was the shadow of something larger, dark and cold, something meant to scare Xích Si and make her back down.

'I fail to see why I should care.'

'About the fleet?'

A shrug. 'We're safe here. But you're not talking about the fleet.'

'I'm talking about your mother!'

'You misunderstand the nature of our relationship.'

'I don't.' Behind Xích Si there was a skittering of bots, a tensing of the guards. She had a few heartbeats, maybe fewer than that, before she lost his attention. 'You fought. Fine. You can't stand each other. Fine. You got her thrown out of the council. Fine.'

His gaze was piercing. '*Rice Fish* is no longer a council member, or kin of mine. And you ... you're not her. You're nothing. Don't presume to lecture me. You've made your point. Now leave. You're lucky I'm letting you.'

The guards grabbed Xích Si, pulled her away. Hồ was turning to look at his tea.

227

'So you're just going to abandon her? Because you think she could have had a different relationship with Huân——'

'Enough.' Hồ made a gesture, and *Mulberry Sea*'s avatar winked out. 'If you're so willing to put yourself in danger, I'm happy to oblige you.'

The guards threw Xích Si on the floor, bots coming to pin her down – and then leaving the room. It was just her and Hồ.

'So.' Hồ stalked closer to her, kneeling by her side. 'Let's talk.'

This close, he towered over her, and his glare could have peeled metal off the wall. She struggled against the bots – they'd linked together to pin her to the floor – like being back in the cell where *Rice Fish* had found her, knowing she was powerless to stop any of the pirates ...

No. That wasn't true. It had perhaps never been true. She was alone, but she wasn't powerless.

'She's your mother.' Xích Si had to crane her neck to look at him, her wrists being pinned down.

'An irrelevant fact. As you point out, I got her thrown out of the council.'

Every moment that passed, every blink she spent arguing with him, was one more moment in which Kim Thông got closer to *Rice Fish*.

'You got her thrown out, but you didn't set her up to be killed.'

'Didn't I?' Hồ hadn't moved. She could only see pieces of him – tiger holos, bots on his knees, the shadows of swords. She struggled, again, but the bots wouldn't move. 'I know what happens to powerless pirates.'

'She's wounded and alone, and you know Kim Thông is going to kill her.'

'Alone. And whose fault is that?' Hồ snapped.

'What ...?'

228

Hồ's smile was all pointed teeth.

'Are you blaming *me*?'

'Am I?' he asked.

The bots released her. She sat up, her own bots — her wedding gift — climbing up her fingers.

Hồ hadn't moved — he was close, too close.

'I'm told you quarrelled.'

Xích Si opened her mouth to say it was none of his business, then stopped. She couldn't have it both ways.

'Yes,' she said. 'We did.'

'And she ran.'

'You threw her out of the council and she ran.'

'You know that's not how it went.' Hồ didn't move. Xích Si dared not move. 'She went to you, for comfort. Isn't that what wives are supposed to provide?'

Comfort. She remembered the fight. Remembered words turning to sharp ice in her mouth. The taste of blood. Being told she wasn't enough.

'I gave her the truth,' she said. And it was the truth, wasn't it, that they had no future. Why did it pain her so much? It wasn't even as though she'd lost something of value.

Hồ laughed. 'You poor scavenger. You can't even save your relationship.'

It was her fault. For dreaming big. For daring to think that she could have more than a scavenger's life. That *Khanh* could have more than a scavenger's life. All that held-out hands got were broken fingers.

Go see the censor, then, if you think so much of her chances. Child.

She remembered *Rice Fish*'s anger. Remembered the trial, and the scavenger Ái Nhân — remembered *Rice Fish* standing up for her, because it was the right thing to do, and the confused and complex feelings she'd had when watching the scene.

She remembered the fear she'd felt, when *Rice Fish* vanished from comms. Remembered the burning rage she'd entered the room with – before Hồ knocked her off course, before he threatened her.

You poor scavenger.

He saw her as someone who could be cowed into silence.

I'm a scavenger.

And *Rice Fish*'s voice, as sharp as a vacuum blade: *No. You're a pirate.*

She found the strength to rise, her bots rising with her, clinging to her robes.

'She disappointed you. She hurt you. You're not the only one. But that doesn't entitle you to hurt others.'

'You're not my mother.'

He hadn't moved; still sounded amused.

'No, I'm not. But have you considered what will happen if she dies? Or worse, if she gets offered amnesty by the censor and turns on you?'

Silence. Hồ's face hardened.

'She would never turn. She's obsessed with this place. With a memory of what it never was.'

'What's wrong with having ideals?' The words leaped into her mouth before she could stop them. Of all the things she'd thought she'd never do, defending *Rice Fish*'s ideals was one of them. 'You think pirates should be able to take what they want with no consequences?'

'No.' He sounded amused again, but beneath it all she could sense the exhaustion: this was an argument he'd had too many times. 'We're not a state, and never will be. We're pillagers. Let's be honest about who we are and what we do.'

'These things can change.'

'That's what *she* thought.'

There was no question who *she* was.

230

'And you admired her for it, didn't you?'

'I *hated* her for it. Both of them.' Hồ was still where he'd been, kneeling by a space Xích Si wasn't occupying any more. Staring at things she couldn't see. 'Everything came second to their dreams. Even their own happiness.'

Even their child's happiness.

She said, finally, 'You sound so miserable. I'm sorry they did that to you.'

'Don't pity me.'

'I don't. I told *Rice Fish* ...' She took a deep, shaking breath, wondering if she had the guts to say it – not just aloud, but to someone who was her enemy. 'That she couldn't do that to me, either. Or to herself.'

A silence. He was watching her, but his bots had relaxed a fraction.

'What do you intend to do about the invasion fleet?'

'The censor? No one has ever taken the Citadel. She won't be able to get past the asteroids. We're well defended.'

'She has Kim Thông.'

'Kim Thông would never ...' He stopped.

'You trust her that much? Is that why she's taken the elite ships of the Green Banner and gone off on some business of her own? Was the invasion part of your plans?'

Another silence.

'No,' he said, finally. 'I assumed it was because we'd riled them up.'

Because of the pillaging. Because of the depredations.

'I talked to the censor,' Xích Si said. 'She knows *someone* will betray the Citadel. She's confident Kim Thông will sell you out.'

'And you believed her?'

'Yes.'

Now Hồ rose. The tigers had gone back to sleep on his robes,

231

the Fire Palace slowly fading out in overlay – setting until the landscape below them became awash with ember-light.

'Kim Thông believes in us. In what we're doing. In the purity of what we are. Pirates. Pillagers. Thieves.'

Xích Si said nothing, because he was trying so very hard to convince himself, and failing.

'She would never ...' He stopped again. 'You don't care about the Citadel.'

'No.'

'No. You want to rescue *Rice Fish*.' Another silence. 'Even after everything she's done to you. After she's broken your relationship past fixing. After you know that it will never work out, and she can't love in the way you love her.'

That one *hurt*.

'Yes.'

'Why?'

Why?

Xích Si said, finally, simply, 'I go with my wife.'

Hổ said nothing. He picked up the discarded teacup, stared at it; it changed in overlay, the celadon cracks starting to shine with the same light as the Fire Palace.

'Your wife.' A pause, as he set the cup on the windowsill – it wavered and became three cups, like three bearers of blessings. 'I can't take the risk of us getting hemmed in here. If they overwhelm the sentinels, we can't defend ourselves while stuck in a dead end. I'll notify the council, call up the Purple Banner and we'll head for the pass. And if we happen to collect my mother on the way there ... well, I won't protest.'

'Thank you.'

An amused laugh. 'Don't thank me yet. You're coming with us.'

*

Rice Fish fixed her comms.

It was slow and laborious. Bots would flicker in and out – sometimes clattering inert to the floor mid-repairs, their awareness winking out, taking out bits and pieces of her consciousness as they did so, like lanterns flickering. It was ... beyond jarring. Jarring would have meant hope for help. She didn't hold out much hope any more.

Tiên was still breathing. Her temperature had stabilised. *Rice Fish* could feel her weight on her floors, the uncanny stillness, with only her breathing separating her from the still-warm debris of the explosion. She wasn't conscious, and some of the warmth, drying now, was her blood. *Rice Fish* just didn't have enough bots to clean it, or to clear the rubble-filled corridors.

There.

Something flickered to life, deep in the lower corridors. A low-pitched whine that resolved into voices as frequencies were scanned: the familiar chatter of ships, fading into the wavelengths that couldn't be heard by human ears; the pulses of stars; the solar wind; the secret songs of dark matter.

Finally. She forced herself to relax; her doors sat a little more easily in their frames, the walls sagged a little more.

Life support was limited, and running out. The bots rummaging in the depths of her systems were just coming up with fried components – while others desperately, futilely, tried to repair her propulsion units. She got the bots to put Tiên in a shadow-skin to withstand the vacuum – holding her breath the entire time. Wounded people weren't supposed to be moved, but she had to do something to protect her. When they were done, Tiên didn't seem any worse. She was still bleeding, and her vitals were degrading. Not much time. She needed to fix her propulsion and find a way to get them both to hospital.

If she couldn't ...

She didn't even want to think about it. It was bad enough

to be drifting, alone in the dark, with Tiên bleeding out – to not have any control over where gravity was taking her – but if she couldn't fix her own emitters ...

An O chatter on the comms, all encrypted. The censor's fleet was moving cautiously, sweeping the asteroids as they went for any sign of hidden pirates. So far, no sign they'd seen her – that vast array of open-the-voids and troop-carriers was steadily moving away. Not that she could be sure, because her sensors were flickering unreliably, but surely she'd see a bunch of ships getting closer to her own position ...

Wait.

There were such ships, but they weren't the censor's.

Still no chatter on her comms, but they were *pirates*. She was saved. Tiên was saved.

Rice Fish opened a comms channel to hail them.

She stopped. The council had thrown her out. It was sharks and orcas out there, and in the atmosphere that Kim Thông had created, there was so little space for comradeship.

The absurd, breath-stilling thought came to her that it was Xích Si – that her wife was coming for her – but no. Xích Si would never have the resources for this, or be prepared to think this large. Of course she would not come back for *Rice Fish*. She didn't care for *Rice Fish* that much. No one did, because she didn't deserve it.

Green Banner.

Those ships were Kim Thông's Green Banner. They were sweeping behind the fleet. They were being careful – hiding, trying not to reveal their position to the censor's fleet. Which meant they didn't trust them. Not a surprise. Kim Thông wouldn't trust anyone.

But they were also, quite unmistakably, looking for something, and she had the feeling that something was her.

Rice Fish could hide. Weather the damage, and wait for a

rescue the chances of which seemed to be dwindling further and further away in likelihood. But if she did so, she wouldn't get what she needed to survive: information.

She opened a different channel – one that wouldn't give away her position.

'Identify yourselves,' she said, quietly and with all the steel she'd brought to ships' boardings and council meetings.

A silence. What felt like a panicked scramble, and then a voice she had entirely expected.

'Child.' Kim Thông wore jade-coloured robes, with a scattering of iridescent scales on her face. The bots on her shoulders and the back of her hands were pure business, sleek and sharp with no concession to aesthetics – clearly weapons through and through. Her topknot was slightly disarrayed – the steel pins askew, a few strands of her grey-streaked hair poking out. 'What a pleasant surprise.'

'Are you with your ships? That's an out-of-the-way place to be.'

'You know why I'm here.'

Mulberry Sea had been correct – and so had *Rice Fish*. The hatred in Kim Thông's voice was unmistakable.

'Running away from your own invasion ships?'

'Taking care of loose ends.'

Rice Fish had humiliated Kim Thông, if only for a moment, in front of the entire pirate tribunal, and then tried a second time in front of the council. That it hadn't worked was irrelevant to people like her. It was the trying that mattered – the refusal to be quiet. The insubordination.

'I see. Like Huân.'

Might as well have it out in the open.

'You've been significantly more annoying than your wife.'

'Which one?'

Rice Fish thought of Xích Si. But surely she would have

235

kept her head down – what she was best at, no matter how inappropriate it might be.

'Jesting? The time is ill chosen.'

Rice Fish was immobile, with an unconscious friend on her floors, and faltering comms – and with no one of her former banner likely to come and help her. Not in the face of an on-coming invasion force and the Green Banner.

'I should have known,' she said. 'You're not going to be here, are you, when those ships hit the Citadel?' *Mulberry Sea* had warned her, but she hadn't listened. Kim Thông wasn't doing this for power. 'You're selling us out. Our deaths in exchange for your redemption.'

Something passed across Kim Thông's face – a darkness twisting it utterly out of shape.

'You're all the same. You, Huân, your belief that the Citadel should be safeguarded at any cost.'

How dare she? Years of building, of sacrifices – how dare she throw it away? A wave of anger rose through *Rice Fish*, tainting everything red. Doors creaked as her entire body clenched.

'Don't cheapen our work.'

Kim Thông laughed. 'Cheapen you? I'm tired, child. Of this life on the edge, this perpetual and perpetually disappointed hope that we don't get caught and summarily executed by An O. You promised us safe places, but the Citadel is just somewhere to bury our heads in the sand. Pirates don't grow old. We're not meant to.' There was venom in her voice now. Disappointment.

Rice Fish heard Xích Si's voice in her head.

You're obsessed with that place, but it's been dead for a long time.

She heard Hổ, speaking of a golden age, of what it had meant to go on adventures. The Citadel was a safe place. *That* was what she had built. The only thing that made sense, that

236

had been worth giving up so much for. But what if it wasn't? What if they were right?

'It's safer here than in Triệu Hoà Port, and you know it.'

Laughter from Kim Thông. It had an edge.

'Is it? I'll take my amnesty and my chances. And in the meantime . . . you'll burn. All of you. If I can't have the Citadel, neither can you.'

Empress of the ruins, except she didn't even think the ruins were worth salvaging. It hurt. *Li'l sis*, *Rice Fish* thought, but Huân was dead – and she realised, with a feeling like ice freezing her heartroom, that she would to be dead, too, soon.

'Do they know? Your crew.'

It was too much to hope that anyone else was watching this – anyone not already loyal to Kim Thông.

'Those who need to.' Kim Thông smiled, and it didn't reach her eyes. 'As I said – I have a few loose ends to tidy up. Enough to merit my personal attention.'

She wanted to be there. She wanted to be the one who killed *Rice Fish*. She wanted her to suffer.

Rice Fish wasn't going to give her any of those satisfactions . . . although she wasn't in much of a position to deny Kim Thông anything.

'You'll not find it easy.'

Kim Thông smiled. 'I don't know where you are, child. Not yet.'

And she cut the comms.

In *Rice Fish*'s faltering sight, three ships peeled away from the Green Banner – small open-the-voids. Like Kim Thông's bots, they were sleek and sharp, weapons built for only one purpose.

Rice Fish gritted her teeth, and focused again on her bots, and on the slow and hopeless repairs. She needed to be able to move, or to speak, or both. And she needed that *fast* – before those ships found her.

Because it was only a matter of time before they did, and when they did she was a stationary, utterly defenceless target.

As they emerged from the labyrinth of rocks that protected the Citadel, Hồ called Xích Si to his cabin.

He didn't so much call her as move her, abruptly – one moment she was in a cabin in his flagship, and the next she was standing in an unfamiliar space, staring at a sea of stars beneath her feet, with Hồ watching her from a raised dais.

'What do you think?' he asked, without preamble.

Xích Si missed *Crow's Words* – he'd tagged along with the Purple Banner, but Hồ had insisted Xích Si come aboard his flagship, an obvious way of making sure she wouldn't vanish in the middle of the expedition. She'd left Khanh with Tấm and Cám, ignoring the child's protestations that she didn't need to be babied, and *Mulberry Sea* had gone wherever it was that fleeing ambassadors went.

Around Hồ was a crowd that she couldn't quite make out: all blurred faces and silhouettes, a reminder that she didn't have elevated access. But then, she hadn't expected it. And in the centre of the room was an overlay showing the asteroid field, with small dots marking every ship.

'Where is she?' she asked.

'*Rice Fish*?' Hồ smiled, and it was ... both predatory and almost disappointed. *Demons take him,* she didn't need the judgement of his kind. He gestured, and something lit up at the back of the mass of ships. *Ancestors.* There were so many of them, scattered throughout the field, so many, and most of them didn't look like they belonged to the Purple Banner. 'I think she's around there somewhere. There are three Green Banner ships combing through those asteroids, looking for something.'

238

'Somewhere?' Xích Si's heart stuttered in her chest.

A shrug. 'Hiding. I can't find a signature, but that probably means she's cloaked.'

Which would not protect her for long against the Green Banner ships.

Hồ gestured, and a single person detached themselves from the crowd. A mindship – her avatar was small and sleek. 'This is *Hidden within the Persimmon*. She's volunteered. She knew my mother.' He sounded ... disappointed again. 'And you have *Crow's Words*.'

'I don't understand.'

'You wanted to rescue my mother. You can go.'

'You'll just let me?'

Hồ's face was hard. 'I don't *need* you.'

'Funny how you went to all this trouble bringing me on board, then.'

It was unwise. She wasn't sure when in the past few months she'd gone from being terrified of pirates to arguing with the head of a banner on his own ship.

'I just wanted to be sure of where you were.' He was looking at the fleet scattered between the asteroids. 'This is going to be delicate enough without having a loose element in the middle of the operation.'

There was something in his tone. Xích Si looked, again, at the ships on the overlay – blurred points of movement. The Purple Banner had positioned itself out of scanning range of both the censor and the Green Banner ships. They were pirates, of course; they wouldn't want a head-on fight. But ...

She thought, again, of the battles she'd taken apart to get at the truth – the Red Scholar's last few. Her last stand.

'You're outnumbered,' she said.

'Hardly.'

'Outgunned, then. Those are open-the-voids, aren't they?

And I see a couple of hail-wreckers, too.' Those were massive ships, and she'd only ever seen them in dramas or in vids, certainly not in the Twin Streams or in the pirate fleet. 'Not to mention you don't know if you can rely on the Green Banner ships.'

He didn't move. 'I can take the Green Banner ships.'

But not the fleet. Certainly not both. He didn't need to say any of it out loud.

None of that should have concerned her. *Take his offer and leave. Take the easy way. The scavengers' way. Focus on what she could control: on evading those Green Banner ships and getting to Rice Fish.* She knew how to do that. She knew how to survive — she'd run in the escape pod and left Ngà behind, and their dreams with her. *Think small. Think doable. Do not involve herself in the affairs of the powerful. Do not reach out.*

In her thoughts, she could hear *Rice Fish*'s voice, excoriating her. *You're a pirate. You married one. You chose to marry one.*

And Hổ's voice, sarcastic and tearing away at all her defences. *You want to rescue her. After everything she's done to you. Why?*

I go with my wife.

She thought how much it had hurt, when Hổ had said *Rice Fish* would never love her back. She'd told herself she was rescuing *Rice Fish* out of duty, to repay some debt, but that wasn't it, was it? She thought of *Rice Fish*, drifting alone in the dark — of the Green Banner going after her. She thought of what would happen if she rescued her wife and let the censor's fleet lay waste to the society she and Huân had built.

I love you.

She didn't think she'd even ever said the words.

If she left, *Rice Fish* would never forgive her — but nor would *Rice Fish* ever forgive herself. She'd be a hollowed-out ghost of herself, just as adrift as she was now, emptied out by grief.

240

It's high time you accepted that you have responsibilities. That you can change things. That you must change things.

Xích Si said, finally, 'I can tell you which ship the censor is on.'

That got Hổ's attention. His head came up sharply, the tigers on his robes flowing out, becoming ghostly beasts prowling on the floor amid the overlay of stars, their claws swiping through small models of ships and asteroids.

'Why would you help us?'

Xích Si said nothing.

Hổ snorted. 'You really think taking the censor out will change anything?' Pity. Anger. Bitterness in his tone.

'For you, or for the Citadel?' Xích Si said.

This time, he was the one who was silent.

Xích Si said, 'Take her hostage, and the fleet will leave.' The censor's righteousness would not have made her many friends – but she was still an envoy of the An O emperor. They would not risk losing her. 'Take her hostage, and negotiate.'

'What's your price?'

'You know my price.' She faced him, with no fear – all of her fears were for a wounded ship adrift in space, for a child in a citadel under threat of invasion. 'I want *Rice Fish* reinstated on the council. I want her back at the negotiating table, at the head of the Red Banner.'

'That's not my decision to make.'

'With Kim Thông gone, you know you and your mother will be the poles around which pirate society turns.'

She didn't know if Kim Thông would be gone, but she acted as if she were certain.

'And for you?'

A wave of panic. She didn't know. She didn't have a plan. It didn't matter. She was going to save everything she could, and then leave. Run away as she'd always planned to.

'Hmmm.' He watched her, for a while. 'On one condition.'

She waited. His ghostly tigers prowled in the space between asteroids.

'You're coming with us to get the censor.'

Of course. He'd offered her ships for a rescue mission, but of course he wouldn't trust her. He needed her to be intimately tied to the mission's success. She'd known that, on some level, when she offered.

'*Rice Fish*—'

'*Persimmon* and *Crow's Words* can go and look for my mother.' It was an order couched in barely polite terms. He was angry. 'So?'

She'd already made her choice.

'Yes,' she said, and closed her eyes, because she wasn't sure if saving *Rice Fish*'s world – the dark, flawed, frustrating construct that only seemed to exist in her thoughts and dreams and memories – was worth any of these risks.

19

Imperilled

On board a smaller shuttle, Xích Si closed her eyes. She accessed her comms archive — the bots on her hands went still as she accessed the data stored in them — and dug up her last conversation with the censor.

She tried not to *remember* it — tried not to remember the sick fear in her belly or the shaking — going straight from the conversation into her fight with *Rice Fish*, and everything that had transpired since. She could do this. She could ignore Hồ — who was sitting next to her on the bench, far too close for comfort — and the other forty or so scowling pirates who were part of the strike force.

She dug up the address the censor had last hailed her from — not a ship's address, but a personal one — and pinged it, once, twice. Listening for the return echo and the way it moved and was distorted by its own momentum, the slight shift of frequencies that betrayed its speed. The transmission had been encrypted, and too far away to untangle. But now they were close to the fleet.

She was in an open-the-void. On a vector aiming slightly from them, a little sideways — *not this one, not this one. That one.*

'Here,' she said, and pointed to a ship that was slightly off-centre within the formation.

Hổ's grin was wolfish.

'Let's cut it out,' he said.

In the overlay, five Purple Banner three-plates veered away towards the fleet, engaging the outer layers. And then another three — a series of feints that grew more and more confusing, a random dance that had all the imperial ships switching off their long-haul drives, trying to change their momentum fast enough to meet the three-plates. They were hunks of metal, as she'd said to *Rice Fish* once — not fast enough, not armoured enough — but enough of them together could be a nuisance.

'A temptation,' Hổ said. 'They think they can take us. We'll use the gap in their defences to sneak in, and then we're on a clock to reach the censor before those ships can turn around to face us again.'

His voice was matter-of-fact. Of course, he must have done this dozens of times. Whereas Xích Si ... she'd been on the other end of this, once. One moment her ship had been fine, and the next pirates seemed to be everywhere — and Ngà had pushed her towards the escape pods and she'd run, and only seen afterwards that she was alone. One moment she was on her way out of scavenging, and the next she was drifting in space.

And now she was on the pirate ship. *With* the pirates.

Xích Si nodded, not trusting her voice.

Hổ's expression was serious. 'Suit up,' he said, to everyone. He handed her a shadow-skin. 'You as well.'

Xích Si stared at it. Shadow-skins protected against the vacuum of space. She was habitat-bound; a simple shadow-suit like this, without a glider or any other mode of propulsion, was for emergency, in cases of breach causing loss of oxygen.

'Why?'

The prospect of being adrift in the dark, even with something to make sure she could breathe, was utterly terrifying.

'It's necessary. For protection.' Hồ's voice was curt. He gestured to one of the women, a hard-faced older one who nodded back at him, minimally bowing to Hồ. 'This is Hạnh. She'll watch over you.'

And make sure she didn't run away. She wasn't sure how to feel about that. Xích Si slipped into the shadow-skin, feeling the slickness of it over her skin. They were making sure she'd survive, in their own way. But she still felt alone and adrift in hostile circumstances.

'And one last thing.' Hồ handed her a gun, watched her slip it into her sleeve. 'When we go in, stay with Hạnh. I'm not explaining how we lost you to my mother.'

If they found his mother. If they succeeded in taking the censor hostage. If if if.

It all ran in circles in her head. If only she could hail *Crow's Words* – but Hồ's ship was running dark, because there was no way under Heaven they were going to broadcast their approach to a fleet they were trying to avoid and a ship they were hoping to board.

Hồ was watching the overlay in the centre of the shuttle. Xích Si saw it, suddenly: the way the An O ships were moving faster, burning all their spare orbital fuel for fast changes in direction, a gap slowly opening around the censor's ship. A tiny one, but soon – with inertia and gravity – it would leave them just enough room. They didn't need to win a battle; they just needed to sneak in and get the censor.

'Now!' Hồ said.

Their ship moved – the centre of the overlay moving with it. It was smooth and sleek, pure orbital fuel being burned much faster than the An O ships, weaving its way on some odd trajectory ... Blind spots: it was using the larger ship's blind

245

spots, weaving its way between shots fired from the turrets. *Ancestors, please please. Please keep us safe.* Xích Si's heart was in her throat, beating madly through her vocal cords until her voice shook with its rhythm.

A jolt as the ship attached itself to the larger ship's hull, somewhere near the engines. The temperature was going up – faster and faster – this was why Hồ had insisted everyone wore shadow-skins, not because they were going to end up in the vacuum of space. Because they were thermal insulators. *Of course.* The ship's turrets wouldn't fire on their own engines, and there was no need to, because the temperature was so high anyone who neared them would be burned to a crisp. The air felt on fire around her. The shuttle's insides hadn't even changed – no metal buckling or melting, or visible distortion. It had to be made of something highly resistant to heat.

A clunk of metal on hard floors, and a hole opening in the side of the shuttle – human-sized, and then dilating larger and larger, like a door being created out of nothingness.

'Adjusting pressure seal,' one of the pirates said. 'In twelve, eleven ...'

Hồ said, to Xích Si, 'This is going to be very fast, confusing and lethal. Remember what I said – stick with Hạnh.'

'... three, two, one.'

The pirates rose, went through the door. Outside, the sound of running feet, then someone screamed, and the sounds of fighting started. Hạnh, Xích Si's escort, pulled her towards the door, and they climbed out into a mass of confused movement and smoke. There was a body by the door, clothes already crinkling in the heat – Xích Si almost stumbled on it, except that Hạnh pulled her upright.

'Keep moving,' Hạnh said. 'Let's not overstay our welcome.'

Corridors, and gangways. Glimpses of a ship that was too large, that was too confusing – vids and holos and pathways

246

wending between huge machines. The heat, dropping, almost bearable now. Bodies, scattered in the pirates' wake, blood pooling on uniforms and rank insignia. They weren't fighting so much as running – forward, always forward – while around them the ships' systems screamed a piercing alarm, calling all crewmen to repel the invasion.

The public overlays flickered in and out of existence, so one moment Xích Si was running through a forest of stone pillars, and the next between passengers' cabins – one moment a bridge over the void of a black hole, the next a simple gangway in a small hangar – and it was even more disorientating as none of the associated sensation filters seemed to have any effect, so the size of the room never changed and nor did her depth perception. But she didn't know where she was any more.

When they finally stopped – Xích Si, exhausted, breathed unexpectedly cool air into her stinging lungs – they were in front of a set of doors shaped like an âm dương double-teardrop. Dead bots littered the floor – and dead pirates, and dead crewmen.

'Wait,' Hạnh said.

She raised a hand. There was a sound like a sigh, and Hạnh crumpled, mouth open and blood pooling on the front of her robes, her bots falling to the floor in a crunch of metal.

Dead.

How ...?

The corridor was devoid of life – only scattered bodies, dead bots. Maybe one of those?

Wait.

There was one blood-soaked bot on the frame of the door. It turned towards Xích Si and started *glowing*. Xích Si threw herself on the floor. Another of those sighing sounds – she got up, shaking, still alive, and started running, just as a shot rang out, the bot falling like a piece of dislodged foil. In front of the bot, against the wall facing the door, was one of the pirates, grinning at her.

Xích Si nodded at them, ran towards the doors, and dived through them.

She recognised the large room on the other side, as one would recognise a familiar nightmare. An overlay of a scholar's study, the windows opening on a garden with a pavilion – the same room from which the censor had commed her, back in that other lifetime before she'd lost *Rice Fish* and her refuge all at once.

There were five dead pirates on the floor – the overlay covered them in translucent parquet slats, and virtual birds hopped on their corpses. Hổ was there, too, his gun in one hand, unerringly trained towards the furthest corner of the room, robes flowing in some invisible wind.

And in front of him ...

Censor Trúc. She held herself ramrod-straight, her topknot impeccable, and the overlay, flickering, covered the blood on her robes. She was also holding a gun – and it was pointed towards her own throat. Her gaze flicked to Xích Si, held it for a few blinks – which Xích Si felt resonate all the way into her ribs and her throat.

'Ah. Child. In retrospect, I shouldn't be surprised to see you here.'

Behind Xích Si, a sound: the pirate who'd saved her, moving to block the doors.

Censor Trúc said, quite levelly, 'We seem to be at an impasse.'

Hổ said, 'I told you. Call off your troops.'

A raised eyebrow. 'And I told you. You mistake me.'

The dragon-bots on her shoulders and on her hands were very still – but she was shaking.

Oh.

248

She was very much like *Rice Fish*, wasn't she? An ideal-ist. She did what she did not for power, not for greed, not for money, but because she believed in it. And this, in turn, meant that faced with a choice between yielding and life, she would never, ever yield.

'You can't,' Xích Si said.

Another raised eyebrow. 'The Dragon Throne will appoint another censor. I'm hardly irreplaceable.'

'Do you care so very little about your life?' Hổ said.

A laugh. 'I care very much. Which is why I won't sully it by dealing with pirates.'

'You dealt with Kim Thông,' Xích Si said, more sharply than she meant.

Sharper laughter from the censor. 'As a means to an end. One pirate to destroy all of them.' Her gaze was raking Xích Si. 'But you've chosen to sit with them, haven't you?'

'She married them.' Hổ's voice was curt. His aim on Censor Trúc didn't waver. 'Well, one of them.'

The censor's hand raked the room – the bodies, the overlay, the bots.

'And you think *that's* an acceptable cost. That's all you do. That's all you deal in.'

Hổ said, 'We're not an easy target any more. Moving against us worked while Kim Thông was distracting us, but you're now facing a pirate banner, and you've cornered us. You'll find this fight costly.'

A banging against something – a sharp crack of metal – a barrage of sighing noises. Xích Si, startled, looked back for a mere blink, just as the pirate at the doors folded under the onslaught of an entire swarm of those small, glowing bots.

What? No!

When she turned back, Censor Trúc had already moved – in that mere blink when she and Hổ were both distracted. The shot, as it went through his shoulder, made no noise — Hổ didn't, either, his mouth open, falling backwards, landing with a thunk, his eyes closing and not opening again, blood pooling under him. *No time*. With a coldness she hadn't known she possessed, Xích Si reached her gun and levelled it at Censor Trúc, her bots steadying her aim. Wordless, shaking.

Censor Trúc looked at her. She was a forearm away from Xích Si. Her own gun was back at her throat, gleaming in the darkness.

Behind her — where Xích Si couldn't see them — was the swarm of bots. She could hear them — a faint, high-pitched sound of servomotors held taut. And — through her own bots, a jumble of sensory input, including Hổ's fast breath. He wasn't dead. Was she relieved about that?

'You're wondering how fast I can shoot,' Xích Si said. 'Your bots have a slower reaction time than mine. I'll get to the trigger before you do.'

She didn't have many choices left, now. It was all sheer desperation — a bad idea turning into a worse one. Just her and the censor in the middle of an invasion fleet, in the middle of an imperial ship.

Censor Trúc looked at her, cocking her head.

'It's a terrible bluff.'

'I'm sorry?'

'You distracted the other ships, but they'll be turning around now. You have perhaps one centiday before they blast us out of the sky.' Her mouth quirked up. 'Though I'll grant you, most of the people on this ship are already dead.'

'You expect me to feel sorry for your soldiers? They knew what they were getting into.'

'As merchants do?' The censor's voice was sharp. '*You* know what you're getting into, don't you?'

Xích Si tightened her grip on the gun.

250

'You want to die.'

A shrug, from the censor. 'You don't. And yet . . .' She spread her hands. 'Quite honestly, I'm not seeing other outcomes.'

'Not even trying to talk me into betraying the Citadel?'

A sharp look. 'Would you? I had the feeling that question had been asked and answered already. Love does funny things, doesn't it?'

'Don't call me funny.'

She barely knew what she was doing. She was alone in some kind of weird stand-off surrounded by only dead or wounded pirates, and she wasn't even sure why. No, she knew — because she loved *Rice Fish*. Because it mattered. Because . . .

She didn't know if *Rice Fish* was alive or not. She pinged *Crow's Words*, because she could, and because silence wouldn't help her any more.

'We're not doing great,' *Crow's Words* said.

'How so?'

A sound she couldn't identify on comms.

'The Green Banner is . . . ah . . . hindering us.'

Fighting them. Which didn't sound good. But also meant that they hadn't found *Rice Fish*. They had to know that a Red Banner mindship and a Purple Banner one could only have one purpose. But if they were attacking them, they hadn't found *Rice Fish* either. She was still giving them the slip.

There was still hope. Something so complex, so fragile to hang on to — a lifeline in the vacuum.

'Do what you can, ' she said to *Crow's Words*, and cut the connection.

Xích Si's bots glinted on her hands: the bots that *Rice Fish* had given her, once upon a time in what felt like a far away land. She thought of what *Rice Fish* would say — some kind of impassioned speech that would turn things around, like she'd done in the tribunal? Xích Si had never been that kind of talker.

But Censor Trúc was like *Rice Fish*, wasn't she? An idealist. A believer. And like Xích Si herself – she'd understood why Xích Si had had to go back for Khanh. And Xích Si knew some of the words that would mean something to Trúc. She said – shaking, exhausted, nothing left in her but the core of who she was, 'You know what's going on in Triệu Hoà Port. You know it's just as bad as what we're doing. You know it's about strength and power and greed. You want to end all that, as much as we do.'

Censor Trúc had gone curiously still, her gaze unerringly fixed on Xích Si.

'Yes.'

'You *trust* them to change?'

'Of course.'

'Then why not us?'

'You? *You?*' Censor Trúc's free hand swept through the carnage on her doorstep. 'You, who make a living pillaging ships?'

Xích Si's hand on the gun hardened, her bots clenching around her fingers.

'You, who think it's legal to sell children into indenture?'

Censor Trúc recoiled as if she'd been physically or virtually hit. That disturbingly piercing gaze – the bots lifting their heads to look at her, magnifying it all ten-thousand-fold.

'Touché.'

Xích Si said, slowly, haltingly, 'Pirates can become enforcers. Escorts. Bodyguards.'

As they should have been to the scavenger Ái Nhân.

Hổ would never stand for this, but Hổ was wounded and perhaps dying on the floor, and now it was just Xích Si and Censor Trúc negotiating. And *Rice Fish*.

252

Silence.

'The depredation will end. The pillaging will end. We'll make sure ships go in and out of the Fire Palace without damage – to the Numbered Planets and the rest of the empire.'

And this would end the taking of prisoners and the indenturing of captives the society ran on. People would join them willingly, not because they had no other choice. She was feeling giddy, as if she'd drunk too much rice wine at a party – and yet this felt right. Much like going to retrieve Khanh had. Inescapably, irretrievably right, words that grounded and rooted her like a banyan tree on the moon.

Censor Trúc hadn't moved.

'You're an idealist. What are your idealistic pirates going to defend against?'

Xích Si laughed, bitterly, thinking of Hồ and the Purple Banner.

'Those who'll refuse. Bandits. Do you truly think we'll all live under the blue sky of justice after this? That no one and nothing will dare threaten wealthy merchants?'

Surely she wasn't that naive.

A silence.

'And you'll stand for this?'

Would she? What would *Rice Fish* think? Xích Si opened her mouth to say she didn't know, but what came out instead was the simple truth.

'We can try,' she said. 'You can stand down, and we can try to change. Or we can all die here. Your choice.'

'Change.' Censor Trúc stared at her, and said nothing more.

They stood, in silence. Xích Si had no more words – and the censor didn't look like she wanted to talk any more. She just stared, the gun held at her own throat – tall, regal, unwavering.

At length – after what felt like an eternity in one of the

Courts of Hell, Xích Si wondering if they'd get blasted out of the sky before coming to an agreement – Censor Trúc lowered the gun. Xích Si saw the tensing of her shoulders. She expected to be shot, though, really, what would that gain Xích Si?

Behind Xích Si came a sound like a sigh; she turned slightly, her bots keeping the gun up, and saw the bots deactivating one by one, falling to the floor like a rain of apricot-flower petals.

Censor Trúc said slowly, evenly, 'I accept your terms.'

20

Ideals

Rice Fish hadn't expected the entire Purple Banner to show up. Why was Hồ there? Was he twisting the knife by assisting the censor, to bolster Kim Thông's plans? Surely he would not be so short-sighted ...

And then his ships moved, towards the open-the-voids. Small and agile, weaving and dipping and trying to take down as many of the An O ships as possible. They were outnumbered, outgunned. Doomed.

But it was Hồ all over: her son had never admitted defeat even when faced with it. He wasn't with the censor. He'd seen, finally, what game Kim Thông was playing, and what it would cost them. And he would go down trying to defend the Citadel and everyone within it.

Her son. Huân's son.

She was so proud of him she could have wept. Even if they never reconciled – and it was looking more and more likely she'd die there – he was doing what she'd raised him to do. The right thing. The moral thing. The dutiful thing.

And ...

Rice Fish held her breath, watching the ships. Surely ...

surely those two ships peeling away from the formation, one Purple Banner, one Red Banner, couldn't be what she thought they were? She looked at their identifiers. *Persimmon. Crow's Words.*

A rescue party. He was sending a rescue party for her.

Except that Kim Thông knew it, too. It looked like the entire Green Banner was moving to fight those ships. They would never get through.

Of course. She should have known there was no hope there.

And the Green Banner ships looking for her were too close. In fact, with the heartroom and the life support still flickering and giving her a faint but discernible heat signature, *Rice Fish* had perhaps a centiday or so before they found her, and she'd be an easy enough target.

Kim Thông would be on one of those ships; she was so angry, so arrogant, she'd be there personally to make sure *Rice Fish* was gone.

At least Xích Si and Khanh were safe. Angry at her, betrayed – which hurt like a knife twist deep in her heartroom – but safe. As much as *Rice Fish* wanted Xích Si to be there – to hold her, to look at her and pause with breath held, as if she had seen something, no someone, infinitely beautiful – it was better that she wasn't. Better that she didn't witness this, or be caught in its ugly aftermath.

Rice Fish had had a long stark look at her options. She had a centiday before she got into a battle she couldn't win, and there would be no rescue. She could try to fix the propulsion, or modify her weapons. Both options were terrible: she didn't have enough bots, or spare parts, or repairs knowledge, for any of them. The motors felt like open wounds, part of the pain she was desperately trying to obscure.

The weapons ... The trouble was they relied on her being mobile, which meant they weren't fast enough and didn't cover enough angles to pose any problem to three open-the-voids flying in close formation.

I don't know where you are. Yet.

Whatever option she took, she needed to get Tiên somewhere safe. A mindship in the middle of a battle for her life was a terrible place for a wounded human. *Rice Fish* still had working lifepods, and they came with a low-range transponder. After the battle, pirates would search for them to rescue or ransom, and Kim Thông didn't have the same fanatical hatred for Tiên she had for *Rice Fish*. Putting Tiên in a lifepod was her best chance for survival.

She'd be angry, of course, but it was very likely *Rice Fish* wouldn't be around to be angry with.

Rice Fish didn't allow herself to dwell on this. She had a few of her bots move Tiên into one of the working lifepods, and set it adrift. It took only a small effort, and then the lifepod was no longer part of her, and she couldn't monitor it any more – as if she'd dropped off a chunk of herself, leaving an oddly shaped hole in her hull.

'I'm sorry,' she said, even though she knew that Tiên couldn't hear her. It was probably for the best; at least she wouldn't get a tongue-lashing.

She stared at the reports from her bots. Making some weapons modifications was the best of two terrible plans. At least she had a chance of getting something to work, even though it'd require the ships to be in really close range, and she wasn't sure how much movement she'd actually get before her structural integrity was compromised.

Rice Fish looked outside. The Green Banner ships were weaving closer and closer. She checked her own infrared signature: with Tiên gone, she could turn off life support. But there still was the residual heat of the heartroom, and of course the lifepod itself would be detectable.

A centiday.

She recalled her bots from all the corners of herself – a scuttling of legs into the vacuum, an unsettling sensation, pinpoints of metal unblunted by air – and sent them outside, to the weapons arrays. She had so few of them left; so many were non-functional little corpses left in empty corridors, in rooms stripped of all holos and vids. Everywhere hurt – from the gaping holes where her motors had been, to the debris gouging her floors, to that faint space where the pod had been: a feeling of loss she couldn't quite encompass.

Outside, the censor's fleet kept moving, smoothly weaving between asteroids that should have crushed it, towards the Citadel. Hổ's ships were engaging it, again and again, but they weren't in a position to do any significant damage. Kim Thông was going to win. And she was going to kill *Rice Fish*, too.

No.

She could at least make sure that Kim Thông was no longer in the picture. She'd have liked to be noble and pretend that it was so she could no longer hurt people, but the truth was, she was so angry, and there wasn't much left to her but revenge. If Kim Thông was going to destroy the Citadel, then she'd destroy Kim Thông.

'There you are.' It was Kim Thông's voice.

The ships veered, moving towards *Rice Fish*.

Endgame.

She tried to steady herself, however powerless – and afraid – she felt.

Outside, the bots were welding the weapons array, frantically trying to add new degrees of freedom to mechanisms that had never really been designed for this. A few more were rejigging her propulsion: not fixing the engines so much as putting together something that would swallow up her metabolised fuel and her own storage space in exchange for a small but crucial burst of speed.

Endgame, and she was at so much of a disadvantage.

'You're doing really badly,' Kim Thông said.

Of course: she'd known *Rice Fish* was damaged, but not the extent of it until now. In the comms, she no longer had dragon scales on her face – instead, her skin was flaking away to reveal a bleached skull, and bone-white antlers around her face. Even her bots were gleaming, and not a hair was out of place. A pirate, preparing for a final boarding. She was very sure she'd win. And how could she not be? *Rice Fish* was incapable of moving.

Keep her talking. And then somehow convince her to come within range. Which meant goading her, making her so angry she'd want to personally make sure *Rice Fish* was destroyed. So angry she'd want to prolong the pain, to be close enough to feel the agony.

Somehow.

Rice Fish wasn't sure what she'd be able to do when Kim Thông got closer – it all depended on so many things: vectors of approach and respective ship positions. She was going to have one small short burst of speed, and a couple of shots. That was it.

'You're not doing great yourself,' *Rice Fish* said. 'The council knows what you did.'

'Told by that brat of yours?' Kim Thông laughed. 'He'll be gone soon. Do you really think he'll hold out against a fleet? He knows he can't.'

Rice Fish forced herself not to dwell on Hổ, or on his own losing endgame. But the idea that everything was lost – that Huân's death had only been the beginning of wholesale destruction – ached within her.

'Do you really think Censor Trúc is going to trust you?'

'You assume I need her to trust me. I just need her amnesty.'

'If you don't already have it, what makes you think she'll grant it to you? She has everything she needs from you now, doesn't she?'

A blink. A touch of fear in Kim Thông's eyes, swiftly replaced by blazing anger.

'You know nothing. You're blind. I stole the council out from under you, and you never even saw it. Neither you nor Huân.'

'Don't talk to me about Huân.'

'Why not? She was as blind as you are.' A pause as the ships moved into position, closer and closer. *Rice Fish* could almost feel the heat of their motors and weapons. 'Believing you could build us a haven. Look at it!'

'It kept you safe, didn't it? For thirty years.'

It had kept Hổ safe. It had given him a childhood where he didn't have to learn about corruption and greed, or the ten thousand ways the laws would be used to hurt him.

'We got *lucky*. You got lucky.' Laughter from Kim Thông. 'There's not enough safety in piracy to keep the censor at bay. There's nothing to stop the empire from crushing us unless they choose not to. Look at it. Just look at it. Even if the Đại Việt came back, even if the censor left, it's only a matter of time before it all comes apart.'

'It's not.'

The bots were still taking apart the weapons batteries on *Rice Fish*'s sides, a distant and numbed sensation compared to the waves of unrelenting pain from her destroyed insides – now without any kind of life support to soften the feeling. She had to make a bet on which side Kim Thông would approach from – left, or right? She didn't have time to make adjustments to both.

Left. Kim Thông was impatient. She wouldn't want to circle *Rice Fish* to shoot at her.

'Isn't it?' Kim Thông laughed. 'You know what I did? You know why the censor is headed towards the Citadel.'

'Because you made us too big to ignore.'

'Because I made us too *successful*. You think I made the banners forget their principles? I made them *live* them. That's all.'

'You destroyed us.'

'You assume there was anything there to destroy! You and Huân had a vision,' Kim Thông said. 'But that's all. You *talked* about safety, about building a haven. You built nothing but fear and instability. I did nothing but take what was already there, and you know it.'

'You made us cruel. Petty-minded. No better than what we fled from.'

'Perhaps, but what did that matter? It's not cruelty that drew the censor here, and you know it.' The hatred in Kim Thông's voice was as cold as the vacuum.

'We built something,' *Rice Fish* said. It wasn't true. It wasn't . . .

But it was, wasn't it? How stable was the Citadel – poised between starving to death and being so successful a censor was sent to hound them out of existence? How needle-thin was their margin of survival? How *flawed* had her and Huân's ideas been from the start?

She couldn't keep anything under control. Her bots were skittering and falling away from her – she cut them off from her perception, left them to fend for themselves on their own subroutines. Every word of Kim Thông's opened up more wounds in the trembling mass of her debris.

'Not any more,' Kim Thông said, and the ships, close enough now, opened fire.

For a moment – a single, suspended moment – *Rice Fish* hung, weightless, not in the vacuum of space, but near a habitat, tethered by multiple restraints. For a moment she was thirty years younger, a captive of the pirates; she knew, with absolute certainty, that she was going to be killed – or worse, completely rewired, dying piece by piece until nothing remained of her.

Big sis!

In her memories Huân was smiling sadly – turning away from her on the docks, looking away as they kissed.

Passions destroy. We'd stare at each other in the ruins of a relationship. There are people depending on us, big sis.

People she'd failed. Except they'd never set them up to succeed in the first place, had they?

A fiery burst of pain, stronger than anything she'd felt – an all-consuming fire that burned as bright as a supernova. Her engines kicked in, delivering a burst of speed that moved her far enough that the other shots intended for her hit asteroids instead. She felt the distant heat of their explosions – and the more pressing one of her ruined propulsion. She wasn't going to get anything more from there.

'Impressive,' Kim Thông said. 'But how long can you keep that up?'

'For as long as needed,' *Rice Fish* said, smoothly, easily, as if she weren't burning and the only thing keeping her whole was a swarm of dying bots she was barely able to access.

'I would wager not much,' Kim Thông said.

The ships moved closer, coasting on their own momentum. They would need to reload their weapons – a time *Rice Fish* knew down to the blink.

She had one chance. Fuel was costly, even more so for pirates. These ships were on bright drive, but burning more than they needed still wouldn't come easily to them. They'd come in range of the modified weapons for about ten blinks, give or take. Taking a shot would be impossible for a human pilot to pull off, and it was a high risk for a mindship, but it wasn't as though she had any other options.

Which meant she needed to keep Kim Thông engaged – when it was the last thing she wanted. She didn't want to trade barbs again and again, not when every one of them sank so deep. And revealed how comprehensively she and Huân had failed.

'We built something,' she said, because she had no other words left.

A snort from Kim Thông. 'Such misplaced pride. But I suppose it would be, when you both sacrificed your own happiness for it.'

That one hurt *more*, and she hadn't thought it was possible. 'Don't.'

'Oh, a sore spot, is it? It's not that it was a secret. Good partners, maybe. Terrible wives.'

Xích Si's voice, lashing out at her in the middle of her heartroom, instants before she left. Before *Rice Fish* drove her away.

If Huân was such a paragon of virtue, then tell me – why did she teach you to be so unhappy?

She did not. Huân would never. She did not.

Huân was dead.

Huân had left. Huân had walked away. She . . .

The ships were in range now. Ten blinks.

Rice Fish needed to . . . She . . . She was struggling to breathe in her heartroom, and those blinks were slipping away from her.

Eight.

Seven.

Six.

She couldn't break free. All she could see was Huân flinching away from her.

Five.

263

Four.

Three.

If nothing was going to survive and everything had been ashes from the start, she could at least have vengeance.

Rice Fish fired on sheer instinct — one last desperate attempt to gather the right mạt chược tiles into her hands, all the weapons on her left side turning on at the same time and moving alongside her hull, raining a hail of destruction in her wake that none of the opposing ships had expected. She had time, barely, to feel Kim Thông's surprise and fear and pain, and then there was nothing.

Three ships, all destroyed.

Rice Fish had won.

It didn't feel like a victory.

The censor's fleet was still headed for the Citadel, and all she had was a hollow victory — and pain she no longer bothered to keep at bay: every hole in her hull, every destroyed cabin, every dead and dying bot. Her comms were flickering and dying; in between bursts of static she could see the Green Banner was still keeping Hổ's rescue ships away. Not that it mattered: Hổ seemed to have boarded one of the imperial open-the-voids on a suicide mission to deal as much damage as he could before the end.

It was over, and not just for her.

Momentum was carrying her further and further away from Tiên's lifepod, deeper into the nooks and crannies of a larger asteroid. She saw, over and over, Huân's face, heard her say they couldn't be together because people depended on them. Saw her turn away.

Why did she teach you to be so unhappy?

Rice Fish had no answer, but it didn't matter any more.

*

Xích Si sat on a chair on the censor's flagship – what was left of it. The censor was sending brisk orders to the fleet. Xích Si's bots were stabilising Hồ, who was still unconscious; he was stable, but didn't look as though he would wake any time soon.

They had barely spoken since they'd both lowered their weapons.

On her overlay, the ships were weaving some sort of incomprehensible dance, actors with coloured make-up on a stage too vast, too dark and frightening, for her to apprehend – a world that had turned and changed on her.

No. She had changed the world. Again and again, and she would do it as many times as it took.

Big sis . . .

Where was *Rice Fish?*

Nothing from *Crow's Words*, but the overlay showed him and *Persimmon* still engaging Green Banner ships. The censor's ships were moving – inflecting their trajectories via minute long-haul drive adjustments.

Censor Trúc said, at last, 'I'm not calling up more people to storm this ship.'

Xích Si looked at her, for a while – dishevelled, shaking.

'I know,' she said, and it was odd she felt more kinship with her than with Hồ. 'You gave your word.'

A short laugh from Censor Trúc.

'What now?' Xích Si asked.

Censor Trúc raised her head, briefly. 'We find a place to negotiate, do we not?'

'Yes,' Xích Si said.

'Good.' Censor Trúc's gaze hardened. Her ships were arcing towards the Green Banner. 'Now if you'll excuse me, I have some unfinished business.'

Xích Si opened her mouth to say something and then closed

it. When mould set into a craft's engines, sometimes the best thing was to dump it all and scour every trace of it from the tanks.

It felt unreal. Negotiate with an invasion fleet, on behalf of a banner she wasn't mistress of. A good thing, she guessed, that Hồ was still unconscious. She needed to find *Rice Fish*, and she needed to find her now.

Though in honesty, having support against Hồ wasn't the real reason she wanted to find her wife.

Her hands were shaking; they felt naked and vulnerable with her bots busy on Hồ's body. Finally she said, 'There's something I need to do, too.'

A sharp and altogether too penetrating gaze.

'I can guess. Of course.'

A gesture towards the further end of the room, where a flimsy privacy overlay flickered on and off.

Better than nothing, she supposed.

She walked to it, trying not to shake – and it took all of her energy not to simply collapse on a heap on the floor once it surrounded her, muting the steady hum of the motors and the distant chatter of Censor Trúc's voice.

Child.

A silence. A burst of static. Then *Crow's Words.*

'A bit busy here, younger aunt.'

'You're about to get help,' Xích Si said.

'We are about to . . .' Another silence. 'What did you *do*?'

'Later,' Xích Si said. 'Tell *Persimmon* that Hồ is wounded, the censor surrendered, and they need to stand down.'

The ship's voice, when he answered, was drily amused.

'I see. I'll tell her.' Curt laughter. 'It's not as though we can take on a full imperial fleet, anyway.'

'Later,' Xích Si said. 'Where is *Rice Fish*?'

'I don't know!' *Crow's Words* said. Something lit up on the overlay. 'Somewhere here, I think. Three Green Banner ships exploded about half a centiday ago. Non-standard weapons signature. And ...' A silence. 'There's a lot of debris in that area, and a lot of residual heat.'

Which meant something large and living was slowly falling to pieces. Which meant time was running out.

'I see.' She kept her voice level with an effort.

'Hard to figure out where she is, exactly, unless she tells us.'

Big sis ... Xích Si forced herself to breathe, *one two three four, one two three four*, again and again. She thought of the words she'd said to *Rice Fish*.

I'm not a child.

Go.

They could sort out whatever they meant to each other another time. No, that was a lie. She already knew, didn't she?

'Unless she tells us. Understood. I'm going to need your comms array,' she said.

All their comms had been routed through the antenna on the Purple Banner craft that was still attached to the censor's ship, but for this, she needed the Red Banner.

'Of course, but I don't understand.'

'I can't signal her from the Purple Banner. She wouldn't understand. It needs to be from me.'

'Ah.'

Crow's Words granted her access privileges, and she was staring at her own upgrades – the protocol she'd installed a lifetime ago, the safe and secure one that enabled their ships to talk to each other. She needed to change identities to broadcast as herself – *Rice Fish*'s wife, the Red Banner consort. She input data smoothly, easily, giving her credentials, waiting for her preferences, identity and accesses to activate.

There.

She was about to find out if *Rice Fish* was there. If she was conscious. If something – anything – of her could still be salvaged.

Xích Si took a deep breath, and started broadcasting.

21

In the Void

It was dark, and cold, and the darkness was comforting.

Rice Fish was drifting further and further, leaking oil, fragments of walls and floor and hull arcing away from her, glistening in the darkness – a lessening of pain as each one broke loose from the mass of her body and ceased to hurt.

If she let go – if she gave in to the urge to disconnect from her sensors – she'd see, not the explosion that had finally ended Kim Thông, but that moment beforehand, when she'd felt again the weight of the restraints tying her to the dock in the pirates' hideout. That moment of utter clarity that she was doomed, that they would do with her as they wanted, that Huân wasn't there to save her, and never had been.

Her whole being was curled up in her heartroom – her avatar sitting on the dais at the edge of the throne that held the Mind, where she and Xích Si had made love. It seemed as good a place as any to wait for the end. She had nothing left but an intense weariness: the butterfly bots weakly fluttering on tarnished surfaces, the oily sheen fading into nothingness, the door barred by a mound of bots' corpses.

At least Tiên was safe.

There was something — an insistent sound at the edge of her hearing, on her comms system.

'*Rice Fish?* Big sis, big sis.'

She ignored it at first, but it kept insinuating itself into her thoughts. As she drifted further and further — into darkness, and wasn't darkness preferable to witnessing the end of the things she'd valued most? — it kept poking at her like meteor shrapnel.

'Big sis. Big sis.'

It was Xích Si's voice.

That jolted her awake. In the heartroom, Xích Si's image flickered in and out of focus. She was breathing hard and dishevelled, with blood splattered across the front of her robe, and her avatar made no effort to disguise any of those facts. What had happened? Behind her was an unfamiliar ship, a classical layout of lacquer and some kind of impossibly green garden with a pavilion in the distance.

An O. That was an An O ship.

Oh no. She'd defected, hadn't she.

'I don't know where you are,' Xích Si said. 'Please.' She seemed to be holding the comms unit in her hands, like a fragile celadon masterpiece or the fragments of a broken cup. 'Come in.'

I know where you are, Rice Fish thought, but didn't say anything.

Xích Si grimaced. 'I know you're hurt. I know you're drifting. At least, I hope you're drifting and not dead, because Khanh just wouldn't forgive either of us. Please, big sis. Where are you?'

An An O ship. How could she? But of course it was hopeless. She was hopeless. Xích Si had said it so many times — that *Rice Fish*, removed from her power and unable to protect her, was not worth a second look.

'Things ...' Xích Si spread her hands, as if unsure what she could encompass. 'Things changed a lot. You saw the rescue ships, didn't you? Hồ came for you. Well. Partly for you. And he didn't object to my tagging along for the rescue.'

Why? It made no sense. They'd been at each other's throats, and he'd made it abundantly clear what he thought of her and her legacy.

'You matter.' Xích Si spread her hands. 'Just because we were angry at each other doesn't mean I'm going to let you die. Or that Hồ is. Please, big sis. Where are you? There are too many ships and too many asteroids to search, and we're *definitely* not going to find you in time. Not without your help.'

We. Xích Si and the Empire. Xích Si and the censor. So she could sell *Rice Fish* out? She should have known. Xích Si had never cared for more than herself and her little world. Nothing had changed since their quarrel.

'Please, big sis. I know we've got a lot to work out. But that's not going to happen unless you say something. Anything. Please.

'You probably can see that I'm on an imperial ship. I ... Well. I did something.' She looked over her shoulder and the privacy overlay behind her flickered, showing Censor Trúc sitting on the edge of a desk and looking as frazzled and as dishevelled as Xích Si. 'We're going to negotiate. We ...' She breathed in, hard. 'We're going to surrender. We're going to change. We're going to survive.'

Surrender.

'The censor is turning the fleet around, in exchange for our ending the piracy.'

She made it sound so easy. So casual. Hollowing out their entire way of living and ending their haven, a thing of so little consequence. She'd never understood, had she?

Or was it *Rice Fish* who'd never understood?

271

It's not cruelty that drew the censor here.

'I don't think Hồ is ever going to agree, but with you re-instated and Kim Thông's power broken, he won't have much of a choice.' Xích Si laughed. There was no joy in it. 'The censor is busy taking the Green Banner apart. Since they came here hunting for you I thought, if nothing else, you'd appreciate the irony.'

Rice Fish did not. She was so angry she could barely think. Was this Xích Si's idea of politics? Finally reaching out in order to get the censor to do her dirty work and never understanding how this — how any of this — was an abomination?

Better to let go. Better to die than to have to endure more of this.

'Please, big sis. The things we said to each other ... They were unforgivable, but they were the truth. Nothing you did — no rules you made, no fairness you upheld — could disguise what you were doing. You bought your haven in blood. In the indenture of your captives. In the deaths of ships and passengers.'

Kim Thông's voice, dripping with hatred: *You built nothing but fear and instability. I did nothing but take what was already there, and you know it.*

They had not told each other the truth. Xích Si had told lies, cutting deep but without any truth or solidity. Huân would never have allowed it. Huân would never.

I don't need to know Huân, because she's here. She's all over here, big sis. You're so obsessed with what you built together, with the perfection and pristineness of it.

'You didn't set out to do this. You set out to be safe. To make others safe. To build a haven. It can still be a haven.' She smiled, and she looked straight on, as if she could see the heartroom and *Rice Fish*. 'I go with you, because you are my wife. Come back. We can rebuild it together – the way I need it, and the way you want it, to be.'

Because you are my wife.

'We can't!' *Rice Fish* screamed, and she realised she was crying, great big gasps that wracked her entire Mind, twisting the heartroom, floors buckling, dying poetry displays twisted out of shape. 'We can't! She's *dead*! Huân is dead! There is no hope. There was never any hope.' She struggled to breathe, but it was still twisting within her – nothing, no thoughts or memories or regrets, just an emotion coming in wave after relentless wave until she shook with it and nothing she did made any difference or offered any respite. 'We can't!'

Xích Si – who couldn't hear her because the comms were off – was still talking, her mouth shaping words that *Rice Fish* couldn't hear. *How dare she – how dare Xích Si – take everything apart and then pretend she could fix it all? How dare she think that she was in any way equal to Huân?*

We can't, we can't, we can't.

Xích Si was standing now. She'd stopped speaking, but the last thing she'd said hung in the air.

'I love you, big sis. Please. Tell me where you are.'

The pain crested, broke – the waves shaking *Rice Fish*'s entire body receded, and all that was left was the thing at their heart, dark and ugly and as hurtful as a vacuum blade drawn across the walls of her heartroom.

Not sorrow, not despair, but anger, pure and simple and unadulterated.

How dare Xích Si care?

Rice Fish was worthless. She was nothing. She was not *desirable*. How dare Xích Si come back, not for political calculus, but for love? How dare she understand what had motivated *Rice Fish*? How ...?

When we kissed, here. When we made love. When you thought

273

you were unworthy of being desired. Who taught you that, big sis?

Huân would never do that. She would never hurt *Rice Fish*...

But she had, hadn't she?

She could have said no. She could have told the truth: she wasn't interested in romance. She never had been; all she'd seen in *Rice Fish* was a business partner. That would have hurt, but it would have been fair. But instead, she'd said ... She'd said ... partnerships and passions couldn't coexist. She'd said love destroyed relationships. She'd made *Rice Fish* believe all love was doomed, now and forever.

She'd lied, and *Rice Fish* had believed her.

Rice Fish tried to breathe, to steady herself. She couldn't. The world was spinning, thrown out of orbit and hurtling towards an irreversible change.

She'd *lied*.

Rice Fish had always believed she could trust Huân — that she knew what she and Huân had had: a deep and abiding partnership forged from that moment Huân had walked on board and laughed. A shared goal and shared skills, and Huân there to steady it all, because she always knew better. Because she was right.

And yet she had lied, and *Rice Fish* had never questioned it, not even when Xích Si had hurled the truth into her face. She had never once looked things in the face, whether it was the truth of her relationship with Huân or the truth of what they had built together. Because Huân was right. Because she had to be — else where did that leave *Rice Fish*?

It wasn't Xích Si she was angry with.

The world spun and spun and Xích Si still stood, watching her, with that same expression of awe she'd had when she'd said *Rice Fish* was beautiful.

I love you.
Come back.
We can rebuild it.
You matter.
I love you.

All of it was true, and it hurt so much.

She was younger and restrained at the docks of the pirate stronghold, knowing the best she could expect was a fast death – she was older and Huân turned away from her, and Hồ screamed that she was nothing but contracts and fairness – older still, and Xích Si turned and looked at her and *saw* her.

Come back.

Please, big sis. Come back.

Rice Fish opened her comms channel, and said – trembling, struggling to breathe, her entire awareness contracted to that small space in her heartroom where Xích Si stood looking at her, 'Li'l sis. I hear you. I'm here.'

22

Aftermath

Xích Si almost got all the way to *Rice Fish*'s heartroom before the little courage she'd scrounged together deserted her.

'Mommy?' Khanh, holding her hand, frowned.

Xích Si shrugged. 'I'm OK,' she said.

Khanh made a face.

'I'm not,' she admitted, finally. 'But I will be.'

There was no one on board: just an army of bots crawling over every available surface, but even they couldn't disguise the amount of the damage the ship had sustained. The Citadel's masters of wind and water had been horrified when *Rice Fish* had been towed back into the docks, though by that time the banners were in disarray, there was an imperial open-the-void and its escort sitting in the middle of the asteroid field, and the council was scrabbling to figure it all out.

Everything was damaged, and hollow. It was all wrong, in a way that Xích Si couldn't quite articulate. *Rice Fish*'s avatar was absent, and even the bots felt as though they were on automatic routines rather than personally invested with the ship's attention. She hadn't realised how much it mattered until it was gone.

She'd almost died.

In front of the heartroom, the small fountain with the silver fish was still there. It was the only overlay active in the whole ship – but the room was thick with flights of butterfly bots; they were so dense they masked the arch leading into the heartroom. Xích Si stopped, Khanh staring at the bots with wonder.

'Come in,' *Rice Fish*'s voice said, from beyond the arch.

'Mama!' Khanh, heedless of propriety, ran in. 'Mama Mama Mama . . .'

Giggling and running, and a distant set of voices. Khanh sounded delighted – Xích Si couldn't hear the tone *Rice Fish* was using.

They had so many things to fix, and she wasn't sure where to start. But she wasn't running away this time.

She squared her shoulders and walked under the arch, through the clouds of butterfly bots.

Inside, the heartroom looked almost unscathed: the scrolling text was the same as she remembered, and butterflies danced everywhere. Except that there were too many of them: the flights hung in successive veils in colours ranging from an imperial yellow to the peach sheen of loyalty.

'You know, I was so scared,' Khanh was saying, and *Rice Fish* laughed – it was meant to sound fond and faintly indulgent, but there was an edge to it.

'Yes, I got quite scared, too. It's not pleasant, is it?'

Xích Si crossed the last veil of bots – they hung on her shoulders and on the nape of her neck for a moment, like a distant caress, making a sound like paper crinkling – and then they were gone, and she was in the centre of the room, in the middle of a circle of lights. Beneath her, characters changing and twisting, An O to Southern to Việt, an ever-shifting kaleidoscope.

Khanh was sitting at the foot of the throne, between the Mind and *Rice Fish*'s avatar, all her attention on the latter.

'No,' she said, in a small voice. 'Being scared is not fun.'

'You would know.' *Rice Fish*'s voice was gentle. 'You remind me of someone, you know.'

'My brother?' Khanh said, and Xích Si held her breath – bracing herself for cutting cruelty, but *Rice Fish* merely laughed.

'A little, yes,' she said, and it was fond and sad at the same time.

Rice Fish's avatar was wearing the same long flowing robes, the topknot with part of the hair flowing down, and the red cloth merging with and taking on the colour of nebulas. Her eyes were black, her face dark and wrinkled. She seemed the same as always – she could have been at the negotiating table with Censor Trúc and the rest of the council, as the Red Scholar now, the head of the Red Banner in her own right. Except that now, in her own heartroom, she seemed smaller and less commanding, and her eyes, when she blinked, lost all colour.

She turned, and saw Xích Si.

'Ah. Li'l sis.'

But when she moved – slow and smooth and graceful – Xích Si felt her breath stop in her throat.

'You look stunning,' Xích Si said, before she could stop herself.

A silence – what was she going to say? Had Xích Si managed to hurt her all over again with the very first words out of her mouth?

Rice Fish inclined her head.

'Thank you.'

She gestured. Xích Si hadn't even noticed the tray of tea and fried rolls at her feet.

'Can I?' Khanh said, and helped herself to one under *Rice*

278

Fish's penetrating gaze, wrapping it in salad and herbs before dipping it into one of the small cups filled with fish sauce.

'There are some toys as well,' *Rice Fish* said.

They were in an overlay, alongside a gleaming bot that lifted its serpentine head when Khanh got closer, and curled around her.

'Oh,' Khanh said, entranced, and kneeled to peer at the toys — miniature spaceships which could be moulded and decorated, as well as a turtle that told stories. Khanh got out her plush turtle and set it beside the overlay turtle. 'Now, be nice to each other, turtles.'

Xích Si kneeled and picked up one of the buns. She watched Khanh for a while, trying to calm the beating of her heart. When she looked up, *Rice Fish* was standing next to her, her face unreadable.

'How is Tiên?' she asked.

'Recovering,' *Rice Fish* said. 'And complaining a lot, which is to be expected. They got to her just in time.'

'And to you,' Xích Si said, trying not to think of the chasm that had opened in her belly when she had seen the ruin of *Rice Fish*'s body.

'And to me.'

Rice Fish's black on black eyes shifted to translucent. She let the moment drag for just a little too long.

'I wasn't sure you'd let me back on board,' Xích Si said.

A silence. *Rice Fish* kneeled, picked up the overlay teacup, and stared at it for a while.

'I wasn't sure either,' she said, finally.

At the negotiating table with the censor, they'd stared at each other in much the same way Hổ and *Rice Fish* stared at each other: the tension and uncertainty palpable in the air. Xích Si had patched up her relationship with *Crow's Words*, apologising for lying to him over her fight with *Rice Fish*, and

279

the smaller ship, who wasn't really the kind to keep a grudge, had accepted her apology. But fixing the much larger hurt she'd inflicted on *Rice Fish* was another matter entirely.

'I'm glad you're alive,' Xích Si said. It felt awkward and inadequate.

'I don't know if I am.' *Rice Fish* drained her cup, stared at the fine network of cracks at the bottom. 'But thank you. For calling me back. And for starting this.'

This ... was a mess, to put it charitably: a tangle of conflicting interests where half the banners saw the wisdom of more legal activities in exchange for stability, and half of them were likely to secede. Censor Trúc wasn't too fussed about either outcome; she got what she wanted, which was fewer pirates – and those possibly at one another's throats.

'Are you happy about *that*?' Xích Si asked, more sharply than she meant.

A silence. *Rice Fish* wasn't looking at her; even the Mind behind her, and the bots, seemed still.

'No,' she said, finally. 'Not entirely.'

Xích Si's heart twisted.

'I did what I had to,' she said. 'I meant what I said, but I can't always be subservient to you.'

Another silence, then: 'No. You're not.' A sigh. 'You're correct. I value the Citadel as a haven more than I value the thrill of piracy. You're also correct that it's not everyone's stance.'

Among the people who did not believe that – as they both knew – was Hồ, who was attending most meetings as an avatar because he was still in hospital, but there was no way Xích Si was going to get closer to that particular black hole.

'So you—'

'I'm not happy about it all, but I understand. Indenture was unfair. We'll end it across the banners. And ...' Another silence. 'It is the only way to make this viable, isn't it?' She sounded desolate, and something broke in Xích Si – and before she could think, she'd reached out and was hugging *Rice Fish*. She felt a faint flinch of surprise, then a blink before the overlays engaged and Xích Si felt the warm, sharp flesh beneath hers. *Rice Fish* hadn't expected to be touched.

'I'm sorry, I shouldn't have . . .' She withdrew, stared at *Rice Fish*.

Silence stretched, with the bots flitting lazily between them. Khanh giggled at something the overlay turtle had said. Xích Si found she couldn't breathe.

'You still expect me to hurt you,' *Rice Fish* said.

'Physically?'

'That's not what I meant.' She looked genuinely at a loss for a moment. The veil of blue butterfly bots moved to settle on her shoulders. 'You're still afraid of reaching out lest you're hurt.'

Xích Si turned the words over and over. She thought of their last fight.

'Yes. But that's not what matters. It's being afraid and doing it anyway. And . . .' She hesitated, but what else could she do other than fling herself bodily into the void. 'Love means we're always going to know how to hurt each other. We choose not to. Or to repair our hurts.'

'Love.' *Rice Fish*'s voice was flat.

'I meant it. Every word I said on the broadcast.' Xích Si reached out again, towards *Rice Fish* – the avatar holding herself uncannily still, black on black eyes unmoving and unblinking. There was a moment's pause, and *Rice Fish* gave a slow, imperceptible nod of her head. Xích Si's hand brushed *Rice Fish*'s cheek, slowly, gently – like brushing the edge of a knife, barely touching. 'I want you. I'm just not sure it's enough.'

'Love?' *Rice Fish*'s voice was light, unbearably so.

'I'm sorry for hurting you. I'm sorry for losing faith. But—'

'But it was the truth?'

'Yes and no. The truth isn't a licence to hurt. I just ... I think you deserved better.'

'Better than Huân.'

Rice Fish stilled again and Xích Si withdrew her hand – but *Rice Fish* reached out and kept it pressed to her cheek. Her bots came to settle on Xích Si's shoulders – nothing more than a touch, but it set her aflame. A sigh.

'We were great partners, but then we ...' She stopped. 'She just didn't know how to say no.'

Xích Si said nothing – just held her breath, leaning in to that touch – waiting the way she would have for an apricot flower to open.

'I ... I wanted more out of the marriage. I ... kissed her. It ... She told me ... She lied. She told me love destroyed partnerships. It tore us apart. And it estranged Hổ from us.'

'Oh, big sis.' A yawning chasm of grief in Xích Si's belly. 'I'm really sorry,' she said. 'No wonder you reacted the way you did when I told you how beautiful you were. I didn't know.'

Rice Fish's gaze was distant. 'It doesn't matter.'

'It does. It should.'

And Hổ – all that bitterness, not at his parents' lack of relationship, but at their unhappiness – Huân, whose lie had festered, and *Rice Fish*, teaching herself over and over that she wasn't worth happiness. Xích Si would almost have pitied him, but she wasn't feeling quite that generous.

Rice Fish's hand was warm against hers, and she felt the ship's attention turning her way. For a moment, everything was back to the way it had been before, the feeling of a vast presence with her – here, now. She leaned in again – watching *Rice Fish* carefully and, when nothing happened except a stretching towards her, went in all the way, kissing *Rice Fish* slowly and deeply and drinking the heartbeat of the stars.

A stillness — a breath that tightened everything from the floor beneath her to the walls of the room. Then *Rice Fish* kissed her back, and the bots around her tightened, a cocoon holding her tight in the ship's embrace. Xích Si breathed in motor exhaust and a trembling, icy heat like a burning comet's tail — and for a moment everything receded, and the world spun and spun with the warmest of glows.

They pulled apart, staring at each other. Xích Si struggled to bring her breathing under control.

'Khanh is here,' she said.

In fact, Khanh was pretending very hard to be engrossed in her turtle overlay, but Xích Si knew she was probably watching everything with bated breath — hoping as hard as she could that they would mend their relationship.

Laughter — tight but genuine — from *Rice Fish*.

'I hadn't forgotten. Well, maybe I did for a blink or two.'

In spite of herself, Xích Si laughed. It felt good to finally relax.

'I don't know where we go from here,' Xích Si said slowly.

'You said it.' *Rice Fish* reached out, her bots touching the ones on Xích Si's hands. 'We change. We survive. We build a safe place, all over again.'

'And us?'

'I don't know. What do you want?'

It stopped her — the question opening up a vertiginous chasm, that feeling of being in space in a shadow-suit and staring at Triệu Hoà Port from afar, seeing it small and utterly dwarfed by the Fire Palace. But she only hesitated for a blink.

'You. If you'll have me. If you'll forgive me.'

Rice Fish didn't move for the longest time. Nebulas and stars wheeled in the depths of her robe, and her eyes gleamed a faint, dark red like a sun. Her bots quivered against Xích Si's.

'If you will forgive me,' she said, finally. Her words were slow and deliberate. The butterfly bots danced around her, lightly brushing Xích Si's hair and cheeks and lips. 'I don't know if love is enough. But if we're both willing to work for it, then it's worth finding out.'

'Worth it.' Xích Si repeated the words, gathering them to herself, like a rare delicacy in her mouth. 'Yes. Let's.'

As they all left the meeting room, Hổ asked *Rice Fish*, 'Do you have a moment?'

Rice Fish looked at him, startled. His avatar was flawless, showing none of the wounds Xích Si had described. He was belligerent and unpleasant in meetings; he wasn't willing to abandon piracy, no matter the price, and he showed no willingness to compromise. Not so changed then, in spite of what Xích Si had said.

'Yes,' she said, 'of course.'

Xích Si had already headed back to her rooms, relieving *Crow's Words* of childcare duties.

Behind him, Censor Trúc – her avatar short and stately, with dragon's antlers over her topknot – threw them both an amused glance, and then went to say something to *Mulberry Sea*, the ship bending towards her to listen. She'd stayed for a while now, and it was still unknown how the Empress of Đại Việt would respond to the agreement.

'Somewhere private?' She gestured, opening up a room of her body to him.

'That'll do,' Hổ said, and relocated to it.

It wasn't the heartroom, which meant it was bare: it was more or less intact with only faint scoring, but she didn't have the energy to run all the repair bots and maintain the decorations at the same time.

'Tea is on its way,' she said.

It had to be run from one of the rooms where power was still running.

Hồ opened his mouth – to say something about not bothering, likely – but then closed it. He seemed unusually subdued.

'What did you want to talk about?' she asked.

A sigh. 'I wanted to apologise.'

She must have misheard.

'I'm sorry?'

Hồ's face was set. 'You almost died, and I let it happen.'

Ten thousand thoughts pressed themselves through *Rice Fish*'s processors – he'd known what would happen, he'd endangered them all – and she weighed and swiftly discarded each of them. Never respond to an apology with anger.

'Thank you,' she said. 'And thank you for coming.'

'You're being very generous. I'd be a lot angrier if I were you.'

That was new. He'd seldom been attuned to what she felt. But then neither had she to him. She and Huân had hurt him a long time ago, and the wound had festered, and neither of them had ever had the courage to air it all. She thought of what she'd told Xích Si.

'I'm sorry,' she said, finally.

'What for? You're the one who got hurt.'

'I'm not talking about recent events.'

'Oh.' Hồ's expression – swiftly switching from neutral to wounded to guarded – would have been almost comical if it hadn't hurt so much to watch. 'That.'

Rice Fish hesitated. 'Huân and I quarrelled. I . . . tried to kiss her, and she told me that it was impossible, that love would doom our partnership. It wasn't true, but I believed it. And well . . .' that, too, had festered, '. . . we failed to address it.

285

We'd never have behaved the way you wanted, but there were ways to not hurt you.'

A silence, broken by the arrival of bots dragging a low table and a set of teacups with cracked turquoise glazing. Hổ crouched to watch them. She felt his weight, his solidity relayed through the overlay: an unsettling reminder of what it had felt like when he'd been there, first as a child and then as an enemy. She couldn't read his face.

'You were a child, and we should ... I should have found the right words for you. The right knowledge.' *Rice Fish* felt as though she was alone and wounded and drifting in space again, every part of her hollow and hurting. 'I'm sorry,' she said, again.

A silence. Hổ lifted one of the cups, staring at it.

'You could say it was all Huân's fault, in the end.' His voice was level.

'No,' *Rice Fish* said. 'She hurt me. But you were a child. What to tell you, how to answer your hurt, regardless of who was to blame for it? That was on both of us.'

'She's dead,' Hổ said. Tears glinted in his eyes.

'I know,' *Rice Fish* said. Something was choking her, too. She moved, kneeling by his side and laying a hand on his shoulders, squeezing. He let her. The spill of her hair surrounded them both, creating a pool of stars within which they faced each other. 'She's still here. Here and everywhere. She's still my wife. Your mother.'

He cried in silence, very still – nothing like the choked sobs *Rice Fish* had let out in the darkness of space. She held him, just as she had when he was a small child, staring ahead, feeling her sadness well up and turn the walls as pale as mourning white. Beyond them, there were bots scrabbling to mend her, Xích Si's distant presence in her heartroom, Khanh's laughter as she challenged butterfly bots to follow her, all of it merging into a maelstrom with them at the centre.

It tapered off. For a moment longer she held him, and then he shrugged her off, gently.

'Mother.'

'Child.'

'You all right?' It was Xích Si, on her comms. 'Everything went a little weird here.'

'Yes,' Khanh said. 'All the butterfly bots turned white!'

'I'm fine,' she said. 'Just sorting out a few things. Sorry I scared you.'

She didn't say any more – she didn't need her wife running to defend her.

He was still looking at her, head cocked. At length he said, 'Do you think that fixes anything?'

'I don't know,' *Rice Fish* said, truthfully. 'You tell me.'

'Later, perhaps.' Hồ sighed. The bots on his neck glinted. 'I'm also here to say goodbye.'

'I'm sorry?'

'It's not going to work out, and we both know it. The terms Xích Si set are unacceptable.'

'You won't give up piracy?'

It wasn't surprising.

'No.' He pursed his lips. 'I understand why Xích Si did it, but I disapprove. I thought you would, too.'

Rice Fish sighed. 'I do. A little. But the benefits ultimately outweigh the costs.'

'The banners are following you. I can see why.' He sounded angry again. No wonder. His fall from grace had been spectacular: it was one thing to advocate for piracy, another to ally oneself with Kim Thông, the woman who'd tried to destroy them all. The other banners and the newly elevated head of the Green Banner had turned to *Rice Fish*. Not that they agreed

287

with everything she suggested, but she had her former influence back. 'But I'm not bending my neck to imperials.'

'What are you going to do?'

'Take the Purple Banner and leave. We'll find somewhere else.'

And become pirates again, attack merchant ships again. They might well end up fighting each other across the Twin Streams.

'I see,' she said.

'You disapprove.'

Rice Fish picked her words carefully. 'I think it's the best thing for you, and I respect that. You're an adult, you have to make decisions you can live with. I love you.'

Hồ jerked back as if she'd burned him.

'You—'

'Of course I love you. Now and always. And you're always welcome here, regardless of where you stand.'

He looked as if he was about to break down again, his heartbeat wildly erratic, his skin temperature rising, a blink before the flush reached his dark skin. She reached out, held him briefly – feeling the roiling warmth of him, the cutting edges of his bots – and then she was the one who pulled away.

'I love you too, Mother.'

Hồ rose, shaking. He disguised the tremor well, but she was more observant than that.

'I'll see you, then.'

She didn't know if she would. She was afraid he'd get killed or be captured, a fear vast enough to squeeze her innards all the way to her heartroom. She was afraid he'd never return. But it was his choice to make, and he was her son, not an extension of her.

So often, being a parent was about letting go.

'Yes,' she said. 'You will.'

He walked all the way to the door instead of instantly leaving — stood, for a moment, on the threshold.

'Mother?'

'Yes.'

Her avatar was still kneeling in the room — it was all she could do to maintain it there instead of simply having it fade, because too many things had happened, too many knots had loosened, and all she wanted to do was cry.

'Give Xích Si my regards, will you? You hardly need my approval, but ...' He paused, the long hair streaming from his partial topknot and billowing in an invisible wind. 'She's something, all right.' A tight smile. 'A fierce wife for the Red Scholar.'

And then he was gone, and she broke down and cried and cried and cried.

When *Rice Fish* came back to her heartroom, Xích Si was waiting for her.

'What was that?'

She'd been poring over some documents while Khanh played — and all of a sudden the walls flashed white, and the entire atmosphere in the room had become taut and unbearable for a blink or two, before something broke and it felt as though the entire structure was melting down.

'Mommy ...' Khanh had said, and clung to her until the tremors passed.

Rice Fish stared at her. 'Just Hồ. He sends his regards.'

'Does he.' Xích Si clamped down on the first hurtful words that occurred to her. And then she looked — really *looked* — at *Rice Fish*: at the taut way she held herself, the uncannily still cast of her face. She turned, and looked at the Mind on the dais, and saw the way she quivered. 'Wait. Were you crying?'

'Maybe. Yes.'

Xích Si's anger evaporated.

'What happened? No, wrong question. Come in.'

She steered *Rice Fish* to sit on the dais.

'Are you sad?' Khanh asked.

'A little.'

Xích Si's bots scuttled on the floor, touched *Rice Fish*'s ones briefly in order to get access to the overlays – she didn't need to, she had the access permissions, but *Rice Fish* needed to be reminded that her own heartroom was still hers and sacrosanct. A cracked celadon teacup materialised in overlay, straight into Xích Si's hand.

'Drink that.'

Rice Fish took it, stared at it before draining it.

'I'll be all right,' she said.

'Here,' Khanh said, and held out her plush turtle to her. 'This'll make you feel better.'

Rice Fish looked as though she was about to cry again.

'Child . . .' Xích Si said.

'It's all right,' *Rice Fish* said. 'Thank you.' She took the turtle, balanced it on her knees. 'I'm sure she'll be of great help.'

Xích Si wasn't about to be fobbed off with a turtle.

'What did he do?'

'Nothing. He's leaving with the Purple Banner.'

'Oh.' *Of course he would.* 'I'm sorry,' she said.

'You hate his guts.'

'I do, but I know what he means to you.'

'He'll come back,' *Rice Fish* said. 'Eventually.'

Eventually . . . and how would they deal with that, when he did?

Xích Si sat down by *Rice Fish*'s side, bots touching her, touching the Mind on her throne.

'It's going to be all right,' she said – leaning to kiss her. 'You'll see.'

290

'Eventually.' *Rice Fish* laughed, and the sound twisted in Xích Si's gut. 'Who knows what the future holds.'

'I don't.' Xích Si held *Rice Fish*, feeling the warmth of her under her fingers and all around her in the heartroom, watching Khanh settling down with the overlay toys, trying to convince them to make some soup dumplings. Something bubbled up inside her, irrepressible and carefree. 'But we're building it together. Our future. Our family. A space where we can be safe. Where we can all thrive.'

And sitting there in the heartroom with *Rice Fish* against her, black hair spilling over her shoulders, bots entangled with hers, Xích Si thought she was going to cry the same way *Rice Fish* had, but they were good tears, of relief and gratitude – and, ultimately, of profoundly serene happiness.

Return to the Xuya Universe in

A Fire Born of Exile

Coming soon

1

The Tiger Games

Minh had carefully thought out her disguise for the Tiger Games. She'd planned out every detail of her physical and virtual appearance, picking out clothes with embroidery that was highly realistic, and an avatar that included fine dragon's antlers around her face and slowly whirling galaxies on her chest and back – the work was rough and detailed, clearly produced by automated routines or a new designer's brush. The bots on Minh's shoulders and wrists were middle of the range: spider-like and designed for show more than practicality, their crowns of sensors glittering with jade and silver inserts, and their multiple legs beautiful and fragile, unable to really withstand any kind of exposure to vacuum. There was nothing that would signal Minh as anything other than an ordinary candidate – a scholar without much money awaiting yet another opportunity to successfully pass the imperial examinations. She'd disguised her authentication token, making it look like a student's. There was nothing that would suggest her mother was the prefect of the Scattered Pearls Belt – one of its foremost and most powerful dignitaries, her shadow following Minh everywhere she went, tainting every interaction she had.

Unfortunately, Minh and her friend *Fruit of Heart's Sorrow* hadn't been out for more than a couple centidays before she made her first mistake.

'One, please,' she said to a seller of steamed buns, a bot descending to circle her wrist.

The seller — an auntie who must have already been old during the Ten Thousand Flags Uprising and who had a stall in the Harmonious Dream marketplace — looked at Minh, frowning. 'What did you say?' she asked.

'One, please,' Minh said, slowly and loudly.

The seller was still frowning, looking at Minh, and at *Heart's Sorrow* next to her.

'What's the problem?' *Heart's Sorrow* asked. He'd already strolled on further ahead into the crowds: now he blinked, making his avatar reappear next to Minh. He had the advantage of being a mindship: his body was parked in orbit around the asteroids, and he was projecting his avatar into the habitats, without having to worry about a physical layer. He'd modified his usual small likeness of his own body to depict a merchant transport, a much larger and bulkier ship, and masked his auth-token. In physical layers he was only large enough for a three-person crew: he was one of the newer, smaller generation of mindships, better suited to the transport of goods than of troops.

The seller was looking at them both with growing suspicion — and any moment now Minh was going to see it, the fear and the craven desire to please them, or rather to please their parents through them. What had they done wrong? They'd both changed their appearance, physical and virtual, they'd taken care to work on their body language ... She asked her bots to play back the scene that had just occurred, looking for ...

Oh.

Their accents. Not only was hers pure Serpent diaspora,

the one all her tutors had drilled into her, emulating the imperial court on the First Planet, it was also entirely wrong for a scholar without means. What could she do? There had to be something—

A distraction, and a correction.

She pitched her voice lower. 'Sorry, I wasn't clear. Make that three buns, with pork. And overlay one for my friend here. We're meeting friends later. Bit of a busy festival?' As she spoke, she shifted the vowels and pitch of her words, moving seamlessly into something far lower class.

The seller cocked her head. She looked for a moment as though she wanted to argue with Minh, but she gave up. Not worth the trouble. 'As good as it can be, I guess. Too many people still afraid the uprising will come back. Too many imperial soldiers – *they* don't pay market prices for street food.'

'Well, that's my first mother covered,' *Heart's Sorrow* said to Minh via their private comms channel. 'Hope she's not going to cover yours too.' *Heart's Sorrow*'s first mother was the Peach Blossom Lake General, the military administrator of the Belt.

'It'd be a good distraction,' Minh said. He was joking, but he was tense, and she didn't need that to be obvious. Neither of them had, per se, permission to sneak out in disguise.

'There,' the seller handed Minh her pork buns. 'Enjoy the festival!'

'Thank you, elder aunt,' Minh said. The bot on her wrist sent money to the seller, and then she and *Heart's Sorrow* were on their way.

'So much for our plan,' *Heart's Sorrow* said. His nervousness made him sarcastic.

Minh made a face. 'I could quote you Tôn Tử's Military Lessons on plans.' They both knew them by heart – the Old Earth strategist, the one from a dead planet the scholars nevertheless insisted on teaching like he was one of their own ancestors, as deserving of worship as they were.

Heart's Sorrow laughed, but it had an edge. 'Don't. That's dreadfully boring.'

'Boring the same way we are?' It was Minh's voice who had the edge now. Their first mothers were a general and a prefect, Serpents so senior their origins had ceased to matter. Minh and *Heart's Sorrow* had grown up in a rarefied circle of the wealthy and influential, their paths in life determined as surely as if a fated thread had been pulling them in. Safeguarded, sheltered, privileged.

Preserved as carefully as dead things in scholars' display cabinets.

'Oh, shush,' *Heart's Sorrow* said. He was eating his virtual pork bun: a skillful aggregation of layers that would trigger pleasant memories. Minh bit into hers. It felt like drowning, her mouth full of over-flavourful cotton, a riot of conflicting tastes from crumbly egg to the sweetness of the pork. 'Come on,' *Heart's Sorrow* said, floating further into the crowd, the sheen on his hull flashing under the lights of the habitat. 'We're going to miss the best of it!'

Minh followed him, away from the Harmonious Dream marketplace and the wide plaza, with its stalls spread under the overlay of the whole Scattered Pearls Belt – into smaller and smaller spaces, corridors crammed with people, mind-ships and humans both, a riot of avatars wearing shimmering fabrics in multiple layers both physical and virtual – and not just humanoid or ship ones, but kỳ lân and lions and mixtures of organic and electronic with multiple legs and elongated bodies, scales and fur and the sheeny, oily light of deep spaces on human skin. Every few measures marked a new ambient poem or music from zither to flute, a new environment – Minh was surprised again and again, as sight and sound and smells abruptly changed, an all-out, all-invasive feast for her senses that threatened to drown her at any moment, an utter exhilaration in every bone of her body, every pore of her skin.

It was everything she'd dreamt of. Not tame, not sterile – as vibrantly alive as the pulsing stars, and utterly uncaring of who Minh was. A person whose avatar was briny mist pushed against Minh – their touch a spray of cold water that smelled of pandanus and salt – and then they were on their way down the corridor. And then another one, with metal arms bristling with bots, and a mindship, bringing with them the fractured coldness of deep spaces – and another and another in a ceaseless dance. Minh laughed. *This* – this was freedom. This was wildness. She could dance and scream, and no one would think twice or be afraid of her.

This was like finally filling her lungs after too long holding her breath.

'Come on!' *Heart's Sorrow* said. He was ahead, so far away Minh could only see him in a tracking overlay, his position a blinking marker over the variegated crowd. Obviously, he would be above everyone: his only physical footprint was the cluster of bots in the shadow of his avatar.

Ahead was a slightly larger space in front of a series of compartments: the sort of space that would usually be claimed by a middle-sized lineage. Now it was filled by a crowd in front of a huge public overlay, an enhanced-depth opening showing the Tiger Games arena. As Minh wended her way through the crowd, struggling to join *Heart's Sorrow* near the front, the view in the overlay moved, panning over the higher tiers of the arena, and Minh had a moment of nausea as she saw Mother in the prefect's private space, wearing the jade belt and tasselled hat of her rank. A blink only, and then it had moved on, showing the other dignitaries, but for that single moment it felt – overlay, perception adjustments and all – as though she stood not an arm's length away from Mother, close enough to see the disapproval on her face.

Or worse, the disappointment.

A touch, on her hand: one of *Heart's Sorrow*'s bots, nestling into the crook of her palm, the sharp, pulsing warmth of its legs steadying her. She glanced at her friend: he was beside her with absolutely no hint of anything in his posture.

'Thanks,' Minh said.

'Pff,' *Heart's Sorrow* said. 'Don't spend days preparing for this outing, and then waste it all on *her*.'

He didn't need to say who he meant. Sometimes, she envied him so much it hurt like someone twisting a fist into her belly. He seemed to have taken his own first mother's measure early on: he loved her but didn't expect her to be anything more than she was – status-obsessed, always yielding and taking the easy way, always seeking to make herself attractive to the powerful. Minh wished she had his clarity when it came to her mother, who was sharp, navigating politics and calling in favours as easily as she breathed, extending the shadowed cloak of her protection to her intimates and subordinates. But sharpness also meant cruelty, and distance, and . . .

And, sometimes, Minh felt scared that Mother just didn't love her.

The bot bit into her skin. 'Hey!'

'You're daydreaming! Look!'

On the screen, the first of the Tigers was coming in, next to their data artist. It was a huge, translucent beast with five pairs of iridescent wings, a maw large enough to swallow suns, with diamond fangs and glittering eyes – a sleek, smooth shape like an atmospheric shuttle, meant to cut through the air, the wings sharp and weapons gorgeous. It moved fast, seemingly answering the least of the data artist's commands, their fingers twitching as the Tiger moved.

300

Their opponent was closer to the Old Earth animal: a faint, huge mist that suggested stripes, and the vague idea of fire. Its data artist was a young woman with plain, unadorned brown robes that made her seem almost monk-like. She was sitting cross-legged on the arena floor – not a movement, not even a blink, as her Tiger moved to stand in front of its opponent.

'She's *good*,' *Heart's Sorrow* said, his voice filled with awe.

As the two Tigers sized each other up, the camera moved across the people seated in the arena: the non-scholar classes packed, standing, into the lower seats, the scholars in their booths, and then the higher-end dignitaries with privileged virtual booths, and the corresponding visibility and access, enabling them to watch the games from the privacy of their own homes while being seen. *Heart's Sorrow* snorted when the camera stopped, briefly, on the booth where his two mothers were: his first mother, the general, wearing her finest formal uniform with the peach blossom insignia, and his second mother the retired enforcer, muscled and fit and looking hungrily at the fight beneath her.

Minh squeezed the bot in her hand, gently. *Heart's Sorrow* didn't answer: his attention was all on his mothers.

'This is the start of the first playoff of the day, with Black Water facing Crimson Rain. A really interesting match, with one of the opponents being brand new to the Games—'

The camera panned again, as the sound of two Tigers clashing drifted from the arena floor. Couldn't they focus on the fight itself? Dignitaries were so boring.

And then Minh saw her.

She was sitting in one of the dignitaries' booths: one of the fancy ones with both physical and virtual access, a privacy screen half up – but as the camera panned the screen wavered, and Minh could see her clearly.

She was a woman of indeterminate age: jet-black hair

gathered in a topknot and topped with a small golden crown in a butterfly shape, with the rest of the hair falling around the topknot in a cascade of blackness. Stars winked in and out of it in virtual overlay: a subtle touch. Her clothes were similarly subtle, a faint overlay of stars shimmering over a richly embroidered fabric. Her face was ... well there wasn't anything specific about her face, but it was the way she looked at the arena, the way she carried herself – like the entire world was an egg that needed to be broken open to release the hatchling within. The face of someone who'd gladly set things afire with a shrug.

Minh realised she'd forgotten to breathe. 'Who's that?' she asked in private comms.

'Who's what?' *Heart's Sorrow* wrenched his attention back to the screen. 'Her? I've never seen her before.' He made a clicking noise. 'Mmm. The network says "Sương Quỳnh, the Alchemist of Streams and Hills". She's not sharing a family or lineage name.'

The Alchemist of Streams and Hills. A literary name. A scholar, then, but she was obviously not from the Scattered Pearls Belt, or Minh or Mother would know her. Next to the Alchemist was a mindship: a larger one than *Heart's Sorrow* but from an older generation, their avatar a bulky metal shape with a profusion of actuators and fins, looking cobbled up from the rejects of other mindships. *The Guts of Sea*, the network said. The woman turned to *Guts of Sea*, and said something which was caught by the privacy filter. She smiled, her lips the perfect, unsmudged red of a vermillion seal, and turned back to watching the arena. Her gaze, for a moment, went upwards, and Minh was transfixed – as if the Alchemist of Streams and Hills could see her through a camera and a public overlay. As if she *knew* Minh.

A sharp pain stabbed her hand. 'Big sis! Big sis!'

She came back to the plaza where she and *Heart's Sorrow* were standing. 'What was that for?'

'Look,' *Heart's Sorrow* said.

'I don't see anything.'

'On the edges.' There was some faint fuzzing on the edges of the overlay. And then the camera blinked — and she saw that the fuzzing wasn't transfer corruption at all, but bits and pieces of the second Tiger, the faint, undistinguished shape of mists and stripes. It had been slowly growing and expanding, and was now filling the arena.

Heart's Sorrow's voice was distant. 'The data artist has lost control of her Tiger.'

Minh watched, unable to tear her gaze away: the Tiger was still growing, officials on the lower tiers scrabbling to evacuate, while in the dignitaries' booth, the Alchemist of Streams and Hills herself sat utterly silent and composed, as if nothing could touch her — and then the mist filled the camera, a glitter of stripes in the darkness for a mere blink before it swallowed up the field of vision.

'Well, that certainly stopped the fun,' *Heart's Sorrow* said.

Minh was still staring at the camera. It showed nothing but that hint of stripes. Around her, the crowd was watching too — speechless and tense, like a piece of metal stretched too much, in that moment before it broke.

'We should get moving,' *Heart's Sorrow* said. 'It's not going to—'

Someone screamed.

Why?

'It's here! Run!'

What?

'Run!'

The crowd was pressing against her, and there was more screaming. The tension had broken and now it was just a mass of jumbled bodies all blocking her. She couldn't breathe, or move – she was suffocated by the thickness of the crowd, a multitude of textures – there was screaming and smoke and a press of bodies around her. 'Li'l bro, what—'

Minh was being pushed right and left – she teetered, lost her footing, caught herself at the last minute. Panic. They were in the middle of a panic. Something had upset the tightly packed crowd, and suddenly they all wanted to get out. And they'd trample anyone to do that.

Breathe. Breathe, but she couldn't, not when pressed on all sides. She struggled to look up – and finally saw why the crowd was running. The Tiger was in the habitat. And not just that, but it was growing and growing, its contours expanding – and where they touched, metal bent, shrieking with the tortured sound of souls bound in the Courts of Hell.

If it touched people, it wasn't just going to be metal that died. *How—?*

No. How was irrelevant. She had to get out.

'Run,' *Heart's Sorrow* said. His bots were skittering, dancing under the crowd's feet. Minh struggled to stay upright. She could barely see him: people had shoved straight into his space, and his body shimmered in and out of existence over a man's brocaded robes, then a woman's, then over two small children.

What was he still doing here?

'Leave!' she screamed at him.

'What? Am I supposed to just leave you?'

'Obviously!' Minh said, pushing her way towards the corridor she'd taken here. The overlays were bleeding into each other with the stress on the network – the ambient music and sounds a cacophonic mixture drowned by the sound of the crowd, swelling like the motors of an atmosphere shuttle about to take off. 'One of us has to make it. Be sensible!'

'Sensible?' *Heart's Sorrow* floated, not next to her, but *over* her, as the crowd surged and pushed, a compact, bristling mass of too many people, too much noise, too many clashing overlays. 'And how am I supposed to explain to your mother that I just left you?'

'I don't care!' More screaming, a shriek of tortured metal — and a high-pitched human wail echoed by others. Something pattered over them — water from the sprinklers in the station? — but when she brushed her hand against her lips, Minh saw that it was blood. She managed, struggling, to turn her head. Behind them, the Tiger had swallowed up the whole plaza, its mist covering the now-still forms of those who hadn't pushed hard enough to escape. Some of them were too small to be adults. How — how dare it? How dare it be there, on her turf? Her anger was white-hot and searing, a feeling that hollowed Minh out like a lantern stretched over its light. 'Do something, demons take you!'

The small, translucent shape of *Heart's Sorrow* hovered over her chest, his hull plunging between her ribs, his turrets passing into her neck. Minh didn't feel anything: her perception filters for that overlay were off. Small mercies.

Heart's Sorrow said, softly, 'I can't. I've tried. I can't recall my avatar, and I can't send an emergency signal. Comms are down. Flooded out I think.'

Or attacked. Minh followed the push of the crowd into the corridor, struggling. Someone brushed against her, too high to be a bot, too small to be an adult. A small girl, no more than three years old, staring at her with panic in her eyes — in that suspended moment before everything became too overwhelming and she utterly broke down. 'I can't find my mommy!'

Minh swept her up, wedging her around her hips, using her bots to provide added stability and support. Ancestors, she hadn't carried small children since her cousins had become too heavy. 'Let's go look, child,' she said.

Heart's Sorrow was now utterly focused. 'Looking her up.'

'You said the network was down.'

'Yes. But I do have the cache for a lot of things. Hang on ...'

A man in a dragon mask tried to push a little too close. Minh glared at him. 'You related to her?'

The man looked startled, then shook his head.

'Then move!' And when he didn't, she sent a bot to sting his feet. He yelped, which was petty but was mildly satisfying.

The child burrowed into Minh's neck. It made her job easier, but also she was way too trusting. When they found the child's mother, she was going to have *words* with her about teaching her child to be wary of strangers, especially at a major festival.

'Sweetie, what's your name? Do you know what your mother looks like?'

A sniffle. 'I'm Nhi Nhi. Cầm Nhi. Mommy—' she flailed. The noise of the crowd was getting unbearable: Minh asked her bots to set up a noise filter at weak strength. She was half expecting it not to work, with everything down in the sector, but it did, and the sound around them receded to an almost bearable level. She couldn't keep it up for long: it was exceedingly unwise to try and drown out noise while being pushed in all directions by panicking people.

A high-pitched screech, a tortured noise cut off by the filter. Nhi finally managed to send Minh an image: a small and chubby young woman alongside an auth-token. A Belt one, thank Heaven. Ah-ha. Minh sent it on to *Heart's Sorrow* and asked her bots to scan the crowd at the same time. She pushed back against her neighbours again. The man with the mask glared at her. Let him.

Her bots couldn't find Nhi's mother. Worse came to worst, she could find her once she was back home, with the tribunal's resources, though she would never hear the end of it from her mother.

'Can't find her,' *Heart's Sorrow* said.

Tendrils of fiery mist floated their way: the air was stingingly hot, and Minh's hands were starting to burn and turn red. Nhi wailed in her arms. She could dial the pain down, but she needed the adrenaline rush. She pushed instead, into the crowd that seemed to have reached a complete stop — and then abruptly they were out of the corridor, and back in the Harmonious Dream marketplace, and Minh pushed and pushed and pushed. With the shape of *Heart's Sorrow* super imposed on her chest — it was oddly like carrying two people, the ship and the child — and they were through, the crowd thinning out at last.

They were in a side street close to the market. Minh stopped to catch her breath and heard only the distant roar of the crowd. 'It's gone,' she said, slowly. 'The Tiger.'

Heart's Sorrow blinked away from her chest, reappeared above a heap of abandoned steaming baskets, his bots climbing the various neighbouring stalls. 'The network is still congested, but it's easing. They say—' he sounded dubious '—there was an accident during the first match. The Tiger broke free of the arena restrictions, and the data artist's control.'

'Mother—'

'They're all safe. My mothers had already evacuated, but looks like your mother barely escaped being mauled.' He laughed, and it didn't sound amused. 'It'll probably make for an entertaining vid.'

'Auntie—' Nhi said, in Minh's arms.

Minh sighed. 'I know. We need to find your mother, and to get you home. Li'l bro,' she started, and looked up, to see that *Heart's Sorrow* had completely frozen on top of the baskets. 'Li'l bro?'

'Don't bother,' a voice said. 'He's stuck, and he's not going anywhere. Neither are you.'

There were five of them in the street, two women and three men, with barely any ornamentation to their avatars: they were *here* in the physical, unpleasantly close, the loose circle they formed around Minh and *Heart's Sorrow* tightening.

The one who had spoken — a squat, commanding woman with the wings of a phoenix — smiled, and it was fanged and unpleasant. 'Poor little rich girl, so lonely.'

'Me, or the child?' Minh asked, tightening her grip on Nhi.

An eyeroll from Phoenix Wings. 'I don't care about the child. I care about how much your mother will pay to get you back *whole*.' She had a knife: it shone sharp and wicked, and Minh's bots very unhelpfully told her it was a vacuum blade, the kind used to cut through metal to maintain the habitats. Which meant it would shear very neatly through skin and bone.

Shit. Shit. That was *bad*.

'You've got the wrong person,' Minh said.

'How dumb do you think I am?'

'I can only tell you the truth,' Minh said. She glanced again at *Heart's Sorrow*.

'He's not going to help you,' Phoenix Wings said. 'We hacked his link to his body. All he can do is watch.' She laughed, holding the blade. 'Now come gently, will you.'

Minh was feeling distinctly ungentle, but she didn't have a vacuum blade. Or four other people with her, also armed with vacuum blades, too. This must be some kind of bandit gang she'd fallen afoul of; opportunists looking for a quick way to get rich. She eyed them again, forcing herself to breathe. They were a few handspans away now, their heavy, armoured bots even closer than that.

Minh said, 'I'm going to set the child down.'

Phoenix Wings laughed. 'The child can come with us. Probably not a great ransom, but she'll fetch something, one way or another.'

Which meant the bondspeople market. 'No,' Minh said. 'If you let us go, I can get you the money when I get back home.'

Nhi gripped her. 'Old Auntie—'

Minh forced herself to breathe. 'It's going to be all right.' And that made her angrier than anything else – that she had to lie to reassure a child.

Another eyeroll. 'When you get home? You must really think we have no brains.' A minute tension: she was going to signal for the attack, and Minh wasn't going to be able to meet it head-on. She set Nhi down, a fraction of a blink before Phoenix Wings actually gestured – and then her bots moved to intercept the bandits' bots, except that they were crushed in a blink, their input feeds suddenly going black in Minh's brain.

Bad bad bad, she had the time to think, before the bandits' bots leapt on her, and their combined weight pulled her down.

Minh hit the floor with a thunk, her head ringing – her avatar wavering, the dragon's antlers blinking in and out of existence as everything around her seemed to fold into throbbing pain. Someone grabbed her by her arms, hauled her up: it was one of the men, towering over her and holding her like she was nothing but a ragdoll, clasping restraints on her wrists. They bit as they closed, like ice encircling her. Minh struggled to break his hold, but her legs didn't even touch the floor and she had no purchase on him.

'Old Auntie!' Nhi wailed and wailed.

'Bring them,' Phoenix Wings said, and the man holding Minh threw her over his shoulder.

She was bent double like a sack of rice. Even looking at the floor required her to lift her head, which was too hard and too painful to do. She tried to raise the network, to send a signal, any kind of signal, to anyone, but the restraints were blocking her access, and everything seemed to be fuzzing over the gaping emptiness of her destroyed bots. She must have hit her head badly when she fell.

Phoenix Wings laughed. 'Looks like she's going to behave without my having to break anything. Good. We'll send a ransom demand to the tribunal once our shuttle reaches the hideout.'

Shuttle. Hideout. They'd be going out of range of the habitats. No one was ever going to find her, because these were outsider bandits. They'd just come in for the festival, and she'd handed them an opportunity on a jade tray.

'Don't—' Minh tried to say, but her tongue felt glued to her palate. At least she'd set Nhi down. At least . . .

'Kidnapping people in broad daylight is a terrible idea,' someone new said. It was a woman's voice. Not the bandit's, this was low and cultured, with the faintest suggestion of an accent – from the shipyards, maybe?

'Who under Heaven are you?' Phoenix Wings snapped.

'Someone who makes it her business to interfere in other people's business.' The voice was cool and collected. Minh tried to hold on to anything, but she felt darkness encroaching on her field of vision. She was going to pass out. Or vomit. Or both.

'Please,' she said. 'Help the child.' It was a bare whisper, physical and with no network broadcast.

And yet, when the answer came, it was said right next to her ear, softly and deliberately. 'I will.' *How—*?

The woman said to Phoenix Wings, 'Put her down, and release the child. I won't ask twice.'

Phoenix Wings laughed. 'Making empty threats? She tried that, too.'

'These aren't threats. They're demands.' Matter-of-fact and cold.

Something clinked: bots' legs, pattering on the floor. One

of the bandit women cursed, something fell, and there was a rapid shift in the air – then *something* happened, and Minh was falling. She flailed, bringing up her bound hands to break her fall, and *bots* caught her and gently cushioned her. The restraints opened, hitting the floor with a resounding clink – their insides gleaming with blood. Minh's blood. They must have been pumping some kind of chemicals into her. Her head felt stuffed with cotton: she tried to pull herself up, managed to stand up for a blink, and then fell back to her knees, vomiting all over the station's floor.

The network came back online – and as it did so, *Heart's Sorrow*'s anguished scream filled Minh's ears. 'Big sis! Are you all right?'

What does it look like? Minh tried to say, but she wasn't feeling well enough.

She was groggily aware of someone coming to sit beside her, waiting patiently until she was done: her rescuer. Minh could only catch glimpses of rich brocade. She opened her mouth, gagging on the taste of her own vomit. 'Nhi. The child.'

'We have her,' her rescuer said. 'Take your time. It's under control.'

Slowly, carefully – wincing at the pain in her neck – Minh raised her head. The bandits were lying dead or unconscious on the floor. Phoenix Wings had her own vacuum blade rammed into her chest, and the woman who had screamed was lying on the floor, nursing an arm bent at an unnatural angle. The man who'd held Minh was dead, unfamiliar bots crawling over his body: one of them came out of his throat, dragging up mucus and blood. The bandits' bots were all inert, as if someone had cut their strings. *Heart's Sorrow* was beside Nhi, whispering comforting words. 'What ... what happened?'

'I did warn them.' Her rescuer sounded distant. 'Pity they didn't listen. Those who survive will have to face the slow death.' There was a dark, vicious satisfaction in her voice that sent shivers up Minh's spine.

Minh tried to breathe. The air felt raw and painful in her lungs. Was it only a few bi-hours ago she'd put so much thought into her dress and disguise, only a few centidays ago she'd seen the Games start? It felt like a lifetime ago.

'Thank you,' she said — and turned to her rescuer, and stopped. 'You're—' she paused, swallowed. 'You're the Alchemist.'

'I'm Quỳnh,' the woman sitting next to her said.

'Minh,' Minh said, reflexively. 'Pleased to meet you. Not the best of circumstances.'

'Alas,' Quỳnh said. Up close, she was even more of a presence, someone who simply drew all the attention without much trying. Her skin was dark, stippled with a light starlight tan, that great mass of hair spread around her on the floor in a pool of darkness. The golden crown atop her topknot glinted under the habitat lights.

'But. You were in the arena. Physically,' Minh said. 'I saw you.'

'I left early.' Quỳnh's voice was cool. 'It looked like it was going to turn ugly, and why stay under those conditions?'

'I don't understand what you're doing here.'

'You sounded like you needed help,' Quỳnh said, simply.

'The network was down.' Minh struggled to gather her thoughts together. 'How—'

'Your friend managed to broadcast a message before he got frozen out of the network.' Quỳnh gestured, and Minh suddenly noticed the mindship hovering behind her. 'It was garbled and incomplete, but *Guts of Sea* is good at deciphering.'

Guts of Sea inclined their avatar in a bow, but said nothing.

'Thanks for coming. Sorry. Not to sound ungrateful, it's just—'

'You've had a nasty shock. It's quite all right.'

'My ear. You spoke in my ear. Like you had the network.'

'I have *Guts of Sea*.' Quỳnh sounded amused. 'She helps with those little tricks.'

Guts of Sea did the mindship equivalent of glowering. 'Slipping comms between the shards of a broken network is more than a *neat trick*.'

'A miracle, then.' Quỳnh's mouth turned up, in a small smile. 'Satisfied?'

'She's alive and didn't break her spine in the fall,' *Guts of Sea* said. 'And they didn't have time to harm the child either. Better than I expected.'

'How did you—?' Minh asked.

Another smile. 'Tricks. Miracles.'

They were deflecting how exactly they'd rescued Minh – she knew it, and it should have annoyed her, but instead she just felt exhaustion and relief. They both sounded utterly in control and relaxed – and having Quỳnh next to her made Minh feel perversely safe, even though they'd barely even met.

'Miracles,' she said. Minh tried to get up, but Quỳnh put a hand on her shoulder to prevent her.

'You're pumped full of sedatives, on top of the shock. Don't move. The militia should be on its way.'

The militia. 'No!'

'It's a tribunal matter,' Quỳnh said, and she sounded puzzled. 'And your friend sent them a request as soon as he was unfrozen.'

Of course he had, if he'd panicked. And of course he wouldn't have thought that he and Minh would both have to explain being out of the family compound, in the seedier areas of the habitats – and not only almost being killed by a stray

313

Tiger, but also how Minh had come so close to being carried away from the Belt and held for ransom by bandits.

The punishment for that was going to be horribly creative and costly.

'You don't understand,' Minh said. 'Mother is going to kill me.' And, when Quỳnh still looked puzzled: 'She's the prefect.'

'Ah. I haven't had the pleasure of meeting her yet.'

She was newly arrived then, which explained the faint ship-yard accent.

'Well, don't worry,' Minh said, more viciously than she intended. 'You'll have plenty of time to become acquainted.'

Contrary to Minh's expectations, when the militia showed up a centiday later, neither of their first mothers was there. Instead, it was Đình Diệu, the aide to *Heart of Sorrow*'s first mother, and Minh's stepmother Hạnh.

Minh had managed to sit down, Nhi on her knees, while *Heart's Sorrow* tried to contact Nhi's mother. Quỳnh had with-drawn a little way, clearly giving Minh some space; but she wasn't intending to leave. Not that she could, since *Heart's Sorrow* had called the militia.

Minh was singing Nhi a song from her childhood, and Nhi – who obviously had Serpent classmates – was nodding along.

'One, two, Serpent in the Heavens,
Three, four, the azure cloth over us,
Five, six, official's robes,
Seven, eight, the sky afire . . .'

'Nine, ten, white birds in flight!' Nhi said, triumphantly, completing the sequence of hand movements by making wings with her outstretched hand. 'Again, Old Auntie, again!'

'One, two, Serpent in the Heavens,
Three, four, the azure cloth over us . . .'

One minute Minh was sitting in the deserted alleyway – the

next an overlay descended, all harsh and blinking lights and jarring sounds, as if she were a criminal being arrested. It ought to have thrown off her focus and coordination: but her throat was still burning from the vomit, her wrists covered in her own, drying blood, and she didn't have the energy to care.

'Child!' Stepmother looked positively outraged as she rushed to Minh. 'What in Heaven did you think you were doing? That's utterly unsuitable for the family.'

Well, if nothing else, Stepmother was thoroughly predictable. Minh bit down on the obvious answer.

Đình Diệu was grimmer. 'You gave us all quite a fright,' she said, running a hand through her close-cropped hair.

'How are they?' Minh asked. 'Mother and the general.'

'Better than you are,' Đình Diệu said.

Minh sighed. 'I have no regrets.'

'Oh, you're going to regret this,' Đình Diệu said.

Minh had no doubt of that.

'You look like something the scavengers dragged in,' Stepmother said. She sniffed.

Minh winced. She held out Nhi to one of the militia people. 'Can you see her home? We know her mother's auth-token, but *Heart's Sorrow* can't raise her.'

'Of course.'

Nhi wailed. 'I don't want to leave.'

Minh hugged her. 'I know,' she said, softly. 'They're scary, and your mommy told you never to mess with the militia. But they're good people.' Well, some of them were. And most of the corrupt, power-thirsty ones wouldn't stoop to harming a toddler for no political gain. 'They'll take you home, I promise.' She hugged Nhi again. 'And then you can tell her about your adventures.'

Nhi sniffed. 'I hated the adventures.'

'Yeah,' Minh said, and winked. 'So did I.' Nhi made a face,

315

but let herself be handed over to the militia woman who came to pick her up.

Stepmother looked, for a moment, as though she was going to lecture Minh, but then she softened. Her daughter Vân, Minh's stepsister, wasn't much older than Nhi. '*That* was well done,' she said.

Minh didn't say anything. There wasn't anything she wanted to say, to be honest. She and Stepmother didn't get on and never would – not with Stepmother's insistence that Minh lacked the decorum befitting to her position in the family, and her favouring of Vân instead.

'I got the full lecture from Đình Diệu,' *Heart's Sorrow* said on the private comms channel. 'That *hurt*.'

Minh was reasonably sure her lecture was being saved for Mother. 'Lucky you. At least you're done. Mine is still in abeyance.'

'Are these dead people?' Stepmother's voice was suspicious. 'You *killed* people?'

'That was me.' Quỳnh interposed herself, smoothly, between Minh and Stepmother, *Guts of Sea* by her side. 'I apologise for any inconvenience, but these bandits were about to kidnap your stepdaughter.'

Stepmother cocked her head, suspiciously.

'And who are you?' Đình Diệu asked.

'The Alchemist of Streams and Hills. My name is Quỳnh.'

'Yes. Yes, I can see that from your display,' Stepmother said. 'Aside from that.'

'A concerned passerby.' Quỳnh's voice was smooth. She recounted, quickly, how she'd come to rescue Minh. She still didn't provide any details on how she and *Guts of Sea* had managed to take out five, armed bandits.

'You did that by yourself?' Đình Diệu said, eyeing the slim jewelled bots on Quỳnh's shoulder, the nacre inlays on their crowns of sensors. She looked impressed, and Heaven knew she was hard to impress: she'd fought in the Ten Thousand Flags Uprising, and at the battle of Cotton Tree Citadel.

Quỳnh shrugged. 'We've travelled. Bandits are a common occurrence outside the numbered planets, and they've not grown less bold since the end of the war.'

Đình Diệu cocked her head, assessing Quỳnh. Something unspoken passed between them – and then again: Đình Diệu reporting via a comms channel to her general.

'The General will want to see you both,' Đình Diệu said, curtly.

Quỳnh inclined her head. 'It will be my pleasure.'

'And mine,' *Guts of Sea* said, angling her squat body to align with Quỳnh's.

Stepmother looked from Minh to Quỳnh. This was a different calculus: it took in Quỳnh's speech, the price of her clothes and the elegance of her bots. 'Where are you from?' she asked.

Quỳnh bowed. It was deep and correct to within an eyelash-width, everything Minh's tutor ever despaired she'd learn. 'The shipyards,' she said.

'You've been to court,' Stepmother said.

'It has been my privilege, but sometimes one requires solitude,' Quỳnh said. She smiled, and there was little of joy in it. 'I wanted the streams and the hills, the hollow bamboo's pleasure. A pine, a plum tree and the moon's reflection can be their own fulfillment.' She was mixing together literary metaphors, quoting on the fly from the poetry masters. Not just a scholar, but the kind that became high official – the kind of dazzling talent that the ministries would fight over, the same path Mother had traced out for Minh despite her lack of enthusiasm. She was *so good*, and it was *so* effortless.

Why was she here? With that kind of talent, she should be at court.

'I suppose,' Stepmother said, slowly and grudgingly, 'that you should come visit us as well. You sound like the kind of person my wife would love to meet.'

Another talented and wealthy person for Mother to obsess over, to try and win to her side for more influence and more power. Quỳnh inclined her head, but by the glint in her eyes she probably wasn't fooled. 'I would be honoured,' she said. It was exactly the same tone she'd used earlier. Minh reached for her bots to replay Quỳnh's conversation with Đình Diệu – but no, her bots were dead, killed by the bandits. But she was sure it was the same tone. It had an edge to it, and no wonder. Stepmother had been about as subtle as a tiger in a cattle pen.

Minh felt grubby. 'I'm sorry,' she messaged towards Quỳnh on a private channel. 'You probably thought we were better than this. The adults are all status obsessed.'

A sound, crystalline and good-natured, only for Minh's ears. It was Quỳnh's laughter. 'I've travelled. I'm not surprised. How much trouble are you and your friend in for sneaking out?'

Minh started. She hadn't expected that answer. 'I don't know yet. I never really thanked you for the rescue.'

'You're welcome,' Quỳnh said. Her voice was grave again. 'Tell me, Minh ...'

'Yes?'

'Can I ask for a favour?'

Minh frowned. 'What kind of favour? Mother is the one you want to ask. I'm pretty sure she'd give you something for the rescue.'

'A gift with, ah, barbs? Your mother is a born politician.' Outside of the private comms channel, Quỳnh was making arrangements to come to the tribunal, and Minh was walking behind Stepmother, eyes respectfully averted – headed home, to Mother and her inevitable punishment. *Heart's Sorrow*

– who had recalled his avatar straight home, leaving only the glowering Đình Diệu – was repeatedly messaging Minh, but Minh put his messages on hold until she could focus on them. 'I need somewhere,' Quỳnh.

'Somewhere?'

'I'm new here, and I don't know much about the habitats. I'm interested in moving into a compound—' she gave Minh the address, somewhere in the inner rings, on the edge of dignitary space '—but I want to know if it's suitable.'

'Suitable for what?'

'I'm going to be here for a while,' Quỳnh said. 'And, well.' She paused. '*Guts of Sea* is looking for a match.'

Minh stopped, so abruptly that Stepmother pushed her. 'She what?' Whatever she associated either of them with, it wasn't marriage.

'We all reach a point in our lives when we want stability. An end to the toil and roil around us. A reckoning with our mortality,' Quỳnh's voice was edged and ironic. '*Guts of Sea* would like to settle down.'

A mindship, looking for a match. That was quite a catch. Mindships were either affiliated with the empire, or free of their engagements. If the former, they would bring connections with high-rank officials – if the latter, a formidable capacity for quick travel. A mindship could make or break a family's fortune, especially an official's or a merchant's. 'Does she have a family speaking for her?' She didn't think so. *Guts of Sea* looked old, and old in a mindship meant centuries of life. It was quite likely she was the eldest of her family, and therefore the one making the decisions.

Quỳnh made a sound in private comms, like a delicate cough. '*Guts of Sea*'s family ... didn't survive the uprising, I'm afraid.' She put a peculiar accent on *survive*.

Ah. No wonder *Guts of Sea* didn't speak much. Quỳnh was

desirable, but *Guts of Sea* would be a liability in a world where everyone sought to distance themselves as fast as possible from the General who Pacified the Dragon's Tail and her rebellion. 'And you're speaking for her?'

'Yes. You can see why I want — why I *need* — to make a good impression.' There was hunger and worry in Quỳnh's voice. 'We're talking about *Guts of Sea*'s future.'

The future. Minh thought of her own. It had been traced for her: the metropolitan exams, a career as a scholar, a courtship with a spouse whose family connections were approved by Mother and Stepmother. It was a certainty: a comfort and a cage. But *Guts of Sea* wasn't Minh. She was from a reprobate family, and she needed a good match. And, in order to get that, to offset the taint of her family's actions, she would need to bring a lot more to the match. 'I see,' she said. 'Looking at a compound and telling you if it sends the right kind of message isn't really a great favour.'

'I know,' Quỳnh said. 'I was in the right place at the right time. I'm not asking you to return a gift of food and shelter by lending your spouse.' She sounded amused again as she referenced an Old Earth tale. She really was a scholar: no one else would have known such an obscure metaphor. 'And I'll meet your family, one way or another.'

'You don't need me for that. Or ever did,' Minh said.

'No,' Quỳnh said, inclining her head as she pointed to one bandit after another for the militia. She was wealthy, and smart, and she'd been to court. Every single dignitary would line up to seek her company.

'If that's all you want—' Minh said.

'It is.'

'Then of course, I'll be happy to have a look.'

'Perfect.' Quỳnh smiled. 'Until then.' She left, *Guts of Sea* by her side.

Minh followed Stepmother to the shuttle that would take her back to the family's habitat. She rubbed her wrists, feeling the hardness of scabs under her fingers. Her disguise was torn and bloodied, her avatar unable to disguise the damage to her clothes.

It all felt like a dream – but was she entering one, or being awoken from one ...?

Credits

Aliette de Bodard and Gollancz would like to thank everyone at Orion who worked on the publication of *The Red Scholar's Wake*.

Agent
John Berlyne

Editorial
Gillian Redfearn
Rachel Winterbottom
Claire Ormsby-Potter

Copy-editor
Steve O'Gorman

Proofreader
Andy Ryan

Operations
Sharon Willis

Editorial Management
Jane Hughes
Charlie Panayiotou
Tamara Morriss
Claire Boyle

Audio
Paul Stark
Jake Alderson
Georgina Cutler

Contracts
Anne Goddard
Ellie Bowker
Humayra Ahmed